Challenge

Warwick Collins has led ....
of his poems were published in the magazine *Encounter*
while a student, he has combined a literary interest with
earning his daily bread. Amongst various occupations
have been those of defence specialist and yacht designer.

In 1979 he was invited to address the House of Lords All
Party Defence Study Group on future airborne anti-tank
systems, and the House of Commons Defence Committee
on the same subject in 1980. He counts yachting as his
main obsession and is the inventor of the Collins Tandem
Keel.

Challenge is his first novel and is soon to be followed by
the sequel, *New World*.

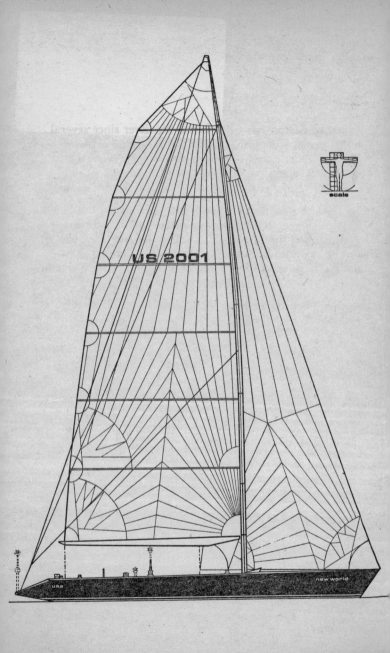

Warwick Collins

Challenge

Pan Books
London, Sydney and Auckland

First published in hardback 1990 by Pan Books Ltd
This paperback edition published 1991 by Pan Books Ltd,
Cavaye Place, London SW10 9PG

9 8 7 6 5 4 3 2 1

ISBN 0 330 31624 9

Phototypeset by Input Typesetting Ltd, London

Printed in England by Clays Ltd, St Ives plc

Acknowledgements

I am grateful to the following for help with aspects of this book: to Alan Gill, director and actor, for his invaluable assistance with dialogue: to Francis Spencer, writer and poet, for clarifying aspects of the plot and structure: to Howard Letty and Capt. Simon van der Byl RN, both owners of boats I have designed, for their shrewd and constructive comments on many aspects of the text: to Andrew Hurst and Bob Fisher for expert help on sailing matters. Any errors or inconsistencies which remain are entirely my own.

to Patricia Collins,
for giving me time and
space to write

Book One

One

US Embassy, Moscow, year 2000

How Glick hated the Safe Room.

Positioned in the heart of the embassy, two floors underground, with its lead-sealed walls, ceilings and floors, it was hidden away for most of the time like a family secret. But over the past forty-eight hours it had lost its unused character. The heavy metal door, with its computer locking device, had now become activated.

The cardholders were all intelligence men, members of the odd little community which lived, much as a city precinct will harbour its group of gangsters, in the labyrinthine interiors of the embassy's lower floors. This community was now in full operation. It seemed to Glick, who occasionally had recourse to the library not far away, that every few minutes one of this subculture placed a cardkey in the door, which opened noiselessly on its vacuum hinges, and then closed with only a low hiss of hydraulics.

The intelligence community were night-people. It was as if their sallow skins had never seen daylight. Their eyes were bloodshot from cigarettes, the cheap, powerful local variety that was their stock-in-trade. To Glick, who functioned as second-in-command, they always seemed to talk out of the sides of their mouths. Their guttural language was as pungent as their cigarette smoke, filled with an incomprehensible combination of obscenity and intelligence patois.

They had systems of communications which bypassed those of the embassy, even the secret ones. Their own highest secrecy communication was called G2, referred to as Fast-Track. Glick had only a vague idea of its precise whereabouts or means of operation, except that there was a room on the first underground floor which was also high security card-operated, where a small red warning light was often evident. He expected this held some sort of clue. That red light was now on constantly. Messages were coming and going. Members of the subculture moved through the underground corridors with the menacing ease of operatives with a purpose.

To Glick the women of the intelligence community were also strange. The gaggle of secretaries in the small intelligence typing pool were like the gangsters' molls that he had seen in old movies. They had that same hard exterior. By day they were relegated to the roll of soulless functionaries. For though the intelligence community might possess the most modern of equipment, their cultural mores seemed to Glick to be sunk way back, to derive from a time when Prohibition was in force. There were two female personal assistants, but they were simply a token of the time. One, Grace Saski, was a hard blonde in her mid-thirties. The other, Charlene Brigson, was a breathtakingly beautiful graduate on her first posting. Sometimes he would see one of the two women walk along the corridor balancing a coffee tray, always with those cheap, disposable plastic cups. They were the only women who had access to the main intelligence room.

There were other outstations. At the end of one corridor on the lower underground floor, nearby an emergency exit, was an automatic coffee dispenser. Sometimes several of the minor figures of the subculture – couriers, sidewalk artists, gatherers of local information, pigeonkickers – would assemble there. As they waited their turn to be served by the grumbling, oddly surly machine, they conversed in low voices in their impenetrable jargon. Even here, Glick noted, there had been an increase in the intensity of operations.

The intelligence machinery had been running at speed for two days. Passing the ambassador in the corridor the day before, Glick had said, 'The Indians are restless,' and the ambassador had looked upwards, towards heaven. At the same time he notified Glick that there was to be an emergency meeting in the Safe Room the following day. It was to be early, starting at five forty-five, so as not to

4

alert the other embassy staff about unusual activities. At this Glick had felt like laughing, for the staff were, on the whole, as keenly aware as he of the ebb and flow of the intelligence community, the odd peaks of activity which built up occasionally, and then died away as mysteriously.

'How restless?' asked Ambassador Brent. Glick said simply:

'Fast-Track room going the whole time. Continuous meetings in the Safe Room.'

'Safe Room,' hissed Ambassador Brent, 'the only room in the whole place where I feel unsafe.' Glick watched Henry Brent's short, square frame walk down the corridor and press the door to his suite of offices. Before he pushed the door, Brent turned and shouted back, 'I want you there, Charles, as a witness.'

The Safe Room walls were lined with cork. It gave the room a bizarre aestheticism, a strange combination of wine bar and torture cell. The only drinks were a carafe of Ambassador Brent's mineral water and several glasses on a silver tray. Otherwise the room, with its long glass table and plastic chairs, was as functional as an operating theatre.

There were only three of them: the Ambassador, Glick and Brad Hinckley.

Head of Intelligence at the American Embassy, Brad Hinckley was a short man, cut square, with close-cropped red-grey hair, and metal frames to his glasses. His squat hand spread out the pages of the document in front of him carefully, with a certain gentleness.

At the head of the table, Ambassador Brent watched Hinckley with that studied patience which is the sincerest form of impatience. There was a meeting Brent had to attend at nine on the other side of the city, a delegation of senior businessmen and trade representatives.

The third member of the party, Charles Glick himself, was thin, tall, stooping even in his chair. He was one of those academic men who gravitate naturally towards the minutiae of protocol. Almost everything in that room

5

offended him. He looked at his watch under the table, pressed his lips. But Brad Hinckley, the intelligence chief, refused to be hurried. His hour had come. He merely said to Glick, 'Could you repeat that bit about the delivery?'

Glick refrained from looking down at his hands. In a voice deliberately couched in monotone, he repeated again that the document had been posted at the embassy by a courier in a black Fiat. The Fiat was local registration, about six years old. They'd taken the number and immediately investigated it on their own internal systems. 'No luck with identification,' said Glick. The receipt of the bag was through Corporal Silvestri. Silvestri had been questioned about the precise appearance of the courier and had written a report which now lay beside the document.

Glick was determined to strike first. 'The courier has been identified,' he said, 'without the use of your intelligence library, I might add. He's Petrov Zutin, one of the Estonian Trade Delegation's four chauffeurs.'

'Zutin's one of their operators,' Hinckley said, perhaps a little too rapidly. 'MVD. A trained ghoul. Your records tell you that?'

'My, my,' the Ambassador interposed. 'You two certainly are lively this morning. Perhaps,' he added in a tone of measured unctuousness, 'you could tell me just what's got you so excited this early.'

Brad Hinckley looked sideways at the Ambassador, as if recognising his presence for the first time, and paused just long enough to be short of contempt. The ambassador thought they would never change, these intelligence men; give them a piece of information and they behaved like a dog with a bone.

Brad Hinckley removed his glasses and rubbed them with a handkerchief. They looked at his red eyes, his two-day growth of stubble.

'I've never seen anything like it,' said Hinckley.

'That's a promising start,' the Ambassador said, 'like what?'

But Hinckley would not be hurried. He placed his

glasses back on his nose, put his handkerchief back in his pocket.

'Maybe it's just poetry,' said Glick. 'Maybe that chauffeur, Zutin, has a literary side to him.'

Hinckley's squat hand reached out again to cover the document.

'It's a document signed by an official in the Soviet Ministry of the Interior. It's addressed "To whom it may concern". The translation's good. They've used high-grade personnel.'

Ambassador Brent reached forward and poured himself a glass of mineral water from the carafe in front of him. He wasn't going to give Hinckley the satisfaction of enquiring further as to what precisely were the contents of the document. It was enough trying to play poker with the local politicians and the staff of the other embassies, he thought to himself, without having to double-bluff your own intelligence chief in an irregular early morning briefing.

At this hour, everything seemed so oddly disconnected. Family men, professional men, forgot these stray times of the day. He had crossed the quadrangle a few minutes earlier and seen shift workers, post deliverers, early cleaners, people he did not know existed, except as names on a list. Five fifty-five, he saw his watch indicate as he turned his wrist to pour the water.

At this time of the morning too, everything seemed unnaturally clear. The ice squeaked and clicked in the tumbler. Brent poured a glass for Glick. He made a polite movement of his head towards Hinckley, but Hinckley said he'd already ordered coffee, and the Ambassador suspected that Hinckley had won another obscure point. He picked up his own glass and drank. If Hinckley didn't offer his information now, the ambassador determined, he would start the day's discussions with his number two and freeze Hinckley out.

Brad Hinckley's blunt fingers continued to rest on the document almost reverentially, but it was Glick who spoke first.

'Translation?' Glick interjected, and the Ambassador

looked at him in surprise. Glick obviously felt as out of place in this early morning briefing as he did. He regarded the hour as absurd, a time for intelligence men and other disreputables. The time alone made him an unwilling party to the ritual.

'Effectively,' said Hinckley, ignoring Glick, 'it's addressed to the highest authority.'

'Why not say the President?' asked Glick, with a sarcastic edge.

'If you say so,' replied Hinckley smoothly. He had drawn first blood. He watched as Glick stooped further to drink from his glass, the rise and fall of Glick's prominent Adam's apple.

'We're treating this as Code Thirteen,' Hinckley continued, 'only two of my men have been cleared to look at this. They were up all night.'

Hinckley knew that the thought of his men working through the night would irritate Glick further. Hinckley hadn't wanted him at the meeting, but the Ambassador had insisted. Now Glick was here, Hinckley couldn't resist firing off a few further shots.

'It's in code?' persisted Glick.

'We needed to be sure that it didn't contain coded elements.'

At this point the ambassador's patience ran out.

'If it's not coded,' he said, 'and it's in English, perhaps you could tell us what it says.'

Hinckley was unmoved.

'The contents are mighty strange. It's a set of conditions based around a challenge.'

'Challenge?' The ambassador's voice took on an accentuated cutting edge. 'Who's challenging whom?'

'The Russians are challenging us.'

'Us being the President?'

'Us being "To whom it may concern".'

At this point the Ambassador felt he might reasonably give way to apoplexy. Here he was being called out for an early meeting, baited by his head of security, and made to look a fool in front of his second-in-command. Perhaps it was the early hour. Perhaps the rules were different. Maybe at these times the intelligence community really did operate an alternative administration. Suddenly he no longer cared. He said, with a trace of his Southern origins, 'What the hell are you talking about, Hinckley?'

If Hinckley had more than enough reason to smile, he did not show it. He still had a final salvo to come. He said:

'It seems to be about a yacht race.' He kept his face straight. His blunt fingers picked up the document in front of him and passed it to the Ambassador. He said, 'Perhaps you'd better read it.' And then, to start his day happy, to put some gold into the morning, he added gratuitously, 'Sir.'

Two

Winter, 1985

Granpa Shaw walked along the causeway, carrying two cans of kerosene, one in each hand, for balance.

It was cold, below zero, but the sun was out. He liked that walk, especially when the snow lay thick and the sluggish traffic, not risking the sliding ice along the shore road, moved inland.

Agnes Chednik's store was open. Business appeared slow in this weather. There were hardly a dozen sets of footprints in the snow. But Agnes Chednik was always cheerful. 'Only the important people come in this weather, Sam,' she said. 'No timewasters, no representatives.'

Inside it was warm. Unfrozen moisture moved downwards, gathering on the windows and window sill, the hanging garden tools, the greenhouse packs, the rows of brooms that betokened an order the neighbourhood hardly aspired to. Those items corresponded to Agnes Chednik's dream, and like a dream, they were untouched by the reality of buying. Her real trade was in groceries, nails, strings, hammers, drying cloths, rubber washing gloves, paint, preservers. She did a flying trade in condoms with the local whores in Cale Street. Sam Shaw walked round an exercise machine which occupied the centre of the room and which had been unsold for more than a year. He said:

'How are things, Agnes?'

In the recesses of the store, Agnes Chednik was leaning over the counter. Only the parting of her hair, thick and black as a Mohican's, showed. There was a moment's silence.

'Seen Maria?' asked Agnes, without looking up. 'Little scamp. Said she'd be out just a few minutes. Skipped out the door as pert as you like.'

Sam Shaw knew when to keep his information to a minimum.

'No.'

Agnes Chednik gave a click, perhaps of irritation, perhaps of triumph at a small task done. She looked up. Her face, though chubby, was pretty. She put her accounts aside.

'You looking after yourself, Sam?'

'Yup.'

'And that grandson of yours?'

'He's fine.'

'Living up in that house like a pair of old batchelors. Jim's gonna end up like you, Sam.'

'Yeah, he's making fine progress for a ten-year-old,' said Sam Shaw. 'He's got the makings of an old coot already.'

Agnes and he always sparred over Jim as if they were estranged husband and wife. Agnes closed the red accounts book in which she had been writing and placed her short, plump hands on the counter. 'What can I do for you?'

Sam Shaw produced a list, a piece of exercise paper

with items in a left hand column, and the number or weight of the items on the right. Agnes Chednik put a cardboard box on the counter, took the list from Sam's hand, studied it, and began to move about in the rear of the store, pulling certain items down from shelves. Sam Shaw was aware of the enormous bulk of her, the hands which dexterously gathered items as her feet shuffled softly. Though large, there was something pleasingly fastidious in her dress, always ironed and pressed, in the tortoiseshell clasp which held her hair at the back.

Sam Shaw was not averse to her size. Fishermen, home from the cold sea, tended to like their women big. In the old days, he would watch the crew go home, the small wiry men to their large women, and he to his. Bless her memory. Agnes said: 'You forgot soap.'

'Yeah, three bars.'

'Toilet paper.'

Agnes did not wait for him to reply. Three double rolls, brought down from the shelves, was answer enough.

She went through several other items. Naming each item, her enquiry was purely rhetorical. Unless Sam objected strenuously, her small hands of their own accord would lift the objects in question from the groaning shelves and place them by the counter.

'I'll fill the kerosene cans,' Sam Shaw said, and went round to the back of the store.

Arriving there, he opened the stopper on one of his cans. The tank was in a small annexe of its own. He knelt down, placed a funnel in one of the cans, positioned it under the tap, and opened it. In the background he could hear Agnes moving about in the store-room, the steady thump as she piled objects on the table.

A flying shadow crossed the low small window. A small figure skipped past, rattled the door, came in. In her furs she looked like an eskimo child. She paused to watch him.

'Hi, Maria.'

She turned her head away out of shyness. It is a strange thing, he thought, how you sometimes look into a small girl's eyes and you see the woman she will become. This one was fiery. She would be some handful.

'Your mother's looking for you.'

Maria turned to stare back at him. He was uncomfortably aware that his words had no effect. He continued to pour kerosene into the funnel of the second can, while she stood her ground and watched him.

'That you, Maria?' Agnes called. Maria looked at him a while longer, at the kerosene being poured, splashing, into the plastic funnel.

'Coming.'

Off she skipped, a small flying wedge. 'Let me help you, ma.'

Back in the house, Sam Shaw made some coffee.

From his kitchen he could look down the row of houses, which stopped abruptly and began again, to the small wooden shed built with A-Frame beams, all slanting roof, with McLuskey's old bicycle leaning up against it.

Through the window he could see across the tarmac parking area to the shoreside, to the small boathouse where he stored his things. The metal chimney of McLuskey's shed was smoking. McLuskey was there, perhaps doing repair work on his skiff or one of the other vessels stored there. He knew his grandson Jim would be down there too, passing up tools to McLuskey as he worked on one of the old vessels, handing pieces of wood to McLuskey while he worked on the bandsaw, or sweeping up the shavings that gathered behind McLuskey like the white wake of a moving boat.

Jim borrowed McLuskey's equipment to work on his own boat. It was an Optimist dinghy, an old one which they had found abandoned, filled with water. Sam Shaw had seen it in one of the small indents on the north side of Weepeq Bay. It seemed rotten, but he and Jim towed it home and dried it out in McLuskey's shed. Once the mud had been scraped off, and they could assess the damage, they found that the mast thwart had suffered, and the central plank was rotten in its forward third. But the skin, surprisingly, was still intact. Sam Shaw found replacement timber for the mast thwart, and he and McLuskey and Jim began the hunt for a mast and sails.

At the weekends Jim would work on the boat, stripping off its coats of paint and varnish. In the afternoons, Jim was often to be seen at the sailing club, studying the placement of gear on the Optimists, watching the way they were sailed in the little fleet. Occasionally he was asked to crew in one of the other dinghy classes, and once or twice was allowed to helm.

Over the weekends he worked for McLuskey, at an unofficial rate of one dollar fifty cents an hour. Bit by bit he accumulated the various fittings for the dinghy.

McLuskey it was who found the spruce for the mast and boom. The following week he lathed the basic shape, so that Jim could finish the task of fairing, sanding and varnishing. McLuskey gave advice to Jim on how to dry out the hull. ('Not too dry, son,' he would say. 'Trees ain't meant to be without water.') McLuskey found him varnish at trade prices. 'Use epoxy to seal the wood, polyurethane varnish on top to protect the epoxy from sunlight. Rub down between layers to key the next coat.'

When Jim first started to work on the hull, McLuskey admonished him: 'Strip off everything, right down to the bare wood, and then some.' He would sometimes walk over from his repairs of the other boats in his shed. 'Keep stripping down to the wood,' McLuskey would say. 'You gotta start from scratch.' So Jim worked on stripping the paint away from the hull with the tools that McLuskey lent him. Sometimes McLuskey would walk over, with his cigarette between his teeth, and watch Jim working away, saying nothing, just smoking.

It was cold on the concrete floor of the shed. One day not long before Christmas, Jim entered by the side door and found his boat had gone from its usual place. His heart skipped a beat. But McLuskey had cleared a place on the upper section of the wooden platform. It was noticeably warmer up there. In the cold weather which closed over them that winter, Jim had cause to thank himself for McLuskey's benign interest.

McLuskey said to Sam Shaw one day. 'He's a determined little tyke, Sam. He's got something of you in him. Just hope he doesn't turn out quite so unpleasant.' And McLuskey gave one of his rare, wide mouth grins, as if he was in pain, and leaned over at his own joke, thumping the working bench so hard with his big flat hand that the paint tins at one end jumped and clattered against one another.

'The trouble with you, McLuskey,' said Sam Shaw, 'is that you don't know the meaning of work.' At which McLuskey doubled up further, hitting the workbench with all the abandon of a sealion slapping the ground with its tail. Breath escaped from his lungs in painful, short wheezes. Sam Shaw watched him with detachment.

It was colder than usual that winter. The sea froze, and pack-ice from the Highton river filled the bay. During the Christmas holidays Jim worked in McLuskey's workshop, helping him to refit several small yachts for the summer.

Once McLuskey had fitted out commercial vessels entirely, mostly fishing boats, in his premises across the bay. But the sea around had been overfished, the fleet had died, so he'd shrunk his operations, dismissed his workforce of twenty-seven men over several years, and worked on his own again. Though the returns were small, the pleasure of moving from administration to handwork compensated for the loss of income.

In the evenings Jim returned through the snow to his grandfather's weatherboarded house, and helped him with repairing the nets he used in summer. The use of the nets was barely economic. It was Sam Shaw's silent protest against the loss of the fleet. It wasn't possible to make a living out of owning a fishing boat any more, but one man with a skiff and nets could just about support himself if he was flexible. At the back of the house was a room full of lobster pots, lines and floats. Jim would also help with their repair.

It was possible, Sam Shaw believed, assuming one made everything oneself and bought only the materials of fishing without the labour costs involved, to make a peripheral living.

In winter Sam Shaw made new lobster pots for the following season. He bought rushes and set to work on the kitchen table, and Jim would help him weave, sitting on the other side of the table, pulling the wands down into the weave, and making the special, powerful twist of a group of fibres that would make an attachment point for the rope. When Sam Shaw and Jim made the lobster pots they would work silently, the small stove hissing in the corner, the tears of moisture streaming down the window.

Sam Shaw became a one-man protest industry against the pollution of the harbour and bay. He would pore over the newspapers, carefully cutting out the pieces that interested him. In the evenings he took down from the shelves the files of correspondence he kept. He wrote laboriously in long hand, though soon after beginning he had kept a carbon copy of each letter. The return mail was small measured against his own effort, but every now and again he received an acknowledgement from a local bureaucrat, or a committee wrote to him with its findings, enough to sustain his effort. Even when he was young, Jim knew that Sam Shaw wrote not so much because he believed it would achieve an effect as for the peace of his own soul, the satisfaction of one small private effort against the forces of darkness.

Gradually, as he began to establish his new way of life, Sam Shaw's entrenchment against the forces of modernity deepened. There had been a television set in one room of the old house, but he had grown to so dislike the faces of the politicians, rich, doughy, infinitely adjustable, that he had unplugged the socket and turned it to face the wall. Jim could never remember it being on.

Sam Shaw became more extreme still. He always had spare kerosene lamps in the household. In the early spring of 1983 there had been a freak weather pattern, a hurricane followed by a return of bitterly cold weather. The power was cut off for three days. The kerosene lamps were lit. When the power returned, Sam Shaw wrote to the electricity company that he could no longer rely on their continuing supply of electricity, and notified them that he would cease from using it forthwith. The kerosene lamps stayed out. The switch was turned off at the mains supply. Thereafter he worked, cooked and ate by the light of his kerosene lamps.

In the records of the municipal corporation, there was mention of an elderly eccentric who had cut himself off voluntarily from electricity. Such are the dry records of the authorities. There is, however, a subjective truth which perhaps is deeper still. When Sam Shaw finally turned off his mains supply, in his own mind he had turned off the whole city and its ways.

In the fullness of time, some several months later in fact, it was thought right to check on the situation of the elderly eccentric, who in the meantime had perhaps perished from the cold. A representative of the municipality, a tall, stooping man with an earnest expression, was sent to visit.

He hovered in the driveway for a moment, and then took the decision to walk around the side of the house and knock on the door. On his way there he came face to face with Sam Shaw carrying some tiles which had been blown off the roof in the previous night's gale. His visitor regarded Sam Shaw with interest.

Sam Shaw could smell a municipal man when he met one. He said: 'Need anything, son?'

For a moment, the official stood his ground.

'The point is, Mr Shaw, do you?'

'No, I don't think so,' said Sam Shaw, advancing towards him along the path. The official backed away carefully. They moved slowly thus, down the path, like two careful crabs in a territorial display, until the municipal man was no longer on Sam Shaw's property.

The official, to save the day, said. 'Pleased to meet you, Mr Shaw.'

Surprisingly, perhaps, Sam Shaw held out his hand and shook the young man's. 'Goodbye, son, and good luck.'

'Thank you,' said the official, and moved away.

Jim was not raised in an orthodox household. If anyone had been brought up to respect no one's views but his own, to distrust the judgement of society against his own judgement, it was he. Granpa Shaw saw to that.

Three

In the early spring, shortly after the thaw, Sam Shaw rowed Jim out to recover some lobster pots. They set out in the early evening. With a small tide helping them, it was perhaps an hour's journey of nearly three nautical miles to a part of the bay where a movement of tidal current maintained a fresh flow over the seabed. Granpa had discovered, in the sinuous wind of the current, a more rapid recovery of lobsters and shellfish in an area of about a square mile. It was deep, and the currents took a toll of the pots, but it was worthwhile.

They reached the site and set about gathering the pots. Night was coming on. A calm extended over Weepeq Bay, so quiet that the water was glassy. They hauled the pots up from their cork floats, piled them high in the stern. It was already dark and the tide would be against them if they stayed longer. Sam Shaw said, 'That's about enough.'

'Can I row?' asked Jim.

'No, son, I need the exercise more than you. You just sit there and take note.'

The rowlocks creaked. Behind them the lights of the city began to twinkle across the bay. They were reflected in the water, so that the oars themselves seemed to dip into their effulgence. Sam Shaw, never one for speeches,

17

commented, 'God said "Let there be light", Jim. But it was the devil who invented lights.'

To Jim, they seemed to be floating in lights right now. As they closed with the shore, Sam Shaw said, 'Your father travelled towards those lights, Jim. Thought he could make his fortune. Never did. Guess you know about that already. Your mother . . . well, I ain't seen her since she left you with me so she could follow your father . . . ' The water from the oars dripped in the reflections. Sam Shaw said finally, 'It's those lights, Jim, they can drive you mad. Weren't nothing wrong with either of them.'

Sam Shaw, having delivered his view of the world, commenced rowing again, shaking his head slowly, and did not speak again until they touched the land. It was that evening that Jim knew that Sam Shaw had drawn up his portcullis on the world; he now felt so far outside it, outside all its modern manifestations, that it no longer existed for him.

A decade earlier the local school at Weepeq had closed down after the fishing industry had disappeared, and the younger families had moved on to other areas seeking employment.

At the Highton High school, several miles inland, Jim was taught the rudiments of reading and writing amongst the children of the upwardly mobile from the district of Holmont. The children reinforced his isolation. Their bright voices reciting declarations of loyalty to the flag depressed him. In all such matters he was subject to the deep cynicism of his grandfather. He learnt at an early stage to keep his own counsel, not to create unnecessary waves, and to maintain only the minimum presence necessary for his education. As soon as he was able, he would slip off to McLuskey's shed to help him with his labour, or to work on the small upturned hull of his dinghy, gleaming now with varnish.

In only one respect did Jim have any attraction to the world his grandfather rejected. The school had a small computer, a Macintosh, moderately powerful, even for those times, with software programmes for three-dimensional display.

In the afternoons some of the brainier kids would play computer games. Jim was quicker at these than others, and soon established himself as champion. It was a matter of reflex and timing, and in both these he was inordinately fast. So he established a small area of predominance. Since most of the afternoon games were knockout competitions, he would often find himself alone with the computer, all the others having disappeared, and he would continue for hours in small experimental operations. Only when the janitor changed for the night watchman would Jim relinquish the small keyboard.

'Time to go,' said the janitor kindly. 'No one allowed here after seven. Watch the ice out there.' On Wednesday evenings Jim turned from the grey screen to the grey dusk which had settled over Weepeq Bay, and walked through the snow to the one house in that city without electricity.

'You staying late at school, Jim?' Sam Shaw asked.

'I've been on the computer.'

Sam Shaw paused to apply a lighter to the frayed ends of a nylon net. Jim smelt the slightly acrid aroma of the melting strands.

'You're kinda taken with that thing, aren't you?'

Jim said: 'I like it more than the kids.'

Sam Shaw considered this information for a while. Inside Jim flinched from the expected rebuke about the playthings of modern man, the emptiness of electrical contraptions. Instead he experienced the silent weight of his grandfather's contemplation. Sam Shaw did not mention the subject again.

The last few, lonely chunks of ice went down the Highton river, melting rapidly. With their departure, the sailing season started.

The sailing club reminded Jim of a termite mound. At a certain stage in the season, when the weather conditions were propitious, the first flying ants would be helped from the winter storage by smaller worker ants. Half a dozen

19

dinghies, usually Lasers and Snipes at first, would be put in the water, and rigged with their colourful sails.

The Optimists at the club started to form their own fleet as the spring progressed. On a clear day in late March Jim Shaw and Sam McLuskey lifted Jim's dinghy down the slipway and into the water. Jim tethered it to a post on the old pontoon. He set up the mast and sails. There was a light breeze blowing onshore, sending small ripples across the flat water. McLuskey pushed him off. Jim tightened the sail and felt the little craft begin to move. He lowered the daggerboard and hardened the mainsheet in a little more.

McLuskey watched for a while, standing with his bandy legs apart, his hands in his trouser pockets. It was an attitude of detached cynicism. A small gust hit the dinghy and McLuskey watched Jim simultaneously move outboard and ease the sheet, a single, fluid act. He felt, he sometimes claimed afterwards, that he had seen in that moment the birth of a champion. And when his companions roared with laughter and patted him on the back, shouting, 'Another one for Mac,' McLuskey would say, 'Like a cat, he moved just like a cat.'

Apart from the school computer, there was another area of potential confrontation with Sam Shaw.

After a dinner of clams, Granpa pulled up some nets for repair, heaving them over the chair. Putting on his gloves, he began to work through them.

'Do you really want to win, Jim?' Sam Shaw asked through lips clenched on a piece of thread.

Far off, a steamer called out in the fog. A buoy rang out in the bay. The fog was thick at the windows, pressing at the house.

Jim thought he heard disapproval in the question. He nodded his head.

Sam Shaw pulled at his nets in the pool of white light thrown by the kerosene lamp. He would roll out the slow workings of his mind, balancing one side against the other, and finally reach a conclusion. Once reached, he hardly ever returned from that position.

'That's a hell of a strange outlook on life, son.'

'Is it, granpa?'

Sam Shaw paused to turn over a piece of net. A few days before a sliver of metal had found its way into the net and had entered his thumb. He was a little more cautious now.

'You're innocent, that's your trouble. Innocent.'

Jim waited for several moments.

'What's innocent exactly, granpa?'

But Sam Shaw was not in the mood for explanation. His reply had a certain circularity.

'Wanting to win, son. You'll see what I mean.'

Sam Shaw pulled at his nets, sitting in the pool of white light like some rare sea-monster. The brightness of the light and the deep shadow behind him made him seem monumental to Jim, who sat watching him on the other side of the table. From his position opposite, Sam Shaw seemed to him monolithic, like a picture Jim had once seen of an old Navaho indian.

It did not matter about Sam Shaw's disapproval of his desire to win. By one of those strange manifestations of will, Jim knew he had Sam Shaw's backing, as long as he wanted it.

Four

Sam Shaw watched Jim's departure from the back window of his house.

A few minutes earlier, tired suddenly, Sam Shaw had stood up and stretched his legs. The cold had a way of sneaking into his bones. He went to the stove and put a kettle on the woodburning stove. Leaving a pile of fishnets on the chair and table, he watched Jim's progress across the Bay towards the little fleet of Optimists whose sails fluttered around the Weepeq Sailing Club.

The day was sunny, but the clouds had a way of hovering over the hills to the north of the bay. A small breeze had started to rustle the surface, picking up slowly as the morning progressed.

On the first day, Jim did not enter the body of the fleet. He sailed some two hundred yards away, shadowing the group of sails as it jostled before the starting gun. As the starting gun went, he turned and sailed a parallel course, far enough away not to incur the wrath of the starting officials, near enough to compare speeds.

Watching him from the house on this first day, Sam Shaw learnt several things about his grandson. Firstly, Jim's pride would not allow him to mix with the fleet in a race until he had 'tuned' his own boat. Secondly, as Sam Shaw watched the small white sail moving parallel to the fleet, always apart, he let out his breath in a sound like a sigh. His grandson was alone. Even Agnes wouldn't be able to reach the boy.

Absorbed in these thoughts, Sam Shaw did not miss a third aspect, one that emerged only slowly as the little fleet made its way to the first buoy, shadowed by a single sail. Jim was already fast. Although two lead boats had broken away from the pack, Jim was running parallel with the third and fourth boats.

At about eleven Sam Shaw grew restless. He put aside his nets, put on his coat, and drew the door carefully to behind him. Setting out on his walk, he skirted the coast road until he reached a stairway from the sea wall to the foreshore. He made his way along the shore below the tideline, through the weed and the plastic detergent bottles, the discarded ice-cream cones and the occasional condom, courtesy of the girls on Cale Street.

The wind was cold, blowing the tufts of the cooch grass, sending trails of smoke from some of the better houses in Highton across the bay.

That evening, after Jim returned, Sam Shaw said: 'You

were pinching a little upwind. You should sail a little freer, especially when the wind is light.'

Jim did not answer. Sam Shaw went on with his repairs, using a candleflame to singe the frayed nylon strands.

'I was watching the lead boats. That's what they did: eased sheets, sailed fast, got out of the pack. No good pointing up if you aren't going anywhere.'

Then Sam Shaw snorted. He felt with one hand for a pair of clippers, trimmed another stray end. 'Guess you got yourself a coach, son, whether you like it or not.'

Jim made several small models from wooden wedges which he had begged from McLuskey and shaped to the rough outline of sailing vessels. The sails were constructed of triangular cardboard. He plied Sam Shaw with questions about tactics. But his new coach, warming to the role slowly, unfolded his knowledge without haste, in his own time. In the evenings, with the kerosene lamp in the middle of the kitchen table, they would eat their supper, and then, when they had cleared the table, Sam Shaw would take out his pipe, fill it, and start to work on his nets again.

On one corner of the table, Jim set out his three small craft, working through a book of sailing instructions. Sam Shaw watched him for a while. He said:

'Euclid taught that the shortest distance between two points is a straight line. Well, that may be so, but it isn't necessarily the fastest.'

'Why not?' asked Jim, looking up from his handbook and his models.

'Breeze just isn't the same in two places. It's got as many holes as a piece of cheese. Euclid wasn't a sailor, or else he'd know that when you're sailing a boat, it's finding that little bit of extra wind that counts. And sometimes, to get that wind, you have to take a longer route.'

'How do you know where to find it?'

'That's what it's all about. The best sailors have a feel for it.'

'How?'

Sometimes Sam Shaw was dismayed by the intensity of Jim's interest. He preferred not to be pressed.

'They've got to find an indication. They look at the other boats, particularly the lead boats, and see what the breeze is doing ahead. They look around at the water, for the different shades of colour on the surface. Dark patches mean more wind.'

Sam Shaw paused to examine a piece of damage that had been caused to a net by a larger fish, a shark maybe.

Jim moved the models about relative to a salt cellar, representing the windward mark.

Sam Shaw reached out a hand to move one of the small models. 'Here I come in on the same tack, down to leeward. Now I'm exercising my rights and luffing you up. OK, now what are you going to do?'

'Tack away, granpa.'

'That's it, son, keep out of trouble on this leg of the course. Get ready to come back at me when we reach the downwind leg.'

They manoeuvred the yachts round the buoy.

'See, son, when we're sailing upwind, and I'm ahead of you, I can put myself between you and the wind. That puts you in my bad air, so you slow down.' Sam Shaw moved the trailing boat back.

Jim said, 'I'm tacking away.'

'That's right, keep away, try and find clean air, get ready to come back at me on the downwind leg.'

'How, granpa?'

'Downwind, the boat that's behind can get between the wind and the leading boat, take his wind, roll right past him, like this.' Sam Shaw showed on the models.

He returned to his nets after his demonstration. He had talked enough. He went back to his customary silence. After another half an hour of mending nets, he stood up to make some coffee.

On another occasion, several days later, Sam Shaw said: 'There's another side to it, son. You have to get to know your competition. To do that, you have to learn to respect your rival. That's the first lesson. Give him the

24

benefit of the doubt. Watch his every move. If you can respect him, you can learn from him.'

'Do I have to respect him, granpa?'

'You're a cussed so-and-so, son. You could be a sailor if you learned how to do that.'

'What do I do when I've learned to respect him?'

'Well, Jim, that's just the time.'

Jim waited. He knew Sam Shaw didn't like to be hurried. He wanted to ask 'time for what?' but he knew it would get him nowhere to press for an answer.

Sam Shaw considered the situation, biting off a thread cleanly. He was concentrating hard now, repairing the damage to several strands, working with slow consistency. Jim thought he had decided against saying anything further, and slid slowly from his chair so he could go to his room. As he passed the doorway, Sam Shaw said, as if speaking to himself:

'That's just the time to blow the sonofabitch right out of the water.'

Five

It was a bright day, but there was a hint of lightning in the sky in the far west, one of those days which could turn dark suddenly, hurling wind and fistfuls of thunder.

At the ten-minute gun the small fleet fluttered like butterflies at a waterhole, passing one another randomly, as tension built. The cordite from the five-minute gun sailed into the air, followed a second later by the boom. Jim chose the pin end of the line, circled the buoy, and came in a little late but fast, in his own clear air, as the starting gun went.

The breeze was filling. He could feel the urgent slap of the wavelets as he hardened in the sheet. He remembered

Sam Shaw's advice to sail free and fast. Though he was not pointing as high as the boats close to him, his snub prow was edging ahead of them, his transom was abeam of their masts. He let out sheet as a gust hit him, leaning out, easing up, keeping his speed up, bearing away a little in the lulls. The fleet were closing with the weather mark and only one blue hull, driven by a red-haired boy he did not recognise, was ahead of him. He drove around the buoy as close as he could. The third boat, close behind, swung a little wider, keeping upwind on the reaching course. Two others passed him on the reach to windward. He caught up on the second boat, but tacked a little too late, over-reached the buoy, and another slipped through. At the finish he was fifth boat in a fleet of eighteen.

'Passable,' said Sam Shaw that evening, as he stowed away the washed dishes. 'I don't want to hear what you did right. We can leave that well enough alone. Just what did you do exactly that made you lose ground?'

In his bed that night, with the slow light of an occluding moon shining through the skylight, Jim went slowly over the race, piece by piece.

In the summer nights that followed, he lay awake and worked through each race as his grandfather taught him. Slowly, as the season progressed, he began his march to the front of the fleet.

By the following season he was winning most of the races that he entered. Sam Shaw said, 'Now you're alone you've got to keep up the pressure, Jim. Now's the time most people would get complacent.'

So Jim took to starting late, putting himself in a position to work his way up through the fleet, skirting the others' dirty wind, trying to slide through at the mark.

Herbie Krieg, the son of a computer expert from nearby Hoken, took a special interest in these self-imposed restrictions. He liked nothing better than to place a cover on Jim, sailing him out to a corner of the course, blocking his path to re-enter the race. After a while Herbie's villainous grin began to haunt Jim as Herbie tacked ahead of him, matching manoeuvre with counter-manoeuvre, shouting comments like 'Caught you there, Shaw.'

Wherever there was a scrimmage at the mark, Herbie's red head could be seen at the centre of it, calling out his scabrous insults, standing in his boat to shake his fist at another. 'You know what my dad'd call you, Shaw? A *shitespiegler*.' He shook his fist. 'A total *shitespiegler*.'

'You put just one foot wrong and I'll get you with the protest committee, you just wait,' shouted Herbie Krieg, his pale eyes and lashes fluttering with rage. 'They'll get the drop on you, you . . . ' Jim raised his index finger to Herbie Krieg as they manoeuvred at the pre-start. 'Excuse me, sir,' Herbie Krieg shouted at the race officer, 'did you see what Shaw just did? I couldn't believe it, sir; did you see that? This is a family show, sir. If my sister saw that, she'd faint, sir.'

Grandfather was excited that autumn. Monday 19 October, 1987. Black Monday, The Dow Jones had plummeted.

Sam Shaw said, 'Just like I always predicted, Jim, the whole goddamn economy is rotten, just a bubble of air. One little shudder and the entire system is ready to collapse. Saw it on a newspaper hoarding outside Agnes's place.'

That evening, when Jim came home from school, Granpa was writing in his painstaking slow hand to the municipality. Once he stood up to look out of the window, as if he were surprised the lights were still there.

The following day Sam Shaw began the task of replacing the tiles on the roof. He had obtained a supply of red tiles from an acquaintance who worked on a building site. He was working on the roof for most of the week. When the day of the national championships in Weepeq Bay arrived the following Saturday, Granpa climbed the long wooden ladder to the roof, and began to lay the final sets of tiles.

His activity gave him a vantage point over the race which could hardly be bettered. He looked out over the other roofs, the wharfside buildings, McLuskey's shed, the disused derricks and cranes, to the starting line where the fleet was already gathering.

Lying on the roof, his thin legs straddled for purchase, Sam Shaw, with his long sight, noticed briefly and in passing the tall figure who emerged from a battered Studebaker and walked, with a pronounced limp, towards the quayside.

He was casually dressed, a man who took no special pride in his appearance, in a red pullover and grey corduroy trousers. Around his neck he carried a pair of old Zeiss binoculars and a handbearing compass. At the water's edge he leaned backwards against the sea wall to steady himself, and took a sighting of the course, checking the wind direction as he did so. It was impossible, in the shelter of the wall, to gauge the speed of the wind, but whitecaps were just showing on the bay. He guessed force four, gusting five.

A dark day, with spectacular clouds banking up in the east, over the sea, and the wind rising slowly.

Jim felt he could detect a bias on the port side of the line. The five-minute gun went as he reached up the line to the starboard side, a hundred yards below it to avoid the huge fleet of over two hundred boats gathering along the starting line. He hardened up, glanced at his watch, and began to count down the final minute in his mind, checking at forty seconds with his watch. He had to duck three other boats, using his greater speed to break through their windshadow. Twenty, nineteen . . . A group were bunched on the start line ahead. There was no time to duck or go round them. Nine, eight . . . there seemed no way through. He was blocked by a raft of boats, as solid as an icefloe. Then two groups seemed to drift apart, a split emerged. He eased sheets and raced for it. Three, two, one . . . Smoke appeared from the starting boat, a boom followed, and he was through, accelerating, winding in and out with each gust. Only three other boats were level with him, one slightly ahead and to windward. He looked over his shoulder at the windward boat and his mind froze. Staring back at him beneath the familiar red hair were the pale eyes of Herbie Krieg.

'Got the drop on you now, Shaw,' Herbie shouted. '*Dimblehoffer.*' He was already edging over, the better to take Jim's wind. Jim tacked to port, lost ground, was forced to duck two boats coming in on starboard. Herbie Krieg tacked with him. A large group was now coming in on starboard with right of way. Jim knew he'd lose himself entirely if he was forced to duck that phalanx. The manoeuvre would suck him back into the centre of the fleet. He tacked again, trying desperately to keep out of trouble. But there was Herbie Krieg, ahead and to windward.

In order to cover Jim, Herbie was also beginning to lose his initial advantage over the rest of the fleet. There was only one way to get rid of Herbie Krieg, and that was to tack onto port again. The phalanx of boats approaching on starboard had spread a little. Jim could see gaps. He decided to risk it and maintained his course.

As he feared, Herbie Krieg stuck to him like a limpet. Jim found a gap and managed to slide through it. Behind him Herbie Krieg was less fortunate. Jim heard the commotion behind him. Glancing back, he saw Krieg's blue hull duck one boat, narrowly miss a second, and strike a third. Herbie Krieg's screams of rage split the air, and his language rose to new levels of inventiveness.

Jim was through and out the other side, but about thirty boats down. He settled in, managing to overtake two by the windward mark. But the leaders were streaming ahead, the first two over a hundred yards away. He could only bide his time and try to remain in the game.

On the reach the wind seemed to fall off a little. He duelled with a small group of three. He managed to find his way past them by the third buoy, but it was laborious. The wind was falling, becoming one of those calms which occurs, on an unsettled day, before greater wind. On the second beat, in light airs, he managed to pull back several places. But there were still at least twenty boats ahead of him. He swung around the windward buoy, slipped through on the inside of a dinghy which had sailed too wide. The breeze had fallen off further. Now it was light, almost drifting.

Through his binoculars Hal Johnson, national Olympic sailing coach, peered at the race. There were several promising youngsters in the fleet. He'd been told to watch three in particular. He'd found two, as he expected, at the top of the fleet, but the last one, Jim Shaw, wasn't in the first fifteen. He guessed he'd had a bad race.

Out on the course, one of the sails had separated off, was sailing away downwind of the fleet. An eccentric course, thought Coach Johnson. He homed on the sail number, and something clicked in his mind. He glanced at the sheet of paper on his clipboard. He thought so. The mystery figure. He raised his binoculars and began to size up the situation again. He whispered to himself. 'No way you're going to do any good there, boy. They'll just bury you.' The sail nevertheless continued to separate from the fleet, pursuing its lonely course.

There was a gaggle of spectators on the foreshore. A stocky man, standing alongside another, pointed at the hawkish, leaning figure of Hal Johnson. Further along, a middle-aged woman walked, weaving from side to side as if in a trance; not far from her, a child threw sticks for a dog.

Some flies had been attracted to refuse on the area of mud between sea and shore. Hal Johnson paused to beat off a couple of big ones with his hand. He took the opportunity to look around the bay, and the deserted foreshore, the empty wharves, the disused cranes behind them on Spillers Point.

Jim was now three hundred yards wide of the fleet, speed slowed to less than a knot, hardly able to hold steerage way. On one side of him the whole fleet was virtually motionless. On the other a front of dark cloud was building. It was a curious sensation, being so detached from the fleet.

Beneath the forming bank of cloud, curving streams of rain and wind spread out fanwise. It was so quiet he needed to work the tiller just to maintain steerage way. The surface of the sea was now so smooth it was almost oily.

Coach Johnson peered through his binoculars again at the arrested fleet. The single sail was now, if anything, even further away from the body of competitors. Coach Johnson swung his glasses further to the building cloud. For the first time that day, he started to feel interested. 'My, my, just look at that. Is that what you're after, son?'

Glancing back to the body of the fleet, Coach Johnson saw that the front fifteen boats had found a zephyr of wind, and were beginning, slowly, to pull away from the main sector of the fleet, opening up a larger lead. 'They're gonna bury you, son,' Coach Johnson said amiably. 'Better cut your losses, get back to the fleet.'

Jim's wind died completely. He had lost steerage way and could only keep on course by occasional sharp pushes on the tiller. The leaders were beginning to move ahead slowly. About the first thirty or so boats began to detach themselves from the main body of the fleet. The race was over for him. He looked towards the cloud bank in the east. It seemed to hang there, arrested, with its spokes of wind like decorations.

He could see the sky's reflection in the still water.

On the foreshore, Coach Johnson said to himself, 'God-damn lottery.' But it was a sign of irritation more than any statement of fact. He knew that the lighter wind races were the most tactical and the most difficult because they were the least predictable.

The flies were louder in the silence. They were starting to get aggressive now, no longer intimidated by the sweeps of his broad hands. He moved back towards the sea-wall, away from the foreshore, and leaned back against it. He raised his binoculars to study the thundercloud.

Wind, when it arrives, can be as refreshing as rain, its

touch on the cheek like the first drops hitting a dry desert floor. A feather brushed Jim's face and hands. The new breeze brought a change in direction of a hundred and eighty degrees. He let the boom swing across, switched sides, felt the boat heel and begin to ride forward.

Coach Johnson, returning from his study of the thunderhead, said, 'Well, I'll be . . . You got your wind, boy. Now let's see what you can do with it.'

The chuckle of the bow wave began. Apart from that sound, the boat was silent when strung. The fleet were still becalmed. Jim leaned out a little further as more breeze came in.

Coach Johnson said, 'Harden up and come in, son. Cut your losses. Come on back into the fleet. Maybe you can get back into the first ten.'

But the small white sail continued on its lonely path, separating further. 'You're crazy,' said Coach Johnson amiably, 'crazy.'

But results are the arbiter of all tactics. In keeping his distance, Jim kept inside the draft of wind fanning out from the cloud. For several minutes he maintained his own private breeze. Only when the wind touched the front sail of the fleet did he change direction and begin to move in on the others. There were twenty seconds of confusion as booms swung across and the other boats began to heel in the opposite direction. Every second Jim gained. He was parallel now with a group of four boats behind the two leaders.

Coach Johnson let his binoculars hang, rubbed reflectively the skin under his eyes, peered around him at the almost deserted foreshore. His mouth was dry. He could do with a drink. He raised his binoculars again.

The single sail was now closing with the leaders of the fleet.

Coach Johnson glanced at his list again. Abrams and Jankowski were the two lead boats, Abrams twenty feet ahead.

The single white sail was running parallel with the two leaders, bearing down on them. He watched its casual, lethal approach. The second boat's sails collapsed suddenly as Jim took its wind. 'Can you believe this?' Hal Johnson said to no one in particular.

But Abrams, the leader, kept his nerve and was first by ten feet at the buoy.

They split tacks after the buoy. 'Good tactics,' said Coach Johnson as Abrams tacked again after twenty seconds to keep a loose cover on Jim. 'Give that upstart some professional opposition.' Jim tacked almost immediately. The leading boat tacked with him. There was a flurry of tacks and counter-tacks, fourteen in all. Jim was still ten feet away, sailing lower but perhaps a fraction faster, making leeway to keep out of the other boat's windshadow.

Jim tacked yet again, but this time Abrams did not try to cover him. Instead he continued on his course. Now it was based on sheer speed.

After four hundred yards Abrams tacked in again. Coach Johnson said, 'You did right, Abrams. You're sailing by the book.'

Jim did not cross tacks. Long before they met, he tacked and sailed parallel, with at least a hundred yards between them. It was difficult to see who was ahead. Jim sailed on another fifty yards, then tacked.

Coach Johnson licked his dry lips. He resolved to consume a six-pack that evening.

Abrams and Jim were closing. Coach Johnson watched as Jim came in on port, Abrams on starboard with right of way. Jim crossed five feet in front of Abrams, tacked immediately to place a close cover, and the two crossed the line in formation, Jim half a boat length ahead.

The sound of the gun dispelled itself on the shore and the empty wastelands of the dock.

Unfortunately, Coach Johnson realised, there would be no six-packs that afternoon. There was work to do.

Six

Coach Johnson carried a limp from 'Nam. He'd been luckier than many. Now he was aware of it because of the irregular echo of his footsteps along the sea wall. He followed several flights of stone stairs upwards, climbing above the first level of houses. The road was called Weepeq, like the Bay. Twenty steps up a final incline and he could see the house, an old wooden building with shutters. As he drew closer he smelt paint and turpentine. The garden was neglected but the house well-kept. The brass door-knocker was polished and the hinge well oiled. He could hear its thump echoing through the rooms. A few moments later, chains were drawn back and the door was opened.

'Mr Shaw?' he heard himself ask.

'Sam Shaw.'

Coach Johnson held out a hand. 'Hal Johnson, national Olympic sailing coach. Wondered if I might possibly have a word with you about Jim.'

He watched Sam Shaw hesitate, study his hand for a moment like a householder receiving a piece of unwelcome mail. They shook hands. Sam Shaw's grip was powerful, as if in warning.

'Come in.'

Coach Johnson removed his hat in the porch. Out of the bright sunlight, it seemed dark inside. He looked around. Pine floors, tall ceilings, no curtains. There was the same smell of upkeep in the big kitchen. The rest of the interior that he could see was clean but spartan. He could begin to believe that luxury was not a big part of Sam Shaw's life.

Sam Shaw drew a high-backed chair away from the table, pulled out a chair for himself, indicated for Coach Johnson to sit down, and sat down opposite.

Coach Johnson decided that, quite apart from the austere nature of the house, this was someone who didn't much care for the preliminaries. He leaned forward in his chair, holding his hat in his hands, and said as casually as he was able. 'Watched Jim sail today, Mr Shaw. Think your boy's got promise.'

'My grandson,' corrected Sam Shaw.

Coach Johnson nodded. 'How old is Jim, Mr Shaw?'

'Thirteen.'

Coach Johnson paused. From where he was sitting he could see, through one of the tall windows, part of the east side of the bay. A group of dinghies was making its way back towards the shore. Like a prefect, a support boat was herding another small group.

'Mighty young.' Coach Johnson heard himself say. 'He's got his education to consider.'

'He certainly has, Mr Johnson.' Sam Shaw paused, then struck hard. 'He's too young to be any kind of professional sailor.'

Another man might have quailed, but Coach Johnson answered amiably enough:

'I grant you that, Mr Shaw, I grant you that.'

Nevertheless, Coach Johnson wanted to think about what Sam Shaw had just said, to recover. He'd let Sam Shaw do the running for a while.

The house had a curious quietness, a silence which seemed built into the surfaces of the paint. It was one of those houses where everything said was like a form of intrusion – a lonely place for a child to live, he thought. An image came to him, of a sail separated from the fleet.

But Sam Shaw wouldn't talk. The silence started to become embarrassing. Coach Johnson took a deep breath. He, too, was not a man for the niceties.

'Right now we're training one of the best sailors I ever did see. Boy named Jack Peabody, aged fourteen. Just the finest natural sailor I coached.'

Sam Shaw saw the pitch coming. He said, 'Coffee?'

'Thanks,' replied Coach Johnson.

In the corner Sam Shaw poked the coal stove, filled a tall kettle with water, set it on one of the hot plates. Coach Johnson looked briefly at his back, meditated on his own position for a while, and decided, for no good reason, to continue.

'Well, the long and the short of it is, Peabody's so damn good, no one there can give him any competition. Sure, we can train him, we can teach him theory, but short of tying a bucket behind his boat, he just isn't being given a hard time at all.'

Sam Shaw continued to make the coffee.

Coach Johnson heard his words move through the house, become lost on the paintwork, felt the place return to its natural state. He looked about him cautiously, noticing, through an adjacent doorway, the nets piled in one corner of the next room. In any normal house, that other room would have been the living room, filled with furniture, books, personal things. Apart from a single high-backed chair, it was as gaunt as a monk's cell.

'You think Jim might be able to help you, Mr Johnson?'

Coach Johnson's mind snapped back to the present. He had lost concentration for a moment. He'd been ambushed again. There was no way of ducking that last question.

'I got this feeling he just might.'

Coach Johnson paused again. He wasn't sure whether Sam Shaw wasn't testing him making him work.

'Thirteen's too young,' Sam Shaw said decisively.

Coach Johnson knew he was defeated. He could have kicked himself. He said: 'Guess you could be right. Yeah, I'll just have to put up with Jack Peabody for another year. Just have to accept the fact that he'll become a complacent, spoiled brat . . . Well, it's been nice talking to you, Mr Shaw. Maybe I'll be calling by next year.'

Coach Johnson stood up. He felt a pain travel from his leg to the base of his spine. If he had been alone, in his bathroom or bedroom or somewhere else without an audience, he would have cried out.

But Sam Shaw was still facing away from him, watching the kettle boil.

The pain subsided in Coach Johnson's leg. Standing there stupidly, it occurred to him that he had been outmanoeuvred again. Sam Shaw was not inclined to acknowledge his presence and was instead resolutely continuing with the coffee. Coach Johnson sat down again.

Sam Shaw set up a filter for the coffee, wetting a glass funnel under the tap and placing the disk of white filter paper inside it. Coach Johnson hadn't seen a filter like that for years. He didn't know they could be bought any more.

Sam Shaw poured the boiling water into it, watching the dark fluid collect in the glass container beneath. He lifted two mugs from the cupboard and placed them on the metal sink.

'This Peabody's pretty good, you say?'

'Best young sailor in the country, to my way of thinking.'

Coach Johnson paused, waiting for Sam Shaw to say something further. A tall clock ticked loudly in the background. He was again reminded that silence was the natural state in this house. He had an idle intuition that words, whoever spoke them, favoured him, and that silences were the natural ally of Sam Shaw. To keep the conversation alive, perhaps just to keep the nervous silence at bay, Coach Johnson said:

'Do you know much about helmsmen, Mr Shaw? I'm just asking that question because I've known plenty. I've known some pretty good ones too. And I have to say, not one of them's going to have an easy path to heaven.'

Sam Shaw said nothing, setting up the coffee cups. Coach Johnson was again forcibly reminded of the weakness of his position, of the absurdity of his reasons for coming here. He wished now he'd taken his own advice, driven home, taken out a six-pack from the back of his small fridge, worked up a presentation he was going to have to give the following week to a sailing school down the coast. Now that he was here, he had nothing better to do than continue.

'The good ones have all got something pretty strange going on inside them. I've had to listen to them, act as their adviser, hear their complaints, try to work out what's going on. Inside every one there's that little devil who wants to win despite all the odds. I say devil because the fella I've glimpsed occasionally sure isn't any angel. And that's not the worst of it. Imagine if you took one of these guys to a really good psychologist. Suppose he put one of these guys straight, showed him it didn't matter a damn in the world who won the race, that'd be the end of him as a helmsman. Sure, he could win club races, show up well in a few nationals, but once that devil goes, why, he isn't any use to me.'

He could smell the coffee now, and for some reason a curious hope began to grow inside him, a conviction that, in the end, he would win the argument with Sam Shaw, that his host would start to see sense.

'That's what coaching is, at this level. It's bringing out that devil, feeding him, making him grow, not so much that he takes over the personality, you understand, but enough to keep that guy on edge, so that something inside him is howling to win.'

Coach Johnson paused again, heard the silence close in, then continued:

'I'm not complaining. That's my job. I chose it for myself, and I don't delude myself about what I do. If I took over Jim's career, that's what I'd be aiming to do, free that devil and let him grow. It's the diametric opposite of what a psychologist or priest does.' Coach Johnson allowed himself the rare pleasure of a fleeting smile. 'I know which side I'm on.'

He waited, waited for what seemed several minutes, while his host moved the coffee jug about slowly, making sure it didn't settle. Finally Sam Shaw said:

'Well, you're honest.' Then he added slyly, choosing his words. 'Maybe that means you're not quite as devilish as you claim, Mr Johnson.'

Coach Johnson said: 'I'm making no claims for myself, Mister Shaw. What I'm saying, I guess, is that helmsmen aren't normal people. A good helmsman has ice in his blood and anger in his heart.'

Sam Shaw was quiet, pouring coffee into the two mugs,

placing a spoon in each. He said finally: 'You think Jim's like that?'

'Maybe,' replied Coach Johnson. 'Maybe you know better than anyone.'

'If he isn't,' said Sam Shaw with satisfaction, 'you can't put it there.'

'And if he is,' Coach Johnson replied evenly, 'maybe it's best to put it to good use.'

'Well,' said Sam Shaw, 'I guess the devil knows his own. You haven't persuaded me, speaking for myself. Jim's going to find out what he wants to do, and I'm not in the business of trying to stop him.'

Coach Johnson shrugged his shoulders, but said nothing.

Sam Shaw continued: 'Myself, I've been trying to move in the opposite direction. I've come to the conclusion that's a pretty unimpressive world out there, everyone competing, driving each other crazy, climbing over one another. I'm pleased to be out of it. But Jim has to learn his own lessons, whatever they may be. I can't teach him.' Sam Shaw added, 'You'll have to ask the boy yourself. Ain't my decision.'

Afterwards, Coach Johnson would wonder when Sam Shaw had changed his mind, when he had decided to let Jim go.

'If Jim's the guy I think he is, Mr Shaw, I'm afraid that's a foregone conclusion.'

Sam Shaw put the cups on a tray. He felt more relaxed now. Perhaps, at the same time, he felt a little older.

'What exactly is your set-up, Mr Johnson?'

'We're sponsored by a charity, the Summer Sailing Foundation. It pays for all our youth training. It's an organisation funded by Mormons. One of the rules is that there will be no alcohol on the premises, and no tea or coffee, because they are the devil's artificial stimulants.'

But Sam Shaw had one final thrust.

'How do you take your coffee, Mr Johnson?'

'Strong and black,' replied Coach Johnson evenly, 'like the devil. And I'd appreciate it if you called me Hal.'

Seven

When Jim arrived at the training camp, nestling in a hollow by the foreshore, Coach Johnson made a point of introducing him to Jack Peabody.

Right from the start, Jack Peabody stood apart from the rest. Tall, somewhat gangling, with reddish hair and freckles, he kept his own company. The others did not seem to concern him.

Jim watched as he walked down the wharf alone, carrying his rolled sails, observed him as he eased himself into the boat, spreading his spidery limbs carefully. One long hand took the tiller extension, another the mainsheet.

The first day it was gusty, blowing fresh. The wind picked up around the little gaggle of buildings grouped around the wharf, producing sudden bursts which caused the sails of the tethered Laser dinghies to flap. Jack was not the first to leave. He allowed his craft to slip back, waited until a gust struck him, picked up speed rapidly as if he was about to ram the wharf, then bore away with cool inconsequentiality. His accelerating wash thumped the sterns of the parked boats. Another gust struck, and instead of letting out the sail, he climbed the side of the dinghy as the power came on, trimmed sail by steering closer to the wind, and like a car on two wheels, powered down the flat stretch of water into the open sea. Jim, watching, turned away with an effort, mesmerised by Jack's confidence.

The first day was spent indoors. Coach Johnson lectured on rules and sailing tactics. There were seventeen of them. Each was, in his own right, a champion. Jim looked round at them. They seemed to drink up Coach Johnson's words. He was, after all, some kind of legend in the sailing community, having sent team after team to outstanding success.

They were all attentive, except for one. Even in the

classroom Jack Peabody seemed detached. The others were eager to ask questions, to display their knowledge. But Jack's brown eyes hardly showed a flicker of interest. He was slouched in his chair, in an attitude so much at ease that he would have been reprimanded as slovenly if he had not been who he was.

Coach Johnson stood with a loud-hailer in his left hand, balanced on his feet with one foot braced on the floor, the other on a thwart, rocking on his soles against the movement of the cutter in the small waves. He shouted instructions through the loud-hailer. 'Come on, you characters,' he yelled. In his right hand he held a starting pistol loaded with blanks.

Charlie Grist, his sidekick and shore manager, sat at the back of the boat. Small, dark, wiry, his body crouched like an animal, Charlie Grist deftly tied on the shapes that he would run up the little mast in the stern of the cutter. A big clock, with a face the size of a carving plate, swung on the arm of the cutter's mast, tied with a cord to the gunwale in order to avoid swinging too much. It signalled the countdown of minutes with one hand, seconds with another.

Coach Johnson fired the starting pistol again for the five-minute gun. A second shape was pulled up by Charlie Grist. The boat rocked as Coach Johnson shouted through the loud-hailer and waved his pistol like a gangster. Through it all he kept his footing, swaying lightly on the soles of his feet. Charlie Grist, having run up the shapes, would light one of his home-rolled cigarettes, crouching nonchalantly in the stern, and the puffs of smoke would float out behind the cutter like silent gunshots.

Charlie was the only person allowed to smoke in the entire camp. He was beyond the pale, one of those sinners whose affliction is too great to be healed. Matron had long since given up chiding or abusing him. He would simply nod his head, say, 'Sure is a fine thing to have good intentions, ma'am.' And he would continue to his

41

uninterrupted smoking, letting slip from his cupped hands the Indian signals of his private thoughts.

Dear Granpa, (Jim wrote)
I have been here over a week now. There's seventeen of us altogether, and Coach Johnson, and Miss Higham, our matron.

We get up at six in the morning, take a cold shower, and do exercises until seven-thirty. Then Coach Johnson runs through the programme for the day. After that we have breakfast, then we have a lecture on tactics or rules. When that's over, we go sailing.

The guys here are really good. On my first practice race I came eighth, then sixth, then ninth. Yesterday I was fourth. I know I'm a long way from being good here, but I'm starting to learn how these boats handle.

Jack Peabody is the one I have to beat. He gets in so far ahead of everyone else he has to hang around on the finish line for the others to come in.

It's real nice here. The weather's good, and we have an interesting mixture of winds.

Coach Johnson asked me to send you his regards.
Love,
Jim

Already Jim was cultivating the art of detachment, already he had begun to imitate Jack. Who but Jack would have described the extraordinary changes of weather that week, from oily calm to black storm, as 'an interesting mixture of winds'?

Eight

Early morning sunlight slanted down the side of the hill, the long shadows so dark they were almost blue. Small white buildings, wood-shuttered, reflected in the water. From a long way off came the smell of Charlie Grist's coffee.

Charlie kept the maintenance equipment, the buoys and the racing marks which bobbed slowly in the bay. The smell of coffee mixed with the more pungent smell of the barrels of tar which Charlie used to protect the wood wharfs.

In the early mornings they walked up the hill in single file, Coach Johnson limping ahead of them, Miss Higham bringing up the rear. On the hill they exercised, push-ups, deep-knee bends, running on the spot. Behind them, to their right, the athletic figure of Miss Higham went through her paces.

They were as much in awe of Miss Higham as they were of Coach; of her apparently tireless energy, her seeming detachment from their overheard comments, her unfailing good humour like armour. Surreptitiously, they studied her high cheekbones and almost squat, eskimo nose with its flared nostrils.

Coach Johnson walked up and down the staggered lines in the early morning, cajoling them.

Jack Peabody was, as always, naturally apart, staring occasionally with his puzzled brown eyes out to sea, sniffing the wind, trying to assess the day's windshifts. Coach said, 'You seen a breeze, have you, Jack? Something to hitch a ride on?'

Afterwards, when Jim's thoughts returned to the summer sailing school, it always returned to the primary figures: Coach Johnson, Jack Peabody, Miss Higham. Like the lines connecting the corners of a triangle, the hidden associations lay between these three. It was as if they held some sort of clue to his being there. Yet the lines that connected them were also the lines of careful disregard, as if each, in ignoring the other, was emphasising the others' existence in some way Jim could not understand.

Everything else seemed like shadows, the quiet explosive shadows of training youths, Charlie Grist's coffee, the group of white buildings below the hillside.

'Don't reckon he even knows he's doing it,' said Charlie Grist, sending a used match sailing out into the water with a flick of his finger. He puffed silently on his cigarette.

Jim noticed that Charlie Grist, when he talked to you, always looked away. When he wasn't talking to you he sometimes looked at you with his slanted, almost sightless brown eyes. You knew he was studying you when he wasn't looking at you, when he beamed at you the strong sideways focus of his regard.

'Doing what?' asked Jim.

Puffs of smoke emerged from Charlie Grist's mouth, quick as a semaphore. 'He's challenging you,' said Charlie Grist. 'You don't know it. He don't know it, maybe. But he is.' He said this with something like satisfaction.

Jim looked at the waterway. Jack had used the strong breeze to pitch the boat up on its side. Then, with a half movement of his hand, he eased pressure on the mainsheet, and the dinghy settled down, like a bird on the water. Jack sat out, drew in the mainsheet, and began to drive her flat and hard.

Charlie Grist said: 'Look at the centre of that boat. See where its centre is? I'll tell you. It's Jack's head. The whole boat just moves around his head. If it's on its side, upwind or downwind, that's where the centre is.' Charlie Grist had removed his cigarette to deliver this, one of his longest speeches. He put his cigarette back in his mouth, picked up two half filled four-gallon tins of wood protecting agent, and set off across the waste ground to his hut, with the occasional puff from his cigarette as he snorted under the weight of the cans.

Nausea rose in Jim's stomach as each race ended and his adrenalin died down. Jack's talent was like a cliff face which he would never climb. By the time he reached the shore he felt sick with depression. He stripped the sails and folded them, keeping to himself, some distance apart from the others. His mouth was full of the slightly salty saliva which precedes vomiting. Above everything he did not wish to throw up in front of the others and allow them to see his misery.

He stood up, feeling shaky, and walked over to a small outhouse which had been placed, like an afterthought, at the end of one of the long white buildings. Someone shouted, 'Going to take a leak, Shaw?' But his mind welcomed the distraction. A few seconds later his stomach started to heave and he vomited behind the little outbuilding, amongst the old and rusty ironwork that had been placed there. It made him feel immediately better, almost lightheaded. He was about to return to the others when he became aware of a figure standing hardly ten feet away, small, dark, leaning against a shed with a cigarette in his mouth. 'How ya doing?' said Charlie Grist. Jim felt a wave of misery return. He had been seen, and he had already developed an odd respect for Charlie Grist.

'OK now,' he said.

Quick puffs of smoke emerged from Charlie Grist's mouth. He seemed to accept what Jim said at face value. He nodded, and walked away with his odd, almost completely silent tread. Jim watched him moving quickly and quietly across the waste ground towards his own shed, which stood about fifty yards away. Jim knew he should go back soon, or one of the others would come to investigate. He felt shaky, but good enough.

On the wharf he picked up his sails, carried them through the shed and set them down on the rack in the long shed which was kept dry by a series of old radiators and waterpipes along the north wall. In the washrooms he rinsed out his mouth, splashed cold water on his face. In the background he heard Coach Johnson shout, 'Come on, you men, let's get through the debriefing.' He dried his face and crossed to the little schoolroom which had been built of pine and which served as the lecture room. 'Take a seat, Shaw,' said Coach Johnson. He turned to someone else. 'OK, Pringle, what went wrong?'

Jerry Pringle was small and fat. Jim had noticed how he had got away to one of the best starts, reached the top mark second or third, and then slumped away. 'I tacked into trouble, I guess. Henry took my wind,' he added.

'Well, if it's your wind, don't let Henry take it.'

The class laughed, discomforted. Coach Johnson said: 'You are one of the best, Pringle. You lost your concentration and attack. Those two are the same thing. That's just the part of the race, when you've rounded the weather mark, where you have to be careful. OK, don't let it happen again.'

Coach Johnson went through each individual's race, occasionally referring to the notes he'd made. His memory was prodigious. He said to Henry Cole, 'There was an opening there at the third mark, Cole, and you could have made it through on the inside. It's good to keep out of trouble, to clear your wind, but sometimes you've got to cut in.'

There were two whose performances he did not analyse, those of Jack Peabody and Jim Shaw. And in a curious way, the others were given to understand that this silence about performance connected them, that judgment was being suspended, and the real fight was just starting.

In the evenings they ate on the long pine boards of the table, Miss Higham bringing in the food, serving Coach at the head of the table first, then Jack, who sat at his right hand. Jim chose to sit at the other end, where Curly Shinwell held court, bantering away.

Coach Johnson hardly spoke at table. Jack, as always, looked detached. But they seemed like father and son who know each other. A familiar wariness separated them. Miss Higham hovered about those two like a mother or perhaps a dutiful daughter. The rest of them were merely guests at the family meal.

46

Like those who have been brought up by the old, Jim felt ill-at-ease in his own age group. It was an odd thing, but Jim never grew entirely to like his peers. His greatest friend was his grandfather. He preferred the company of the elderly. In some ways they were like children too, returning to the pure unthinking egocentricity of the child. But their childishness was tinged with the comical, terrible wisdom of experience. If Jim was hungry for knowledge, he preferred to find it among the old.

'Now listen, Jim,' Coach Johnson said, appearing beside Jim in the early morning before the exercises started. 'When you first came here, maybe you felt it was going to be easy. I mean, you just walk over all the guys back home, so you think you can do the same here.' Coach Johnson stood beside him, looking out to sea where the first ruffle of wind turned the water a darker shade of grey.

'The other guys who came here started like you. They thought "these guys aren't any different from the guys I beat back home". But they are, Jim. These are the guys that beat the guys back home.

'Now you're starting again. You aren't any better and you aren't any worse. I don't care if you come in at the tail-end of the fleet. I'm watching to see what you do after that. Are you going to just fade away. Or are you going to crawl back?

'Because that's what it takes. Talent sometimes isn't enough to beat the guy that you can't put down, that learns by his mistakes, that comes back for more.

'Any real champion has that quality. Why, you just look at Dennis Conner, Jim. Big, fat guy, looks like a softy. Talks as if he's somewhere else. But what happened when he lost the America's Cup in 1983. Why, he just got down to it and came back. It's what's inside that counts.'

Coach Johnson looked out to sea, at the racing buoys bobbing like cormorants out to sea. He said:

'Never give up. If you don't give up, you ain't beat.'

On the hillside the others were gathering. Coach Johnson shouted. 'Hey, you guys, what is this, a picnic? Let's move it.'

Jim had said nothing. He watched Coach Johnson walk away, shouting to the tailenders who were gathering on the hillside before the exercises. He felt an odd wave of sympathy for Coach Johnson, forced by his position to act out a certain role.

Down the hill the short figure of Charlie Grist leaned over some items of brass Miss Higham had asked him to clean. The smoke drove away from his mouth in short bursts as he concentrated on the task. There was precious little role-playing where Charlie Grist was concerned.

'Coach eggin' you on, Jim?' Jack Peabody was beside him, speaking softly with his Southern accent. Jim couldn't make him out against the rising sun, his face in shadow. It was a day of surprises.

'Yeah, I guess so.'

'All that stuff about never letting go, always coming back?'

'Yeah.'

Jack paused. His brown eyes took on their wistful puzzled look. 'You believe that crap?'

'Some of it, I think.'

'That's perverted values, Jim. I'm going to have to keep a fatherly eye on you.'

Coach Johnson was at the other end of the line. About forty feet away, Miss Higham was exercising in her leotard, running on the spot, swinging her knees up in swift jerks.

'Holy cow,' Jack said under his breath.

In a pause between exercises, Jim said, 'What do you believe in, Jack?'

'Big tits, man. Big tits.'

'That's not serious.'

'I am totally serious, believe me. My faith grows deeper every day.'

Behind them and to their right, Miss Higham started

48

on an especially energetic series of arm swings, thrusting her breasts forward. Jack said fervently:

'My cup runneth over, man.'

Coach was suddenly alongside, striding up the line.

Jim and Jack started to work harder. To their right Miss Higham stopped exercising. She stared out to sea for a few seconds, hands on hips, then reached down to pick up her jumper and throw it over her shoulder. She walked off down the hill.

Coach Johnson walked up and down the line, shouting, 'Move it, you guys, move! One two one two one two. Keep on your toes there, swing your arms.'

Coach walked away, and Jim noticed that Jack gave his departing back a concentrated look, difficult to decipher. Jack said:

'Coach thinks he's found a stick to beat me with, Jim. He thinks you're that stick.' He did not look at Jim.

Jim said nothing. He put on his sweater. They fell in with the other boys as they walked down the slope towards the small group of white buildings.

Jim started to bring in thirds and fourths. Only once in the course of the following week did he manage a second. Always ahead of him was Jack, never looking back. But a curious thing happened that second week. Jim had felt his heaviness disappear. Instead he felt a peculiar lightness, like hunger. At the same time he felt detached. On the quay he would linger longer than the others, rolling up his sails, thinking about the race, going through his moves one by one while it was still fresh. The others scampered ashore to play games of darts and billiards in the rest room before the afternoon debriefing with Coach Johnson. Jim preferred to linger on his own near the boats.

He liked to help Charlie Grist in his work. Charlie had stripped the paint from the walls of one of the wooden houses, and was painting on primer. He had several spare brushes beside him, and Jim started to paint with him.

One day Charlie Grist said, 'I been watching you.' His eyes were small, widely set, curiously sightless. His face, the colour of grey smoke, had crease lines running down from his eyes and mouth. 'You're on the track.'

'What track is that?' asked Jim.

Charlie Grist directed at him the beam of his sideways regard, blowing once or twice a cloud from his cigarette. He said: 'Not watching him, not thinking about him.'

When not holding a cigarette, Charlie had the fingers of an addict, constantly restless. They patted his pockets, pulled out keys, screws, odd scraps of paper. Rumour had it that his shed was piled high with pornographic magazines.

In the races which followed Jim concentrated on the others, on their strengths and weaknesses. Larry Sparkes, for example, was brilliant at sail handling. He could create extraordinary turns of speed, his quiet hands on the sheets and the tiller, his eyes constantly flickering from sail to the surface of the sea. Jim tried to match him on the reaches, where Larry was supreme. On that point of sailing you didn't need weight so much, you had to get the sails and the trim of the boat just right. On the reaching legs he attempted to draw close to Larry Sparkes, trying to match against him his own peculiar, elusive thread of connection between the balance of the boat and speed.

Little Curly Shinwell was the master of tactics. Every second race his start would be the best. In some ways the study of Curly's tactics was the most difficult; his approach to the start line was unexpected and wholly original. If there was an opportunity to be exploited, Curly was nearly always uncannily there. So Jim took time to watch Curly carefully in the final two minutes before the starting gun, his almost instinctive positioning. He noted one important feature of Curly's starts. Curly always reached fast in the few minutes before the gun, building up maximum speed so that when he swung into wind, he could use this superior burst of speed to punch out into a lead of half a boat length or so.

These lessons were absorbing. But always out ahead,

after the first two or three marks, would be a single white sail.

'You'd think he'd get lonely out there, wouldn't you?' said Charlie Grist. He was thinning a pot of old paint, adding spirit as he stirred it with a stick. Jim said nothing. Charlie moved his cigarette around his mouth. Jim knew that Charlie was driving in the challenge, that sooner or later he would have to show his hand. It was odd how calm he felt.

In the afternoons, after debriefing, when they had an hour to themselves, Jack went walking. He vaulted a low stone wall and made his way up the seaside path along the low cliffs. Jim could see his thin figure flicker like a flame in the wind. Charlie Grist noted, with only the faintest shadow of a smile, that Jim did not watch the figure disappear behind a dip in the land. Instead Jim seemed to be internally preoccupied, to be working on something inside himself.

In the evening, after their meal, Coach Johnson retired to his office to work for an hour or so on paperwork, and to plan the details of the following day's schedule.

Most of the boys lay on their bunks and read. It was Jack's habit to sit out on the porch of the sailing house for half an hour before the bell went and lights were turned out in their dormitory.

One evening Jim went outside. The crickets were chirping. Against the darkness he could see Jack lying against a wooden pillar, chewing a piece of grass. Jim sat down on the portico steps.

Jack said: 'There isn't anything to do here at night.'

Jim was silent. Jack indicated a window, with curtains drawn, in one of the other buildings.

Jack said, 'Miss Higham lives there. She's already booked, though.'

'What do you mean?' asked Jim.

'Coach.'

'Coach Johnson?'

A bell rang inside. Laconically, Jack raised himself to

51

his feet. Jim looked at the window, then at Jack. He followed Jack inside.

Coach Johnson stood in the cutter, loud-hailer in one hand, starting pistol in the other. Charlie Grist sat in the stern, tying the starting flags in. Around them the dinghies milled.

Jack was about fifty yards distant, detached. Coach Johnson shouted through the loud-hailer. 'Jack, you take the pin end this time.' Jack, without looking at him, hauled in his sheet, accelerating away towards the pin end.

'OK, you men, get ready to start,' shouted Coach Johnson.

The five-minute gun went. Charlie Grist was crouched over in the stern of the cutter, lighting up a cigarette. Jim crept over towards Jack at the pin end, easing out sheet so that he wasn't going fast. The minute hand of the big clock face swinging from the yardarm of the cutter indicated two minutes to go. Jim felt an odd, unexpected calm inside him, as if he were an observer.

Jack was forty yards away, cruising back and forward across the line.

With thirty seconds to go, Jim hardened in sheets and began to work up speed. He turned now towards Jack, easing away from Curly Shinwell and Jerry Orlovsky.

Nine, eight, seven, six . . . He no longer watched the clock hand and was simply counting. He hardened in and swung up closehauled. The starting gun went and he crossed the transit about four seconds later. It was a safe start, not brilliant. Jack elected to tack away. Jim tacked towards the fleet. There was a small avenue of disturbance between him and the rest of the fleet, a darker patch on the water. He was in it first, ahead of Curly, who was close behind. A quick surge of power filled the sails, and the sheer of the wind allowed him to point higher. It lasted hardly more than a minute, but he had been lifted into the lead of his own group. He was aware of Jack parallel to him, about a hundred yards away, tacking back. Jim tacked again, trying to find the avenue of wind. It seemed to have blown itself out, a tiny local eddy. But once again he saw the water round him become darker, he felt through his arm the extra power in the sail. Leaning out further, he drove the dinghy forward as fast as he could. Now he was pointing a little lower than the group, but going much quicker. He emerged on the other side of the wind gust and tacked again, still hunting for the little wind corridor. This time he was lifted again, sailing higher and faster.

At the weather mark Jack cut in across him two lengths ahead, and Jim, still in a trance, followed him round for the reaching leg.

Almost immediately Jack began to pull away. But Jim, accepting this predominance, sailed a higher course, a little faster than if he followed Jack, hunting for advantages. Jack did not look back, relying, as he preferred to do, on his own speed.

Jack swung round the next mark six lengths ahead. Glancing behind him, Jim saw the others were now nearly two hundred yards behind, dark triangles on a sun-blasted surface. Curly Shinwell was leading the pack. Several duels were going on within the pack. Two boats were bearing away to get out of the ruck.

Round the buoy, almost directly downwind, the sudden knowledge of Jack's vulnerability went like a howl through Jim. A little hesitantly at first, Jim began to hunt back and forth, searching for Jack's wind. Still Jack did not look back.

After a few moments Jack's mainsail shook and lost wind, filled. Jim hunted him down again, collapsed the mainsail. The sun was behind them, shining on Jack's back.

Jack's sails collapsed, then filled with a sudden bang, and collapsed again. He looked upwards and turned slowly to gaze into the sun. In that moment Jim sailed through to weather of him, moving almost two knots faster, thinking that for the rest of his life he would remember the sightless, uncomprehending stare.

Back at the dock, Jim rolled up his sails and, as he always did, ran through the race.

After he had passed Jack, he had deliberately sailed as high as he could, to discourage Jack from sailing upwind of him and stealing his own wind. But Jack had not attempted to match him. Instead Jack had continued on his course, picked up speed, and slowly overhauled Jim to leeward. Jim knew that if the finish line had been a further hundred yards ahead, Jack would have beaten him. As it was, he had scraped into a win by hardly more than a yard.

Jack was second into the wharf. He stripped his sails and disappeared into the rest room. Jim heard a record being put on, a heavy metal group whose name he could not remember.

A shadow fell across Jim's sails. Small, changing patterns of cigarette smoke broke from the shadow. Charlie Grist stood beside him for a few seconds, saying nothing, and Jim knew that he approved.

Nine

Jim thought they'd let him forget his victory that day. He didn't want any fuss. Charlie Grist had understood that, as he understood most things.

In the debriefing, Coach Johnson performed his usual autopsy on the results of the others. Jack's and Jim's performances seemed exempt.

Coach Johnson finished his comments. He looked towards Jim Shaw. He said, 'I guess there isn't too much I can say about your performance today, Shaw.' The classroom was silent. Coach Johnson looked towards Jack Peabody, leaning back laconically in his chair. 'Any comments, Jack?'

Jack must have felt the attention of the class turn towards him. The quietness which had descended on the room seemed now to focus on the pencil Jack was gently tapping on the desk.

Jack's expression hardly changed. They watched the pencil gently rising and falling. They waited until the tapping came slowly to a halt. Jack seemed to pause, to gather his thoughts. He appeared to shrug slightly, and said, 'He beat me fair and square.'

'I guess he did,' said Coach Johnson gravely. 'I guess he did.' They watched Jack's face, because it is in defeat that one sees the colour of a champion. Perhaps they hoped to find some trace of consternation, of anger, at the very least some small loss of poise. But if such feelings were present, no one could perceive them.

After a few moments, Jack yawned. It broke the spell. They turned away. Coach Johnson issued some instructions for the following day, and they left the little school-room.

At the evening meal, Jim was about to take up his position at the end of the table next to Curly when Coach Johnson caught his eye, gestured to him to sit on his left-hand side at the top of the table. Jim Shaw, who had no compunction about fighting on the water, winced at this ceremony.

They stood silently while Coach Johnson said grace. When they had seated themselves, Miss Higham brought in the plates of steak, boiled cabbage and potato. She put the first plate in front of Coach Johnson, but he said: 'Jim first, Nancy, if you please. He won the race today.'

Miss Higham leaned over Jim to serve him. The table was quiet for a moment, and then gathered its usual babble of voices. But Coach Johnson was unwilling to lose one final opportunity to torture his two protégés. He whispered to Miss Higham, who filled the glasses with water, then tapped the table with his knife:

'Now listen, you men. Today Jim Shaw really sailed like a champion. I know we aren't supposed to swear here, but it takes a hell of a good man to beat Jack on any day. I want you to raise your glasses and drink a toast to Jim Shaw.'

The rest of the room, drawn like any restless crowd towards the spectacle of this bull-baiting, raised their glasses and roared out, in approximate union, 'Jim Shaw'. Then they broke into loud applause.

That night, on the dormitory porch, Jack took up his usual position leaning against the portico. Jim sat down on the steps.

Jim said, 'I'm sorry about today.'

'What about?'

'All that stuff afterwards.'

'It's fine by me. Keeps Coach amused.'

Jack turned away, looking in the general direction of the sea. Far away, they could hear Charlie Grist's little primus stove whistling as he boiled some coffee.

'You weren't trying today, Jack.'

The crickets shrilled.

'Wasn't I?'

'You got something on your mind.'

'Maybe.'

A shape moved across the window opposite. Jim caught sight of Miss Higham's voluptuous shape. The curtains were drawn together, as if shutting them out.

Jim said: 'You serious about her and Coach?'

'She's a Mormon, ain't she?'

'What do you mean?'

'God,' said Jack, 'you don't know anything. You ever met any Mormons?'

'No, I guess not.'

'They don't drink, they don't smoke, they don't even take coffee or tea. There's precious little fun for a Mormon.'

'So?'

'So what's she got left, huh?'

'What?'

Jack leaned forward: 'I once got up real early, you know, to take a leak. And I crept by Coach's door, and there wasn't a snore or a sign of breathing. I didn't take much notice, but then when I was on my way back I saw him coming out of Miss Higham's room, in his pyjamas. He was creeping along the tiles.'

'You mean?'

'I mean,' said Jack, 'Miss Higham would just tear you limb from limb. That's what these big, healthy girls are like.'

Jim said nothing.

'Mormon girls are almost as good as black girls,' whispered Jack.

'Really?' said Jim.

'I'd put them on a level with Italian girls,' Jack hissed.

'That so?' said Jim, doing his best to sound knowledgeable.

The bell rang. Coach Johnson shouted from his open study door. 'OK you guys, go inside now. Go to the bathroom and hit the sack. Parade at six-thirty.'

Jim followed Jack inside. Before he closed the door he took a last, careful look at Miss Higham's window.

In the race which followed, Jack pulled out a five hundred yard lead on Jim. Jim was second, about forty yards ahead of Curly Shinwell, who stuck doggedly to his heels through the race, and almost overtook him, by expert exploitation of a windshift, in the last leg.

Jim rolled up his sails, and went through the race. He felt he could have gained a few yards here, a few there. But five hundred? As he finished folding the sail, he felt the familiar nausea rise inside him at the scale of Jack's victory. He made a detour to his place behind the shed. He was grateful that Charlie Grist was nowhere to be seen. As usual, he felt almost immediately relieved.

In the course of the race, he had gybed rapidly in the pre-start mêlée, and had been struck a glancing blow on the left side of the head by the boom. He felt with his hand gingerly over the bump that had formed there, and found his hand sticky with blood.

At the washrooms he rinsed out his mouth, washed his

hands, removed most of the blood on his head. He looked in the mirror and saw that he was still bleeding there. It didn't look serious to him, but he felt obliged to take precautions against infection.

He knocked on the door of Miss Higham's office to ask her whether it needed attention, but there was no reply. He looked around for her in the other buildings but could not find her. Shrugging his shoulders, he went into the debriefing room and sat on the left side of the room so no one would see or be able to see or comment on his bloodstained, matted hair.

Coach Johnson conducted his usual post-mortem. Jack took up his customary laconic position in the chair in one of the far corners. Mercifully, Coach Johnson undertook no detailed analysis of his own performance, except for a comment that Curly Shinwell was on the point of overtaking him on the last beat, a comment Jim knew to be just. He had forgotten the state of his head when he walked out.

Outside, Miss Higham turned towards him and gave a small, low scream. 'Look at your head.'

She seized him by the wrist and marched him smartly to the small surgery. 'Why didn't you notify someone?' He wanted to say that he had called by the surgery earlier, but some intuition told him this was unwise.

Miss Higham clucked over the state of his head. When he saw himself in the mirror, he could partially understand her reaction. The side of his head was a caked mass of blood. The blood had dried his hair together. Miss Higham used small scissors to cut away the mat of dried blood and hair. She disinfected the gash carefully, laid a dressing on and bound it round his head with a bandage.

If his headwound had looked impressive before he was subject to the ministrations of Miss Higham, his new situation virtually gave him the status of a war hero. That evening Jack said, on the dormitory porch, 'Shaw, I thought I was racing you today, but you'll do just about anything to get in there with Miss Higham, won't you?'

Jim shrugged his shoulders in what he hoped was a good imitation of a victim of the Somme. 'I guess so.'

Each day they raced, fighting each other on the course, and over the period of that summer's sailing school, Jim established his place as second to Jack Peabody. He won no further races in the week that followed, so that Coach Johnson had no further opportunity to chastise Jack with toasts to the winner.

One morning, before they broke off their early morning gymnastics for a shower, Coach stopped him on the footpath. 'You did well, Jim. You made Jack up his game.'

There was no further commentary from Charlie Grist. When Jim worked beside him, painting two final layers of topcoat on the buildings, Charlie Grist merely puffed at his cigarettes. One day Miss Higham approached them while they were painting. She stood behind them for a while, as if waiting to be noticed. Charlie Grist paid no attention to her. Jim felt the tension. He didn't know what to say, so he continued painting.

After a few moments, Miss Higham walked away to her office. Charlie Grist glanced once at her disappearing back, changed his cigarette from one side of his mouth to the other, and continued to paint.

It was on the second to last day of the sailing camp that Jim was able to lock antlers with Jack Peabody.

It began as a blustery day. The wind settled to a strong force four, occasionally lifting to force five. The starting line had been almost perfectly set to the top mark, leaving no perceptible bias. In such conditions the fleet split virtually evenly along the line, with Jack choosing the pin end. Jim was used, by now, to focusing on Jack. At any moment in a race, even amongst the mêlée of boats, Jim was aware of Jack's position at almost a subconscious level.

Prior to the start, Jim drifted over to the pin end, keeping Jack in his outer sights, reaching fast to pick up speed, keeping behind the others while he looked for a place to strike the start line. At twenty seconds he turned into wind, hardening up the sheets. His momentum carried him through the lee of Curly's main. As Jim came through, he felt the surge of wind in his sails, heeled, and hit the line about two seconds after the start gun. He was in clear air. He drove hard and fast. In the corner of his mind he watched Jack's sail swiftly tack about fifty yards away. A small but quite sharp swell had been whipped up by the wind. The Laser was a responsive dinghy and he pumped and feathered the boat over the swells, concentrating on keeping up speed.

Jack, who had kept his distance, now closed with him. Jim, aware of the rhythm of Jack's sailing, knew that it was a conscious decision, that Jack was driving deliberately towards him. Jack was bearing down now on starboard tack with right of way. They were neck and neck. Jim swerved to duck Jack's transom, luffed up to take advantage of the swerve of the wind in Jack's windshadow. Jack tacked immediately on top of him. In all his previous racing experience, Jim had never seen Jack choose to close with a rival. The sudden aggression of these tactics was unnerving.

The two dinghies were sailing parallel, Jim eased down to leeward to drive himself out of Jack's bad wind. He lost ground at first, but the stronger breeze that suddenly filled his sails told him he had succeeded in gaining clear air. They sailed neck and neck for perhaps a hundred yards, pumping and feathering their boats over the swells. Jim hit a small patch of flat water, and took the opportunity to ease up towards Jack, squeezing him, causing him to luff up. Jack was forced to tack away. It was a small moral victory, which he compounded by tacking with Jack, trying to ride over him to windward.

But Jack fought back, holding his ground. They engaged in a flurry of six further tacks before Jack managed to shoot the buoy a boat length ahead and drive away on the reaching leg.

Jim immediately struck back by trying to take Jack's

wind. Jack counter-attacked by luffing up. The two fought closely down the leg.

Coach Johnson and Charlie Grist, following in the cutter, studied this intense ballet of aggression, where one and then the other seized the advantage. When Jack, in the final beat, scudded across the finish line half a length ahead of his rival, Coach Johnson turned towards Charlie Grist.

Charlie Grist stared back levelly, puffing a short, staccato commentary on his cigarette. Coach Johnson said:

'You been casting your Indian spells, Charlie?'

'Jim don't need no Indian spells, Coach. He's got his own.'

'Maybe it's time we put these boys on a two-handed dinghy next season. We could let them loose in the 420 fleet. Or perhaps we'll let them continue as they are, so they can tear each other apart next season.'

'Who's going to steer if they go to a two-hander?' asked Charlie Grist.

'Interesting question. Isn't so obvious now, is it?'

'Not so obvious as it was, Coach,' agreed Charlie Grist.

Ten

Even though he had come in second, Jim was elated. At last he had been in a race on equal terms with Jack. In his heart he knew it could have fallen his way just as easily as Jack's.

After the race, the others would dawdle about for a few minutes in the area of the finish line, playing the fool. Jack steered a course into wind, practising his fast tacks. Jim set sail directly for shore, covering the half mile to the sailing camp as quickly as he could. Coach and Charlie Grist in their cutter were counting the stragglers behind him. He could hear their motor revving up as they turned toward shore, caught him up and passed him.

He tied his boat up, lifted the mast, and folded the sail. Beside him, the empty cutter floated. He felt suddenly an overwhelming wish to talk to Charlie Grist, to thank him for helping him, for his steadfast support.

The slipway was empty. Long afternoon shadows were starting to join up the quiet buildings. The other sails were still some distance off.

The path to Charlie Grist's little shed was through stacks of barrels, old machinery, pilings that had been dragged out, dried, and were due to be re-treated. He crossed the yard and made his way through these various obstacles to the grey-painted door. He knocked, and heard no answering call. He would wait for Charlie to return. Gingerly, he opened the door and went in.

On the floor, two bodies separated. Charlie Grist stood up, his trousers down, and turned around. Behind him, Miss Higham rolled away, covering herself with a blanket. Charlie Grist said nothing, just looked at him. Miss Higham had put a hand across her face. In the gloom of the corner, where the newspapers and magazines had been pushed aside to make a space on the floor, and a tarpaulin laid there, he saw her sit up, draw up her knees, hunch over herself.

Jim said: 'I didn't mean . . . ' He felt sick, and backed away. Charlie Grist merely stood there in his nakedness. It was the fact of Charlie's silence that unnerved Jim. He backed out of the shed and started to run away, but he didn't get to the main buildings before he felt, like the culmination of all bad races, the nausea inside him. This time, when he threw up, the unpleasantness did not diminish. It was not what he had seen, but the unthinking stupidity of his entry into the lives of two people he liked, two people he wanted to see happy, that would haunt him.

Feeling wretched, he went to the dormitory to lie down.

That night it was difficult at the dinner table. Coach Johnson insisted that Jim sat on his left at the top of the table, as if he had won the race. Miss Higham leaned over to serve him. When the dinner ended, Miss Higham said, 'You better let me take that bandage off. It needs a fresh dressing.'

In her little office, with its big, wall-mounted medicine cabinet, its first-aid kits, its smell of disinfectant, she removed the head bandages. He watched her hands in the mirror, capable hands. He felt as if her silence were a kind of condemnation. She said suddenly: 'You shocked?'

He said, 'No,' but it was a mumble, a betrayal in itself.

She did not seek to justify herself. When she had put on a fresh dressing, she came round to his front, faced him, looked directly into his eyes, as if searching for his thoughts.

'You sure you're not shocked?'

He wanted to say that what shocked him were her questions, the act of mentioning something that should not be mentioned. In an obscure manner, he felt she had wilfully committed a second transgression.

He tried to meet Miss Higham's eyes levelly. The corners of her mouth had a smile, as if she was amused by his struggle to express himself. He thought she was about to say something else, something that he also feared would be shocking, but instead she said, 'When that dressing comes off we won't need to replace it.'

'We've got a day off coming up,' Jack said to Jim. The day before end of camp was a free one. 'Why don't we go into town?'

Jim felt honoured. 'Town' was, however, Gatesby, about fifteen houses and a single shop on a small high street.

They had to walk several miles, a good hour's walk, to Gatesby. On the way, Jack said: 'This is a really amazing place we're going to. Absolutely incredible. It's full of Swedes.'

Jim now knew Jack sufficiently to realise that his cue had been called.

'Swedish girls?'

'Jee-sus,' Jack said, 'you should see them.'

They quickened their pace and almost started to run, Jack was so keen to get there.

Gatesby was approached around a small hill. The town looked a little empty. But Jack was not going to let a little thing like no people destroy his vision of Swedish girls.

'Where are they?' said Jim.

'Hiding away in those houses,' Jack said. 'They have fair skins. They don't like the sunshine.'

At the outskirts of the town a man was carrying a grey sack in a wheelbarrow. Jack walked up to him and asked, 'Excuse me, is there a shop here?' The man looked at him for a moment, showing neither friendliness nor hostility. 'Sankey's Stores,' was all he said. He used his thumb to gesture behind him, picked up his wheelbarrow, and drove stolidly past them.

'They're shy,' Jack said. 'They have a funny language. They don't know how to communicate.'

Jim stopped. He said, 'There's no one here.'

But Jack had gripped his arm. The strength of Jack's grip indicated the fervour of his idealism. 'The first thing you have to learn with women,' said Jack, 'is how to persevere.'

Sankey's Stores had several of the letters missing. The weatherboarding had fallen off on one side. But inside, with the tinkling door closed behind them, it looked clean. The room smelled of oiled hardwood, a little like a school-room or church, but more homely. Jack pressed the bell at the counter.

A middle-aged woman appeared with slightly myopic eyes, features which were once fine, but now had a great many lines.

'Can I help you gentlemen?'

'Do you sell . . . ah . . . liquor?' asked Jack.

The woman looked at them without smiling, as if she had not heard him, and for a moment Jim thought that she was deaf.

'What sort of liquor would that be?'

Jack was taken aback.

'Whisky,' Jack replied.

For the first time the woman smiled. 'Ed,' she called into the interior. 'Ed, would you come out here?'

There was a rustling inside one of the rooms. Someone was putting down a plate or glass. Jim felt nervous. A square, balding man came out, rubbing his eyes, putting on his glasses.

'What'd you say?'

'Ed, these young gentlemen have asked whether we sell whisky.'

The man looked at them.

'Hell, they aren't old enough to piss in a pot.'

'Bourbon,' said Jack, standing his ground.

'Bourbon if you please,' said the man. 'What you going to pay with, young man? Stamps?'

Jack reached into his pocket, and drew out a ten dollar note. He looked at Jim. Jim had three dollars fifty.

'Thirteen dollars fifty,' said Jack triumphantly.

'You boys have come well prepared, I see,' said the man. But the woman it was now who stood between them and their goal.

'You can't sell it to them.'

'They're on the limit,' the man said. 'I have to admit.'

'Limit?' the woman replied, and suddenly she became animated, suffused with indignation. 'They're about as far from the limit . . . '

'It's a difficult case,' said the man. 'Real difficult to tell their ages.' He looked at them hopefully. 'You got identification?'

'No,' replied Jack.

'You see?' the woman said.

'You certainly are making things difficult,' the man said. 'However, I'm gonna have to give you the benefit of the doubt.'

At this the woman turned away and went inside. They could hear her talking to herself, or perhaps to someone else.

The man was unlocking a large cabinet behind the counter. He put the bottle on the table.

'That'll be twelve ninety.'

But Jack was on the warpath. He lifted the bottle off the counter, surveyed it with an air of considerable expertise. He nodded confidently at Jim, and held out his hand for three dollars. He put the combined sum of thirteen dollars on the counter with a flourish.

'You're a man of knowledge, I can see,' said the man. 'I could see that straight away.'

He gave them their change and wrapped the bottle.

Inside they could hear the woman talking to someone in a patient, scolding voice.

A curtain was drawn back. A girl came out, ducked under the counter and walked towards the door. The voice of the woman rose behind the curtains. 'And don't forget the bread.'

The girl turned back to look briefly at them. They had an impression, a brief impression, of blue eyes, a turned up nose, long blonde hair.

'Thank you,' said Jack.

'My pleasure, sir. Always pleased to meet a connoisseur.'

Outside the sun shone brightly after the gloom of the little store.

The girl was walking away.

'Time we were getting back,' Jim said.

But Jack had only one thought. 'Did you see that?'

He was already walking fast after her. Jim had to almost run to keep up.

She turned a corner and they followed. The empty houses seemed to stare at them.

'Excuse me,' Jack said. At first the girl didn't seem to hear them.

'Could you help us, Miss?' Jack asked. He was almost abreast of her.

The girl continued to walk until they were round the corner of the houses. She turned round with an impatient movement of her head. They saw that she was older than they first imagined, several years older.

'We're lost,' said Jack. 'Could you tell us the way back to the Summer Sailing School?'

At first they thought that she too would not speak. She looked at them carefully.

'You from there?' the girl asked. Her voice was high-pitched, amused.

'From that direction,' said Jack.

'You from there or not?' persisted the girl.

'Those parts,' replied Jack.

'They're just kids,' she insisted.

'They certainly are.'

The girl looked towards Jim. Her eyes were penetrating. 'He from there too?'

'He's from there,' affirmed Jack, and Jim knew the pang of betrayal.

Jim said, 'I think we ought to be getting back.'

'I think you'd best be,' said Jack, and Jim knew clearly this time that Jack was asking him to get lost, to leave him alone with her. He was aware of the girl's fixed gaze. He nodded to her.

'See ya, Jim,' Jack said.

Jim started to walk back.

Jim was fifty feet away when he heard the girl ask, 'How'd he get those bandages on his head.'

'It's a rough place,' Jack replied. 'I'm worried about the treatment he gets there.'

Jim heard their voices behind him, but by now it was difficult to make out what they were saying. He thought he heard Jack say, 'Jim's my nephew,' but he couldn't believe Jack would say that. Not for a moment. He tried to think of words that sounded like 'nephew'. But there weren't many. 'Nephew' was quite a distinctive word.

When he looked back, Jack and the girl were walking on. Jack was holding the whisky bottle in one hand, waving his free hand, explaining something.

Eleven

When Jim reached the camp, it was nearly midday. Some of the boys were packing. Several had been commandeered by Coach Johnson to put the dinghies on their trailers ready for winter stowage.

Jim walked around the buildings, and entered the camp undetected. He used a path between two buildings to reach his dormitory. Charlie Grist was on the wharfs. Out of embarassment, he wanted to avoid Charlie. But Charlie called out, 'How you doing, Jim?' and waved him closer.

Jim could not escape. With misery in his heart, he walked over. Charlie was painting preservative on the last of the wooden piles. Charlie Grist indicated a spare brush. Jim picked it up and started to help brush the preservative on to the wood.

After a while, Charlie said, 'I'm not asking you to forgive me, Jim. But I think you ought to forgive Miss Higham. She's a nice girl, a fine girl.'

Jim wanted to ask why she needed his forgiveness. In an obscure way, he felt he was being made an accessory to what he had briefly witnessed.

'She likes you a lot,' said Charlie. 'I hope you aren't going to hurt her.'

'How could I hurt her?' asked Jim, rebelling.

'Just be nice to her, is all I'm asking.'

Jim continued to paint in silence, watching the light wood become darker as it soaked up the preservative. The sun was getting hotter now. Coach Johnson's shouting, swirling gang of supporters were hauling up dinghy after dinghy. Another group were parking them alongside the buildings, pulling tarpaulins over them to keep off the rainwater.

Charlie was his habitual, silent self; his thoughts expressed in brief puffs of cigarette smoke.

After a while Jim settled in to the painting of the wood,

the rhythm of the brush strokes, the air growing hotter as midday came on.

The cries of the boys storing the boats stopped. They went in a body towards the buildings. He knew it was time for lunch. He was about to make his excuses and go when he was aware that Coach had approached him, was standing in the sunlight.

'Seen Jack?' he asked.

Jim felt again the complicity of the act, the curious sensation of being separate and, at the same time, being drawn in against his will.

'Not recently,' he said.

Coach paused for some time, and then said, noncommittally, 'Time for lunch.'

Jim put down his brush and walked to the washrooms. He felt the eyes of Coach and Charlie Grist on his back. He heard Coach say to Charlie Grist, 'You seen Jack anywhere, Charlie?'

'Ain't seen him today,' he heard Charlie say.

Inside the washrooms it was cool. Most of the other boys were in a mass, struggling to put Curly Shinwell's head under a running tap. The battle was raging back and forth. Sometimes Curly managed to get a leg against the wall and propel himself away from the basin and the running tap. Then the pack would surge back with its victim. The lunch bell went. The pack dropped Curly unceremoniously on the floor and walked out in a group. Curly picked himself up, smeared down his wet hair with his hand, and said, 'How're you doing?'

'OK,' said Jim.

He walked with Curly over to the eating room. When they were all seated round the table, Coach asked, 'Anyone seen Jack?'

No one answered. Miss Higham served the food, a big last-day meal of bacon, eggs, steak, mashed potato.

Coach Johnson took the opportunity of issuing final instructions on packing up the gear, putting the sails and masts in the store-room, checking over the inventory so that what had been broken could be replaced next season.

After lunch, when they were all about to leave the room, Miss Higham said to Jim: 'You better let me take a final look at your head.'

Jim followed her to the surgery. Inside it was cool, a single slice of shadow. The green Venetian blinds were drawn against the sun. Miss Higham's hands removed the bandages carefully. She put her hands on his head to tilt him so that she could see against the light. 'It's healing well,' she said. She went to the big medicine cabinet, selected an antiseptic, moistened a piece of cotton wool, and dabbed it against the healing cut. It stung a little. Miss Higham continued to dab and rub.

'OK now.' she said.

He stood up, facing her. She smiled at him. By some curious process his heart lightened and he could smile at her, smile without pain or guilt.

Outside the sun was bright. As he passed the door of the washrooms he could see the gang had got hold of Curly again, had upended him, and were carrying him in a shouting, surging pack towards the toilet cubical so they could flush his head in the bowl.

During the afternoon Jim helped Coach Johnson with the inventory of broken equipment, calling out the names of items from a pile of broken gear, twisted blocks, broken lines, frayed sheets, bent screwpins, a broken dinghy oar, torn sails. A detailed list had to be filled out in duplicate.

When they had finished Coach Johnson and Jim went outside. At the edge of the wharves the pack had suspended Curly Shinwell upside down over the water, holding onto his ankles. Curly was wriggling like a worm so his hair wouldn't touch the water.

'Leave off, you guys,' Coach Johnson said.

They let go of his ankles one by one, until only two hands held Curly. It was too much weight for one person. Curly hit the water with a splash.

'Shinwell,' Coach Johnson said, with the tone of a man whose patience has been tried too much. 'Stop showing off, will you? Get out of that water.'

'Yessir,' said Curly. He swam round to the ladder.

'Look, men,' said Coach Johnson. 'Can we start to act with a little maturity?'

'Yessir,' they chorused.

'Why don't you go and exercise up on the hillside? Take Shinwell with you. Dry him out, will you?'

'We will, sir,' they chorused. Curly Shinwell had clambered out of the water. The pack picked him up like a battering ram and carried him off in triumph towards the hillside.

'I do not believe this,' Coach Johnson said under his breath. 'These last days are always a nightmare.'

Jack was still not back by supper that evening.

After they sat down, Coach Johnson said, 'Anyone seen Jack?'

There was silence. Several faces turned towards Jim. Coach Johnson did not look directly at him, but Jim knew at whom the question was directed.

Miss Higham brought in the food. She seemed happy. Her eyes shone. Jim realised with an odd turn of his heart that his forgiveness of her had helped her. At the back of his mind some nervousness remained, a fear that his own miserable private opinion was able to so affect her.

The last days of the summer sailing camp brought so many conflicts, so many types of turmoil, that their very proliferation precipitated a kind of detachment. It was as if his mind, no longer able to cope with them individually, floated free of all.

He was to find this later in his sailing, where such a plethora of crises converged that his mind seemed to rise free, almost unconcerned, as if the answer to one crisis was another.

He was not to know that this was a strange gift, that to the majority of minds crises are cumulative, that one weight adds to another until the mind sinks below the surface.

Somehow, with his subtle instinct for pattern, Jack got through the camp in a drunken stupor without detection, and climbed onto his bunk in the dormitory. Jim only heard him when, passing the dormitory window, he thought he could detect a low singing.

There was no one about. He slipped into the dormitory. Once inside, his eyes adjusted to the darkness. He could make out Jack on his dormitory bed.

Jack's hands were folded over his chest. As Jim approached him, he became aware that Jack smelt strongly of bourbon. When Jim drew closer still he saw that Jack's face was composed, that he had a slight smile.

'How you doing?' asked Jack. It was the third time that day that Jim had been asked that question. It seemed to Jim that he knew how he was doing, that the people who asked him the question didn't know how they themselves were doing.

'I'm going to have to tell Coach Johnson you're back. He's worried. He was going to send out a search party soon.'

'Sure,' replied Jack. He paused, then added. 'Tell him I'm real sorry if I caused him any worry.'

Jim wanted to ask about the girl, but something prevented him from asking. Besides, Jack closed his eyes, and was soon snoring gently.

Jim walked over to Coach Johnson's small office. He knocked on the door. Coach Johnson was leaning forward over his desk, filling in reports. He came to the door.

'Yeah?'

'Jack's back.'

There was a moment's pause.

'Damn him,' said Coach Johnson quietly. 'How's he looking?'

'He's asleep,' said Jim.

'He seem all right to you?'

'He's OK, I think.'

'Let him sleep,' said Coach Johnson. 'Tell Miss Higham he's back, will you?'

Coach Johnson went back to his reports, leaving the door ajar. Jim saw him pause, lean over his desk, start filling in the columns.

Jim knocked on Miss Higham's door. There was no sound. Jim knew where she would be. He went back to the dormitory, and searched among his things for a pencil and paper. Jack was snoring quietly. Jim wrote:

Dear Miss Higham. Coach Johnson asked me to tell you Jack's back. He's fine. Yours sincerely, Jim

He slipped the note under Miss Higham's door.

The absence of Curly Shinwell and his gang made the place quiet. Long, afternoon shadows poured between the buildings. He could sense, in the claustrophobic afternoon, the scratching of Coach's pen through the open door, Jack's snoring, and somewhere, in the background, the gasps of Miss Higham in Charlie Grist's little shed. It started to close in on him.

Jim set out for a walk along the hillside. The pressure inside his head seemed to ease with the evening air. There was no wind and the bay was silent. The racing marks had already been collected, re-labelled, stored. The bay seemed empty now. Below him the camp was a tiny group of white buildings, hidden by the dark mass of promontory as he turned the corner.

Curly and the gang were playing football on one of the sloping fields. Jim walked down the hillside, avoiding them, and walked along the shore.

Jack never did talk about his day out with the blonde young woman from Gatesby. The following day he had a hangover, but the smile of detachment was on his face again.

Coach said to him, 'Don't ever do that again, Jack.'

Jack nodded.

At breakfast Jack took up his position on Coach's right hand. It seemed to Jim that Jack had once again moved away, into another world.

Twelve

Jim went home that summer to his grandfather's house.

He was one of the little group of boys not picked up by their parents. They were put on a bus to the closest Greyhound Station and made their different ways home. Sam Shaw, taking his broken down pick-up van to the bus terminal to meet Jim, exercised that careful, discreet courtesy of adults towards children who are changing so fast that the relationship needs to be started from fresh.

Agnes Chednik continued to chide Sam Shaw about Jim's isolation and independence. Jim Shaw persevered in his ploy of exaggerating these characteristics when he talked to her in order to cause fresh outbursts of criticism.

Jim continued to sail through the rest of the summer whenever the opportunity offered, setting out behind the fleet where he needed the extra competition. Sometimes he crewed on two-man 420 dinghies. Then, through a contact at the club, he was introduced to a young executive called Sean O'Neill, newly arrived at Highton to install a new computing system in the district's largest accounting firm.

A 250-pound powerhouse who was relatively new to sailing, O'Neill pumped Jim's hand while he smiled through newly capped teeth, the result of an accidental gybe in a race early that year. His accident had not diminished his ardour for racing. He thought maybe Jim could help him to learn.

Through Sean O'Neill Jim became versed in the normal psychology of yacht owners and their crew. O'Neill sought his expertise, but insisted on applying it himself. Like all competitive men, he wanted to win, but not at the expense of handing over the helm of the yacht to someone else. He was proud of his young crew, but also jealous of his own position.

Their collaboration did not yield immediate results. In a fleet of fifteen boats they were generally in the last five.

Jim gave advice where he could, but itched to take over the helm himself, and put his own advice to direct practice. He was the lighter of the two by a long way. It made much better sense if Sean O'Neill went out on the trapeze as crew, where his extra weight would add power to the boat, particularly on the upwind legs.

Matters resolved themselves in due course. O'Neill had to undergo several vaccinations and injections in his right arm preparatory to a business trip to South America, where his accounting firm was setting up a new office. They were in the middle of a series. O'Neill asked Jim to take over the helm while O'Neill's younger brother took over as crew for the missed race. They came in third.

O'Neill returned the following week. They dropped once again to twelfth place out of fifteen. On a day in late August, O'Neill asked Jim to steer for one race. They came in eighth, but they had led the fleet for two exhilarating legs of the course before tangling a spinnaker hoist. O'Neill, driving home that evening with fresh memories of being out on the trapeze as they thundered to windward in a freshening force five, was placed in the classic owner's dilemma. Should he continue to helm, and firmly place the boat in the stragglers of the fleet, or concede the helm in favour of winning? He decided he could grow used to the trapeze.

Jim found the big, powerful dinghy a handful at first, and it would take another season before he developed the physical power to play the mainsheet and kicker with the brutal alacrity of the leading experts. Sean O'Neill's own physical strength partly compensated for Jim's early shortcomings. The few races they won in the falling summer were won by careful tactics and luck, as much as by any sailing virtue. But they provided Jim with an invaluable opportunity to develop his skills on a two-man dinghy, to learn something of coordination with his crew, and pick up confidence.

The leaves started to turn gold. They kept racing, even though the fleet was diminishing with the onset of cold weather, right up until the morning of the first ice in

Weepeq Bay. Then he helped O'Neill put the dinghy under cover in the club's big storage shed, and took up his spare time work once again with McLuskey.

Throughout the winter and the early part of the following year, Jim's mind kept returning to the days of the summer sailing school, to the unexpected conflict of emotions that occurred there in the final few days.

Before he left in Coach Johnson's old Studebaker for the Greyhound Bus station, he was carrying his canvas carrier bag with his clothes and, rounding a corner, had come face to face with Charlie Grist.

Charlie Grist leaned against the side of a building, smoking. He said: 'Thanks for what you did.' He drew in and exhaled several times in short, staccato bursts. It took Jim a few seconds to realise that Charlie was talking about Miss Higham, about the fact that he had been kind to her.

Charlie Grist turned sideways, and Jim knew he was under intense scrutiny. Charlie was clearly perplexed by Jim's unresponsive, almost sullen look. Charlie said:

'You may be a fine helmsman, Jim, maybe one of the best. But don't ever fool yourself that you understand women.'

He smiled, stubbed out his cigarette on the ground, and disappeared in the direction of his small shed.

When the winter came in sharp and cold in early November and racing in the little fleet ceased, Jim laid up his Optimist in Sam McLuskey's shed, and put a notice of sale in the yacht club. An offer was made several weeks later for it, which he accepted. It was the first time he had any real money of his own.

In the limbo of the winter he read every book on sailing from the library that he could. His favourites were the books of Paul Elvstrom, perhaps the greatest competitive sailor of all time. He also read everything he could about the Olympic dinghy classes, Finn, 470 and the Flying Dutchman, fastest and most powerful of these three

76

classes. His imagination was gripped by the legendary figures who inhabited the sailing pantheon. He found a biography of the eccentric English sailing genius Uffa Fox, designer of the Flying Fifteen, friend and companion of royalty, who died in poverty on the Isle of Wight.

There had recently been a biography of another sailor, hardly in his early twenties, a rising star in the East, the helmsman Ivan Illich. Someone had ordered the book, recently printed, and Jim had seen it on a pile of other books ready to be returned to the main state library. Jim had to sign a form to take it out.

Ivan Illich was already, at the age of twenty-two, a legend. He had recently achieved his second Olympic Gold in the Flying Dutchman class. He had won his first Gold in the Flying Dutchman at the unbelievable age of eighteen. On the front cover of the little book, Ivan Illich's face, handsome, poised, stared out with cold intensity. Jim found another photograph of this same face on the cover of a yachting magazine. The photograph was an action shot. It consisted of Ivan Illich's Flying Dutchman crossing the finishing line of the final race at the Olympics. Illich's huge crewman, out on the trapeze, was raising a fist in a victory salute. But Illich, showing no signs of emotion, simply looked backwards over his shoulder at the fleet he had left behind him.

When he was not doing spare time work with Sam McLuskey, in the winter evenings Jim helped Sam Shaw to repair his nets, lines and lobster pots. Sam Shaw had had his best season as an independent fisherman so far. There were signs that the fish were returning to Weepeq Bay, particularly now the government was exercising a more effective control on industrial pollutants. There had been a legal action against a big upriver company, a subsidiary of the Ericson Traction Corporation, by a local environmental group, and the costs had been so swingeing that other companies had been forced to follow suit with respect to their own pollutants.

The reduction in subsequent pollution had helped Sam

Shaw. But another discovery also helped him. Sam Shaw had found, like a rich mineral artery, a winding current of purer water which bypassed the concentration of industry on the southern bank of the river. From this seam Sam Shaw drew forth big crayfish, crabs and lobsters, healthy cod. He began to become nervous that the commercial fisheries would return, despoiling the resources as they had done in the past.

In the evenings, while repairing the nets and pots, Sam Shaw would work through tactics with Jim, particularly the strange patterns of wind caused by land masses, the bending of air currents along certain features of the coast, the inshore and offshore winds created by the heating and cooling of the land in its daily cycle. Then there were other things, the effect of storm clouds, wind against tide, in all of which he could draw upon his rich experience as a life-long fisherman and wanderer of the ocean.

Owing to Sam Shaw's lack of enthusiasm for modern gadgets, they had no telephone in the house. But one day a message arrived from Jack in the form of a letter. Jim at first did not recognise the confident, clear handwriting. He looked at the postmark, but it was indistinguishable. He opened it at the table.

Dear Jim,

I've been sailing two-man boats last season. Someone has loaned me a 470 for December. The weather here in Florida is a bit too hot for my liking.

Care to come along? We've got accommodation.

Jack

Jim worked out that with the money he had received from the sale of his Optimist, he could just about afford the transport to Florida and back by coach.

Sam Shaw, appraised of Jack's invitation and Jim's wish to go, offered no objection. He even offered Jim the fare, but Jim showed his first signs of independence in his sailing career, and travelled without financial support, arriving a little tired and bedraggled at the bus terminal in St Petersburg. There he called Jack on the telephone, and waited in a bus shelter for Jack to meet him.

Thirteen

The grey Lincoln Continental, moving slowly past the seedy square, seemed out of place there. Jim could not see the occupants, hidden behind smoked glass.

The glistening machine made its way through the discarded cigarette packets and beer cans. A spring-loaded door opened and a tall figure in T-shirt and Bermuda shorts stepped out from behind the clouded glass. Jack was tanned and fresh-looking, if anything an inch or two taller than when they had last met.

It was difficult, Jim realised, to greet someone wearing dark glasses. He could see nothing of the expression in Jack's eyes, while his own uncertain smile danced in the two reflected lenses.

'Let me help you with these,' said Jack. They piled Jim's canvas bags into the boot. 'Sit in the front,' said Jack.

'Jim Shaw,' Jack said inside the car. 'My father.'

Alvin Peabody reached a large, dry hand across the front seat.

'Pleased to meet you.'

Seated beside Alvin Peabody, senior partner of Peabody and Levine, attorneys at law, Jim cruised along the wide street, past the tall buildings with their single palms, down to the seafront and the St Petersburg Yacht Club. On the seafront the limousine wheeled right along the coast road, and moved on purring tyres past the magnificent Poynter Institute building and the Salvador Dali Museum. Through smoked grey glass he watched pelicans flap and dive into the bay. The car's whispering air-conditioning protected them from the seething heat.

Jack's parents had a holiday home on one of the St Petersburg bayous. A bony, grey-haired man, Alvin Peabody had the peculiar gravity of the ascetic. He enquired courteously about Jim's trip down by bus. Jack was silent in the back seat, staring out dreamily across the bay. After a drive of only a few minutes, they turned into a wide driveway flanked by two towering palms. Mr Peabody pressed a remote control switch and the large gates opened on soundless hinges. Behind the high walls a set of sprinklers was showering the lawn. The car drew up, with a rustle of gravel, at the porticoed doorway.

A tall, blonde woman, her hair drawn back in a bun, came out to welcome them. An unruly spaniel jumped at her heels. So Jim was introduced, firstly, to Mrs Peabody and, secondly, to the ambience of the rich.

'Pepita,' Mrs Peabody called, addressing a dark-haired young woman who hovered politely in the hallway. 'Could you see Jim to his rooms? Lunch is in twenty minutes, if that suits you.' It was that final phrase which Jim remembered, the elaborate courtesy of the family. Pepita took hold of the two canvas bags and began to walk up the stairs. Jim's bedroom, of vast size, overlooked the bayou and their private jetty, in front of which a large motor-cruiser was moored. A new 470 dinghy was drawn up on its trailer in front of a launching slipway. Pepita pointed out towels and soap, and left quietly.

Lunch was held on the patio. Pepita, whom Jim soon came to recognise as a mainstay of the household, hovered quietly in the background. Today she would serve lobsters, followed by the largest, creamiest of steaks. Jim, who had eaten very little on his journey down, moving from bus shelter to bus shelter like a refugee, pleased Mrs Peabody by cleaning up everything that was put his way. Jack ate virtually nothing.

'Jack,' said Mrs Peabody. 'Please take off those dark glasses. Then we can see who you are.'

Jack removed his shades, folded them carefully, and placed them in his shirt pocket.

'If you want to stay in my mother's good books,' whispered Jack, after they had left the table and were walking down to the slipway, 'You just carry on and eat like a horse.'

'Me?' Jim asked. 'A horse?'

'Like a horse out of a nosebag,' Jack assured him.

In the hard glare of the afternoon they rigged the 470 and launched it from its trailer. Jack took the helm. In the shelter of the bayou there was little wind. They drifted out into the bay. The horizon was hazy with white heat.

Rounding a promontory they picked up a breeze, and began to trim sails. Jim practised spinnaker hoists and drops, fast reaching under spinnaker, beating. They went through sailhandling drills all through the afternoon, until Jim's hands were blistered with the ropes. The wind continued to fill. They worked the big dinghy to windward, driving through the short swells that were starting to come in from the south. Jim tried to become used once again to the trapeze, to leaning out with the jib sheet over his shoulder, while beneath him the spray punched out from the bows. They practised rapid tacking, bearing away around a small fishing float with a rapid spinnaker launch, emergency gybing.

When they returned to the bayou the light was fading. They could see Pepita walking through the ground floor rooms, turning on the lights of the house.

The evening air had a softness which both attracted and repelled Jim. Far away they could hear the small surf breaking. Mrs Peabody's voice, issuing instructions to Pepita in the kitchen, was murmurous, as soft as the air itself.

Drinks were served on the patio, followed by a light salad supper, the air so quiet they could eat by flickering candles. A moon tiger sent up curls of smoke against the mosquitoes. Half way through the salad an animal, a large rat or some other rodent, crossed the end of the garden.

Mrs Peabody said: 'Maine must be cold now.' She shivered, as if in revulsion.

Jim nodded. Mrs Peabody had that striking beauty which commanded attention, and which seemed to show more clearly as, with age, the bones began to dominate the skin.

Her husband leaned back in the chair and went to sleep, snoring gently. Jack excused himself from the table and walked to his room. Mrs Peabody filled Jim's cup with a second coffee and asked him about the town in which he lived, his grandfather. Jim, guarded at first, began to talk more freely as he became aware of her unaffected interest.

At one stage she said: 'Jack tells me you beat him in the last race at summer school.'

Involuntarily Jim looked towards Jack's room, where a light was shining, for some explanation of this statement.

'No, I didn't beat him.'

'Really? He said your boat was chasing him all summer, that it was like being overtaken by a bus.'

She must be teasing me, he thought suddenly. He said instead: 'Jack is so much better than me, it hurts.'

He saw her eyes were watching him closely, without expression. Mr Peabody snored softly on. Whatever was out in the garden came closer, crossed a piece of moonlight, disappeared. He wanted to mention it to Mrs Peabody, this scurrying presence in their midst, but he thought she might be forced, by courtesy, to react to it. He decided not to mention it, if only because he feared it might break the spell of quietness.

'What do you intend to do with your life, Jim?'

He knew the question was well-intended, and in the struggle to answer it as best he could, he realised that he had never thought of anything else but sailing, had never considered any other aspect of his career.

'I don't know.'

He felt the weight of her eyes studying him.

'Curious. You give the impression of someone who really does know what he wants to do.'

Outside the line of light, the creature scuttled.

'It's a tree-rat,' said Mrs Peabody, watching his eyes. 'It's quite friendly.'

'You're right about me,' Jim admitted. 'I do know what I want to do.'

Mr Peabody drew in his breath, shifted his position in his chair, started, after a few more seconds, to snore again. Her eyes moved to her husband's face, then back to him. The moment for replying to her question had been lost. He was aware, suddenly, of her loneliness and boredom, of the crushing certainties of her existence.

A few minutes later she graciously excused herself, stood up, and helped Pepita to clear the plates. Jim helped them carry the last few plates to the kitchen, then went upstairs. In his room he could hear Mr Peabody snoring gently below his window.

That night he slept between deep blue sheets. He remembered the cushioned ride from the bus station, the extraordinary quietness of the gates opening. The exotic images of the day poured through his mind softly, like smoke.

Despite, or perhaps because of, the richness of his dreams, he slept fitfully. His mind kept returning to consciousness, to the room, with its strong moonshine, as if constantly seeking assurance of its existence.

At the centre of his existence as the guest of the Peabody family, the late afternoon races organised by the club were like small, intense fragments of reality, as crisp as spray.

Day by day, and then into the second week, they began to claw their way through the fleet. But there were several boats that were consistently better than theirs, sailed by crews in their young twenties with several years of experience. Against these crews they made slower progress, sometimes managing to beat one or two, but almost never all at the same time.

It was in the third week, when they had settled into a pattern of finishing in the first four or five places, that Jack abandoned the helm without warning one afternoon, clipped on the trapeze, and Jim found himself steering upwind towards the start line, the pain of anticipation in his heart.

They came in eighth, their worst result for almost a week. After the race they steered home, neither Jim nor Jack speaking, accepting that tomorrow it would once again be Jack's turn to helm.

But the following day Jack clipped on the trapeze line, said 'bias towards the pin end,' and as Jim took the tiller, levered himself out on the trapeze in the rising breeze. Perhaps it was this unexpected gift to Jim, when he was temporarily reconciled to his failure, which gave him an unforeseen advantage. Their sailhandling was better than the previous day. At the start they were up with the first two boats, tacking effectively and proficiently. Jack's greater height and weight gave them more power than when Jim was on trapeze. They were second round the top buoy. Jack launched the spinnaker and they planed in the wake of the lead boat. The wind was rising. Around the leeward mark they were still in touch with the first boat. They tacked away to clear their wind. The leader tacked with them. They tacked again, initiating a flurry of tacks and counter-tacks. As they neared the line, they were neck and neck, their rival to windward. Jim, exercising his rights, eased his boat up towards them, until Jack on his trapeze could have reached out and touched their opponents' mainsail. Their manoeuvre forced the other boat to tack, temporarily slowing their rival. Jim crossed half a second ahead, punching at full power through the finish line.

Jack gave a whoop as fierce as an Indian war-cry.

'You eat like a horse, and you win races,' said Jack. 'My mother thinks you're some kind of hero.'

They were working on the 470, shining the underwater section with very fine sandpaper.

'Why did you tell your mother I beat you in the summer in the last race?'

'Did I tell her that?'

'That's what she said.'

'Maybe I don't like my parents looking too closely over my shoulder. You know, I'm always supposed to be the best at school, the best at sports, the best at learning a classical instrument. They don't seem to care much what I do, just as long as I'm the best at it.'

'They seem nice to me.'

'Yeah, they're nice,' said Jack.

Jim realised that he had said too much. He asked instead, 'What's that strange creature that runs around us when we're eating in the garden?'

'Pepita?' suggested Jack.

They burst out laughing. Jim said:

'She seems nice too.'

'Yeah,' said Jack. 'She's nice too.'

The following day, Jack said: 'I'll be crew and do tactics. You helm.'

So the pattern became set. That day they came in second, the following day second again; then first, then second: then first, first, first.

Fourteen

Several days' journey from shelter to shelter in Greyhound buses had given Jim's eyes a red rim, and an air of fatigue, but it had hardly rubbed the bloom off his healthy tan. He seemed to have put about ten pounds extra weight on his thin frame. When Sam Shaw had made a cup of coffee, and they were seated at the table, Jim recounted their victories in the 470. But he omitted to mention to Sam Shaw that he had helmed. Sam Shaw was left to assume that Jim had been crew. Jim exercised a peculiar propriety, a reticence which he had learned from his grandfather.

As spring came and progressed into early summer, Sam Shaw noticed with a certain wistfulness how Jim had increasingly detached himself from his school and his friends, how, never gregarious, Jim now developed an even stronger shell of independence. He became one of those strange creatures, a being lit by internal motivation. He appeared to require no one to help or support him. Sam Shaw felt the child growing away from him. He supposed that in growing into one's own skin one grows away from other people, one kicks away one's supports. He himself had run away from home to work on a fishery ship when he was hardly older than Jim was now.

But in Sam Shaw's case it had been physical separation, a single act fiercely committed. Once committed, it required no other sustained effort. In Jim's case it was a matter of will, constantly expressed.

Maria Chednik often came up to see Sam Shaw, carrying supplies for her mother after school. Like her mother, she had taken to chiding Sam Shaw to keep up-to-date with his housekeeping, his store of groceries. Thirteen years old, he said to himself, and already she's organising me. He liked her bright, open face, even though she liked to get her own way. She was already starting to show that flashing temper of a woman who knows she is beautiful. Sam Shaw considered with a certain sadness how she and Jim were growing more in opposite directions, Jim towards self-reliant solitude, Maria in the direction of confident sociability. Vivacious already, she would be popular, the centre of attraction at parties.

Jim clearly puzzled Maria. He resisted all her overtures of friendship. For once on Maria's face Sam Shaw could see a trace of self-doubt. Sam Shaw wanted to say to her, 'Don't take it personally, he's like that with everyone.' But he could see that it would explain nothing.

Her mother, Agnes, continued to chide Sam Shaw constantly about allowing Jim to develop into such a solitary. 'I can't help it, Agnes.' He would reply. 'That's just the way he's turning out to be.'

'It's you, Sam,' Agnes Chednik insisted. 'He's just like you.'

And he could see that it was at least partly true. Now that the fishing grounds were coming back slowly to normal, now that he was able to earn his own living, not in comfort, but with sufficiency, Sam Shaw had continued to pursue his inexorable isolation from the rest of the modern world. He had survived several winters with no electricity, without any intercession from the municipality. He so hated the municipality and its works that he was even thinking of cutting himself off from the municipal water supply. He planned instead to draw his own water by hand from a small well several houses away, in a garden belonging to an elderly widow, Mavis Blatsky. He would have done so, and was only held back by the consideration that, if Mavis Blatsky's property were sold in due course, its new owners would not be obliged to maintain the agreement.

Sometimes, on those rare evenings when he felt he had worked enough for the day, Sam Shaw would commit the indulgence of accepting an invitation from Agnes Chednik to a glass or two of slimoviz or vodka in her parlour behind the store. Once there, he would slyly encourage her to talk about Russia, a country which held for him a strange fascination. Agnes's mother had emigrated from Estonia with her parents when she was six. Her father had died shortly afterwards and her mother spiritedly had kept herself and her two younger brothers by working out. She remarried, but died in due course at the age of thirty-eight, worn out from a life of toil. It had fallen to Agnes, at the age of sixteen, to take charge of her family.

Sam Shaw carried a great admiration for Agnes, who in turn (since her stepfather had taken to drink) was mainly responsible for bringing up her own younger sister. With the responsibilities thrust upon her by her situation, Agnes had sustained the two of them for ten years. Single until she was twenty-five, she married a fisherman. She had a son and a daughter. Her son had been a trial. Her second child, Martha, was already married and now lived in Philadelphia with her husband. Her second daughter, Maria, was born in Agnes's late thirties. Sam refrained from asking Agnes about her husband, who had left one day on a cargo ship and reportedly was now living in California with a younger woman. He knew that Agnes and her husband had separated twelve years before, but little more than that.

So Sam Shaw would sit in Agnes's small lounge, with its two icons (all that had remained of the family's possessions). And taking care not to disturb her sensibilities, he would ask her about a mythical place called Russia, about a country where they had attempted to banish commercial competition, a country where those who needed help were provided for, a country of simple workers – mechanics, fishermen, farmers – magnified into giants by the dignity of labour.

But to Agnes such a country did not exist. She described instead the hardships of her mother's youth, and repeated what she had been told, when only a child, of the lack of food, the infinite queues, the bitter winters without fuel for heating, and worst of all the continuous, draining fear of a knock on the door early in the morning when, as her mother put it, 'the soul itself is asleep'. And she described to him instead a mythical place called America, where if you worked, you could provide for yourself and your family, a place of opportunity for the poor. In America you did not need to talk in whispers for fear of being overheard.

In the snugness of Agnes's parlour, with the bills lined neatly on the table, the smell of kerosene and wax, these two great, shining myths slid past each other like two liners in the night, all lit up, each impervious to each other's existence.

Even though Sam Shaw chose not to believe in this myth of America, he loved to listen to her, to joke with her about her vision, to accept her chaffing over the absurdity of his own beliefs and ideals. He enjoyed the vodka, too. Usually abstemious, he appreciated its quiet introduction, its self-effacing nature, its friendly backward kick. It was only when she turned her attention to Jim, began slyly and mercilessly to tease and upbraid him for bringing him up a lonely boy, and Jim such a nice kid, that Sam Shaw grew restless, and maybe said a few things about there being some advantages in the independence of the American way of life.

The solitary, antisocial individual Jim Shaw continued in his activities of sailing through the summer. Sean O'Neill would shout: 'Tack,' and when the boat spun, O'Neill would fling his powerful bulk across to the other side, swinging out on the trapeze. Jim learnt to time the haul on the mainsheet to perfection, powering up the mainsail just as O'Neill's frame, leaning out, exerted maximum leverage.

O'Neill began to insist that as helmsman Jim should keep half of the silverware they had won. Jim's small room under the eaves became so cluttered with these trophies that Sam Shaw erected a shelf for them to stand on in the sitting room.

Maria commented on them, enquiring of Sam Shaw which had been won where. She delivered groceries after school, putting her bright face round the door, always with an eye out for Jim. Sometimes she would deliver things to McLuskey's, where Jim continued to work in the evenings.

McLuskey said: 'What eyes that young lady has! One look fires a full load of buckshot through my heart.' Jim, sanding down a hull, did not pause to answer. McLuskey wondered if Jim had heard him, then shook his head and went back to his own sanding.

'Maria was here today,' said Sam Shaw that evening. 'Asked after you.'

'Oh, really?' said Jim, and went upstairs.

'She likes you,' said Sam Shaw up the stairs. 'You should be nicer to her.'

He heard nothing from Jim's room except, in due course, the pages of a book being turned.

'I hear,' said Sam Shaw, 'that this evening they're showing some sailing on the television. Some guy called Ivan Illich is winning all the races.' There was a prolonged silence upstairs. 'Agnes asked me over to see it tonight. Don't suppose you want to come, do you?'

In about five seconds Jim was standing beside him, his hair combed.

'Do I understand that you would like to come?' asked Sam Shaw. 'May I assume that this is the case?'

Sam Shaw put on coat and tie. Jim hadn't seen him dress like this for years.

'Before we go,' said Sam Shaw. 'I have to tell you something about Estonia, where Agnes's family comes from. It's considered very rude to refuse extra helpings of food. Understood?'

Jim nodded.

At the Chednik house, with the store safely locked up below, Agnes and Maria made supper for them, a dish of salted halibut, oil and a vegetable sauce.

'Just couldn't keep Jim away,' explained Sam Shaw. 'This is amazingly good, Agnes, Maria. Just excellent.'

Jim kept eyeing the television screen.

'Just magnificent,' Sam Shaw said.

'Like another helping, Jim?' asked Agnes. Maria watched his face. Sam Shaw turned towards Jim, head on, and stared. Jim took his cue.

'Yes please, Mrs Chednik.' Jim said.

'What'd I tell you, Agnes. Little devil could smell it cooking a mile off.'

Jim cleared his plate again, with more difficulty this time. The meal was heavy.

'Like another helping, Jim?' asked Agnes Chednik. Jim glanced at the television screen. Sam Shaw looked at Jim.

'Yes please,'

'Goodness, you certainly are a hungry young man,' said Agnes approvingly.

'When Jim's finished that plate, Agnes, I guess we'd really like to take up your offer of watching a little of the sailing on television.'

'Be a shame to waste this,' said Agnes, piling Jim's plate high.

'He'll eat all of it,' said Sam Shaw contentedly. 'Don't worry about me, just give my helping to Jim.'

Maria watched Jim as he ate the food on his plate. Jim managed to get it down. He even smiled at Maria. It was a heroic performance.

When the television was switched on, and the screen flickered, Jim felt his stomach churning like a washing machine.

'May I be excused?' he asked politely.

'Why certainly,' said Agnes Chednik. She added almost coyly. 'You want to know where the men's room is? Just down the corridor, second on your right.'

Jim found the room, closed the door and locked it. Salty saliva filled his mouth suddenly. Over the drone of the announcer in the other room, the jingle of the sports news, he regurgitated his dinner in hot, sultry surges of colour into the porcelain bowl.

After he had flushed the toilet, he rinsed out his mouth, placed a piece of toothpaste on his finger, and swilled his mouth out with water.

He took his place in front of the television, hoping no one had heard.

'Just in time,' said Sam Shaw cheerfully.

On the screen a single sail seemed to detach itself from the fleet as it approached the finish line. A large spectator craft interposed briefly, frustratingly. But the dinghy appeared on the other side, clearer now. The camera's telephoto lens zoomed in. Ivan Illich's handsome, wolf-like face turned to look over his shoulder at his pursuers as he pumped the mainsheet in two savage bursts of his left hand. Jim felt that his evening of genial torture at the hands of Sam Shaw had been worth it, after all.

Fifteen

At summer school the same gang assembled, except for a few new faces.

Coach Johnson, his face already burned by the summer sun, picked up Jim and Curly Shinwell from the coach station, transporting them over the bumpy road in his old, swaying Studebaker. His head with its red-grey, spiky hair swayed in front of them as the car rolled over the bumps and potholes.

The base, when they arrived, was bustling. A group of boys was pulling the dinghies out of their shelters and launching them on the water.

Jim stowed his gear in the rack above his bed. Returning a second time to the camp, he felt like a veteran.

Jack arrived by taxi from the airport, carrying his bag over his shoulder, looking like a tourist with his dark glasses. 'Hi,' he said, and carried his gear into the dormitory.

Jim followed him in.

Jack unpacked in silence. Jack said: 'And now for the important things.'

He removed three bottles of whisky from his carrier bag and said: 'Where am I going to store these?' He was like a man in a trance. He walked towards the toilet cubicle. It had one of those old-fashioned high cisterns. He stood on the toilet seat and peered in. Carefully he unloaded the three whisky bottles into the cistern and replaced the lid. 'Saves water when you flush,' he said. 'Environmental concerns.'

Now that the important matters had been arranged, he was freer to talk. He took off his dark glasses, lay on his bed, and looked at the ceiling. 'God, what a holiday. St Petersburg in summer. At the sailing club. On the beaches. Danish, Italian, Polish, Spanish, Dutch, Brazilian, French . . . I'll need months to recover . . . Months.'

Jim saw that he was asleep.

'Just wonderful,' Jack said later, out of his sleep.

Jim left the dormitory and went outside. The sun beat down strongly on the wooden jetty. Black shadows stood at acute angles. It took his eyes a while to accustom to the light.

The gang who had been launching dinghies had temporarily put aside their labours in favour of the more pressing task of launching Curly Shinwell. They were swinging Curly by his legs and arms, shouting in unison. They liked particularly to see Curly go flying out over the surface, hover (flapping his arms like a duck) for a few gratifying moments over his own reflection, and hit the water with a splash. After the first launch, they were momentarily undecided whether to haul Curly out for the pleasure of relaunching him. Coach Johnson appeared outside his study. The gang scattered to the boats.

Coach ignored Shinwell sputtering in the water. 'Charlie!' Coach Johnson shouted. Charlie Grist put his head out of one of the outhouses, where he was unlocking stores. 'New dinghy arrived yet?'

'Yuh.'

Coach said to Jim as he passed:

'Kick Jack's ass. Get him over to the dinghy park. You come too.'

'Oh, Jim,' Coach said, turning back. 'Tell Jack two bottles of whisky is the maximum in the toilet cistern, otherwise it won't flush properly.'

'Yessir.'

Jack was lying on his face, a pillow lengthwise under him, his arms around it.

'Jack, Coach says to come over to the dinghy park.'

With a grunt Jack turned over so that he was facing the ceiling. He rubbed his eyes and put on his dark glasses.

The wraps were pulled off the 420 by Charlie Grist. It was, Jim remembered, like the best Christmas present he had ever had. The surfaces of the dinghy shone like the varnish on a Stradivarius. Its equipment gleamed, from the mainsheet track to the cleets.

'Gift of the Summer Sailing Foundation,' said Coach Johnson. 'This is what you'll be using this season. You'll work out on Lasers with the others, then you'll work up this machine in the evenings. We really need a trial horse, but we'll have to wait until next year for that. So what we'll do is throw you both in at the deep end later this year, down in Florida at the 420 National Championships. You can cut your teeth there. Sound reasonable to you?' Coach turned away before they could say yes. Jack looked on impassively behind his dark glasses. Charlie Grist had found a dent under the starboard bow flare caused by a knock during transportation. He ran the tips of his fingers over the area, working out how to fill and fair it with epoxy compound.

Miss Higham walked past in her white matron's uniform. Jim, in his controlled euphoria over the 420, did not fail to notice that she and Charlie Grist apparently ignored each other. Miss Higham unlocked her office and disappeared inside. Charlie's eyes flickered briefly towards her office, returned once more to the indentation in the hull. Jim was determined this season to keep out of the line of fire of any relationship between them.

In the first race in the Lasers, Jack struck back ruthlessly at him. Finding his own private corridor of wind up the first beat, Jack seemed to soar like a bird towards the weather mark. While Jim fought his way through the pack, Jack increased his lead to four hundred yards in the course of the race. Jim, who managed just to break clear after a spirited luffing match with Curly Shinwell, was a poor second.

That evening they practised in the 420, Coach in the cutter, calling out instructions. Coach asked Jack to take the helm, and Jim knew that this was to be the arrangement, at least for a season. He bore no resentment towards Jack, and began to work himself into the role of crew.

Jim's extra weight since last season helped power up

the boat. Though not as tall as Jack, he had developed his physical power over the course of the last year. That first evening, before Coach could instruct them, they did several rapid tacks, building up speed only to tack again. Jack spun the boat back towards Coach Johnson's cutter with insolent ease.

'Goddamn,' said Coach to Charlie Grist, who was seated in the stern, puffing a cigarette. 'What do we have here?'

Back in the Lasers, in the three races which followed, Jack continued to dominate the fleet. Jim was second in each race, pulling out greater leads as time went on. But it was as if Jack had found a new source of inspiration, as if he had freed a further reservoir of natural sailing talent. It was not simply boatspeed, but an understanding of windshifts, of the wind's ineffable moods, inexplicable accelerations, quiet pockets and coiling vortices. In races where Jim found himself close, their speed was more or less even. But as soon as they separated, it was Jack's sublime intuition which seemed to draw him to the marks so far ahead of his rivals.

Accepting Jack's detachment from the matters of the base, Coach began to treat Jim as his second in command, prevailing on Jim to organise the safe return of the dinghies, the storage of sails and equipment, to run messages. Jim welcomed these tasks. They took his mind off other things. In the third week Coach, hurrying to organise some business with Charlie Grist, asked Jim to take a batch of progress reports to Miss Higham's surgery.

It was a quiet afternoon, a little close, with a dark thunderhead to the west. Jim knocked on the surgery door, heard no response, and was about to leave when the door was opened. Miss Higham was officially off-duty. She wore a simple blue dress with a black belt. She seemed pleased to see him and ushered him in. Inside he noticed how radiantly healthy she looked, as if she had just returned from a holiday. She took the envelope, set it down at the small writing desk, and asked, 'How's the head wound?' He had forgotten it, and it took him a

95

moment to remember what she was talking about. She said, 'Sit here. I want to see how it's healed.'

In the swivelling chair, her fingers parted his hair. She could only find a thin scar as trace. She did not comment. In the little room the weight of her presence was like the thunderstorm he had seen building outside, gathering its forces through the afternoon. Her hands, touching him, disturbed him. The light was strange as the thunderstorm approached. The air seemed almost green. Her deft fingers parted his hair along the silvery trace of the scar. He could feel her breath on his ear, the concentration of her breathing. It occurred to him then that this was how she would breathe when she lay next to her lover. When she had finished her examination he stood up, trying not to brush against her. He thanked her and went towards the door, but in the silence of the little room, with the venetian blinds drawn, her breathing seemed to follow him. He put his hand on the doorhandle and paused momentarily in astonishment. Her arms were circling him from behind, pulling him towards her. Her breathing seemed to grow fiercer, louder. Her lips moved against his ear. He twisted his body gently to disengage, but he seemed to twist into her. Her mouth moved across his cheek and sought his mouth. He could feel the warmth of her body through the dress. 'For Chrissakes,' she said a few moments later. 'Let's lock the door.'

So the affair began. Miss Higham was its practical initiator and instructress. He left the office half an hour later, but not before she had carefully cleaned the lipstick off his cheeks and settled his clothes back to her satisfaction.

Over the course of the next week they met several times, always in her little room after hours. The room where she slept was in the main buildings, and his visits there would be immediately noticed.

They made love on the stretcher trolley. It was bare, but it was a source of amusement to them both that it had moved several feet after one of their afternoon meetings.

In addition to the increasingly familiar contours of her body, Jim began to like and admire her. In her passion there was something honest, unhidden. Perhaps it set his taste in the direction of the type of woman who is physically direct. Perhaps, having spent little of his life in male peer groups, with their collective fear of women, he did not fear her power. Instead he began to learn, if not understand, her moods, the explosion of tears beneath her dark eyelashes if he did not promise to see her again soon, her charming but inexplicable gratitude for pleasure when she herself was the expert.

Strangest of all was the ease with which their affair remained hidden. Charlie Grist was Jim's remaining fear. Jim did not know, and did not feel that he had the right to ask, whether she and Charlie were still seeing each other.

One day, when Jim was packing sails, he saw a shadow fall close by, and sensed rather than heard that Charlie Grist was standing beside him. 'Thanks,' was all Charlie Grist said. Jim knew that Charlie was incapable of irony or sarcasm, but he could not bear to be left without an explanation of this strange avowal of gratitude. It seemed both Nancy Higham and Charlie Grist were inexplicably prone to it. But before he could say something in return, could ask for clarification, Charlie had walked away.

Jack knew nothing of his affair with Nancy Higham. Jack continued to move his whisky bottles from place to place as Coach effortlessly located them. Jim learned not to flinch if Jack made remarks about Nancy Higham when exercising, or in the evenings on the patio before they went to bed. Jack's cerebral attitude to women, his classification of them for erotic purposes into distinct racial or religious groups, continued to amuse him.

If anything, Jim's affair with Nancy Higham made him more detached from the others than ever. He had never boasted to a peer group before, and he would not start now.

The afternoons were still the best times to meet, after

the sailing, when the others were relaxing. Nancy Higham's surgery was hidden from the main offices by a storeroom. With his legitimate activities as major-domo of the store-room, Jim could wait until the coast was clear before crossing the few yards of open space between the storehouse and her surgery, tapping on her door. It was only towards the end of the season that he was able to sneak away from the dormitory and spend most of the night with her in her small room, with its scents of a female lair, before returning at first light to the sleeping dormitory.

Jack's heartfelt concern was concentrated, during the summer school, on the whisky bottles in his care. Following Coach Johnson's warning about more than two bottles in the cistern, the dangers of sleeping with bottles in the pillowslip, about stuffing the head of the mattress with bottles, the illegality of keeping bottles in his carrier bag, Jack had asked Jim's permission, as storeman of sails, to hide the two remaining bottles in the sail store. Naturally Jim had agreed. Jack liked to have a 'snort' occasionally. He zealously marked with a pen the level of all the bottles, referring to this as 'quality control'. Jim was allowed an occasional 'snort' for his safekeeping.

It was only in the last few days that Jack, his shades giving him psychological protection, sneaked into the store-room for a snort and happened to catch sight of Jim disappearing into Nancy Higham's surgery.

Jack hovered about the area for an hour.

Jim was creeping back from Nancy Higham's surgery to the others when he heard a hiss from the store-room interior. He followed Jack's beckoning hand. 'You bastard,' said Jack. 'You goddamn polecat.'

Jim shrugged his shoulders.

'How long has this been going on?' Jack hissed.

'Not long,' said Jim. He knew Jack well enough now that understatement was the key to his frenetic imagination.

'Not long? You were in there an hour at least.'

'That long?'

'Jesus . . . ' Jack's indignation put him at a loss for words. 'You weasel. Right here in the camp.'

Jim shrugged.

'How'd you get this going?'

Jim said: 'It just happened.'

'You ferret.'

'Thanks.'

'Don't mention it.'

The following day Jack rammed the windward marker buoy, followed the rules in making a turn around it, and collided on port tack with Curly Shinwell, who was approaching on starboard. Jim scooted into the lead.

Jack set off after him in agitated pursuit. Jim didn't have a great deal of difficulty in holding off his erratic, unsettled rival. This time it was Jack who had to fight off an excited Curly Shinwell, who just managed to get his nose in front of Curly's at the finish line, and who limped back to base licking his wounds. Jack experienced the further ignominy of knowing that in a real, as opposed to a practice race, he would have been protested out for a port-starboard incident.

'You stoat,' said Jack to Jim. 'You didn't tell me, even when I talked about her.'

'Why should I?'

'What I said was offensive,' Jack insisted, 'that's why.'

'I don't mind,' said Jim, 'because you didn't know.'

'You should have told me.'

'If I had told you, you really might have been offensive.'

'I think I should have the right to be offensive if I want to.'

'I didn't want to upset your racing.'

'It's your not telling me that has upset my racing,' Jack hissed.

'You didn't tell me about your Swedish girl.'

'That's different. Swedish girls are different.'

It never ceased to amuse Jim how vulnerable Jack was on the subject of women.

Jack might have known about Jim and Nancy Higham,

but he didn't know about Jim seeing Nancy Higham at night. Jim waited until Jack began to snore. He waited a further ten minutes, then he sneaked out of bed, tiptoed for twenty feet past the other beds to the slatted door with its mosquito netting, and stepped out onto the moonlit portico. It was about fifty yards to Nancy Higham's room. He knocked softly on the door. She had been waiting for him. She opened the door noiselessly and pulled him into the darkness of the room.

He would return an hour or so later, not wishing to risk detection. Nancy Higham would murmur her complaints at his going. When he crept back, he was grateful for the deep sleep of those who have worked hard during the day.

It was eight days before the camp broke up, and in that time, with Nancy Higham fresh in his mind, Jim beat Jack six times.

Morale is everything in a sailor. At each start Jim removed himself from the body of the fleet, sought clear air and, his mind curiously calm, began to find his way through windshifts towards the top mark. Playing windshifts is risky. Even on those occasions when Jack managed to draw ahead, Jim ignored him, searching for purchase in the shifting, infinitely complex breezes. He made several errors, and on two occasions these lost him races. But in the last eight days he began to draw ahead. At the end of the week he had six firsts, a second and a third.

Having nothing to impart to Jack on the subject of Nancy Higham, he kept his distance and his silence.

Coach Johnson took to seating Jim on his right at dinner. At the afternoon race debriefings, since it was Coach Johnson's habit to comment briefly, if at all, on the leader, Jack's racing tactics now came under scrutiny. His natural flair was not enough. Now he was coached. Coach Johnson seemed to relish this new task.

In the evening practices on the 420, Coach Johnson was particularly harsh if Jack's boat-handling wasn't up to scratch. Jack began to join the community, if only by virtue of the fact that he was now treated no differently from the others.

Jim had learned a bit about Nancy Higham. She came from a large family in Utah. Her father was an engineer. Her two brothers were also in the family business. She had trained as a nurse, become a ward sister in her early twenties, decided to travel the world a little. Now she had a job in Philadelphia. This summer job was part dispensation, part holiday.

There was a broken relationship in her background, a fiancé who had left her. Jim began to see that, in spite of her magnificent figure, her air of professional competence, she was vulnerable. The day they broke up from summer camp, she called Jim into the surgery, closed the door without locking it, and sat on the table facing him. He could see that she had been crying, but she now faced him, composed.

She said they both knew it would be absurd to continue. Jim nodded. He had aroused her passions and he knew there would be consequences which he could not now fully comprehend. He also sensed, with a curious certainty bordering on fatalism, that she would be the standard by which he would judge other women, that he would be following her ghost with each girl that he met.

The virginity of women is considered a serious matter, that of men a joke, a small, comical matter best managed in a brothel. Jim Shaw stood up, shook her hand, and walked from the small surgery room that warm morning in late August.

Out of deference, Jim had managed to avoid Charlie Grist until then, or at least to keep out of his way. Crossing the small area of rough ground, he turned a corner of the buildings and found Charlie Grist there, smoking, not looking at him. Charlie Grist continued to block his path. Jim had stopped, and now found it embarrassing to push past Charlie.

Charlie Grist continued to smoke, not looking at him.

Then he smiled to himself, threw the cigarette down, stubbed it under his foot, and with his hands in his pockets, walked off in the direction of his hut.

Jim returned to the dormitory, picked up his two hold-alls, and set off down the road. He caught a lift there from a farmer driving a tractor towards Gatesby. After he had been set down on the road, he picked up a lift inland towards Oldport. From there he caught the Greyhound bus to Highton and Weepeq Bay.

Sixteen

Being so cut off from the world, it was seldom that Sam Shaw received a letter. On this one, the handwriting had a familiarity which he couldn't quite place.

He made himself some coffee and opened the envelope. It was from Coach Johnson.

Dear Sam,

Just wanted to drop you a line to tell you about something, something maybe that will interest you.

As you know, Jim and Jack Peabody have been doing mighty well as a team, with Jack helming and Jim crewing.

The other day, Jack came into my office. He was looking nervous, as if he was about to say something important. I did my best to set him at ease. He said he'd only sail in future on one condition. Hell, my heart sank. I thought he was going to say he couldn't sail with Jim anymore. Saw my most promising team folding up in front of my eyes. That wasn't what he said.

What he did say was that it was his view that Jim should be helmsman and he, Jack, should be crew and tactician. When I recovered I asked him why. He said he thought Jim was a little tougher than he was, he was a fighter. He, Jack, was too easygoing.

102

Now I want to tell you that struck me as an astonishing thing for a fifteen-year-old to say. He had no need to say it, but I knew there was some truth in what he was saying, so I just said I appreciated his concern for putting forward the best team. I'd give due consideration to what he said. Even in something like that it's bad practice to be dictated to.

Wanted you to know how that came about.

Best regards,

Hal Johnson

Sam Shaw looked at the notepaper in front of him, with its neat, almost military handwriting. He was struck by an odd mixture of sentiments. Deepest of all was a fear for Jim, a fear that now nothing protected him from the consequences of his own ambition. In such moments of intense thought he had a habit of putting his hand on the back of his neck, and scratching absentmindedly there. After a while, he said to himself softly: 'Maybe Jack means you're more evil than he is, Jim.'

Sam Shaw opened the door and looked outside, protecting his eyes from the glare. It was a good day for picking up lobster pots, despite the thunderclouds.

Book Two

Seventeen

Nine years later

They leaned against the bar, the two of them, Jack Peabody and Jim Shaw. Jack said: 'Two beers, José.'

The barman put two glasses in front of them and studied them dispassionately. José Ferrara had developed a certain liking for these two. They were good for business, bringing in those who sought to emulate them. The US Olympic trials had now finished, and they awaited the formal announcement of the results.

If there was ever a God of chance, he had not smiled on Jim Shaw and Jack Peabody that week. In the first race they had broken a mast in a freak gust. In the second, with an untuned, inferior replacement mast they had won handsomely, but in the third a spinnaker halyard had split in the middle of a crucial duel, and the sail had wrapped around a competitor's mast, disqualifying them. In the fifth race they led to the weather buoy, then on rounding the mark they seemed to almost halt in the water. The fleet's frontrunners powered over the top of them. A plastic bag had wrapped itself around the centreboard, and by the time they had identified the problem and shaken it loose, half the fleet had passed them. They had regained a fifth place and emerged a poor third overall. The results had been suspended while a committee of enquiry was flown in to consider the position. It looked hopeless for them.

The trials were strictly on points, so the committee seemed unlikely to find in their favour. The barman José Ferrara, having moved down the length of the bar, walking slowly with the slightly crab-like gait of a former fisherman, stopped in front of them, his fingers on the counter, and studied their faces for a moment.

'Think you'll be selected, boys?'

Jim Shaw shrugged: 'Almost certain we won't. We'll know in a day or two, I guess.'

José had never seen them like this. He had become used to a certain manic high spirits. Now they were as listless as zombies.

'If you'll allow me, boys, the drinks are on me.'

'Thanks, José.'

'If you don't mind me saying so, you both look as if you need it.'

José walked to the other end of the bar, and began to wash and polish glasses. Outside in the street lights had started to come on. It was a strange hour, an hour between day and night when everything seemed oddly unsettled. In another hour the streets would be filled with night-lifers, and the stalls and bars down the street would be plying their trade.

Jim Shaw wandered over to the old jukebox, gripped its sides, and stared at the titles of records displayed in lights. There was nothing he could see that would cheer him up. He returned listlessly to the bar and settled down on the stool.

The tables started to fill behind them. José, the barman, served people at the other end of the bar. His assistant, Alice, a tall, thin blonde from Wisconsin, started taking orders from the tables.

'Two more, José.'

'Why don't I just put a crate beside you boys? You can drink yourselves into oblivion.'

'Where's oblivion, José?'

'It's where I came from,' said Alice suddenly.

Jim's and Jack's eyes swivelled towards her. It was the first time they had heard her speak, other than to take orders.

'That so?' asked Jack. 'Oblivion, Wisconsin?'

'Temperance,' said Alice. 'Oblivion's what it should be called.'

'We're being served in this low dive by a nice girl from Temperance, Wisconsin,' said Jack. 'José, you ought to be ashamed of yourself.'

108

'Never mind about Temperance,' said José. 'You just worry about oblivion.'

Jack poured himself another glass from the fresh bottle José had put beside him.

'Jim's mighty silent tonight,' said José.

'He's thinking,' said Jack. 'And believe me, when Jim's thinking, he's dangerous.'

Jim ignored him. He was looking in the mirror. Two girls had walked in.

'What's the talent like out there?' asked Jack.

'Not bad. Not bad at all.'

Jack looked behind him, glancing noncomittally around. The two girls had sat down at one of the tables. They were talking to a pair of large bikers. One look at them made Jack nervous. The girls were pretty, one especially.

'Not bad, like you say.'

'Are we going there, or what?' asked Jim.

'We're staying here, man,' said Jack. 'It doesn't look too healthy over there.'

But Jim was smiling in one of the bar mirrors at the two girls. He was raising his glass to them. Jack rubbed his chin, looked down at his drink, and glanced again at the bikers. One of the bikers caught his eye, gave him a flat stare.

'Here they come,' said Jim. The two girls were standing at their shoulder. Jim turned round.

'Jim Shaw and Jack Peabody.' Jim held out his hand. 'Nice to meet you.'

'Hi, I'm Samantha. Everyone calls me Sam.'

'Hi, Sam. This is Jack Peabody.' Jack turned round. The pretty girl introduced her friend.

'This is Doris Swarze.'

Doris was taller, darker, with a good smile.

'Hi, Doris,' said Jack.

'Can we buy you girls a drink?' asked Jim. Doris looked briefly in the direction of the bikers. They sat facing one another, their faces expressionless, talking only occasionally.

Jack said quietly, 'We could have problems.'

Jim looked towards the bikers. The barman appeared at his shoulder.

'What are you ladies having?' asked José.

'What are you drinking, girls?' asked Jim.

'Oh boy,' commented Jack. He looked up at the ceiling.

'These guys are sailors, real fine sailors,' José was saying.

'We'll have two martinis, please,' Sam said.

Doris addressed Jack. 'Does your friend know what he's doing?'

Jack smiled. 'Does any of us, Doris?'

Doris giggled. It was this laugh that seemed to stir up the bikers. Suddenly they were on their feet, making plenty of noise. They weren't particularly tall, but they were wide. In fact, they were enormous.

'Here comes the cavalry,' said Jack.

The bikers stood in front of them. The taller of the two said: 'These are our chicks, buddy.'

Jack was all innocence. 'Gosh, guys, I didn't know.' He smiled helplessly. 'Well, it was really nice meeting you girls. I hope you have a nice time.'

The two bikers looked at him, faces expressionless. Jack smiled at one and then the other.

The one who hadn't talked put his arm around Doris. Things seemed to cool down a little. The other biker, the one who talked, placed his hand on Sam's shoulder. They turned round and started to walk off with the two girls.

Jack watched them go. He breathed a deep, inaudible sigh of relief. He turned towards the bar. Jim said, more audibly, 'My, don't you just love those tattoos?'

The two bikers stopped in their tracks. They waited, as if listening for a sound. Jack whispered to himself, 'Oh, Jesus Christ, no.'

The bikers started to turn round slowly. Jack swung to face them, smiling sheepishly. The larger of the two walked slowly back towards him, spread his feet, put his hands into his belt.

'You a fag?'

'No,' replied Jack, smiling, waving a hand. 'I just have a hormone problem.'

The biker hit him hard, without seeming to move his arm. The blow struck Jack in the side, close to the kidney, with a sickening thud. The other biker pushed Doris aside, and charged like a rhino. Jim sidestepped and struck him full on the side of the face. The larger of the two bikers grabbed Jim from behind. Jack was buckling slowly, sliding towards the ground. José tried to break it up. The girls screamed.

The shorter of the two bikers recovered, and charged Jim again. Held from behind, Jim skewed and twisted sideways, not enough to break the grip, enough to bring his elbow hard into his assailant's solar plexus, to hear breath expunged and the squeal of a windpipe sucking air. He broke free. The short one charged him again, and this time Jim hit him full on the side of the face with a right hook, throwing everything he could into it.

At the same time, he sidestepped to the right. The force of his blow, and his move away, brought his attacker crashing into the bar. Bent like that, Jim brought up his knee into his solar plexus, so that he went down, clutching his stomach, wheezing and vomiting.

Jim turned to the other biker, who earlier had grabbed him from behind. His face had gone white. He was crouched over, trying to suck air into his lungs. 'Mary mother of Jesus,' he heard José saying behind him.

Jim turned to help Jack, lying buckled on the floor. As he knelt over Jack, he glanced towards the other end of the bar.

There must have been about seven of them, in leather jackets with tattoos on their arms, streaming through the doorway, gathering on the other side of the room like Zulus on a hill. They looked at him, and then at the bodies of the two bikers sprawled on the floor. Sam and Doris stopped screaming and drew back. José was shouting, ineffectually, 'Just keep calm, everybody, keep calm.' Jim said: 'Just a little misunderstanding, guys.' But the consensus amongst the tribes gathered there seemed to be that they didn't like misunderstandings. In fact, it seemed to them that there were too many misunderstandings in the world, and they wanted to put it right. When Jim said resignedly, 'OK, who's first?' they were all volunteers.

Eighteen

It was cold outside, where their bodies had been thrown.

To the left of José's bar there was a small shingle bank, behind which a number of dinghies were stored. Next to that was a car park. The bikers had dumped them unceremoniously on a patch of waste ground between the two.

After a beating, there is security in inactivity. The mind starts to function, puts out feelers, begins, somewhat furtively at first, to try to rearrange itself into a semblance of order. Then a doubt strikes it. Is the body still here? If it is, is it more or less in one piece? Only action will tell.

It was Jack who moved first, turning over slowly, inch by inch, until he lay on his back. It was a reasonable start. It might have been worse.

It was several moments before Jim, lying on his side, attempted the same manoeuvre. When he had completed the long, painful journey from his side to his back, he reached an enquiring finger towards the mask of sensations that had once been his face. The pain leaped towards him like a dog over a gate. He withdrew his fingers. He tried to open his eyes. The blurred light of a streetlamp pulsed. His tongue felt enormous in his mouth. In spite of it, he could speak. He said:

'"No, I just have a hormone problem." God, what a line. We were all right until you said that.'

The streetlamp wavered above him, elusive.

'My hormones really hurt,' said Jack.

They lay there for perhaps twenty minutes. They could hear the sound of noisy drinking from José's bar fifty yards away, the muffled footsteps of promenaders a little inland, the impact and then the sucking hiss of the breakers behind the big shingle bank. Sometimes they could hear, from a distance, footsteps and voices from the street.

They weren't sure how long they lay there. Neither was in a big rush to get anywhere, and it seemed to them that the longer they lay there, the more sensation slowly came back into their arms and legs.

They must have lain there half an hour. Shadows fell across them. Perfume engulfed them suddenly.

'Oh my God,' one of the girls said. Then the one called Sam was trying to lever an arm underneath Jim's shoulders, attempting to lift him. He tried to help her by pushing downwards with his arms, but the pain nearly poleaxed him.

'We gave them the slip,' Doris was saying. 'Better get a move on, or they'll guess where we are.'

Jack said: 'I'd rather die here, if it's all the same to you.'

'It's better if you die at my place,' Doris chided him.

'No one dies on us,' Sam said, laying down the party line.

It was as if they were used to helping men home, as if all their instincts had been trained in that direction, as if it were a normal occurrence in their lives.

Slowly, with the affable determination of women everywhere who have looked after the young, the ageing, the sick, the two girls got them to their feet. Jim had a sprained or perhaps a broken arm. It was virtually impossible to move it. Jack could hobble with his arm over Doris's shoulder.

Like two clumsy four-legged animals, they made their way to the steps that led up to the sea wall. Then the girls struck inland, allowing them to pause now and again to lean for rests against lampposts, the sides of buildings.

It had become cooler. A sea mist had come in.

113

The journey seemed to take hours. They made plumes of smoke with their breathing, stumbling to rest for a while against damp walls, moving across old parking lots where debris lay in dense piles in the corners, through the rear premises of a bus shelter, past the smoking lights of streetlamps. Their footsteps echoed. Their voices were hoarse against the high brick walls and black windows of offices and old warehouses. Sometimes they tripped. Several times they fell down and had to be helped to their feet by the two girls.

Doris's place was a small flat in the working district of the town. By the time they reached it, Jim and Jack were ready to collapse. Doris propped Jack against the wall while she fumbled in her handbag for the key. Sam held up Jim, swaying.

'Thank you, ladies,' Jack said. 'This is real nice of you.'

It was at that point, or so shortly afterwards that memory telescoped the two events together, when two more bodies came out of the night. The two further presences were merely shadows at first, but they heard a voice say. 'OK, girls, step aside.' Jack tried to stand up. Jim, who found himself suddenly unsupported, wavered, turning to face his assailants, afflicted with the terrible slowness of dreams.

They knew, both of them, that this time it was inevitable. This time it would be serious.

But it was not their own voiced fears that they heard, it was the soft and dangerous rise of a female knee between two unsuspecting male legs, a sound as innocuous as the pat of a pillow – except for the sudden, astonished grunt of agony which followed it, the keeling over and staggering about over a bellyful of pain. Other sounds followed; the gratuitous violence of a handbag, full of scent bottles and lipsticks, spare coins and other repositories of weight, on the back of a surprised head. Then the two girls had set upon the other figure from two sides, decorating an incredulous face with crimson nailmarks, raining blows from two handbags (well-made in imitation leather and serviceable for the purpose), on the side of a face and defensively bunched shoulders. Even a belaboured fore-arm, thrown across a face in a life-saving gesture, could not much soften the force of the violence visited upon its owner. The entire counter-attack was accompanied by an explosion and creativity of female language which, even in the less respectable parts of town, would have raised the fright-wig on a Norway rat.

The two figures staggered away. The door was unlocked. Jack and Jim were helped and pushed inside. Then the door was slammed shut with peremptory disgust and the chains were rattled and bolted into place.

'Coffee?' asked Doris, smoothing down her skirt.

Who could refuse?

Doris put on the kettle.

Her flat was small, a neat oasis of order. The kitchen was hardly big enough for two to stand in, but she had soon put out cups and saucers, and the kettle was shriek-ing happily. Sam helped them down onto the easy chairs in the small living room that adjoined the kitchen. From where they sat, they could see Doris moving back and forth in the little kitchen, putting out milk, sugar, biscuits. The flat smelt clean and warm.

After the coffee, the two girls attended to their cuts in the little kitchen, applying antiseptic and bandages. They should go to the hospital for a checkup, said Sam.

In the morning, replied Doris. It could wait till the morning.

'Don't bandage too much,' Jack said. 'Leave a few bits of me showing.'

But the girls ignored these feeble protestations. They were going to deal with the situation as they saw fit.

'Were you guys looking for a fight, or something?' asked Doris.

'Subconsciously, perhaps,' said Jack.

'Don't give me that crap. Were you or weren't you?'

But the question wasn't addressed to Jack. It was directed at Jim. The one thing that they remembered that evening was the cold fury with which Jim fought, pulling chairs and tables together so that the charging mass was forced to come at him in single file, the apparently casual feints as each assailant came on, watching their eyes, the savage, calculated, punishing blows he dealt them as they staggered by him, confused and wrong-footed. There must have been three or four of them lying incapacitated on the wooden floors before they pulled back the barricade of tables and chairs and rushed him in a body. Even in that final mêlée, it was the weight of bodies that carried Jim down.

'What about your friend?' asked Sam but her interest seemed to have lessened. Jack glanced at her. He noticed her lips, concentrated as she patted Jim's face with disinfectant, open slightly with contemplation. His eyes went down. Jim's left arm hung downwards, useless, but his right hand was active under Sam's dress.

'For God's sake, Shaw,' Jack said.

'Keep your eyes to yourself, mister,' said Doris.

Jim went into the small bedroom with Sam. Doris bedded down with Jack on the sofa-bed in the tiny living room.

They went to the hospital early, having done their best to pay back the girls for their protection, despite the pain.

The sunshine produced flat, hard shadows. Doris drove them down the streets in her old Chevrolet to the white-gabled buildings in their neat flower gardens. There was no one about at that hour, but the sprinklers were already on. They called in at the emergency centre. Jim's arm was X-rayed. No fractures were found, but as a precaution a cast was made for the wrist of his swollen left hand. Doris dropped them off at their own lodgings at the sailing base. They kissed the girls goodbye and sneaked in through the side-door to their own small rooms.

There was no sailing that day. They could lie up and recuperate. The emergency meeting to decide on the Olympic team was scheduled for the following day. Coach Johnson, as it happened, had left that morning early for a prize-giving at a university down the coast. It was their one small break in a week of calamities.

Charlie Grist sneaked them orange juice, toast and tea and kept bulletins on the other's progress. They were holed up for the entire day. By mutual agreement, despite the pain and the headaches, they decided to go for a walk in the early evening, during that quiet time before the streetlamps came on. They found themselves knocking on the door of the girls' flat, attempting to smile when Doris came to the door, raising bandaged arms to greet her and trying not to leer out of half-closed eyes as Doris hauled them in and they could see, crossing the open doorway with a towel around her neck, Sam's naked legs and fur across the upper landing as she left the shower for the living room.

They sat on the sofa while Doris brought them wine in plastic cups. Sam dressed behind them, shimmying into her dress.

'You going out tonight?' asked Jack.

'Yeah, we got a date.'

'The guys we fixed last night,' Doris said.

'They phoned up,' explained Sam. 'They were real apologetic. They're nice guys, really.'

'They coming back here?' asked Jim.

They were not so sick, so weak, that they didn't both move towards the door. They were halfway down the stairs when Doris managed to get between them and the door. Placing her well-made behind against the door, Doris said:

'You aren't frightened, are you?'

They paused.

'Look, Doris,' Jack said. 'We just called to thank you for what you did.'

Doris didn't move.

'That's all we are to you? Just a couple of chicks? Easy come, easy go?'

Sam brushed past them and joined Doris.

'They look pretty frightened to me.'

'What are you frightened of, exactly?' asked Doris.

'I think you could say life in general, Doris,' said Jack. 'We don't mean you any harm. We'd just like to leave before your friends come back.'

'That's right,' Jim said. 'If you'd kindly step aside, girls, we can be on our way.'

Doris said. 'Phone them up, Sam. Tell them we can't make it tonight.'

Sam pushed past them, almost contemptuously.

They listened to her talking on the phone upstairs. They distinctly heard her say 'Well, fuck you, buster,' and put down the phone.

'Men,' commented Sam.

Doris herded them upstairs, keeping between them and the door, in case they had second thoughts.

The girls found pasta in the cupboards. Sam went out to a local shop where she could buy mincemeat. The girls laid the small table and pulled up chairs from the kitchen. Two candles were lit. They brought out a carton of cheap white wine and poured out glasses. It tasted good to them. When the pasta was set down on the table, they were ravenous. They both had second helpings, washed down with more wine.

The girls kept up a banter through the meal. Doris was a manicurist, Sam a dental nurse. They earned good money, better than Jack or Jim on their sailing scholarships.

Afterwards they almost repeated the pattern of the previous night. This time Doris took Jack to the small bedroom. Sam gave Jim a demonstration of her foxy athleticism on the small living-room sofa-bed.

Curiously, it was Jim who preferred Doris; he was mocked by her dark eyes and would have appreciated her generous proportions and voluptuous power. It was Jack who preferred Sam, with her small, birdlike ribcage and sweet breasts. So each of them could not help listening to the other through the door, gauging the activities there.

On their way back in the early morning, with the sunlight washing the streets, Jim asked, 'How was Doris?'

'Great,' said Jack, 'Tremendous girl. Maybe a little too passionate for me. You know, all-encompassing.' A knife turned in Jim's heart. 'You?' asked Jack nonchalantly. 'Sam? Yeah. A bit too "little-girl", maybe. I'm not the protective type.' He saw, or rather felt, Jack turn away with a twinge of the same erotic pain.

Nineteen

Jack Peabody groaned audibly.

It was a charity race, but no less hard fought for that. They had managed to break clear of the main group and had spent the first leg of the course scrapping with the three leaders. But every movement of arm or leg was uncomfortable, every haul on the sheets released sharp stabs of pain and to tack was close to agony.

The local television station were filming it for inclusion in their sporting programme later that evening. Flags and bunting had been set out on the shoreline behind the sharply shelving little beach where the dinghies were launched. Several large spectator boats, full of town dignitaries, had been hired to watch the race, and now pulled their folding wakes across the water somewhat indiscriminately. Jim and Jack were forced to sail lower and butt across the waves in order not to lose too much speed.

Neither was immediately recognisable. Jim's left arm was in a sling; bandaids covered his face in several places. Jack hung out on the trapeze; his face was bound heavily in white bandages, with only a slot for eyes, over which he had placed his habitual dark glasses.

Some wags on one of the spectator boats burst into loud cheering whenever they came into view, treating them as an original fancy dress ensemble. They did their best to avoid this spectator boat.

'Tack,' Jim said. Switching from one side of the boat to the other, the pain of movement brought forth a copious stream of groans and obscenities.

They settled on the new tack. A competitor was approaching them on starboard tack. They were forced to tack again.

Another boat sliced past. Two sunswept Californian types looked them over. One shouted:

'Hey, you shouldn't take out those big women.'

The Californian sniggered and waved.

'Did you hear something?' asked Jim.

'No, I don't think so.'

They crossed tacks again a few minutes later.

'What happened, Peabody?' shouted the fairer of the two Californians. 'She roll on top of you?'

Under his breath Jack said: 'Can we get out of here?'

'Tack.'

It was when the dinghies were drawn up after the race, and they stood swaying on the foreshore in their sea-soaked bandages, that Jack noticed a pretty girl walking along the sand, tall, with a wide mouth, close-cut hair. Jim, turning to follow his stare, felt odd, elusive memories strain. He recognised something in that appearance and that walk.

'Who is that?' asked Jack. 'You recognise her?'

It was difficult to say. Jim said instead: 'I don't believe it.'

'Don't believe what?'

But Jim was not yet ready to utter his suspicion.

'Polish chick, my guess. Hungarian, maybe,' said Jack. 'Magyar cheekbones. Wow.'

'Maria,' said Jim to himself.

'Great ass,' said Jack, behind his bandages. He turned. 'What'd you say?'

'Maria Chednik.'

'Maria who?'

'Girl who lived near me. Scrawny little thing.'

'You kidding? That little girl that was always hanging round?'

As they peered out from behind their bandages, one of the Californians, the taller, blonder one, walked up to her and put his arm around her waist.

Jim heard her say 'Chuck' or perhaps 'Hi, Chuck.' The important thing was that he was called Chuck.

Jack said: 'Just look at that.'

'Chuck,' commented Jim. 'Can you believe that?'

The arm was possessive, encircling her waist. They walked away, arm in arm.

'How old is she now?' Jack asked.

'Eighteen, nineteen.'

'That so?'

They watched the two walk away into the late afternoon shadows, their shadows mingling.

'You know,' Jack said, 'Watching that guy Chuck gives me a new pain, I mean somewhere that, well, to be specific, is actually located in my rear end.'

'Let's walk back.'

They walked in silence for a while, skirting the top of the dune, crossing the flat back of an arrested wave of sand.

'I'm really worried about you,' said Jim. 'I've never seen you quite this interested before. I mean, there are levels of interest. But this is what I'd call genuine interest.'

'What makes you think I'm interested?'

'You're interested.'

They were walking parallel to the sea shore. The sun was almost touching the surface of the water. With the onset of evening, the sea-breeze had died. Two deck-chairs had been propped together like drunks.

'What happened to her brother? Doesn't she have an older brother?' Jack persisted.

'They don't talk about him much. He's a bad boy.'

'Oh?'

'He's in gaol, man. San Antonio. Aggravated burglary.'

'What'd he do exactly?'

'Aggravated a burglar, I guess.'

'This is a hell of a time to joke.'

'Like I say, man, you're interested.'

They started to walk over the dunes. It was tough work, walking through the sand. Every footstep was an effort, every effort was painful.

'What happened to her older sister, Margaret?' asked Jack.

'Martha.'

'Martha. What happened to her?'

'She married. She's got three children.'

'Who'd she marry?'

'Boy, you sure got it bad.'

'You sure it's me who's got it bad?'

Jim was flabbergasted. He slowed, but Jack continued to press on.

'Look,' called Jim after him, 'You saying I got it bad?'

'Yeah, I'm saying that. Why else are you so goddamn protective about her?'

'Protective? Me?'

Jack stopped. Jim caught up with him. Static suddenly, their shadows ceased to hobble and sway. Jack said:

'Let's be mature about this.'

'Yeah, let's be.'

'Let's not get worked up about this.'

'No, let's not.'

'I saw her first.'

'I recognised her first.'

'I got a pain in my butt first when I saw her boyfriend.'

'She should be protected from the likes of you.'

'Yeah?'

'What are we going to do? Throw a coin over her?'

'Don't think we're in a position to throw a coin right now.'

'Maybe not,' Jim conceded. 'We couldn't bend down to pick it up.'

They made their way carefully over the dunes, towards the seafront with its little bunting flags, arguing about Maria, Martha, her gaoled brother, nourishing their hatred of male Californians.

122

Back at the camp, Charlie Grist said: 'How'd it go?'

'We won,' Jim said.

Charlie Grist watched them settle down. Jack opened the fridge and drew out a can of beer.

'You sure you won?'

'Sure we won,' Jim said.

'We goddamn won,' Jack repeated.

Charlie Grist shook his head.

'You guys want anything to eat?'

'No.'

'There's a telephone message for you,' Charlie said. 'Those two chicks you're taking out.'

The information did not raise any immediate attention. At length Jack stood up. The phone was in the hallway, an old-fashioned dial-phone. You raised the receiver and put the coins in.

'Doris?' asked Jack.

'Jack?' asked Doris.

'Yuh.'

There was a giggle on the other end of the line. He could imagine them both.

'You and Jim coming over?'

'We were in a race today, girls. We're real tired.'

There was an awkward pause.

'We'll cook supper.'

Jack put his hand across the phone.

'Jim, you want to go out?'

'Get out of here, you miserable sons of bitches,' Charlie growled.

Jim nodded towards Jack.

'OK, we're coming over,' Jack said.

The girls cooked fresh fish in their little kitchen. And as the evening drew to its end, and the two pairs were about to take up their respective beds and sofa, by some odd alchemy they changed partners that night. Maybe the girls had organised it. Jack took the foxy, pretty Sam into the little bedroom. Jim slept with the voluptuous Doris on the sofa, and when they emerged, satisfied and replete the following morning, Jim with a few extra bruises and scratches perhaps, neither spoke as they hobbled their way down the hill towards the sea in the early morning sunshine, crossing the long shadows on their way back to the clubhouse.

'OK,' said Coach Johnson. 'So who's responsible?'

They had never seen Coach Johnson quite that angry. He was one of those people who seem to grow colder as rage increases.

'Responsible for what, Coach?' asked Jim.

'They couldn't help it, Coach,' said Jack. 'We all have our failings.'

'I don't mean them. I mean which one of you dumb, stupid, incompetent bastards did this?'

'Did this, sir?'

Coach Johnson's face jutted out towards them. He had a way of lowering his hands by his sides, as if by some deliberate mental effort, to stop them rising toward someone's throat.

'You just don't understand, do you? This isn't a god-damn joyride. You're training to represent your country at the Olympics, and you go and . . . rough up in some low dive.'

'Represent our country, sir?' asked Jack.

'Oh, you didn't know. God help us, the committee voted last night.' The thought seemed to make Coach Johnson almost angrier. 'They agreed unanimously to take the almost unprecedented step of ignoring the points system. They voted for you two sons-of-bitches. Two good guys, who thought their chances were certain, are now out on their asses because of you. Now get the hell out of here, both of you.'

They turned round. They hobbled towards the door. Coach Johnson was still standing in the same place, staring away from them. They closed the door behind them. They walked down the corridor.

'Did he really say that?' asked Jack.

'He did.'

124

Behind them the door was thrown open. Coach's angry face peered round the frame.

'You got two days off. I suggest you get back here in forty-eight hours, or I'm gonna have your guts for piano strings.'

They watched the door slam closed.

Jack said: 'Underneath, he's a nice person.'

'He certainly is.'

Twenty

Jim sat on the café terrace.

He had placed himself strategically in a position to observe the main thoroughfare to the beach. His newspaper propped in front of him, from behind dark glasses he checked the pedestrian traffic along the walkway.

It was the second day he had haunted the seafront, searching, observing. Brightly coloured umbrellas kept the sun off the tables. Families of holidaymakers settled and left, dragging trailing children.

He watched the passers-by with vague interest. His face was not as swollen as yesterday, but bandaids still covered the unhealed cuts. When another hour had passed, Jim paid for another cup of coffee. Around him the tables were full.

After two further hours of waiting, all the chairs around him had emptied. He stood up, somewhat weary with inactivity, put his hands in his pockets, and started to walk down the now empty street. He was still limping slightly. It was late afternoon. Most of the holidaymakers had gone.

In the town the first lights had started to appear. From the pathway he could see down two blocks of flats to José Ferrara's bar. The memory made him flinch.

Jim walked to the other side of the street, looked in a window idly. Behind the screen were expensive confectionery, bottles, little dolls. He moved from window to window, idly. There was a sports shop there, with photographs of young men and women holding tennis rackets, golf clubs, basketballs. Alongside it was a health-food shop, with the same type of models in slightly different situations. He was about to make his way back to his room at the sailing club when he tensed up suddenly. He reached up to pull down his dark glasses slightly so that he could study the images presented by the hard surface of the glass.

He looked past his reflection. In the centre of the shining screen he studied the image of a dark-haired girl and tall, blonde young man, arm in arm. He waited until they had passed, and then looked casually after them.

His heart raced.

They walked through a turnstile of a park. He followed at a safe distance. He noticed that they walked happily, like lovers.

They paused beside a lake, looking at the ducks.

On the other side of the park, they kissed, parted and waved. Maria's boyfriend, the one called Chuck, set off. He was built squarely, with an almost jaunty walk, and Jim felt his own dislike follow him like an assassin. But Maria was already walking quickly away. He started after her. Her walk was confident. She didn't look back. At a distance, he followed Maria to an apartment building overlooking the park. Maria entered the hallway of the apartment block.

It was early evening: twilight.

Jim walked fifty yards down the street and sat down on a park bench, determined to wait.

It became darker. Lights had already begun to appear in the building into which she had disappeared. Early evening pedestrians walked past him.

Half an hour passed, then an hour.

He felt like all the old hobos and tramps in the land,

sitting in the dusk, waiting. The shadows crawled up the buildings. He took off his sunglasses.

The block which Maria entered earlier was now a great square of light. He saw a tall figure come to the entrance, pause, then turn and walk away. He started after her at a brisk pace. She was on the other side of the road, but suddenly she turned, glanced up and down the road, and crossed to his side.

For a moment he thought she had seen him.

Jim made a detour into the park and started to run. His run was more like a fast limp. To a wounded man, pain increases geometrically with speed. A walk is uncomfortable, a trot is torture, and a slow gallop is hell on earth. He half ran, half limped until he emerged at the other end of the park. For several seconds he gathered his breath. He stepped round the corner and emerged.

Too slow. She had gone past.

He turned to look behind him. A streetlamp as bright as a sun blinded him. He could only see her silhouette at first.

Maria stopped. He said: 'Jim Shaw. I guess you don't remember me.'

She paused only momentarily, studied him briefly, then said,

'I don't remember if I do.'

Maria walked on.

Jim ran after her. Her stride was brisk. He could tell by the set of her shoulders that she was angry. He managed to catch up with her. As he drew alongside, he said: 'Wait a minute. Wait a minute. Please.'

Maria halted, breathing deeply, looking ahead. She still did not look at him. She said suddenly:

'You followed me?'

'Er, yes.'

She breathed again, angrily. He thought she was about to walk away, and this time he wouldn't have the temerity to try to stop her. Playing for time, he said: 'Look, I'm just trying to be friendly.'

'Following someone isn't friendly.'

'How else could I meet you?'

'You could have just walked right up to me and said "Hello".'

'I just did.'

She bit her lip, but couldn't hide the smile. Jim pressed his advantage. He asked:

'May I take you out sometime?'

'I already have a boyfriend.'

'Yeah, I noticed,' Jim said. 'You off to meet him now?'

She paused: 'You certainly are pushy.'

'Look, can we just talk? Will you have some coffee?'

'I don't want to keep Chuck waiting.'

'He never kept you waiting?'

She paused again, breathing audibly: 'Boy, you sure are something.'

Jim pointed to an expresso coffee house nearby, across the street.

'We could go there. Come on, one cup of coffee isn't going to hurt you.' He sensed her stiffen beside him. He said: 'Please.'

He still wasn't sure whether she'd walk away. Instead, Maria breathed a sigh, half way between irritation and resignation, and said: 'One cup.'

Lavazzi's was like other coffee bars in the city, except more so: a little more chrome perhaps, the décor a fraction more self-conscious. The rubber plant was a little greener, the waiters a shade more unctuous.

'Just coffee for me,' Maria said.

'One coffee and one expresso.' He turned to face Maria. 'How long have you been here?'

'About a year. I go to college here. Chuck's also at college. He's doing his MA.'

'Really? I've seen him sailing.'

'Chuck? Yes, he sails a lot. He loves it.' She paused. He was aware of the peculiar seriousness of her expression. 'What are you studying, Jim?'

'I just sail.'

She nodded, but her eyes remained uncomprehending.

'You just sail?'

'Yeah, that's all I do.'

'How do you earn your living?'

'I have a sailing scholarship. I teach at sailing schools in summer. Anything I can do to keep life and soul together.'

'That seems a funny kind of life.'

'Maybe it does to you. To me it seems quite natural.'

'You aren't interested in anything else?'

Jim looked down at his coffee. He couldn't remember being questioned quite like this before.

'What are you going to do when you finish sailing?'

'I've never thought about it.'

'You haven't?'

Jim looked up at her.

Maria glanced at her watch. 'I guess it's time I went.'

She stood up. Jim reached out and held her by the wrist.

'Maria, I'm not going to compete with Chuck.'

'Oh? I thought you sailors liked competition.'

'We do. On the water.'

'Well, listen, Jim. When you come off the water, why don't you get in touch with me?'

Maria firmly pulled her hand free, and stood up to leave. The waiter brought her coat. Maria said: 'Thanks for the coffee.'

Jim started to rise after her, but the pain that went through him suddenly, from a site in his left side, made him want to cry out. After a few moments the spasm subsided.

She had stopped in the doorway and was watching him. He looked away.

'What happened to you?' asked Maria.

'Nothing.'

He heard the door close, and he was certain she had gone. But both of the figures that moved away through the frosted glass were unfamiliar.

He sat down carefully into his seat. When he looked up, Maria was seated opposite him again.

'You don't look too well for a sailor.'

'We all have our problems.'

He looked outside at the traffic shuffling through the streets, determined not to let her see the traces of the pain still slowly subsiding in him.

'When exactly are you proposing to ask me out?'

'Tomorrow night,' Jim said.

'I can't manage tomorrow night.'

'The night after?'

'No,' Maria said. She flashed him an odd look. 'Tomorrow lunch.'

'I'm sailing tomorrow morning.' He added, 'Practice.'

'Then you better get your priorities right. I'll be here, twelve-thirty.'

Maria stood up to leave. Through the glass Jim watched her walk away. The waiter returned. Jim wanted time to think.

'Another expresso, please.'

He looked thoughtfully out through the window. He even allowed himself a wry smile.

Twenty-one

Next day Jim turned up twenty-five minutes late.

It had been a struggle to get away in time. Coach had held him back after the morning's training race. He was exhausted from crossing the park. The minutes seemed to pile one on top of the other by the time he reached the coffee house.

The waiter was busy clearing away used cups.

He looked around in panic. The place was half full, but he couldn't see her. The waiter looked up at him.

'She left.' He shook his head in wonder.

'When?'

'Five minutes ago.'

Jim was out in the street, looking right and left. All the figures were unfamiliar. He peered between the shadows over the trees in the park. He could have howled.

Coach Johnson bustled about beside a slide projector. He wore a green shade on his head like an old-fashioned newspaper editor.

'Sit down, sit down, you guys.' He pointed out chairs to Jack and Jim in the little clubhouse room. 'I'm going to show you a few slides of your rivals, by way of brief introduction. Remember these faces, you'll be seeing them on the race course.'

Coach Johnson switched off the lights, pushed a slide into the ancient machine. The machine whirred, gathered momentum, and threw an image on the white screen of a swarthy young man with dark, curling hair. Coach Johnson paused for effect.

'Fernando Berlini, Italian, twenty-five, national champion of Italy four times, second in last year's world championship. A brilliant helmsmen, he can take his boat clean through a pack as if it wasn't there. Quick, resourceful, a seat-of-the-pants sailor.'

Another slide came up.

'Crewman Luigi Martolo, also a good helmsman. Maybe that's why these two are so good. They seem to think together, as if they're both helming the boat.'

A further change of slides.

'John Sinclair. English. Twenty-three. Last year, he was top-scoring helmsman in the Admiral's Cup series. We came third. This guy's cool as they come, fine temperament. They say he's going to be their next America's Cup helmsman. His problem is he's got too much on his plate. Won't be able to devote himself singlemindedly to the Olympics. This is his crew, John Chapman, good solid guy, maybe a bit overawed by Sinclair. Reckon we can get the edge on these guys.'

Coach paused for breath, moved a slide through.

'Gustav Zimmer. German. Just what you'd expect. Methodical, thorough, infinite patience and preparation.

He's one of the top helmsmen, but not in the top four. The guy that really pulls in the successes is his crew, Johann Zeit.'

The machine whirred again and changed slides:

'This is Zeit here. Tactically brilliant. He calls the shots. These guys have pulled races out of the bag you wouldn't believe. Seems like God created windshifts for these two. Second and third in the last two world championships. Silver medallists in the last Olympic Games. Watch them.'

Like a magician at a magic lantern, Coach fed another slide into the machine. Up came a Slavic face, fair haired, one of those faces which are closed, which give away nothing. Coach paused as if for emphasis.

'Ivan Illich. Russian. Thirty-one. Maybe the world's greatest living sailor. Gold medallist Olympic Games at the age of nineteen. Gold Medallist Olympic Games, age of twenty-three. Seven times world champion in class. Gold Medallist Olympic Games aged twenty-seven.'

'No one has dominated a class like this since Rodney Pattisson in the Flying Dutchman in the late 1960s. What can you say about this guy, except he's some kind of goddamn genius? He's also a chess champion.'

Coach changed slides:

'Here's his crew, Sergei Linkov. He's also just about as easy to read as a cube of ice. Comes from Tallinn, Republic of Estonia. Estonia's one of their main seaboards. Most of their best sailors seem to be Estonians, starting with Timir Pinegin, their first Olympic Gold medallist sailor. Illich also comes from Tallinn.'

Coach went to the wall and put on the light. He switched off the machine.

'I just want to say one thing. I reckon that if we really train hard, and we study what we know of our rivals, we can beat all these teams. Except one. The Russkies.

'Over the next few months, I'll take you through the ways that these guys sail. We've got good videos here. We'll analyse your racing techniques and theirs, and we'll work out tactics that can maybe tip the balance. But I'm not going to bullshit you about those two Russians. If I try to analyse their weaknesses, maybe a preponderance of expertise in one type of wind condition, I just don't get anywhere. They don't have any.

'But we are going to try. We're going to work you to the bone. Physical fitness training first thing in the morning starting six o'clock; sailing in the morning; more training in the afternoon; debriefing in the evening.' Coach Johnson looked at the signs of their recent fracas – the weals, bruises and inflammations that had not yet subsided – and said with something approaching satisfaction. 'You boys won't have any time to visit any low dives.'

From this preliminary introduction to their main sailing rivals, Jim carried away one clear image. The green eyes of Ivan Illich, the strange, detached eyes of a wolf or an ascetic, hovered in the darkness of the small screen. He fixed his mind on those eyes and settled down to wait for their first meeting.

Twenty-two

'Gybe.'

Jim spun the boat about. He flicked the boom across and ducked beneath it as it crashed onto starboard. Jack was already on the other side, hauling in the jib sheet hand over hand as they hardened up on the wind. They swept across the bow of a boat on starboard, realised they wouldn't clear the boat immediately behind it.

'Tack!'

The curved sail thundered as they came through the wind. Jack was easing out on the trapeze, picking up power. They hardened up tight, driving through a flurry of crossing boats. A small gap opened up as the fleet closed with the starting line. Jack counted down. They made up distance on the boat to windward. Nine, eight, seven . . . Time to squeeze up a little further, forcing the boat to windward to tack away to avoid a collision. BANG! They were close enough to smell the cordite of the starting gun.

The front of the fleet was threaded on a single line of concentration. They had cleared a little space. Jack was now full out on the trapeze and they were driving as hard as they could for speed. These were nervous times, when a few inches forward or back could mean clear air or a backward plunge into the undignified mêlée of the pack. Around them shouts indicated where rights of way were being forced. Somewhere there was a collision, an explosion of swearing, then the outraged cough and squeal of two hulls grinding together.

But now their bow was edging slowly out ahead. Jim was working the boat around and through the swells that were coming in from the North. By a tiny fraction of distance they had clear air. Jim glanced behind him. The boat which they had forced to tack away from the start was in bad air from several boats and now was being sucked back remorselessly into the centre of the pack. He looked across the line for forward boats. Like an amoeba putting out cautious pseudopodia, the front of the fleet was sending out its few leading boats into clear air.

This was a time of suspense. Boats were tacking everywhere, trying to break into clear air, shaking off rivals. No one was threatening them immediately.

Jim had time to make a brief appraisal of the sails. He tightened in slightly on the mainsheet now that they were up to speed so that they could point a fraction higher. Two of the leading boats tacked and were now approaching them on starboard, on a converging course and with clear right of way. On the closest of the two they identified the sail numbers of the Italian champions, Berlini and Martolo. Jim waited deliberately until the very last moment, until a collision seemed imminent, then spun the boat through the wind onto parallel tack. Jack seemed to fly across the boat like an owl, through and out on the trapeze on the other side. They came up hard under the lee of the Italians, neck and neck. Jim bore away slightly to pick up speed. They had clear air now, and he could start to squeeze up towards them. But the Italians were experts, and as soon as they felt a loss of power from the backwind of Jim's sails, they tacked and ducked under the stern of the boat to starboard.

The boat behind now came into full view, moving fast, slightly ahead of them.

It did not take Jim more than an instant to recognise, even if only at a subconscious level, the blonde hair of the helmsman, or to remember, in the little darkened room with the old-fashioned slide projector, the image of wolves and forest saints.

'Let's try luffing them,' said Jack.

They started to squeeze up towards them, a bit at a time. But the Russians made no attempt to keep their distance. Instead, Illich eased sheet a fraction, picking up speed, and swooped down towards them, hardening up just ten feet above them, enough to take their wind and start their sails shuddering.

'Tack!'

Jim made his escape as best he could, fighting to bring the boat up to speed again. Benefiting from the manoeuvre they had forced on Jim and Jack, Illich and Linkov fetched the windward mark some three boat lengths ahead of them, without a single further tack. Jim's own forced tack had also allowed the Germans to slip through ahead of them. They were third round the mark.

They managed a creditable fourth in a strong international fleet, behind the Russians, the Germans Zimmer and Zeit, and the Englishmen Sinclair and Chapman. Illich and Linkov were easy winners.

Coach Johnson was waiting for them on the shoreline, ready to take hold of their rigging and steady them as they came in. 'I have an old Russian proverb for you boys, "The bite of the wolf is bad enough, but that of the Bear is even worse.'"

'Amen,' said Jack.

'Good race,' said Coach Johnson. 'You did well.'

Once bitten, twice shy.

Even when ahead, they could not hold off the Russians. Each race that followed pursued a different pattern but produced a similar result. They could keep up with the other leaders, but Illich and Linkov attained a purity of their own. Holding onto the coat-tails of the Russians was like trying to keep hold of a nervous animal. Any momentary relaxation of attention resulted in a loss of distance. Any inspiration or brilliance would merely result in holding them for a short while. It was like trying to climb a downward escalator; you had only to pause to be pulled backwards.

One day they were setting up mast beside the seashore prior to the seventh and last race of the practice series. About twenty yards away, Illich and Linkov were working on their boat. A strong, gusting wind sent shudders through the dinghies. They had been watching Illich and Linkov surreptitiously.

Jim said: 'Coach sure is spooked by those Russians.'

'I am too, I guess,' Jack replied.

Another gust hit them, singing in the rigging.

'They can't be that good.'

Jack did not respond. He continued to tighten a rigging screw. Jim said: 'There has to be some flaw, some chink.'

Jack turned round. Several boats away the Russians adjusted their rigging. The handsome, expressionless face of Ivan Illich looked towards them momentarily, then turned away again.

Jack said: 'There isn't any flaw.'

Twenty-three

The first day of the Olympics was overcast, but with a good, stiff breeze.

Coach Johnson was of that school which believed he should not be too closely present on a launch. It was one of those eccentricities which are easily excused in the great. Instead he preferred to watch from the shore. To help with the progress of the races, he switched on the radio.

JOHN HOUSE
This is John House reporting the first race of the Olympics in the Flying Dutchman class. And we are going to see some very exciting racing here today. Representing the US are the sailing champions Jim Shaw and Jack Peabody, twice national champions and third in the World Championships last year. These two are considered to be the dark horses in the sailing fraternity. They generated a startling number of wins in the youth championships in the 420 racing dinghy, and are now finding their feet in the Flying Dutchman class. They won the US National Championships last year and were selected for the Olympic team by committee decision after unlucky gear failures hampered their Olympic trials. They came fourth in the Olympic practices last year, after the Russian, German, and Italian crews. That's rapid progress for two young sailors.

Intense moments sometimes have the unreality of dreams. In the first race they were fifth, in the second race third, in the third race second, in the fourth race third again. Their averages were sufficiently high to place them in second place.

But Illich and Linkov did not require good averages to place them first. Every time the results went up on the board, Coach Johnson watched that most simple of numerals, the single vertical one, appear against the Russian names. First in race one, two, three and four. This wasn't simple superiority, this was domination.

Coach Johnson watched for signs of a break like a farmer hoping for signs of a thundercloud, with the same deadly patience but with no more control. The fifth race started out slightly differently.

After the brief mêlée of the start, it wasn't Illich's boat which began to pace out ahead of the fleet, but the Germans Zimmer and Zeit. Zeit had found a windshift, struck it as perfectly as a tennis player hitting a ball on the sweet spot, and Zimmer and he were forty yards ahead of the fleet. Illich and Linkov were second, ahead of the ruck. Following them were Peabody and Shaw.

Illich and Linkov closed in on Zimmer and Zeit like dogs in pursuit of a stag. A hundred yards from the top mark they crossed tacks no more than ten feet apart. Zimmer tacked with the Russians and placed a close cover on them. Illich tacked immediately to escape Zimmer's grasp. Zimmer tacked and covered again. There was a flurry of six tacks, until the boats were slowed down to half speed. It was as if, Coach Johnson said later, two dogs had locked teeth on one another, and neither would let go.

In the third boat it was Jack who, sensing blood, hissed 'Now!'

They eased out sheet and picked up speed to punch through the lee of the duelling pair. In the flow of clear air on the other side, they tightened up, feathered through the wind and, springing like a cork from a bottle, were first round the buoy.

From his position on the shore, Coach Johnson let out a brief, uncharacteristic whoop of joy.

Zimmer and Illich continued to scrap down the reach, before Illich managed to shake off his adversary.

Jack, glancing behind, saw Illich break away and come towards them with a shocking burst of speed.

The rate at which the Russians now overhauled Jim and Jack seemed inexorable. Since the boats were moving away from the shore, with the lead boats visually blanketed by the rest of the fleet, Coach Johnson switched to his radio for commentary.

JOHN HOUSE

Illich and Linkov have won their duel against the German pair and are in hot pursuit of the Americans. They have seldom looked more determined and aggressive. Shaw and Peabody are also pulling out a surprising burst of speed on this leg, as these two lead boats open up a big distance between the third-placed Germans.

'Don't look behind,' said Jack between his teeth.

'Don't tell me,' replied Jim. 'The bear's chewing our ass.'

Illich was a boat length behind as they reached back. Illich started to climb up behind them, seeking to take the wind out of their sails, but they climbed with him. Illich's bow was closing in on them. A sudden bang from their mainsail meant Illich had found their wind, and their sails collapsed. Illich and Linkov burst through. All they could do was try to hang in. There was hardly a boat length between them the entire reach.

Up the beat, Illich and Linkov placed a loose cover on them, and when they crossed tacks and shot the buoy they were still only three boat lengths behind.

As they turned onto the downwind leg, they were now between the wind and the lead boat.

Jack said: 'Let's try to hunt the bear.'

But this was a clever bear. Illich and Linkov started to reach-tack down wind. As they turned away from the direct downwind course, their apparent wind increased, and they picked up speed. Illich zigzagged down the course, keeping out of their wind-shadow, gybing with perfect precision every time they were close to stealing his wind. Jim felt like a boxer who steadies to throw a punch, but finds that every time he does so, the opponent effortlessly floats out of reach.

They could only follow move for move, keep their sail-handling crisp, try to make no mistakes, and keep hunting. They were hardly two hundred yards from the lower buoy when they caught the Russians' wind, watched their sails collapse. The lead boat wallowed suddenly. Then

Illich caught the breeze, but only momentarily, before Jim struck again, and the Russian sails collapsed for a second time. It was sweet revenge to bear down on them, sail over them, break into the lead with a knot more speed.

JOHN HOUSE

The Americans have taken over the lead in the fifth race. Illich and Linkov are ahead in the series, but in this race for the first time they're being pressed close by Shaw and Peabody.

These two lead boats have opened up a big distance between themselves and the rest of the fleet. The Russian and American teams are neck and neck now and as they move, practically touching, to the leeward mark, it's Shaw and Peabody who have established an inside overlap. The sails of the Russian boat are pulling again. This is starting to look exciting!

Jack glanced down and his blood froze. Linkov's hand was on the gunwale of their boat, holding them back.

Jim was watching the sails and hadn't noticed. Jack's jaws tightened. He punched out with his foot against Linkov's hand, and heard Linkov's hiss of pain.

JOHN HOUSE

Shaw and Peabody have rolled over Illich and Linkov, and are now placing a close cover on their rivals as they round the leeward buoy and start the final beat. These two boats are so far ahead of the fleet that this almost becomes a match-race. Shaw and Peabody can afford to lose some time in covering, which is exactly what they're doing. Tack for tack, Shaw is covering.

The Russians, who are in the lee of the American boat, are slipping behind, and as the American boat turns towards the finish line and makes a final rush, it looks as though they're clear. It looks good as they approach the finish line.

There goes the finish gun, and Shaw and Peabody have taken this race from the Russian sailors!

The score still puts the Russians firmly in the title spot for the Gold medal, but this is the first time in this series that the Russian pair have been closely pressed. The young American team has given them some real competition.

140

This is John House signing off at the end of the fifth race of these sailing Olympics.

Dinghies were being hauled out along the beach. Jim and Jack pulled a tarpaulin over their boat.

Standing on the other side, Jim could see Illich and Linkov packing up their own dinghy for the night, stowing gear, covering her with a tarpaulin.

Jack, following the direction of Jim's stare, glanced around at Linkov and Illich.

Jack said: 'That isn't going to do any good.'

But Jim continued to stare. Then he stepped round the boat and, hands in pockets, began to walk towards the Russians. Jack followed a pace or two behind, anxious.

Jim halted a few feet in front of Illich and Linkov. He opened his shoulders, looked up at the sun, down at the boat again.

Ivan Illich, his hands busy with the final hanks on the tarpaulin, surveyed him expressionlessly. Sergei Linkov had both hands on the gunwale. Jim focused on these hands. One was badly bruised. Linkov let his hand drop, so that it was hidden behind the dinghy. Jim let his attention wander up to Linkov's face, to the beginnings of a black eye.

Jim smiled, turned and walked away. Jack followed. They could feel the eyes of the Russians on them. When they were outside hearing distance, Jack said:

'See his hand?'

'Yeah.'

'You gonna protest?' Jack asked.

'No.'

They walked in silence.

'Why not?' asked Jack.

'Because they're beating us fair and square. Someone already gave that guy Linkov a black eye.'

'Reckon it was Illich who did that?'

'Yeah.'

'You really admire that guy, don't you?'

'He's the best in the world.'

'Then I guess you think you're the second best in the world.'

Jim shrugged.

'Yeah.'

Jack paused long enough to let Jim get a bit ahead of him, then placed a foot squarely in Jim's back, and toppled him onto the sand.

Jim lay face down in the sand, his hands still in his pockets. Jack said:

'You're a goddamn creep, you know that?'

Jim raised his face from the sand.

'I guess so.'

In the sixth race they were third again, this time behind the Russians and the brilliant Englishman Sinclair. In the seventh and final race, they themselves found that windshift which, like luck itself, seems to favour champions. The same shift that lifted them towards the upper buoy buried the Russians amongst the second echelon boats. Amazingly, Illich and Linkov fought back from twenty-second position to third. Jim and Jack spun across the finish line in first place, with the Germans second. It was a race based on good fortune, but good fortune or not, they were the only pair who had taken two races from the Russians.

On the shore, Coach Johnson heard:

JOHN HOUSE
Russians for the Gold, Americans for the Silver. That's the final score in these races. To come second to Ivan Illich is as good as a Gold in any other fleet. To take a race off Illich, and the Americans have done that twice, is a major achievement. Ivan Illich is widely believed to be the greatest active racing sailor in the world. These two youngsters are starting to look like heirs apparent.

Coach Johnson switched off the radio. He had never expected his protégés to win the gold against Illich, but their performance had exceeded his expectations. Zimmer and Zeit and the Italians would have been Gold medallist contenders in any other fleet, and the Englishman Sinclair would also have been a threat in any field. He stood up and began to walk along the beach to the landing point so that he could offer his congratulations.

Coach Johnson did not attend the medal ceremony in the great Olympic bowl. Avoidance of ceremonies was another of his eccentricities. As he packed to return to the USA, he left the radio on the sidetable next to his single bed.

He folded his clothes neatly into his suitcase. In the Army he had learned neatness. On the tabletop the radio bustled like a boiling kettle.

JOHN HOUSE
The Russian pair Illich and Linkov step up to take the Gold. The anthem of the USSR sounds in the background. This is Illich and Linkov's fourth Gold. Their mastery of this class is more complete than any other in history.

Young Americans Jim Shaw and Jack Peabody also sailed like masters to take the Silver in this fleet of champions. They were well out ahead of the formidable Germans Zimmer and Zeit, who take Bronze here. You're watching a great assemblage of sailing champions.

'Jim,' said Coach Johnson a few days afterwards. 'I'd like you to meet Tom Stuttaford.'

Sitting at the small café table a hundred yards from the sailing school, Jim could only see the outline of a head and face of a big man with grey hair. He stood up. The big man's features were still indistinct from the sun behind his shoulder. Out of the sunlight Jim's hand was gripped in a powerful paw.

'Pleased to meet you, Mr Stuttaford.'

'Watched you sail at the Olympics, Jim. Saw you take Ivan Illich pretty close.'

'Thank you.'

'Maybe we could have a talk sometime. Would you care to have dinner with me on Friday night?'

'That's kind of you.'

Coach said: 'Mr Stuttaford was chief fundraiser for our last America's Cup Defence.'

'I'm a banker, Jim.' His voice boomed out of the sunlight. 'Sometimes we have our uses. I'll look forward to seeing you. Here's my card and address. See you seventhirty, Friday.'

Twenty-four

Jim pressed the door-bell of the expensive-looking town house. As he waited for the door to be answered, he looked around him at the quiet neighbourhood. Other houses were discreetly hidden by trees. Large limousines drew past slowly, almost without noise, and parked in secluded driveways with a quiet rustle of gravel.

He could hear the two chimes echo inside. The door was opened. A middle-aged blonde woman, of fine features, her hair in a scarf, opened the door.

'You must be Jim Shaw. I'm Angela Stuttaford.'

'Pleased to meet you, Mrs Stuttaford.'

'Come right in. Why don't you go upstairs to Tom's study. First landing, first door. I'll be preparing the supper.'

Inside it was quiet, with that quietness of rich houses in which sound itself appears reticent. There was a large, expensive sidetable in the hallway on which had been placed several outdoor hats, an umbrella stand, a two-door cupboard for coats. Following Mrs Stuttaford's instructions, Jim pursued the long, carpeted steps up to the first floor. He knocked on the first door.

'Come in, come in.'

Stuttaford was at his desk, writing.

Seeing Jim enter, he stood up, walked round the table, and pulled up a chair. 'Take a seat.' Reaching down, he withdrew from his desk a box of Havana cigars. He held out the box to Jim. 'Care for one?'

'No thanks.'

'Hope you don't mind if I indulge. Only place I am allowed to in this house.'

Stuttaford lit his cigar in the old way, with a match, pausing with a kind of profound deliberation while the cigar came to life, as if he were lighting thoughts within himself. Jim took the opportunity to glance around the room, with its numerous group photographs of Tom Stuttaford's private school, his class at Yale, his presidency of MacQuorquodale, Bankers. Below a long oar with a painted blue blade were other photographs of rowing teams in which he had been a member. Jim gained an impression of Tom Stuttaford as a team man, a group leader, a corporate animal. Stuttaford puffed several large clouds, flicked his match until the flame went out, placed the burnt match carefully in the ashtray, and sat back.

'I hope you have no objection if I get right down to business before we go down to supper. There are a few things I'd like to say.'

He paused to draw on his cigar.

'I've had word – from unimpeachable sources – that we could be facing a Challenge for the next America's Cup quite soon, maybe a little sooner than we bargained for. I'm not talking about the usual run of challenges, with the challengers' lists open to all comers. I'm talking about a Challenge from a very unusual quarter.'

Tom Stuttaford settled back in his chair.

'My sources tell me that the prospective Challenger will invoke the original Deed of Gift to propose a one-on-one competition. Time will be tight. No other challengers. No elimination trials. Just the two of us.' Stuttaford smiled evenly. 'Like a war – a war without blood.'

Jim would remember that phrase.

Stuttaford paused: 'I'm afraid any further information at this stage is confidential. In the meantime, perhaps you'd just keep that in the back of your mind, would you?'

Jim nodded.

'Good. Now, I wanted to ask you something about Ivan Illich. What I want to ask you is this. Do you think he can be beaten?'

Jim paused, taken aback.

'I don't mean you to think about it. I'm asking what you feel, right here.' He tapped the area of chest above his heart.

'He might just be.'

Tom Stuttaford paused to consider that remark, puffing his cigar. He said finally:

'This is just speculation on my part, as long as you understand that.'

'I understand.'

'Just say, for example, I wasn't talking about dinghies. Just say I was talking about big boats.'

'Big boats?'

Tom Stuttaford paused, and Jim tried to recall afterwards whether in his heart he had ever suspected what was coming next.

'America's Cup boats.'

You could hear the silence; it was palpable, like a separate presence. Stuttaford blew a few small clouds with his cigar, which seemed so heavy to Jim they could almost start raining. Stuttaford said:

'Every good America's Cup helmsman, almost without exception, came from dinghies. Maybe you know that. It's the ability that counts. Between a dinghy and an America's Cup boat there's just one little difference, the matter of scale.'

Tom Stuttaford smiled, puffed his cigar. It was quiet in the room. Somewhere below Jim thought he heard Mrs Stuttaford moving about in the kitchen.

'An interesting subject,' Stuttaford continued. 'I've known quite a few helmsmen on big boats who have achieved fine results. But put them against a dinghy champion on another big boat, and they don't do so well.' Stuttaford exhaled, raising his eyes to the ceiling in contemplation. 'Sharpness, speed of reaction, that's what a dinghy champion brings to big boats. I'm digressing.

'Maybe you'd just give the matter some consideration. In the meantime, Jim, I'd hope that you could start with us in our training camp. We're already limbering up for the next America's Cup, whoever the Challenger may be.'

'Could I think about it?'

'You have to think about it?' asked Stuttaford, gazing at him with detached interest over the top of the table.

'I accept,' Jim said. 'But there's just one condition, sir.'

'My, my. You've just been asked to join us and already you're imposing conditions. I'm going to have to watch you, young man!'

'I'm only accepting if Jack Peabody is also included.'

Tom Stuttaford studied him. 'You sure do know how to negotiate.' He leaned forward to tap his cigar several times in the ashtray.

'We studied this from the various angles. You and Peabody are a team. We want him there too. So you got it. Peabody's your tactician.'

'Thank you, sir.'

Stuttaford smiled: 'You come highly recommended by Coach Johnson. Says you're a killer. Hell, the way he described you, I'm nervous even to allow you in my house.' He smiled. 'You get on well with Coach?'

'He taught me everything about sailing.'

'Maybe he taught you something else, too,' Stuttaford stubbed out his cigar carefully, ' – about survival.'

Jim did not speak, so Stuttaford leaned back in his chair, folded his hands across his stomach, and proceeded amiably enough.

'We were both in Vietnam,' continued Stuttaford. His face, which seemed to Jim on short acquaintance generally to be jovial, became serious, almost withdrawn. He was clearly recalling something of importance to him. 'I was a young lieutenant in those days. We Vietnam people have something in common. We stick together. Some of us felt abandoned, you see, after the Vietnam War. It was more painful to those of us who felt we'd done our best.' He paused.

'Hell!' Stuttaford said suddenly, breaking out of his

147

reverie. 'This isn't a pleasant subject for a fine summer evening. We're not here to talk politics. I guess we ought to go down to supper. Maid's away today, been given a holiday. It's something simple Angela made.'

The 'simple' dish Mrs Stuttaford had cooked consisted of a three course meal. They started with soup, followed by sliced breast of quail, and then some light, fluffy pudding, a whirl of delicate flavours.

Mrs Stuttaford put a coffee tray in front of them and then, pleading that she had to attend to the forthcoming wedding arrangements of one of her daughters, left them in the wood-panelled dining room.

'I have three daughters,' Stuttaford said. 'I guess that's how fate treats someone who has always wanted a son – several sons, actually. Instead, I find myself the only male member of an extensive female tribe. Help yourself to coffee, by the way.' He glanced at the door by which his wife had left. 'Would you like anything stronger?'

'No, thanks.'

'I used to be like you when I was young.' Stuttaford drew forth a decanter of brandy, and poured himself a glass. 'Orange juice. It wasn't as fashionable then.'

Tom Stuttaford referred to this decanter at regular intervals in the course of their discussion. He was like a man who has left behind a golden youth, and who seeks to recreate his past constantly through association. He asked about the training prior to the Olympics, elicited Jim's attitude to the latest advances in equipment, the new sailcloths. At one stage he said:

'Coach Johnson is maybe the best sailing coach this country has ever had. I guess I find any kind of great achievement fascinating. I know him well enough to have had a few heart-to-heart talks about coaching. He has an interesting hypothesis about the nature of the sailors he trains. Maybe you heard it?' Stuttaford raised his eyebrows mockingly.

'What he says is that each man has something of the devil and something of the angel inside of him. People

148

have said things like that before. It's how he puts it to use that is interesting. According to him, his function as coach is to support the devil. In competition at this level, there is no room for the generous, the kind, the courteous, and least of all the humble. You've heard that before?'

'Not put exactly like that, sir.'

'Oh?' Stuttaford refreshed his glass and leaned back. 'And what do you think of it now that you hear it?'

'Sounds pretty close to the truth.'

'You aren't shocked by its, ah, moral implications?'

'Not particularly.'

Stuttaford studied him for a few seconds:

'I don't believe, young man, you know what a moral implication is.'

'I don't think I do, sir.'

'Hell,' said Stuttaford, 'I'd give anything to be young again. Moral implications do not mean much to the young. That's why it's the young who fight wars. They aren't evil, just innocent. When we're older, we learn what moral implications are. Knowledge brings corruption in its train.'

Stuttaford helped himself to another glass of brandy.

'Maybe that's why you're so effective. That's why we need you to smite the Philistine.'

'You mean Russian, sir, don't you?'

'Russian if you will, young man. Russian if you will.'

Twenty-five

The trill of the phone punched into Jim's darkness. He rolled over in the sudden blackness to lift the receiver, to stop its shrill misgivings. A voice on the line said 'Jim'.

He rolled back with a sigh of resignation.

'Jim,' Coach Johnson's voice repeated. 'Something has come up in the programme, something important.'

'Do you know what time it is?'

'We have a meeting at eight tomorrow. We're scheduled to meet in the sailing house building. Be there.'

'What is this, Coach? Some sponsor want to check up on us?'

'You could say that.'

There were several moments of silence, then the line went dead.

Early morning shadows lay long on the road. Jim liked this time of day, the way the light picked out things so clearly.

A whistling newsboy rode a bicycle past Jim, throwing the papers into the doorways.

At the doorway of the sailing house Charlie Grist was sitting on a chair in the hallway.

'Coach Johnson's in there right now, Jim. Requested me to ask you to wait a while. Said he'd call you presently.'

An unexpected flare of rage went through Jim. He didn't like being treated like this.

'So who's in there with him, Charlie? Mr Big?'

Charlie said: 'Something like that.'

Jim sat down on the chair next to Charlie. That morning Jim had made an effort and put on a shirt and tie. He had combed his hair more carefully than usual. Though he didn't like to admit it, he was spooked.

'You keeping well, Jim?' Charlie asked.

'Yuh. How about you?'

'Not so bad. Congratulations on that Olympic medal, Jim.'

'Thanks, Charlie. Tell me you knew I was going to do it.'

'I didn't know that. I guess I didn't think about it.'

'You were always honest.'

Jim noticed there was something missing, something he couldn't put his mind to immediately.

150

'You've given up smoking?'

Charlie Grist looked almost guilty. A smile broke out on his face.

'My wife doesn't allow it.'

'Wife?'

Jim had heard that Charlie had finally married a handsome half-Indian, half-Mexican girl. It was difficult to put an age on Charlie Grist. He realised he had never attached an age to him and guessed he must be in his early forties. He had heard that Charlie had become a little more domesticated. But Jim was flabbergasted that anyone had managed to separate cigarettes from Charlie.

Just then the door opened. Coach Johnson's head appeared. 'Jim.'

'You kidding?' Jim said to Charlie. 'How'd she manage to stop you smoking?'

'Jim,' Coach repeated.

'See you, Charlie,' Jim said.

He stood up slowly. He straightened his tie deliberately, turned round and followed Coach into the room.

Jim paused in the doorway. Seated at the table was a distinguished, silver-haired man in officer's uniform. As Jim approached he rose to his feet.

'Jim Shaw, our helmsman,' Coach Johnson introduced him. 'Jim, this is General Walters.'

After the greetings, General Walters indicated a chair. Jim sat down opposite him. Coach Johnson sat down beside Jim.

'What I have to say to you is a little strange. Maybe you'll bear with me.'

General Walters paused. 'When dealing with the Russians, we find, God knows why, that if they want to send us an important message, they don't like to use the direct links. They transmit it by other means, sometimes through one of the smaller embassies. With really important messages, they send it through our embassy in Moscow.'

The general looked out of the window.

151

'Something about the Eastern mind ... However, that's not our immediate worry. What was in the diplomatic bag, however, concerns you directly.

'The letter I'm talking about was addressed to us by a functionary, some assistant secretary in a department with four numbers. Typically, that's a sign the message is so goddamn important that it gets sent directly to the Secretary of State's office.'

He looked impassively at them.

'OK, now get this. The letter stated the Russians want to put in a challenge for the America's Cup. Well, that's no great surprise. They participated before in the America's Cup.'

A beam of sunlight had crept onto the General's face and he had to harden up his eyes against the glare.

'You have to understand that's only part of it. This was put directly to us, one nation to another, so to speak.' The general looked at Jim, as if he understood. 'A one-on-one competition, no other parties. It was the way it was framed, too. Special rules to be agreed between both parties. A new type of boat, so that neither the challenger nor the defender could draw on any special experience of sailing it. The terms of their challenge also included the banning of exotic materials, where we might have an advantage. Know what material they specified?'

For the first time the General smiled.

'Wood. Wood from trees. Nature's design for swaying in the wind. God's answer to the stress cycle.'

Jim said: 'We accepted their challenge?'

General Walters paused. 'Sure, we accepted their challenge.'

'Holy Cow.'

'Maybe you don't quite understand what this means. As of now, this is a defence programme. Highest grade secrecy.'

Coach Johnson said: 'For the next nine months we're going to be in training. Confined to quarters. No drink, no broads, no going out unless given written permission.'

Jim was aware of Walters' cold eyes on him, assessing him. He felt uncomfortable under the stare of those hooded eyes.

'That clear?' General Walters asked.

Jim nodded.

'I hope so,' Walters said carefully. Jim experienced again the discomforting fierceness of Walters' gaze.

'Maybe I can make something clear to you. This isn't a sport. It's a contest, a contest between two technologies, two systems. The individual isn't the primary factor. The primary factor is the contest itself.'

General Walters stood up, followed by Coach and Jim. They shook hands. Coach Johnson followed General Walters to the door, opened it while General Walters stood aside.

They could hear the footsteps of their guest echoing away.

Coach Johnson walked back towards Jim. He looked pleased with himself. He said: 'The Russians not only named the rules for the construction of boats, they also specified the nature of the course, the sailing rules, and a whole lot of other things.'

'We accepted all of them?'

'We felt obliged to. They made specific reference to the terms of the original Deed of Gift. The challenger proposes the boat and the time. The defender is obliged to accept the challenge.'

Jim's mind was racing. Questions were forming, being pushed aside by others. But there was one overwhelming question. At last he said: 'Who's their helmsman?'

And Coach Johnson waited, waited for the dust to fall, for the room to become silent, for chairs and tables and the old paintings to compose themselves into final peace. Jim might know the answer already, but he was forced to pause until he too seemed part of the oppressive silence. In retrospect, it was only a few seconds, but it seemed at the time like eternity. Into this listening space Coach Johnson injected two words.

'Ivan Illich.'

Twenty-six

'Subject to trials and final selection,' Coach Johnson said, 'these are the crew.'

He handed Jim a slim blue file.

All that week Coach Johnson had been making phone calls. They could hear his voice behind the blue painted door of his small office, talking, arguing. Sometimes, with the door ajar, they could see his palm spread to catch some point, the chop of his hands as he drove home a series of arguments. They could hear him plead patriotism to some, plain duty to others, or the thrill of fierce competition to yet others. Once they heard him say 'Can you kindly ask him to get off her and come to the phone?' They knew he had been tracking down, at shockingly short notice, the best sailors in the USA, wheedling them out of comfortable jobs, out of nicely paid professional lairs, sometimes off streets and out of bars. Several days passed. At last Coach emerged from his office.

'You guys may have an Olympic silver and a couple of world championships behind you, but you're still wet behind the ears compared to most of the people you're going to be sailing with. As you'll see, we've lined up experience in depth.'

Jim read it in the dormitory, beside the beds, empty now, that would soon support the weight of heroes.

Jack had his bible with him, the updated racing rules, and was poring over an abstruse point about a tangle around an upwind buoy.

BOWMAN
Tony Jankovsky. Height 5' 8". Olympic Bronze medallist
gymnastics (parallel bars). National champion, J24s, three times.
5 Admiral's Cup racing campaigns, three on leading American
yacht. Nicknamed 'Virus' (because he's everywhere at once).
Considered best big-boat foredeck man in the world.

SEWERMAN
Marvin Toller. Height 6' 3". US Finn Champion. 6 successful
offshore campaigns. One of the most experienced big boat crew
in the USA. Reserve winchgrinder. Nickname 'Jingle'.

MASTMAN
William Henry Longhurst. 6' 7". Aged 25. Graduate Yale
University (English Literature). Varsity champion oarsman.
Olympic oarsman. 5 Offshore campaigns as crew-boss, successful
Ocean racer 'White Cloud'. Reserve winchgrinder. Highly
stable, resourceful. Responds to nickname 'Big Ape' when
friendly.

WINCHMAN
Gino Compostella. 5' 11". Aged 23. US champion weightlifter
four times. Outright winner US national winchgrinding contests.
University champion discus thrower. 2 Offshore campaigns.
Nickname 'Mace.'

WINCHMAN
Hemdale Sondheim. 6' 3". Age 28. Graduate Syracuse University.
Olympic Gold medallist decathlon. US champion decathlon 4 times.
2nd national winchgrinding contest after Gino Compostella. Sales
manager, Longhaul Winches. 5 Offshore campaigns. Veteran
sailor. Nickname 'Moose'.

('Shit,' said Jim. 'Hemdale Sondheim. I wouldn't even
dare to ask for that guy's autograph.')

PORT TRIMMER
Sidney Grossman. 5' 10". Age 27. Graduate Minnesota
University. World Laser champion 3 times. Senior manager
Feinstein Pugh, Wall Street brokers. 6 Offshore campaigns.
Nickname 'Greenback'.

STARBOARD TRIMMER
George Riga. 6' 1". Age 32. Graduate Berkeley University. Soling world champion 2 times. Vice-president Riga Sails. His loft has generated sails for almost half of the major offshore yachts during the past four years. Nickname plain 'Georgie'.

MAINSHEET TRIMMER
Ian Creel. 6' 1". Age 28. Instructor sergeant, US Marines. 8 Offshore campaigns. Mainsheet on 2 times Admiral's Cup winner 'Crazy Horse'. Nickname 'Sunshine'.

NAVIGATOR
Ernest Milgram Stead. Graduate, MIT, computer design. 6' 5". Aged 24. MSc computer mathematics (Princeton). Trainee executive Honeywell. Navigator on 50' offshore yacht 'White Cloud', champion 50' offshore circuit 3 consecutive years.

Jim looked across at the confident, ebony features of Ernest Stead, and called across to Jack. 'Hey, look at our navigator.'

'Well, I'll be,' Jack whistled. 'I knew navigation was a black art, but I didn't know it was *that* black.'

'No more cheap racist remarks from now on, Jack.'

'Yes, master,' said Jack. He took the file so that he too could familiarise himself with the background of the frightening collection of talents and achievements they were about to sail with to defend the America's Cup.

'What do you think?' asked Jim, when Jack had read the brief summaries.

'Makes me blush to be on the same boat as those people.'

'Same here,' Jim said. 'OK, that's the modesty, now what do you think?'

'After you,' Jack said with mock politeness.

'Mainsheet seems a little weak,' Jim said. 'No dinghy experience.'

'That's a little hard, isn't it?'

'Maybe. Admiral's Cup, too. There are some poseurs in amongst those.'

But Jack didn't rise to that one.

'Maybe Coach knows something we don't know.'

'Yeah,' said Jack. 'We'll see.'

Jim studied the list of the reserve crew. There seemed hardly any difference in quality here. He looked at the description of the opposing helmsman, Ernest 'Sunray' Houseman, a Gold medallist in Stars, one of the three or four greatest big-boat helmsmen in the world. Houseman was another legendary figure.

When he shut down the lights and shadows closed over the dormitory, Jim lay awake, thinking. 9 months! 9 months to shape up against a campaign by Ivan Illich. 9 months to gain the loyalty of a crew most of whom were far senior to him in experience. Would they ever learn to trust his judgment? Would they have time to form that most strange and magical of animals, a genuine team?

The following day Coach Johnson said:

'I've got a job for you, Jim.'

He handed Jim a short, buff envelope.

'Name of shoreboss we want. Next to it, rate of pay we can afford. Want you to seek him out. He's setting up an ocean racer called Big Wheel. Boat was last seen in Chesapeake Bay. You can open the letter.'

Jim read:

Eddie Cantor: $1200 per week.

'Haven't been able to contact him,' Coach Johnson said. 'Never seems to go near a phone. Rumour has it he's preparing Big Wheel in Frigate Harbour. Go get him.'

Twenty-seven

Sunlight lay dense on the harbour. It was not yet hot, but Jim could tell by the seamless sky that it was going to be a scorching day.

The coach ride down to Frigate Harbour had taken several hours. He caught glimpses of the yacht basin, and the forest of masts inside it, as the coach gingerly descended the final hill. He alighted from the coach at the small hidden terminal set between high office buildings. He threw his jacket over his shoulder, and made his way down through the main streets towards the harbour.

Already, although it was only nine-thirty in the morning, he could feel the warmth nestled in the sides of buildings. He walked down the sidestreets towards the harbour.

Crowds had not yet collected along the harbour wall. Stallholders and ice-cream vendors were setting out their displays. An attendant was moving folded chairs from a small shed where they were stowed overnight.

The inner harbour was small, but in the outer harbour a large marina was indicated by the presence of a forest of masts. In order to reach the marina berths it was necessary to cross several walkways and negotiate a bridge to the floating pontoons.

Amongst the seven hundred or so yachts gathered there, Jim's attuned eye picked up immediately the masts of certain yachts, slenderer than the other masts for their heights, with that look of tautness which is characteristic of racing yachts. Several of these were fractional rigs, so-called because the forestay does not reach the top of the mast.

The offshore racing fleet was in. There were about fifteen of these graceful racing masts, and he knew that under one such he would find Eddie Cantor. He had met Eddie on only one occasion before, but had remembered him because he was a kind of legend in the sailing world.

Sometimes Jim felt that the proper analogy of racing crew was with the old pirates or buccaneers. They were equally footloose and fancy-free. In much the same way that the old buccaneering crews brought individual skills such as that of carpenter, metalworker, ropemaker, to the ship, so each crew member on a racing yacht brought his own medley of skills and knowledge, from building to repairing to the infinitely complex art of setting up the yacht in such a way as to optimise performance.

But what truly united the pirate with the modern racing crew was an ability to switch roles, competently, quickly and without prior warning. At sea, things happened so fast and unexpectedly that one person would be called on to do a wholly different task at a moment's notice. Sailing is the final refuge of the all-rounder.

Each of the 'great' crews comprised such individuals, men who could move swiftly from one area of expertise to another, from the intricacies of effecting a repair to the topsides in carbon and kevlar composites before the next race, to the installation and tuning of complex electronics, to the careful management of payments and deals with suppliers, to scaling a mast in a pitching sea in order to unhook a fouled spinnaker halyard. Each of the great racing yachts, moving from regatta to regatta and campaign to campaign over the world, was a moving circus of buccaneers. Each came with very little except his clothes, sometimes only a box of tools, but above all a thirst for competition.

At the heart of half the successful racing campaigns in the previous ten years could be found one figure in particular. Eddie Cantor was a master of the art of the possible, a man who could conjure a new piece of equipment out of thin air, who could make almost anything with his own hands in a short time given the most basic working facilities.

Jim halted beside a small, dark man, leaning forward to tighten a rigging screw.

'Eddie Cantor?'

Dressed in deckshoes and shorts while he worked at the rigging screws of the lower intermediate stays, Eddie Cantor's back tensed slightly. At the sound of Jim's question he paused as if he had heard an unpleasant word.

Eddie did not answer immediately. Instead, he turned to look over the source of this irritating interruption, then turned back to tightening up the rigging screw. He used quick, precise jabs of his fingers to increase the tension.

'You going to stand there annoying me, or you going to explain why you're doing it?'

'Jim Shaw.'

If Eddie paused again, it was momentary, no more than a man shrugging off a fly.

'You're gonna annoy me, I guess.'

'Can we talk?' asked Jim. Eddie leaned back so that he could sight up the line of the intermediates. He said quietly: 'Why don't you go back to Flying Dutchmen, glamour boy?'

'Maybe,' Jim replied. 'But only if you go back to 470s.'

470 dinghies had been Eddie Cantor's great love, Jim knew. Like most of the best ocean racing sailors, he had started in dinghies.

Eddie paused for more than a moment this time, pulling in more tension on the rigging screw. He said: 'Help me with this rigging, then we'll talk.'

Jim climbed aboard. He looked up at the mast. Fractional racing rigs require careful setting up. The top section of the mast can be hauled backwards by pulling on the backstay, which causes a uniform bend down the mast. The degree of this induced bend in the mast in turn affects the sail shape, providing a sail aerofoil which is deep and powerful, or flat and less powerful.

After each short burst of turning with his hands, Eddie moved from the side of the boat to the centre, sighting up the mast. 'Out of column at the lower spreaders. Look at these intermediates,' he said loudly. 'The guy that set this up is an asshole.'

Eddie tightened the screws a little, then went back to the mast. Kneeling down, Jim began to tighten the intermediate stays which Eddie had just left. 'Keep going,' said Eddie. He was active, swift as a bird in his movements round the mast. 'Come on, let's set up this turkey properly. We're just tinkering. There's a quarter of a knot of speed in the goddamn rigging alone. The owner thinks he's some kind of an expert on this rigging.' He paused and looked up at the sky.

'OK,' continued Eddie. 'Release the running backstays. Take everything off the checkstays. Now let's lower the boom onto the deck. That's right. No more influences on the mast, right?' He squinted up the mainsail track. 'Now we'll set up the lowers.'

They worked on the lowers and intermediates for a quarter of an hour, Eddie moving after each burst of turning the rigging screws to study the mast.

It was getting hotter. Their perspiration fell to the deck.

'Look behind me,' said Eddie. 'See there's a small guy there. Bald head, sunglasses, looking at the boat like he owns it?' Jim looked over Eddie's shoulder. 'I hate people like that.'

'Who is he?'

'He's the owner.'

Jim wanted to burst out laughing. 'Want me to wave at him?'

Eddie ignored him.

'We did these inclining tests the other day for the handicap rating. The rating results didn't come out like the owner wanted. Got me moving bits of lead in and out of the boat like there's no tomorrow. Did some more inclining tests. No dice, rating didn't come out as calculated. He phoned up the designer. Some little dude came down from Annapolis with his toupee and his computer. Plugged it in. Fed the readings in. No dice, went away shaking his head. More lead, more inclining tests. God, I hate designers.'

'What *do* you like?' asked Jim.

'I don't like anything about the International Offshore Rule. IOR's the most stupid in the world. These designers don't design, they just let their computers tell them how to work around the rule.'

'So why do you do it?'

'For the same reason people get married. You do it in hope.'

The sun was hot now, a white ball whose reflection danced in the sheltered waters of the marina.

'The boats are crap,' continued Eddie, 'expensive crap, too. Built light, then stuffed with lead on high racks to make them unstable because that lowers the handicap and gives them an advantage. It's crazy.'

'Maybe you'd be interested in joining an America's Cup defence.'

Eddie did not answer. Jim wasn't sure whether his proposal had registered. Perhaps this was Eddie's way of giving himself time to think.

After a few moments, Eddie said: 'We better look at the upper spreaders. Check on the rigging up there. Gonna send you up first with the tool kit.'

'Me?'

But Eddie was already asking Jim to sit in the bosun's chair, and was shackling the chair on the mainsail halyard. He also shackled the topping lift on for extra safety. 'No problem,' Eddie assured him. With one hand he was taking up slack on one of the deck winches, with another fitting a handle in the winch, starting to wind. Jim began to move upwards. 'Hang on to the mast, that's right, steer your way round the first set of spreaders.'

'How are you getting up?' asked Jim, already fifteen feet in the air. Below him Eddie made fast on a cleat, and hauled up the slack on the topping lift. Then he went back to the winch again.

'Under my own steam, glamour boy.'

The second set of spreaders was a good forty feet above the deck. A breeze was rising, and an unexpected gust of wind touched Jim. The marina and its forest of rigging spun beneath him.

When Jim was in position Eddie made fast on both the main halyard and the topping lift. Then he started to shimmy up the mast under his own power, moving from handhold to handhold where he could. Between handholds, he scaled the bare reaches of mast by locking his legs and arms around the mast and inching up more slowly. 'Hell,' he said to Jim when he had arrived at the same level. 'I'm getting older.' He hooked a leg over the spreader so that he was braced. 'OK, hand me the pliers, let's tighten up these pins here.'

Out of the toolbag attached to the bosun's chair, Jim handed Eddie each of the bits of equipment he asked for.

When he had finished, in the pause before the descent, Eddie said: 'You mentioned something down there about an America's Cup defence?'

Eddie's small, dark eyes were level, amused. He added: 'You better be on the level, glamour boy, or I'm going to lower you slowly down the mast upside down by your balls.'

'I hope that won't be necessary,' Jim replied.

'I'll decide about that,' Eddie said cheerfully. 'Guess I'm in a good negotiating position up here. I run the shore support organisation, right? No interference. You rock stars sail, I take care of the boat.'

'Right.'

'Fifteen hundred smackers a week, anything less would be an insult.'

'Twelve hundred smackers.'

'You're up a sixty foot mast with a none-too-friendly Orang Utang. You shouldn't say things like that.'

'You're an addict, Eddie. You run on masochism, like all of us. Twelve hundred smackers. Accommodation and food thrown in.'

'I can see you're not averse to taking risks with your life.'

'Is it a deal?'

Another gust of wind hit them, and the rigging started to sing. Jim could feel the vibrations in the mast.

They shook hands. Eddie Cantor's hands had calluses on the calluses.

'I don't believe this,' said Eddie. 'I can kiss goodbye to the IOR. Know what I'm going to do?'

'No.'

'I'll tell you. I'm gonna wave to that fat guy down there.' Eddie waved to the owner. 'Hi, goofball.' The plump figure on the dock seemed to stir uneasily. Eddie added, 'Yes, you, sweetheart.'

Twenty-eight

They began to assemble, arriving in cars, on motorbikes, or on foot, their carrier bags on their shoulders; in suits and in sweatshirts, in untidy jeans or fashionable Bermudas; the flower of the American sailing world. They were allocated their dormitory beds, their locker room storage.

Every day more faces appeared. Coach Johnson knew most of them, embracing those who had passed through his youth training programmes, shaking hands with his Olympic protégés, asking them about their latest campaigns, who they had sailed with recently.

At breakfast now it became Coach Johnson's habit to stand up and tap a glass with his knife several times until there was silence. He announced the day's schedule of exercise, briefings, and sailing on the several six-metres which acted as sail training yachts until the big boats arrived.

Eddie Cantor arrived in an aged Combi bus, with four of his picked engineers and henchmen. With hardly a word to anyone, they melted away towards the big work sheds. Because their life would be largely nocturnal, a second dormitory had been allocated them so that the sailing crew did not break their pattern of work and sleep. A truck arrived shortly afterwards piled high with machinery, engineering equipment. These and other items started to fill the big repair works sheds. Extra power points and lighting were installed. The plant for temperature and humidity control began to hum permanently. Storage areas were set aside for temperature sensitive resins and other chemicals. Drums marked 'dangerous' began to accumulate inside them. Small extensions to the buildings were constructed of wood and carefully sealed for refrigerant uses. An autoclave was set up in one of the two large buildings to help in making structures such as spinnaker poles or booms. Tackles, booms, hoists began to lean out crazily from the walls.

Behind them, the sail loft was installed in the largest shed of all, some twelve thousand square feet of raised wooden floor. A huge computer cutter was lifted gingerly from a lorry with the help of a forklift and eight men, and installed in a corner of the vast shed. A protective screen was built around it. Fifteen sailmakers and cutters were moved in under the aegis of the presiding sail making genius, Tom East.

Sailmakers were tribal. The greatest of the sailmaking companies had been East Sails, founded by Tom East himself a decade earlier. But every now and then one of his chieftains would split away to form another company. There were always rumours of stolen technology, of computer cards disappearing, of research data mysteriously reappearing in the new tribe. East, faced with these regular palace revolutions, could only keep ahead by constant innovation in shape and use of materials. The cutting of sails had become highly automated, with a high level of computer calculation, but those who so assiduously stole, lifted, or copied his technology lacked one vital element in overcoming him in the market place – the complex intuition of genius.

As sailmaker, Tom East would sit in on their meetings and briefings, hardly speaking. A man of remarkably few words, every phrase or comment was sifted by his henchmen for its hidden or mystical content. It was widely believed that Tom East had never spoken more than three words in a single sentence, and that four words would require the advent of the Apocalypse.

If the support personnel were included in the calculation, the little community had grown to nearly sixty people within the course of two weeks. A new dormitory for the sail cutters was erected by the shore support team, using epoxy-coated wooden beams on an A-Frame construction. The two full sailing teams of eleven men each and eight reserves began to train every morning on the forecourt before breakfast.

There was another level of activity which had been taking place alongside. The security perimeter of the base was being installed, eleven-foot fences topped with barbed wire and surmounted by electricated wires. Army engineers drilled the deep supports through the concrete for the strong iron poles that held the wires. A watchtower was built beside the main complex of offices. A grid of radio reception aerials was erected over its roof. At the entrance, electrically operated security gates were installed, with an aluminium guardhouse nearby.

'Who's organising all this?' Jim asked Coach Johnson, pointing to the surrounding high fences.

'Base security.'

'That's what it's called?'

'Our new base commandant is arriving tomorrow. He'll explain.'

Coach Johnson walked away to his own small office. Jim looked around him. They were sealed in now, in a kind of compound. Wherever he looked, the security fence stretched. There had been numerous access points to the compound, but now there was only one, a system of electrically operated gates on the northern side. The aluminium guard posts being erected there had bullet proof windows and automatic locks.

On one occasion, meeting Coach Johnson accidentally beside the new watchtower under construction, Jim said: 'Coach, I didn't volunteer to join the armed services. I'm here to sail boats.'

'Then keep your mind on sailing,' said Coach Johnson levelly, 'and don't let this get to you.'

A black limousine arrived the following day at about nine-thirty. Filing cabinets, computer terminals, typewriters followed in a small army truck. Several orderlies carried into the office complex a tall, square-shaped object in a cover of dark, heavy plastic. One of the orderlies came to knock on Coach Johnson's door. Coach Johnson was closeted for what seemed several hours in the new administrative offices.

The crew were undergoing intensive fitness training by army instructors while they waited for the boats to arrive. The gym area thundered and pounded as they ran on the spot and lifted weights.

Several days later, when nearly all the sailing personnel had assembled, there arrived at the outer gates a small red Renault. Jim, who was walking past, did not notice until the guard had ushered it through the gates and into the compound. A voice from the car said:

'Hey, honky. Where's the boss man around here?'

Jim leaned over to peer inside.

Out of the small car stepped one of the tallest men he had seen. He might have been a basketball star. He was the right colour too.

Ernie Stead leaned back against the car and took off his dark glasses. He looked around at the security fences, the guard huts, the watchtowers.

'This an occupied zone?'

Jim held out his hand.

'Jim Shaw.'

'Ernie Stead, navigator.'

'Pleased to meet you.'

Ernie Stead's eyes turned to study Jim. Jim said: 'Let me help you with your things.'

Carrying one of Ernie Stead's two bags, Jim led the way down the side of the main building towards the dormitory.

Virus appeared from behind one of the huts, carrying a piece of winch equipment.

'Hi, Ernie.'

Ernie waved a wrist as thin, as distinguished, as a Watusi.

Big Ape shouted:

'How are ya, Ernie?'

Ernie waved a few long fingers.

They rounded a corner, moved out of the way of a jeep carrying a load of metal bars, coiled rod rigging. Eddie Cantor leaned his head out of the car.

'Sonafabitch, it's Ernie Stead.'

'Hi,' Ernie said.

'You popular, or something?' Jim asked.

Now that the personnel had assembled, the following day Colonel O'Reilly gave his official address. The entire crew and support personnel assembled in the briefing room. General Walters and Coach Johnson were seated on the dais. On General Walters' right hand side sat another man, darkhaired, in the uniform of an army colonel.

General Walters stood up: 'Gentlemen, as you already know, we have a somewhat unusual rival for the America's Cup next time. I'm here to ensure that we take appropriate precautions.

'When I say we have an unusual rival, I should really say that you have an unusual rival. For my part, the rival is the usual one. That's why, in this matter of the nature of the rival, perhaps you'd accept a few words of advice from me on his methods and capabilities.

'The Russians have a system based on secrecy and on spying. Recent limited liberalisation hasn't changed these fundamentals in the way they view other countries, or the way they operate abroad. If anything, their espionage effort has increased. Those two aspects, secrecy and spying, complement one another. Their secrecy is devoted to their own affairs. Their spying affects us directly.

'The less information that leaves this compound and the personnel within it, the greater are our chances of winning. I'd advise you to be on guard the entire time against slips of the tongue, gossip and any other disclosure of information which is not strictly necessary.

'We're also placing a strict security cordon around the compound, with some six security guards in attendance at all times. Each of you and the support personnel will be given an identity card which you will show on entry and on leaving the compound.

'The central base area where the yachts are worked will be subject to a further security clearance.

'You may find this all somewhat tedious, in which case please accept my sympathies. That being said, those who do not conform to the security regulations will be subject to disciplinary procedures. It is an axiom of military organisation that once you accept the necessity for these precautions, they do not become burdensome.

'Colonel O'Reilly, who is seated behind me on the dais, will be here on hand as your base commander. If you have any problems, or you feel that security is being unnecessarily jeopardised in any way, please consult him. I'm going to stand aside so he can introduce himself.'

Colonel O'Reilly stood up.

'Thank you, Sir, for your address. I have nothing to add to it, except to wish you all the best of luck in your endeavours. I'd appreciate it if Jim Shaw could report to the briefing room at three o'clock this afternoon.'

General Walters strode down the aisle, followed by Colonel O'Reilly and a respectful Coach Johnson.

A few minutes later the General's big, black limousine pulled out through the security gates.

The austere briefing room, with its bare boards, its high windows, a table, chairs, reminded Jim of a schoolroom.

A security guard had opened the door to let Jim in. He stood on the threshold of the room. A shaft of sunlight from the high windows caught him on the face and he had to screw up his eyes to see the two figures seated at the table.

Coach Johnson's voice said: 'Sit down, Jim.'

Jim moved over to the chair indicated by Coach Johnson. Both remained seated as Jim approached them. Coach said: 'Jim Shaw. Colonel O'Reilly.'

Jim nodded. Coach Johnson pointed to an empty seat in front of the desk: 'Take a chair, Jim.'

Seated opposite him, Jim could study O'Reilly more closely. O'Reilly was smart. Every facet of him glowed. He looked, Jim thought, like a film star's portrait of a colonel, except that no film star could have worn his authority with quite such self-assurance.

O'Reilly added affably: 'I guess you won't mind if I call you Jim.'

'I guess not.'

There was a brief pause.

'Good,' O'Reilly said. 'Before we get down to the routine of training and building up our capability against the Russian challenge, there's something I'd very much like to ask you, Jim, and you too, Coach.

'The point is this. We know the way the Russians operate. When they say they want to challenge, that means in their own minds they're pretty sure they can win.' O'Reilly looked from one to the other. 'So why are they sure they can win?'

It was Coach Johnson who answered: 'They've got the best helmsman in the world.'

'With all due respect, Coach,' O'Reilly replied evenly, 'that doesn't mean a thing. The Russians wouldn't risk their reputation on one helmsman. The individual is frail, we know that. He can be bribed, seduced, blackmailed.'

'Colonel, Ivan Illich isn't human, he's a machine. No disrespect to our boy here, but Illich is almost superhuman. He's not the sort of guy you could bribe, seduce or blackmail.'

O'Reilly glanced toward Jim.

'I agree with Coach Johnson,' Jim said.

O'Reilly nodded.

'I respect your view of him, both of you. And maybe there's something in what you say. You know your rival.

But we also know ours. And we intend to find out why the Russians are so confident.'

Colonel O'Reilly rose.

'I'm going to say my goodbyes. Have to attend another meeting. Perhaps you'd be kind enough to think carefully on what I've said.'

Coach Johnson and Jim rose. They shook hands with O'Reilly.

Coach Johnson said: 'Sir, there's just one question. If you do find they've got something, something which is maybe cheating, what are you intending to do?'

Colonel O'Reilly turned slowly. Jim would remember the slowness of that turn, the way O'Reilly pivoted to face his questioner directly.

'What we do in war, Coach Johnson,' O'Reilly replied evenly. 'Cheat right back.' He smiled. 'Now I bid you Good-day, gentlemen.'

After Colonel O'Reilly had left, Coach Johnson said: 'You better forget you heard that.'

'But I did hear it,' Jim replied.

'There are official and unofficial statements,' commented Coach Johnson. 'That one was unofficial.'

Twenty-nine

The limousine which carried them to the aircraft factory rode smoothly over the country roads.

Colonel O'Reilly came to the outer gates personally to meet them. A corporal from the guard-house opened the door of the shiny, dark grey Cadillac. Coach Johnson, Jim and Jack stepped out, glancing around them in the bright morning sunlight.

'Follow me.' O'Reilly's greetings were generally perfunctory. Today they were non-existent.

A blue side-door was opened by security card. Inside was a small room, overlaid with heating pipes. Two security men frisked the guests. 'Routine,' said O'Reilly. 'Follow me.'

They walked down a long corridor. Various personnel stepped aside to allow O'Reilly and his little group to pass. Occasionally O'Reilly would give a nod in return. Jim was inwardly conscious of O'Reilly's sheen of assurance in this place. He was clearly in control.

The party approached a huge metal door. Bells started ringing. A security barrier in front of the door went up. The door opened, rotating upwards. Several uniformed security guards, standing on the other side of the door, stepped back and saluted when they saw O'Reilly.

O'Reilly strode through.

Inside was a vast hangar. It was clearly in use as a store-room. Hundreds of racks led off to one side. On another was a maze of small rooms, constructed of some insulating material, within which temperature-sensitive materials were stored. Skulls and cross bones painted on several of the doors indicated that some of the contents were highly toxic.

The party continued down this long, central walkway, almost as wide as a runway. The only sound was the background air-conditioning, a low drumming as on the bridge of a liner. At the furthest end of the huge building O'Reilly turned right, in front of another security door. Lights flashed, the heavy, metallic door swung and raised. The little party advanced into the recesses of the room.

The windows were blacked out. The interior of this inner hall was lit entirely by artificial light. It took several moments to adjust to this new level of illumination.

But the contents of the hall made Jim's mind spin. Positioned centrally, lit by powerful arc-lights, two sleek shapes stood side by side like two creatures in a great museum. Apparently identical in contours, together they dominated that large room. Both rested in cradles. A

172

spray of spotlights illuminated their perfect curves. The incongruity of their shapes in this environment heightened their dramatic power. The various cranes, hanging lights, the liana-like streams of power-lines suspended from the ceiling, did not detract from their symmetrical beauty. It was a form which is always both classical and modern, which belongs to the past and the future, the shape of a magnificent racing yacht.

O'Reilly was talking now, but Jim was only partly aware of what he was saying. Instead his mind was trying to take in the scene ahead of him, bringing all his knowledge to bear on the two shapes. As if in a trance, he walked forward. In the background O'Reilly said: 'Our scientists undertook computerised flow-tests for some 4,000 differing keel and rudder shapes in combination with some 300 variants of hull shapes. I don't need to tell you that's over a million combinations. We have expended as much mainframe time on this project as on the preparatory stages of designing a major military aircraft.

'Each of these two yachts is precisely similar in shape, to tolerances of about half a millimetre at any one point. The two hull bodies have a measured weight difference between them of less than ten kilograms.

'The Russians specified wood in their construction. They said nothing about the fastenings. We've used the latest techniques to laminate selected panels of wood together using glues specially developed from our stealth aircraft programme. We've tested examples of this. Frankly, the strength and resilience of the skin structure we've managed to develop has astonished our structural engineers. The destruction tests that were carried out on samples in neighbouring laboratories confirmed what some of these guys have forgotten, that wood is a magnificient structural material, with an astonishing fatigue life. Sandwich wood in the latest chemical hyper-glues and we have a structure which is on a par with virtually anything we might have produced given a free hand.'

O'Reilly paused, but only briefly.

'The boats are identical so that anything you change

on one will be shown as a speed difference in trials. This will give a real indication of the consequences of the changes that you're looking at. Guess you know what I'm saying. If we don't have a "control", in this case another boat that is similar in all respects except the thing we are studying, frankly, we're shooting in the dark.'

O'Reilly stepped towards a sidedoor. But Jim, lost in his own thoughts, moved forward, walking around the closest of the two shapes. The keel, with its two vertical foils separated by a gap reminded him partly of some recondite structure, like one of those modern sculptures one sometimes sees in parks, and partly of some biological shape.

O'Reilly paused. He watched Jim for a moment. He said:

'Best keel shape we could come up with for the various facets of the course was this one. We've refined it a thousandfold using our mainframe and research facilities.

'Our objective was to increase the manoeuvre capability of a match-racing yacht. We were helped in this by computer simulations of one-on-one aircraft combat. Our knowledge of this is extensive. Like aircraft, the important thing is that the keel should not stall in the middle of extreme turns. This type of keel corresponds in certain principles to the shape of a modern fighter. The smaller forward foil deflects the flow onto the rear foil so that the rear foil is virtually stall-proof. This makes the boat come out of a manoeuvre with more speed and energy than a rival yacht. We figure that because you may be racing against the greatest living sailor, if you aren't able to outspeed him, you've got to be able to outmanoeuvre him where necessary.'

Jim traversed the gleaming sides of the closer of the two yachts, running a finger lightly along the mirror-smooth topsides, still held in his own private reverie. O'Reilly, no longer amused at his young charge's absorption, barked: 'We got places to go, young man. Follow me.'

Jolted out of his thoughts, Jim walked to the exit door

behind the small party. He could not help glancing back at the two graceful shapes behind him. Outside once again, they began to traverse part of the complex to their next appointment. The corridors seemed endless. At the end of each one there was some form of scrutiny or clearance. The entire place was crawling with security.

O'Reilly halted. He placed his identity card in a recess at the side of one of the laboratory doors. With a shrill whine of motors it opened. O'Reilly strode through until another door was reached. He knocked. A face appeared at a grille. The door opened.

Inside, laboratory tables were piled with complex electronic measuring instruments and hardware. Several computer screens glowed white.

A short, bespectacled man, studying one of these screens, turned round and came towards them. Doctor Li was clearly of Chinese ethnic origin. At the back of his head he grew his hair long, perhaps as a deliberate assertion of independence against the more abbreviated military hairstyles of the other personnel of this high security establishment.

'Doctor Li,' O'Reilly said, 'I'd like you to meet Coach Johnson and the America's Cup afterguard, Jim Shaw and Jack Peabody. Doctor Li is going to show you the main onboard instrumentation package.'

Doctor Li shook hands with them. Turning, he led them to a white console with, around it, some five different keyboards. At the press of a button, a single screen flowered into life.

Doctor Li's oddly soft, high-pitched voice took them through the initial introduction: 'What we have here is the yacht's nervous system. Computer circuits are so microminiaturised, we're getting down to a molecular level. These new generation computers are called biological computers.

'Central on-board computer is an advanced small biological computer which will give you more than enough capacity to run the system. We've got capacity for twenty times the current load, so we can add other facilities if we want them. Console and operator interfaces are adapted from an F-17A Stealth Fighter. The computer system integrates the information from sensors placed at various points over the boat. Direct measured information includes extremely accurate renditions of boatspeed, windspeed, wind-direction, windshear, and navigational information such as precise calculation of direction and distance of next mark at all times.'

Li looked up: 'Those are the basics. Tactical information is based on a laser windspeed anemometer adapted from a fighter aircraft. The laser anemometer fires at points all over the course. Each laser beam is reflected back from dust particles and records their movement.

'This information is interfaced with the computer so that if you press the "wind pattern" button here, you can see on a grid covered by flowlines what the wind is doing all over the course. If you look at the pattern upwind of the course you have an idea of the wind strength and direction that is going to be affecting the course over the next hour.'

O'Reilly said: 'Thank you, Doctor Li.'

Li shrugged: 'However good the information, the decision in the end is of course a human one. This will provide some of the data that makes for a better decision.'

'Follow me,' O'Reilly ordered.

In the briefing room to which O'Reilly now conducted them, the main furniture consisted of four small rings of seats gathered about a screen. O'Reilly said: 'Could you turn off the lights, Coach?'

The lights were killed. In the darkness, O'Reilly's voice said, 'This information is classified, gentlemen.'

A picture was flashed up on the screen. Like a piece of modern art, a Jackson Pollock perhaps, spidery lines radiated across, joining together dots of colour.

'Photograph from a spy satellite of a submarine base at Odessa,' O'Reilly said by way of introduction. 'OK, now we're going to focus down on the area marked with a small square in the top left hand corner. We're about to focus down yet again.' Another image filled the screen, this time more composed, more like a Klee. 'This is the equivalent of looking down from a very high building. Maybe you guys recognise these two shapes here, to the left of this small building. That's right, two big racing yachts, side by side.'

O'Reilly pressed the button. The same slide came up, this time with a series of small red rings.

'These boats aren't simply being stored. The red rings denote some forty personnel are working in and around them. This is a full development programme. Actually, it's rare for the yachts to be seen outside their storage shed. The time of the photograph is July 1995.

'There has been an interesting pattern over the last decade. At the end of each America's Cup series, one or two of the most competitive boats from the contest seem to disappear. They're bought by obscure syndicates, and then aren't heard of again. We now know where they end up. A large converted hangar in Tallinn contains a museum of these yachts. Russian designers and technicians have analysed the changes that have occurred, and have continued to monitor progress right up to the present time. It's an extraordinary build-up, highly systematic, well orchestrated.'

O'Reilly pointed to the sleek shapes in the picture.

'Careful analysis of the dimensions of these yachts show conclusively that they are built, not to any previous America's Cup rules, but to the new rules proposed for the forthcoming competition. In other words the Russians have been developing their own yachts to this rule for a minimum of five years. That gives them a huge development lead time.

'The terms of the Russian Challenge gave us eighteen months to develop these boats. It's taken us ten months to design and build them, which leaves eight months to go.'

O'Reilly sipped a glass of water, put down his glass, continued.

'There has also been a bjg Russian sail-training programme. In summer the yachts are trialled off Tallinn. In the autumn, before the sea freezes, they're moved down to a special site in the Black Sea. The whole circus is lifted there in an amphibious assault vessel called the *Moscow*. The *Moscow* is a floating base and headquarters for the operation.

'When they made their challenge, we enquired where the Russians would like to put their challenge base. We offered them a variety of options. They made it perfectly clear that they don't need a shore base. They're going to anchor the *Moscow* and other support ships within easy reach of the course and that's going to be their headquarters. They've been acclimatising themselves to running the whole operation from the *Moscow* over the last two years.

'This isn't just a sporting challenge,' O'Reilly continued. 'It's a full military development programme, with a lavish budget, and all the privileges and access to sophisticated design associated with that type of programme. The Soviets announced their challenge with only eighteen months to go. That means they've got years of preparation over us in this new class of boat.

'Starting with their unexpected participation in the America's Cup in 1992, they've been building up their big boat experience to the point where their crews are now thoroughly trained. Five years ago, we might have been expected to predominate because of this. But frankly, they've caught up. This launch of a challenge in a completely new boat to us, on which they've clearly been working for the past five years, is a kind of a lightning attack.' O'Reilly paused for emphasis, 'Unlike their previous challenges, there clearly is a military signature in this operation. To make sure we are on a par with them, we clearly need to respond in kind.

'We've taken six months to do our research and development and four to build the boats. That's working fast.

178

Now those boats are going to be launched in three weeks' time. We've got less than eight months of preparation before the match.'

Coach Johnson said: 'You realise that's an impossible schedule, Colonel, sir.'

'That's right,' O'Reilly replied laconically. 'We have just eight months to train and fully organise ourselves to fight off the best prepared challenge ever seen.'

Questions were starting to rise in Jim's mind, questions which had lurked, and which were only now beginning to form. If the military had known of the challenge for ten months, why had they only recently announced it to the defending crew, when they could have been preparing ever since the challenge was first given and accepted? He looked towards Coach Johnson and saw Coach's face was impassive. Coach Johnson did not speak further. This also surprised Jim. It would haunt him later, when things started to change.

O'Reilly was winding up the meeting, gesturing to an orderly to switch on the lights. A sergeant had appeared at the doorway to escort them back to the limousine which had brought them here. O'Reilly was shaking their hands, wishing them well. The three of them followed the duty sergeant down the lengthy corridors, through the security doors and past the shrilling bells. They were frisked again before they left. And through it all Jim watched Coach Johnson's impassive face, as the enormity of the task they had been set slowly began to dawn.

Thirty

The weather was much as forecast. A haze of light cloud prevented the full heat of the sun. But it was good weather for the launching.

A crowd of twenty-five thousand people gathered around the harbourside to watch.

The new yacht hung in slings, with the customary security screen around the keel and rudder appendages. A Stars and Stripes lay across its decks, flowing over the side with its white star-points, covering the boat's name.

They were gathered there, the full crews, in two lines of blue blazers. Jim Shaw, Jack Peabody and Ernie Stead stood closest to the boat and the launching rostrum with its microphones and speakers. Coach Johnson stood between them and the rostrum. A bottle of champagne hung ready to be catapulted against the yacht's bow.

The military band struck up.

On the other side of the rostrum a group of dignitaries, including the mayor of the town, stood waiting for the military music to end. Jim had seen General Walters standing beside Tom and Angela Stuttaford. A short man in a grey overcoat stood next to them, his hands folded behind his back. The band approached the end of its piece. Tom Stuttaford walked towards the rostrum and mounted the two short stairs to the platform. He waited for silence.

'Ladies and Gentlemen. Shortly I am going to ask my wife to launch this yacht with the customary bottle of champagne.

'Before we begin that joyful ceremony, I'd like to say something about the name of the yacht we are about to christen. As you know, American defenders have been given names which have attempted to epitomise our national character and our political ideals. Past defenders have been called *Enterprise*, *Freedom*, *Liberty*. Others, in expression of our national energy and strength, have been given names such as *Resolute*, *Intrepid*, *Courageous*.

'In our own case, we looked for a name that would signify what this nation stands for, not only to us as Americans, but to others in the world. After all, our country has been host to the oppressed of many nations throughout our history.

'We have found a name that seems to symbolise the American ideal. For this reason we're naming our American defender *New World*, in honour of new beginnings and fresh horizons.'

A cord was pulled. The huge field of stars and stripes slid off the bow, showing the name *New World*. A cheer broke out among the twenty-five thousand assembled. The television crews zoomed in on the newly disclosed name.

'And now my wife will christen and launch the yacht.'

He stepped down to help Angela Stuttaford onto the rostrum. Angela Stuttaford displayed the composure of a senior political wife. She waited until the cheering had died down before enunciating in a clear voice:

'I name this yacht *New World*. May God bless her and all who sail in her.'

The champagne swung through a graceful arc and exploded on the hull. The band struck up again. *New World* was lowered into the water.

'Who's the guy standing next to General Walters?' Jim asked Coach Johnson.

Coach Johnson said: 'Andre Antonov, Soviet Ambassador to the US.'

Jim turned again to glance in that direction. General Walters was clearly in discussion with Antonov. Walters stood with his hands clasped behind his back, smiling like a Sphinx. Antonov was making short, stabbing motions of his hands as he explained something.

The yacht was now fully to her lines in the water, floating easily. Now that the water hid the keel and rudder, the security skirt could be lifted. Jim turned away to study the magnificent object, from Walters and Antonov which he and his crew would soon be sailing.

Later that day, in a private ceremony, *Shadow*, the replica and trial horse, was quietly launched. The two boats lay side by side, as elegant as two doves. Two tow-boats travelled down from the syndicate compound and towed them the five miles to the training complex and compound. The two crews were lined up respectively on each boat as the procession moved upriver.

In the training camp Jim could smell the sea.

Much as a thirsty steer or sheep can sense water over the next fence, he could sniff the sea's tang in the compound. The following day the two crews and the full support team worked with heightened urgency. The two tall composite masts were lifted by crane into the two boats and the crews and support men set about rigging them, installing the winches, setting fittings into the deck, epoxy bonded and through-bolted onto washer plates. The boats swarmed with men like a piece of cheese beset with ants.

At nightfall a reserve group set about the same tasks. Lights were set up on rigging above the boats. The runs of the halyards inside the masts were checked, the boom controls threaded until they moved with perfect efficiency. Eddie Cantor worked with the navigators of both boats to set in the computational and sensor equipment. The connecting circuitry, based on the fly-by-light system of an aircraft, radiated outwards on the underside of the deck like a spider's web.

Doctor Li arrived from the lab to install the central computer, and to coach the three afterguard in its multifarious uses. Eddie Cantor had built a special waterproof moulded housing for both computers, lined with foam against the shock of the sea.

'You think these things are going to survive?' asked Jim.

'They're built to survive nine-G turns in a fighter,' replied Doctor Li, 'and partial destruction by fire.'

'What happens if I get angry and kick it?'

'It flashes up DON'T GET PERSONAL.'

But it was Ernie who struck up the most personal relationship with the computer. Every day he sat by it, loading up, punching in data, listening to its small chirping responses like a father at the bedside of a child. It was operated by a waterproof keyboard which reacted only to the faintest touch. Every input, as it connected, brought the confirmation of a small musical note.

Four days after launch they were ready to set out on the first trial sails of the two boats. The crane lifted both boats into the water of the pens. Sails were loaded aboard. The lines of the two towing craft were fastened and the yachts were pulled downriver, through the harbour entrance and out to sea.

It was hazy, with a force three breeze blowing on land. As the morning drew on the sun burned away the sea mist. Five miles from land the towing craft slowed and turned into wind.

'Up mainsail,' Jack shouted.

Big Ape and Virus hauled up the mainsail, hand over hand, jumping off the decks to take hold of the halyard high. Tom East's masterpiece soared aloft, flowing upwards in slow, thundering curves. Hauled up fully, tightened in, the sail shone luminescent like a dragonfly's wing.

'Genoa up.'

Jim was turning the wheel now, bearing away.

A surge of power went through *New World* as she heeled and began to pick up speed under her huge mainsail.

'Four knots, five knots, five point five, six, six point five,' Ernie sang out.

The genoa, hauled up, thundered slowly.

'Sheet in,' shouted Jack.

Moose and Mace were already bending power on the coffeegrinder, punching in a sustained burst. The genoa came in and the speed started to rise.

'Seven-five, seven-seven, eight, eight point two.'

They were beginning to burn into wind, sending out two hissing foam-trails. *Shadow* swung alongside them, sailing parallel, pacing them. The two boats hardened up slightly into wind and the two crews settled in to tune.

Thirty-one

A maid met Jim at the door and escorted him into the interior of the house. She opened another door and ushered him through into a room hung with chandeliers. A wave of noise struck him. The room was large, but it was filled with people who were talking at the tops of their voices. For several moments, faced with the unknown, he was seized with panic and felt like fleeing. A waiter appeared with a tray of wineglasses and canapés.

In the middle of the room Jim saw a familiar figure. Angela Stuttaford was standing slightly apart from a group, smiling a welcome. Before he could turn towards her, his attention was distracted by a loud hail.

'Jim,' Tom Stuttaford bellowed, 'Come over here. Want you to meet someone.' Tom Stuttaford waved above the crowd around him.

Jim made his way through the crowds as best he could, moving aside as a man waved his arms excitedly to make a point. Standing beside Tom Stuttaford, dwarfed by him, was a short man in glasses, with silver hair, a white complexion, an explosion of veins in his right cheek.

'Jim Shaw,' said Tom Stuttaford. 'Ferocious helmsman, puts terror into the Russians.'

'Hullo,' the stocky man said. 'I'm Henry Brent, Ambassador in Moscow.'

'Henry's back here for a holiday,' boomed Tom Stuttaford.

'I'm really pleased to meet you,' Ambassador Brent said. 'We were the embassy that received the Russian Challenge.' He glanced at Jim quizzically, as if considering his next words. 'Mighty strange business.'

Jim turned to face Henry Brent directly. He seemed an amiable man. Jim noted the physical characteristics; a short square frame, an easy manner, quiet eyes behind magnified glasses. On an instinctive level, the level at which animals peruse each other, Jim took to him immediately.

'I'm gonna leave you two,' said Stuttaford. 'Gotta circulate. Plot, duck and weave.' He pronounced this last motto to the approximate rhythm of 'shake, rattle and roll'. Stuttaford forced his way through the crowd, shaking hands, booming out his welcome.

'Why does it seem such a strange business, sir?' asked Jim, when Stuttaford had gone.

'Well, to give you my honest impression, young man, it seemed more like a declaration of war to me.'

Jim waited for an explanation. Ambassador Brent took a careful swig of his drink, and added quietly:

'I love those Russians. I really do. The finest goddamn people in the world.' Jim was aware again of that owlish, amused glance. The hubbub of conversation rose and fell around him.

'It's my profession, after all, to try to work out what they're thinking and report back to my masters. Now listen, young man, this concerns you. Just let me tell you something, then I'll go bother someone else. It's about the Russian attitude to rules, and the use of force. Applies to everything, society, commerce, war, sport. You ready?'

Jim nodded. In another part of the room someone commented loudly, 'Primaries won't do him any good.'

'Think,' Ambassador Brent began, 'just for a moment, what force means to a Russian. It means something totally different than it does to us. Here, in this country, we think of force as a last resort: it's a kind of final, desperate remedy when all other means have failed. But look at it this way. Suppose the Republicans had come to power,

185

not recently, but in October 1917, like the Communist Party. Suppose that they had achieved power not by the ballot box but by a putsch, a flagrant use of force against the existing institutions. Suppose, further, that having come to power, they just shot everyone who got in their way. Or put them in prison camps, starved their families, burnt their houses and crops. That's what the Communist Party did. Suppose, further, that the Republicans set up a police state, so that even if you whispered something anti-Republican the likelihood would be that you'd be overheard, imprisoned, tortured, liquidated?

'When a Russian looks out at the world, his attitude to force is so totally different from ours, it's almost inconceivable. To a Russian, force is the prevailing reality behind his political institutions. Force is above the individual notions of good and evil; it's the *modus vivendi*, sorry, young man, the very heart of social life. That's what frightens me about *glasnost*, *perestroika* and the election of key figures. I'm always looking for the claw beneath the pretty handkerchief. I'm not criticising them. I'm just saying that's their background. It'll take decades of liberalisation before that's bred out of their assumptions.

'That's what I'm saying to you, when you're facing the Russians. Even in a period of liberalised, late communism. Rules to them are a bourgeois convention, to be used or discarded as it suits them. You might just bear that in mind.'

'"Bear"?' someone said behind the Ambassador's shoulder. 'Haw, haw, Henry. That was an unintended pun. The worst kind.'

'Just look who it is,' said the Ambassador. 'Sam, you old troublemaker.'

'You boring someone again, Henry?' A tall man with startling blue eyes approached them.

'Not that crap about the Russians, I hope.' He winked at Jim. 'Told that one so many times to us old fogeys he's now turning to younger audiences. So just who exactly are you, young feller?'

'Jim,' said Ambassador Brent, 'this insulting old buffer

186

is Senator Sam Hickstead. I take my orders from people like this. Sam, this young man's conducting our defence of the America's Cup.'

Senator Hickstead leaned forward. Jim felt, like an icy tide, the full power of the Senator's concentration.

'Pleased to meet you.' Jim's fingers took the force of a hand that had pressed the flesh from Boston to Arkansas, from Tucane to Tennessee.

'I read in the papers you're a Maine man,' the Senator said. 'Maine men won't use three words where two will do, unlike we politicians. I have heard it said that there are only three sentences that a Maine man needs to carry him through from birth to death. "Hello", "The fish are biting today", and "It's been a good life." Heh, heh.' He turned to the Ambassador.

'Henry, before I say anything more, can we have a little private talk some time about developments on the overseas front? I've got to face a foreign relations committee next month and I want some background on the state of opinion in certain quarters. Some bright boys are gonna be facing me on that committee. Need to protect my ass.'

'You bet, Sam.'

The Ambassador turned toward Jim.

'Nice to have met you, Jim. Remember what I said about the Russians. Finest people in the world but a different historical perspective. Bye, Sam, see you on Capitol Hill.'

'Get your secretary to arrange an appointment with Martha, Henry,' Senator Hickstead called after him. 'I need that information.'

When the Ambassador had gone, Sam Hickstead leaned towards Jim conspiratorially.

'Young man, let me tell you a story to, uh, add a little bit of balance to what my esteemed colleague the Ambassador has just said to you about our friends the Russians. Someone, an American athlete, won a Silver medal at the Olympics. I understand you did too. Now you and I agree that's a fine achievement. There's no doubt about that. But let me continue with the story. This young man belonged to one of those great commercial families, one of the household names that you see on billboards and on television screens. He came home to his family with a justifiable feeling of triumph. They had dinner together. It was a good dinner, an enjoyable dinner. He felt proud to be back in the bosom of his family. He was happy.

'After the dinner the women left the room. Just he and his father remained. His father passed him the wine. They both drank a couple of glasses. They smoked a couple of good cigars. Then his father said. "Now, son, about that Silver medal. I have to tell you that in this family we don't tolerate losers."'

'Haw, haw haw,' chortled the Senator. 'Ain't that something? Pity of it is, it just happens to be true. That's what you're up against. You think the Russians are bad, just wait till you get a good dose of American public opinion. I know, I've been there.' He winked. 'Keep one eye on the Injuns behind you. It's the arrow in the unprotected rear that hurts the most. Heh heh.' He patted Jim on the shoulder and passed on through the assembled guests.

Jim felt faint suddenly. The babble of voices which now assailed him seemed magnified, as if turned up by a switch. He looked around unsteadily to try and find a way to the door. It was hot amongst all these bodies. He heard a snatch of conversation here about newspapers, another about the tribulations of moving house, a third about the social niceties in New Mexico. He wanted to find an area of fresh air where he could breathe.

'Here he is,' Tom Stuttaford said. 'He doesn't look mean, but underneath he's a goddamn terror. Why, he'd sink his teeth into your leg as soon as look at you.'

'That bad, huh?' another man's voice said. Jim turned round. Tom Stuttaford had his hand on the shoulder of a bluff man with hawkish features.

'Jim Shaw, this is General Walters.'

Jim shook hands with the General.

'We've met before,' said Jim.

General Walters nodded. But his eyes were glancing

around the room, assessing the nature of the company. He said quietly to Jim, without looking at him:

'Hope you guys are toeing the line.'

Jim did not reply. There was something about the way General Walters gazed past him, as if he were insignificant, while giving him an obsequious order at the same time. He would have liked to have thrown a punch. He wondered how Tom Stuttaford would feel if, having described him as red in tooth and claw, Jim physically assaulted a serving three star general in his own living room.

'Must move on,' said the General. 'Tom. I see Harry van Hoff standing over there. Need to have a brief word with him on a matter of mutual interest.'

'Goodbye, General Walters,' Jim said to the General's disappearing back.

'Now, how are you enjoying yourself, young man?' asked Tom Stuttaford. 'Pity there aren't any young women here I could introduce you to. It's a kind of a rule that we don't bring our mistresses to parties like this.'

'Hi,' said Angela Stuttaford. Jim was aware of her as a centre of stillness against a background of animation.

'Tom teaching you some bad ideas?'

'I guess after my last sentence I better be on my way,' said Stuttaford. He said to his wife, 'See you later, sugar.'

Jim turned to face her. She wore an elegant, tight-fitting blue dress which showed her fine figure. A simple pearl necklace set off the ensemble. Her blonde hair was drawn back, but its austerity only served to heighten her marvellous bone-structure. 'How are you doing?' She studied his face carefully. 'You don't look as if you're having a good time.'

'Just tired, I guess.'

'At your age? Come on, what's wrong? Something bothering you?'

She turned and made her way gracefully through the crowd. He followed along the path she made.

She opened the door to the hallway. He followed her through another door and found himself in the kitchen.

She pulled a chair out from under the breakfast bar. 'Sit down.' Leaning forward, she undid his tie and opened his collar.

She leaned back against the breakfast bar and studied him.

'Now, what's bothering you?'

'I'm just not used to parties, I guess.'

'Pretty frightening, aren't they? Those politicians, I mean. I'm used to them. They're my brothers, sisters, friends. It's quite refreshing to see someone new in amongst them. Reminds me what the outside world must really think of us.'

Jim felt embarrassed. He hadn't come to the party to criticise her friends.

'The Ambassador seems real nice.'

'Henry,' she laughed. 'He's just like the rest of them. He does by stealth what they do by assault. He's more subtle, of course. That's why he's such an expert on the Russians. He sees himself in them.'

'What he had to say about the Russians was interesting. I didn't think of them in that way.'

'Part of his charm, I guess, making you see things in a different light.'

Jim had the impression that, in her somewhat inebriated state, she was challenging him to say something reckless, something he suspected that she could both agree with and despise. He realised that she frightened him as much as the others did.

She poured a glass of water and offered it to him. A voice, a woman's voice, was calling her name from the hallway. 'One of my sisters,' said Angela Stuttaford. 'Stay here as long as you like,' she added, and left through the open door.

Thirty-two

On the way out to the course, under tow from the launch, they worked through the instrumentation, checking the readings of the wind strengths, the co-ordinating grids. Between checking the instruments and feeding in the figures, Ernie Stead, their navigator, was unusually talkative.

'I went on a trip to Russia once,' Ernie said. 'Saw an offer to go over on a Russian ship, a steamer, real good price because they had left a cargo in Philadelphia and were going back to Leningrad unloaded. Wanted to see Russia so bad.'

'So what happened?' Jim asked.

'Picked up my bags and walked aboard this steamer. I suppose someone like me is a fraction sensitive. I didn't even get down the gangplank before I could see it, smell it, touch it. It just came towards me like a living force.'

'What are you talking about, Ernie?'

'Racism, man. I've been all sorts of places, up North where it's in the glance, the expression behind the eyes; down South, where it comes thick and strong and American as blueberry pie. But nothing like this.'

'The Russians?'

'I could hardly move for it. I was in terror for my life. From the time I showed my face out of my tiny cabin to the time I cowered in my bed at night, I felt I had done well to survive.

'Sometimes, if you rile a waiter or something, they drop the plates a little sharply on the table, just to make a point, you know. I'm not kidding, these guys would lay down the soup from a vertical height of four feet. By the time I had wiped my eye, pretended I hadn't noticed anything, there was hardly anything in the plate.'

'So what did you do?'

'The first time it happened I acted as if I hadn't seen it. The second time I was undecided. The third time I stood up. I said to this guy. "You got something against me?" Damn me if three other crew who were eating at another table didn't come up and stand behind him. I was in the middle of it. You could have lit some kind of torch with it. I said, "Guess I made a mistake, guys," and sat down. That was just the beginning.'

'Maybe they were just anti-American,' Jack suggested.

'There were four other Americans there, all white, three elderly men and one middle-aged woman. They all had relations they wanted to visit in Russia or Poland. The soup arrived in front of them just as softly as a girl's first kiss. Didn't hit the table and jump two feet like a Harrier jet.

'I got so scared I kept myself to my room most of the day. Did plenty of studying. Counted off the days. Like I say, I consider myself lucky to have stepped off that boat still covered in my own skin. May be black, but it's good and warm, and I'd prefer to keep it.'

'Coach is signalling us,' Jack said, interrupting them.

'Teacher's Pets hauling on main,' Jim said. 'Let's go in and get them.'

They cast off from the tow-boat.

'Up sail,' shouted Jack. The mainsail began to rise up. With several knots of momentum left from the towing, Jim kept the boat heading up into wind.

'Code four genoa.'

'Code four,' shouted Jack.

The big genoa in its bag came out of the sewerman's pit like a rabbit on pep pills. Jingle and Big Ape were hauling on the main halyard. Virus was running up and down the deck, clipping on sheets. Jim said:

'Keep talking to me, Ernie.'

'Wind just backed port two degrees. Slight bias other end. Chart flowlines show whirl moving toward us, maybe 2 miles away, right upwind. Looks like wind's going to shift back 'bout eight minutes time. Keep to this side.'

'I'll come back to this side when we've kicked their ass,' Jim said.

'You wanna kick,' Ernie commented, 'you just go right ahead and kick.'

'Jack?'

'Unanimous,' Jack said.

Jim was already turning the wheel down to port, the boat was heeling and picking up speed. Georgie and Greenback were easing out the straining sheets through their gloves.

'Look at them,' Ernie said over the top of his instrument panel, watching the other boat. 'Been kissing Coach's ass all night. Just full of the joys of it.'

The other boat was coming in, pushing out a big wave. Sunray was hauling the wheel with his big forearms, stroking the boat downwind. The Teacher's Pets were looking indescribably mean.

'Get ready. We'll turn and burn,' Jim said. 'One minute closing. You mean that about the Russkies, Ernie?'

'True as God. Give me a bunch of rednecks out on a stag party in Tennessee any day.'

'Coming down the line,' Jim snapped. 'Coming down fast.'

'Collision course,' Jack warned.

'We'll go low.'

Going low was turning downwind of the other boat, Jim's preferred tactic. You could pick up extra speed as you bore away to go low, use that momentum to throw the boat into a tight turn and still come out the other side capable of causing mischief.

'Keep talking, Ernie.'

'Wind headings unchanged for now. Swirl rolls in toward us, closing distance.'

They were increasing speed all the time.

'Eight point five, eight point seven, nine, up she comes, nine point two,' Ernie intoned.

'Boarding party,' Jack said. 'Get in real close.'

Jim was turning the wheel fast, feeling the keel dig in, slewing the boat so hard they leaned outwards on the turn. Moose and Mace were going quietly mad on the coffeegrinder.

193

Now they were locked together, grappling, the winches on both boats screaming, the sails alternately drawn in and eased out through the smoking leads. When this happened there was pandemonium on both decks. Jim barked orders to turn; Jack roared out orders to the trimmers. In a low, sing-song monotone, like an oldstyle crooner, Ernie issued a continuous stream of numbers on heading, boatspeed and windstrength above the winding, squealing sheets and the sudden, angry thunder of the sails as they passed through the wind.

Then they were out the other side. The winchgrinders were slumped momentarily over the winches, breathing hoarsely. Jack remorselessly harangued the trimmers. 'Ease, ease, ease,' as they closed up on *Shadow*'s hip in the pole position.

'Nailed him,' Jim said with satisfaction. In this position they could drive the other boat away from the line.

'Let's just keep forcing him away.'

This was plain evil. They simply ignored any kind of timed start, driving the other boat away down wind in the same way that one maiden aunt, with wholly malign intent, might drive another's croquet ball into the furthest hydrangeas.

After two minutes the start gun banged forlornly behind them. They were at least a minute away from the line, still driving *Shadow* away. The helmsman, navigator and tactician in *Shadow* had their necks screwed round, watching them. Sunray held up a finger in a brief gesture of outrage.

'Ready to roll'. Jim spun the wheel in quick stabs of his hands. Almost instantaneously the other boat spun too. At the turn into wind *Shadow* was only a boat length and a half behind. *Shadow* tacked away almost immediately to try to get out of *New World*'s windshadow.

They hit the start line about fifteen seconds ahead of *Shadow*, then tacked to place a loose cover on their rival.

When they had settled in on the upwind leg, Jack, ever practical, said:

'I've thought of an idea to beat the Russians. When

they're ahead in the race, we drop Ernie overboard. They'll circle back and try to ram him in the water.'

'That's sick,' said Ernie. 'Wind veering one degree. I'd go white with fright, anyway. Wind steady. They'd think I was one of you guys, man. Whitey ain't worth coming back to ram.'

'Cut the crap, you guys' said Jim. 'They're hauling us in.'

Their three heads craned round to look at the sails on the other boat.

'Goddamn mainsail.'

'Yeah,' Ernie agreed. That mainsail looked perfect. It was *Shadow's* engine, and it was sucking the other boat slowly but inexorably up towards them.

'We're being knocked, we're being headed,' Jack sang.

'Keep feeding me the speed numbers, Ernie. Jack, tell me what they're doing.'

'Eight one, eight one, steady, eight two, eight two, down, eight one, eight, eight dead. Wind direction steady,' Ernie intoned.

'Wind lessening at all?' Jim asked.

'We're holding them now,' said Jack.

They could hear the winches grinding on the other boat as the genoa was eased and tightened, eased and tightened in the lulls and gusts. All *New World*'s men were concentrating now. Jim had never seen a more deadly crew.

'They're sailing out from under us in the gusts,' Jack said. 'In the lulls we hold them.' It was a point of pride that they could outspeed the others without performing a close cover. It was part of their attitude of superiority.

New World was a study in concentration now. Jim was engrossed in building up that final fraction of a knot of boatspeed. Jack kept the other boat under close surveillance. Ernie fed out in his low, steady voice the instrumentation readings.

'Ease mainsheet an inch,' Jim said. 'Feels better. Genoa in one inch. No more. No, out again.'

Other than that it was quiet.

'Wind's heading us,' Ernie said. 'Three degrees, four, five. Gusting and heading.'

'More wind out to the right,' called Virus from the foredeck.

'Tack now,' advised Jack.

Jim spun the wheel. The boat shook and thundered with the flapping of the sails. Eight seconds later they were on the other tack, the sails hauled in, the coffee-grinders in slow overdrive for the last few inches of sheet as the boat picked up speed and feathered up into the wind. They were losing *Shadow* now, as they almost always did. It had become routine.

Thirty-three

Several days later Coach Johnson said it was routine too. That made it official.

'You got it too easy, Shaw and Peabody.' Coach Johnson's powerful forearms lay along the arms of the chair in which he sat. Like a big, red-haired spider, he faced them across the top of his desk. The strip fluorescent lighting above them threw a harsh light over the office.

Seated opposite, they waited for him to speak his piece. Behind Coach Johnson was a picture of the President, an official photograph of the incumbent of that office looking young and healthy. He was standing for the photograph in front of the draped Stars and Stripes. Jim estimated that photograph was at least six years old, taken early in his first term.

'Jake and his boys are good, but they're not really pressing you. I've met with the committee and discussed this. Alternative arrangements have now been agreed.'

'Thanks for consulting us,' Jim said.

Coach ignored him, speaking, as was his habit when

addressing more than one person, to a piece of air above their heads.

'We've looked around for the best possible rival crew we can find. The ideal would be a well-trained, highly successful big-boat crew who can function as a team. It sounds difficult, but I think we've found what we're looking for. I'll let you boys know as soon as it's certain.'

'Coach Johnson,' Jim said. 'The defence rests on our shoulders as much as anyone. Why are we being kept in the dark about this?'

'It's on a need-to-know basis,' Coach Johnson stated crisply. An uneasy silence followed.

'The discussion,' Jack tried to lessen the atmosphere of friction, 'is surely how we can raise our performance. Maybe we should have been consulted on that, Coach.'

But Coach Johnson was looking at Jim without speaking, as if reassessing him. Coach Johnson's eyes, for the few brief moments that they studied Jim, were expressionless. Jim felt intuitively that there was an area of detachment which he had not noticed before, or at least not consciously. What thoughts occupied that unseen ground, he asked himself?

Jim had noticed other things recently. Coach Johnson's easy, slouching walk, the walk of a streetfighter, had become more upright, more formal. Even his method of talking had changed subtly but perceptibly, in a manner which irritated Jim. A natural authority had been transformed into something stiffer, more brittle. This was only part of the reason why Jim had begun to question him directly, to challenge his authority.

It was curious, but Coach Johnson seemed to Jim to be in a steady process of emotional disengagement. It was as if the military were in the process of reclaiming his loyalties. Behind that air of detachment he felt Coach was beginning to harbour some antipathy towards him.

Outside, when they were out of hearing distance, Jack said: 'Why are you starting to get edgy with Coach?'

'Because I don't like being treated like a child, I don't

like being kept in the dark, and because I don't know any more where he's coming from.'

'That seems kind of odd to me.'

Jim looked at the old, familiar Jack, his tactician and alter ego, whom he would trust with his life, and it occurred to him that even to mention his own darker fears and suspicions about the way the syndicate was controlled would seem to Jack, standing there with an expression of good-natured perplexity on his face, to be churlish and absurd.

'If it seems odd, then I won't say anything. It's just something I feel.'

Jim turned to go, but Jack said:

'Jim, sometimes those suspicions can cause the thing you most fear.'

Jim turned back: 'You mean I could be driving Coach away from us by acting suspicious?'

'Something like that.'

'You may be right,' conceded Jim. 'But that doesn't stop me being suspicious.'

He walked away. But Jack called cheerfully after him: 'See you about, Jim. Don't dwell too much on things you can't control.'

The mechanisms of psychological conflict are strange, and often only become apparent later. When Jim remembered the expression with which Coach Johnson had regarded him, an expression of cold detachment, he considered what the consequences might be. And it seemed to him clearer what was going on in Coach Johnson's subtle mind. Coach Johnson knew, as a great coach must, that his helmsman, if he is to survive, must be put through fire. And it is easier to commend to the flames someone for whom you feel nothing.

Thirty-four

If Coach Johnson had wished to start a war, he could not have made a better choice of opponents. John Ericson the third was a Harvard Phi Beta Kappa Key, an athlete and sportsman, a golden youth. His father, John Ericson Junior, was a rich industrialist on the Eastern seaboard. For a few months in the year John Ericson the third attended his father's offices as a vice-president of Ericson Traction Corporation. For the other nine months he was a professional sailor.

The family had been founded by Eric Ericson, son of a Swedish fishing captain. He had started his small company in freight, and spread from ships into railways, until he founded one of the great railroad baronies. The family had prospered, but it had never entirely lost its links with the sea. His son John Ericson had owned and campaigned the great J-class racer *Renown*. In turn John Ericson's son, John Ericson Junior, had built and campaigned a series of the huge offshore Maxi yachts, each one called, perhaps appropriately, *Ghost Train*. *Ghost Train 5* was currently the leading maxi-yacht in the world.

Helmed by John Ericson the third, *Ghost Train 5* moved from regatta to regatta, from seaboard to seaboard or across oceans, often attempting to break some ocean passage record in transit.

John Ericson had gathered around him some of the best crew in the world. Although it was claimed that the crew were amateurs, in fact virtually every man on board was a full time professional, on the payroll of Ericson Traction Corporation in some form or another.

It was said that nothing gave Ericson's father greater pleasure than to pick up the newspaper and see, in the morning news, that *Ghost Train 5* had won another race, another regatta. He referred to his son as 'my ambassador'. A stream of telexes and faxes followed around the world as he arranged for his son to meet this industrialist,

199

that politician, and invite him as a guest on one of the big races.

An eighty foot maxi, with a beam not far short of twenty feet, was almost twice the volume of a twelve-metre, the traditional class of America's Cup yachts since the Second World War, and was a substantially larger yacht than the sxity-footers in which Russia had challenged. Whereas the latter had a crew of eleven, a maxi's full complement was twenty. The tradition of big race boats was deeply ingrained over several generations. When Ericson's grandfather, the son of the railroad baron, had campaigned in the 1920s one of the huge J-class racers, it had been his habit, when the designated America's Cup yachts changed from J-Class to twelve-metres, to refer to the latter as 'ladies' yachts'.

John Ericson the third, echoing his grandfather, had cause to make reference to this phrase. The day after the receipt of the challenge notice, Coach Johnson had written:

WE ARE PREPARING AN AMERICA'S CUP DEFENCE AGAINST MAJOR, REPEAT MAJOR, OPPONENT IN SPECIALLY BUILT 60' MATCH-RACING YACHTS. TIME SHORT. WOULD YOU AND YOUR CREW HELP BY TAKING OVER SAILING OF TRIAL HORSE YACHT 'SHADOW'?

To which a reply had been received:

ARE YOU SURE WE SHOULDN'T BE TAKING OVER THE LEAD BOAT? NO, SERIOUSLY, WE'VE BEEN CAMPAIGNING HARD AND WE WOULD LIKE TO HAVE A BREAK IN YOUR LADIES' YACHTS.

Coach Johnson, when he received that, knew that the right choice had been made. The rivalry would be murderous. He had no hesitation in pinning the two telexes up on the board to start things cooking.

Several further stages of negotiation were undertaken. Once more Coach Johnson's blue office door was closed.

Discussions this time were carried out *sotto voce*. Each day there would be a visit from Colonel O'Reilly. Neither Jim nor Jack was party to these discussions.

Several days later, returning from practice, Jim noticed the large black limousine of General Walters, with its military number plate, in the forecourt beside the administration offices. Tapping his gloved fingers on the wheel, a uniformed chauffeur patiently waited. Beside it was another limousine, a grey Lincoln Continental. Another chauffeur sat behind the clouded glass, immobile. Jim had once heard that the chauffeurs of senior men often talked to one another, but that those of the most senior men, party to telephone calls and conversations of a high security nature, became as remote as the men they served. These two men did not even recognise one another's presence.

In the changing rooms Jim showered while he kept his eye on the two waiting limousines out of a small, eye-level window.

When he had changed, an orderly came from the administration offices with a message from Colonel O'Reilly to inform them that Coach would not be at the afternoon debriefing. He was otherwise engaged. Jim looked out at the big, important limousines stationed outside. He had arranged to meet Tom East, the sailmaker, for a discussion on the cut of the sails, but he found himself lingering by the window. After twenty minutes a tall, immaculately groomed man emerged from the offices. The chauffeur of the waiting grey Lincoln Continental opened the door for him. General Walters shook hands with him. Colonel O'Reilly and Coach Johnson each shook hands with him and then stood respectfully to one side. He heard Coach Johnson say, 'Goodbye Mr Ericson.' Jim knew then that this was John Ericson Junior, President of Ericson Traction Inc, father of the man whose team would be taking over *Shadow*. The engine was started, and almost without a murmur the big car drew away, paused at the gates, was waved through by security, and accelerated out into the street.

A few days of dislocation followed. Now that the issue of the rival crew had been decided, Sunray and the number two crew were paid off and left, with an added retainer to remain on standby should they be required again. They had served their purpose well. In any other company they would have been formidable. As it was, Jim had grown to like Sunray, to admire his coolness under pressure, and was sorry to see him leave. Although they liked to needle each other on the water, the crew of *New World* gave the second crew a good sending off. A day's leave was granted. For once the night generator in the workshops was stilled and the crew, support personnel and sailmakers left in a body to get drunk on the town. The two communities, the crew and the nocturnal workers, talked over aspects of the campaign, cleared a few differences, and returned in the early hours of the morning, a little the worse for wear.

When John Ericson the third drove through the gates of the compound in his hand-tooled grey-blue Lagonda sports car, in his leather driving gloves, his high-class blonde beside him, Jim and Jack were standing in the assembly courtyard with most of *New World*'s crew, waiting to receive him.

John Ericson emerged from his car, walked over to the other side to open the door for his girlfriend. Cynthia Lelague was a New York deb: tall, blonde, with a wide mouth full of perfect teeth. Ericson sauntered over with her on his arm to pump Jim's right hand.

Jim said, 'I'm glad you consented to come and sail in our ladies' yachts.' He turned towards Cynthia Lelague and said:

'You must be the crew.'

Cynthia Lelague let back her head and howled with laughter. Jim liked her. John Ericson the third's smile froze on his face.

Coach Johnson rushed to intervene in this embarrassing situation. John Ericson the third said through a smile tight enough to make you think the two halves of his jaw might have wired together: 'I look forward to introducing my real crew.'

Without shaking hands with the rest of *New World*'s crew, he walked away with Cynthia still giggling on his arm. Coach Johnson hovered in dutiful attendance.

It was a fine beginning.

The rest of Ericson's crew came down two days' later, not in buses and old jalopies like the crew of *New World*, but in a double-decker, open-top British bus. Sixteen hand-crafted Ivy League thugs stepped out.

There is a certain air about those who have always been fed a good diet, whose parents have watched adoringly from the sidelines of football matches, whose skin and teeth and hair are advertisements for orange juice and vitamins. They emerged with their leather-tooled suitcases, James and Dan and Henry and Gene, swaggering about the high security enclosure with the assurance of privilege.

They had a private language, one only remotely accessible to Jim and the others.

A dormitory on the south side of the compound had been set aside for them, and there they moved in a body to dump their suitcases, trunks and sailing bags. Their loud, suave voices took over the compound.

It was perhaps inevitable that they were referred to by the crew of *New World* as 'the preppies'.

Jim asked Jack in their own dormitory that evening, 'What do you think of those guys?'

Jack shrugged his shoulders. 'Nice enough.'

Jim said: 'Good old Jack, no complexes, no insecurity. Do you know what those bastards are calling us?'

'No,' replied Jack.

'"The banana street gang", that's what.'

'That's pretty good,' said Jack. 'I guess they have some wit, too.'

Jim nursed the fingers of his right hand after three winch grinders in succession had shaken it. After the first hand shake he thought he'd lost it, but he assumed afterwards you cannot break jelly, and so he had survived the subsequent maulings.

'They're just nice, friendly people,' said Jack. 'They want to be liked.'

It had started as soon as they got off the bus.

'Hi, good to meet you. I'm Franky Haldane, mainsheet trimmer.' Franky Haldane's grip was like iron. 'You must be the helmsman, Jim Shaw. Sure is an honour.' Jim's hand was being pumped. It seemed to him that he could feel the joints of his fingers snapping, the metacarpals being ground together. 'Sure is a fine place here.' Franky Haldane's eyes were friendly as he stripped the cartilage from the bones of Jim's fingers. 'Hell, we're all looking forward to meeting you on the water.' Jim had almost passed out. He withdrew a hand so battered it seemed without feeling. 'Let me introduce you to our three main winchgrinders,' said Franky Haldane, 'Chuck Freeman, Archie Orlov, James Bucholz.'

Jim waved weakly with his left hand. 'Hi.'

But Chuck Freeman had moved in and seized his wounded hand, right friendly.

It was, as Coach Johnson knew it would be, a fine beginning. That night Jim hid his swollen right hand under the dining table and carefully forked food into his mouth with his left. He looked down the table and noticed the majority of the crew were left-handers tonight, except for Big Ape, who resolutely ate with his right, glowering over the table.

At the dinner table the two rival teams lined up on opposite sides. Coach Johnson talked quietly with John Ericson on the left-hand side of the table, virtually ignoring Jim on the right. Ericson discoursed about their various racing campaigns over the last ten years, about the merits of the current *Ghost Train* over its predecessors, while Coach Johnson nodded respectfully.

Ericson shared a dormitory with his men, like Jim. Neither helmsman was granted any privileges. If Jim thought Ericson would buck at this he was wrong. Ericson had seen enough offshore races to know that he was living in relative luxury. The following day, he was up at six-thirty with his crew, lined up on the dockyard in the first filtering light of dawn, exercising with the rest of them.

Jim didn't like him, but he knew he had a formidable opponent.

Thirty-five

Shadow's new crew were given two days to settle in and acclimatise themselves to their new vessel. They were inheriting a tuned yacht. Even so, on their first evening the big searchlights above the yachts were turned on, and her entire new crew boarded her, working through every aspect of the yacht's equipment, familiarising themselves with its layout. Eddie Cantor was on hand to help them.

The following day, in the light breeze, they hauled up *Shadow*'s mainsail in dock and went into conclave with Tom East for several hours to explain how they wanted it recut. It was remarkable arrogance to suggest a tuned sail should be recut without testing on the course, but Jim noticed with interest Tom East's respectful silence as Ericson put over his requests and instructions.

Ericson's navigator, a computer genius called Jim Wren, took instructions from Doctor Li on how to programme their boat's memory and storage systems. He brought from his own trunk certain items of equipment which *New World*'s crew could only guess at.

Coach Johnson, a witness to the exhaustive professionalism of the new team, walked past Jim with a contemplative expression on his face. This expression reminded Jim of a cat considering a tasty meal.

On the third day after their arrival, the two yachts lay

alongside the wharf. The crews clambered aboard and made their final checks of equipment and rigging.

Each crew worked for two hours on tuning up the masts and rigging before the initial day's racing. Each checked thoroughly through a full list of equipment. The tuning of the rig and gear was a process that would continue all the way through training. In this, the first day, each crew watched the other surreptitiously as they went about their business.

It was a fine day with a moderate breeze, ten knots of wind, a clear sky, with a small chop coming in from the east. The two towing launches drew the two vessels eight miles out to sea and released them, about a hundred yards apart. Mainsails were hauled up. On *New World* they could hear John Ericson shouting commands in his Eastern voice.

'More tension on the backstay,' Jim called.

Already the big, powerful animal was starting to generate forward speed under mainsail alone. The speedo started reading five knots, five and a half, six knots. With a flurry of movement on deck, the crew raised the genoa, which now began to thunder in the building breeze. The winchgrinders started to sheet in, driving bursts of energy into the coffeegrinders. Abeam of him Jim could hear the answering thunder of *Shadow*'s genoa. Coach Johnson's voice came over the radio. 'Course laid, bearing of weather mark is 215 degrees, over.'

The muscles of Jim's stomach tightened. He felt that momentary weakness of fear which also clears the head. Adrenalin started to pump through him, swamping his fear. This always happened to him, a wave of terror drowned by aggression, followed by the system settling down. His mind became clear, floating on anger. In no more than a few seconds the process had completed itself. The other yacht was the enemy. By some remote system the individuals on the other yacht lost their identity, became part of that other entity, the adversary.

The seconds ticked by for the ten-minute gun.

A sailor can tell, at a glance, whether a rival yacht is well organised.

The expertise on *Shadow* was immediately noticeable in the sail handling. The speed with which any large yacht can tack is governed by the speed with which the genoa can be released and hauled in on the other tack. On *Shadow* the genoa was released and hauled in like a spring. Studying this performance over his shoulder, Jim watched Ericson take the yacht through three tacks, each forty seconds apart, as neatly as a model yacht on a pond. Each time the genoa was setting within seconds on the other tack.

Ten years of campaigning experience told in *Shadow*'s crew. The gear and the equipment were smaller than they had been used to. They had been fighting bitter duels against up to ten other great maxis in every major regatta over the past decade. Even at this stage, before they crossed swords directly, Jim could sense the same power and confidence in their start manoeuvres. Jack, glancing across at the other boat as they went through their own preparation, simply whistled tunelessly through his teeth. Jim knew that Jack was also under no illusions about their opponents.

The other members of the crew were casting looks in *Shadow's* direction. Jim redoubled his orders. They tacked once, twice, the genoa coming in more slowly than *Shadow*, but the men were working well, improving a little with each tack.

On *Shadow* now they were concentrating on the shape of the mainsail, hauling back the mast tip to flex the mast, working on outhaul and kicker. He could hear Ericson's barks of command as one control and then another was flexed and eased. They mirrored his own and Jack's.

Jack moved up and down the whole length of the boat, transmitting orders, exhorting, cursing, lending a helping hand. They started to feel reasonably well tuned up. Even though it was well short of good, it was enough for the time being. On his loudhailer Coach Johnson was signalling them to go to their respective corners, like boxers in a ring, for the first race.

The ten-minute gun fired, and both yachts entered the starting box. *Shadow* had picked up speed first and was swinging towards him, a bone of spray in her teeth.

No matter how many times he had studied the texts, or Coach Johnson had taken him through the videos to demonstrate the various tactical moves, this was a moment of elation. He felt the yacht alive under the huge wheel, checked the speed rise, bore off slightly to close rapidly with the rival. The two juggernauts, weighing twenty tons each, thundered towards each other.

It was clear Ericson intended to teach him a lesson straight away. He had placed *Shadow* on a collision course, so that Jim would have to swing wide to avoid him. They closed like two jousting knights. He could feel the tenseness of the winchgrinders and trimmers as they closed; shortly, they knew, it would be up to them.

Ericson turned away when they were about thirty seconds from a collision, bore off to pick up more speed, and then swung the wheel in a savage turn, hurling *Shadow* into a close circle. Jim responded by turning with her, trying to keep *Shadow* away from *New World*'s stern. The winchgrinders became frenzied, the huge genoa thundered across the deck as they tacked; the boom crashed from one side to the other.

He could hear the same controlled fury on the other boat. A chop hit the side of *New World*'s wheeling bow and a bucket of water splintered into his face.

When it cleared a few seconds later, he confirmed what he had already sensed, that Ericson's turn had been faster. *Shadow* was lying directly astern, driving them away from the start line. In this situation the following boat had effective right of way. If they turned to starboard, they would have crossed *Shadow*'s path and been protested out of the race for obstruction. If they turned to port *Shadow* would also do so and any further turn on their part would amount to obstruction.

There was no choice but to sail away from the line with *Shadow* in pursuit. Jack said behind him: 'Looks like we're going to have to get back on speed.'

Shadow drove them away from the start line for two minutes. As the start gun went, *Shadow* swung back abruptly towards the start line.

'Gybe,' shouted Jim. The boom crashed across, the genoa was sheeted on port, and *New World* closed up into the wind so that they were pointing towards the port end of the start line.

Ericson tacked to cover. Jack shouted, 'Let's get speed on. Tension backstay, more kicker,' Jack roared out. 'Ease genoa, she's too flat.'

'Leach line,' shouted Jack, 'More tension main halyard.' *New World* was starting to move well. Each of the small adjustments added an infinitesimal amount of speed. Jack kept issuing a stream of orders. 'Slide boom down on track two inches. OK, harden in on mainsheet. Damn it, can't we do anything about the top of that sail?'

New World was starting to fly. They were beginning to gain, but *Shadow* was first across the start line by six seconds.

'We're closing on them,' said Jim. 'We'll keep on this tack.'

Coach Johnson's launch, with its two Caterpillar diesels, lifted and spun across the waves. Coach Johnson was shouting, firing two shots on his starting pistol.

'He's signalling for another start,' Jack said. Jim felt the tension and frustration in his shoulders. He said 'Why doesn't he let us finish the goddamn first leg? We were gaining on them.'

The crew too had begun to ease back. 'OK, men, we're turning back for another start.' He could hear the quiet expulsion of breath from Big Ape and Georgie, the low swear-words of the winchgrinders, picked up and tossed away by the breeze. 'We're bearing off. Ease sheets.'

Ericson won four out of five starts. In the close quarter manoeuvres *Shadow*'s sail-handling superiority proved too much to overcome. The fifth start Ericson overplayed his hand in a turn, Jim made a dummy turn with him, then reversed direction once his pursuer was committed to the gybe, and managed to place himself behind *Shadow*'s counter, driving Ericson away from the line in classic manner. It was the one sweet part of the day.

In the steam of the shower rooms afterwards Jim looked over at Ericson's corner. Ericson's powerful torso was golden with light. His moustache was pale, almost white. His light blue eyes moved slowly about the room in a way which reminded Jim of some strange sea-creature. He deliberately turned away from Jim if they should come face to face.

Nor would Ericson's men talk to Jim's crew. They gathered at the other end of the shower rooms, exercised in a small clique on the forecourt early in the mornings. At the dinner table the two sides ranged on either side and very little conversation flowed. Coach Johnson presided over these two hostile camps with something approaching approval.

On the training course, Coach Johnson was the final arbiter as to when the races started and stopped. If Jim seemed to be gaining an advantage, he would halt the race and restart. If Ericson was ahead, he would let it continue for a while in order to rub home Ericson's advantage. As soon as he was ahead Jim knew the launch would be alongside, Coach Johnson would be firing two shots to signify the end of a race, and loud-hailing him to return to the starting box for another race.

Ericson was perhaps the most aggressive starting helmsman in the world, and Coach Johnson gave him every opportunity he could to practise his art on Jim. For nearly six weeks they did nothing but starts.

The pressure placed on Jim and his crew was enormous. Coach Johnson confined their races to precisely that area where Ericson and his men were supreme, and continued his practice of halting those races in which Jim was ahead. Some of the crew of *New World* began to become despondent. Others seemed to grow under the pressure. Jim noted those who reacted badly and reserved his views.

Over the weeks which followed, Ericson never let up. Every day he emerged full of apparent animus and ruthlessly attempted to bludgeon *New World* with his own seasoned crew. Ericson was developing a streak of ruthlessness in Jim which he did not know existed.

In spite of these differences, Jim was slowly beginning to get the measure of Ericson. His men were beginning to achieve the same co-ordination as Ericson's crew in the turns and twists of the pre-start manoeuvres. Their sailwork was beginning to achieve the smooth efficiency of champions.

But what was more pleasing to Jim were the improvements in speed they were beginning to draw from their boat. Sometimes, when Coach Johnson allowed them to continue up the first leg to the top mark, *New World* could open up a forty or fifty second lead. Helmsmanship was only a part of it. It was largely a combination of Jack and the two genoa trimmers, Greenback and Georgie. They achieved an almost perfect interaction between the genoa and mainsail. In a straight line, *New World* started to fly.

But every day they were under pressure. Ericson's crew were improving, too. Coach Johnson had chosen for the rivals not a group of isolated geniuses, who would have had to assemble themselves slowly into a donkey that worked, but a living, breathing team, full of confidence and elan. They seized on this new sixty-footer and almost literally took it apart, stripping the winches to check every aspect of the mechanism, tensing and re-tensing the rigging until they were satisfied with its set under every condition. They brought their critical gaze to bear on every piece of fitting and deck machinery. They surveyed every part of the boat, from stem to stern, checking the rudder bearings, the trim-tab mechanisms, the egress points of the underwater instrumentation, even the beams and structure of the yacht itself. Their two electronics experts could not be separated from the sophisticated

211

instrumentation and computerised information systems. Their tactician spent several hours every day analysing print-outs of speeds and vectors over the whole of the day's racing.

As part of this professionalism, they brought special areas of expertise which *New World*'s crew could only struggle to match. No yacht is perfect; each has its strengths and weaknesses. But in the case of the great ones, certain features lie at the heart of their success. On *Shadow*, there was one aspect of almost sublime efficiency. On their very first race Jack had commented on it. *Shadow*'s mainsail was trimmed with uncanny intuition. It had the grace of a butterfly's wing; from the aerofoil section at the base to the twist in the upper third, every gradated curve looked good. *Shadow* seemed to pivot around this superbly setting sail, powering and depowering at will in the close quarter combat, picking up speed with an eerie grace once a manoeuvre was completed.

The heart of the power of a fractional rigged racing yacht is its mainsail. The mainsail trimmer, by releasing a fifth of a second too early or too late, can control the tack or turn. At table in the evenings Jack and Jim found themselves looking at the small, wiry Franky Haldane with awe, watching him eat cheerfully, with the unassuming hands that controlled the huge mainsail. They would have cheerfully asked for his autograph if they had not been his opponents. Even heroes have heroes.

Thirty-six

Deep into the night the two crews worked on the two boats. Floodlights were opened up after dark. Each day the boats were lifted from the water and three or four men from each crew would work on them until ten o'clock.

Both crews had access to the workshops, behind the yard, where Eddie Cantor worked his magic in repair and renewal. Even in sails, they had equal access to the cutting lofts, where some sixteen cutters worked in eight-hour night shifts, so that they could have the sails repaired and recut by dawn. In a huge shed nearby, the masts were lifted out every night for checking and repair.

At night more than ever the base was like a military camp. The doors to the outside were manned by military policemen. Inside the base there was tense and continuous activity. Hidden at the centre were the sail lofts, the machine rooms, the instrumentation laboratories. Close by were the store-rooms from which could be produced, at short notice, a bar of alloy, rolls of cloth, titanium sheaves. Like an organism in which all the cells are constantly renewing themselves, every feature of the two yachts could be reconstructed at will.

They might have been on a battleship. Even Jim's sleep was choreographed by the scream of metal being machined in the workshops, the thump of the spare generator like a heartbeat, the odd, eerie blasts of light, like small fireworks, of the lathes and acetylene lances. As April turned to May, and the temperature continued to rise, the workshop roofs were opened, and the smoke and flame of the repair factory was reflected out into the night as if the devil's furnaces were beneath.

Eddie Cantor's crew worked all through the night and replaced gear in the early hours of the morning. They breakfasted and slept during the day, waking up in the early afternoon like strange nocturnal animals. Then they waited for the yachts to come home. Always on the quay to meet them were Eddie Cantor and Tom East, the sailmaker. Already, even before the two yachts arrived back from a hard day's training, the sailcutters were setting up the loft floor in preparation for the incoming flow of sails and requests for newly cut ones.

To Eddie Cantor and his crew, every day provided a new heartbreak, a fresh challenge. One of the spinnaker booms broke in a particularly fierce luff by *Shadow*. Within twelve hours Eddie Cantor had not only replaced the pole by cannibalising, cutting and pop-rivetting a spinnaker pole from a maxi, he had instituted a programme of building four new carbon-fibre poles, lighter and stronger than the original, in one of the outer workrooms.

As the training progressed, the competition grew fiercer. Eddie and his men were waiting by the dockside at four in the afternoon, ready to go through a checklist of work which needed urgent attention. Both skippers looked for nothing less than perfection.

In the ensuing weeks Jim continued to develop his profound respect for the professionalism of the preppies. They did not shirk from working sixteen hours a day to set something right. After each exhausting daily session of racing, the gear on both boats was checked minutely, repairs agreed, a timetable set. The crews ate supper, and then a works crew of three or four from each boat would set down to business, relieved at ten by a second crew. Ropes were changed, halyards examined foot by foot, winches overhauled. In the morning both crews would be out on the quadrangle exercising from six-thirty until seven-thirty, followed by showers and breakfast. Briefing with Coach began at eight-thirty; at nine-fifteen they were in the boats being towed out to sea. Day in, day out, for two months, they worked, pacing each other, driving.

Coach Johnson, having set in train the competition between the crews, needed only to act as referee. Rivalry develops its own momentum. Though there were tensions between crews, arguments with the repairers, under the pressure of Coach Johnson the powerful antagonism between the two crews became like the heartbeat of a living animal, the source of nourishment and circulation.

Far from *New World* being the favoured crew, the banana street gang felt they were being selected against. It was as if Coach Johnson was saying, 'If you can't win at a disadvantage, then you aren't the people we're looking for.'

The strain began to tell. One of the reserve winchgrinders on *New World*, Hugh Logan, was caught by the mainsheet in a gybe and flung against the cockpit side, breaking several ribs. He would be hospitalised for two months. Watching Hugh Logan being carried off the boat on a stretcher, his shirt covered in blood, Jim turned towards the other boat, and experienced again the curious implacability of his feeling. Rivalry, like love, can reach a second, almost transcendental stage, a stage of pure detachment.

More than the physical strain, the remorseless psychological pressure was responsible for removing their sewerman. He started to make mistakes. One of his functions was to clip the bowman into the bosun's chair and haul him aloft, often several times during a race. One day, Virus, the bowman, came down the mast after being hauled up in the routine of checking the halyards in the race, stepped out of his bosun's chair, and held up to Buddy Fleming's face a shackle which had stood between him and a fall of sixty feet. The shackle had not been properly closed; only the tiniest edge had been held in the socket, hardly more than a hair. Buddy Fleming looked at it and his eyes filled with tears. Virus said nothing and went back to his duties.

Buddy Fleming completed the race, and that evening asked to be replaced. Jack spent an hour trying to negotiate with Coach Johnson a payment of three thousand dollars so that Buddy Fleming could take time off to repair some of the psychological damage and start his life again. Coach Johnson replied that someone could have fallen sixty feet; someone could have been killed.

'We all make mistakes,' said Jack.

'Only once in my outfit,' replied Coach Johnson.

Jack said they all agreed a mistake had been made, they felt that a payment would help him on his way. Coach Johnson refused on the grounds that it would set a precedent.

'People are more important than precedents,' said Jack Peabody.

'In heaven, maybe,' replied Coach Johnson.

Jack suggested that heaven was a good place to emulate. Coach Johnson then expressed his well-known view that professional sailors had more in common with the infernal regions.

'Even Lucifer was an Angel,' tried Jack one more time.

'Yeah,' replied Coach Johnson, 'but he fell more than sixty feet.'

Finally the crew of *New World* put together six hundred dollars from their own savings, and bought a ticket for Buddy back to Florida. Perhaps the thought that they had all contributed was of more importance to Buddy than the extra money. They heard several months later that he'd settled in Tampa Bay and set up a small jewellery business with his girlfriend, that he was happy and well.

If there was any aspect of the training camp which resembled the infernal regions in more than simply a metaphorical sense, it was Eddie Cantor's workshops, an area of noise, strange lights, ice-cold fires and shadows flung by acetylene lances. Lathes and grinders were in constant use, sparks flung onto the dark, stained walls. Here Eddie was in his proper lair. Concentrating on his own exhaustive schedules, he moved from area to area like the chief devil, his small quick eyes alight with concentration. Jim would sometimes visit him to ask a favour, some special piece of equipment they had dreamed up. Eddie would be standing at a lathe or grinding a flawless fit in one of the yachts' metal mechanisms. He would act as if he hadn't heard. But a day or so later, rarely more, the part would appear, with a small note attached. It might, for example, be a snap shackle with a locking cap so that the bowman could be winched up in safety. Eddie wrote accompanying notes in his sloping hand. 'Is this it?', 'This what you wanted?', 'Like this, you mean?', always with the question mark childishly large.

In the mornings, when they gathered in the quadrangle for exercise, Eddie would appear owlishly from the recesses of the workshops, his face so white it made his small, bright eyes even darker. Behind him two of his men would wheel a small trolley, carrying parts repaired, stripped or replaced. They'd spend sometimes an hour on the actual boat, going over every part of the mechanism in question, and afterwards they'd eat a breakfast in the main room, at a table on their own, their bedtime meal before they retired to sleep. If Jim thought his own life was one of discipline and tension, he couldn't bear to imagine Eddie's.

The entire crew was feeling the strain. Jim had a pain buried deep in his back from the furious turns on the wheel required in the close-quarters duelling, and a bad rope-burn across his hands from a crash gybe in the pre-start manoeuvres. In one of the wheeling fights with *Shadow* Jack darted forward to help the mainsheet trimmer unjam a coil. Jim had tackled the runners as they gybed, had momentarily lost attention as the wheel spun freely behind him, and found a huge burn across his fingers and the palm of his hands as the leeward running backstay shrieked out in the gybe with the full weight of the boom behind it.

Both crews became dug in, dealing blow and counter-blow. Like heavyweights in training, they came out each day and fought head to head. If too much of a lead opened up between the boats on a race, Coach Johnson would call a halt and they'd start again. Slowly, by degrees, *New World* began to achieve parity with *Shadow* in the pre-start manoeuvres. To counter Ericson, *New World*'s crew were forced to conduct feints, false tacks, dummy gybes. Quite often now Jim was able to outwit Ericson, to turn an aggressive move of his opponent into a trap.

It crept up gradually, but every day the confidence of *New World*'s crew was growing. Jim noticed with a certain amusement how they descended into the boat like the argonauts, this motley band. They were towed out, and silence closed over them as they went through the boat in a final pre-race check.

After three full months of racing starts, Coach Johnson allowed a fortnight of racing around the course. *New World*

217

was given an opportunity to open up the throttle, Jack to set sails. It was odd being able to canter across the seas like spirited horses, to play the windshifts, to open up the game. Away from the frenzy of starts a different rhythm emerged, not the aggressive battleaxe and mace of close-quarter manoeuvre, but the hardbitten one of calculation, when the outcome of a race could be decided by the single rifle shot of a superior decision.

In the races which followed, on a full Olympic course, Coach Johnson scheduled one race a day for twelve consecutive days. The tally, stuck up on the side of the wall nearest the yachts, mounted up. At the end of the series, the banana street gang had won nine out of twelve races. It was the final collapse of Ericson's camp.

Jim was interested to see how Ericson would take his defeat. He had come to respect both Ericson's talent and the unremitting fury of his commitment. As the weeks progressed, his rivalry with Ericson had become almost impersonal, a force which drove him because it had settled into his own character, had aligned him like a compass. At the same time it became almost devoid of any feeling of animosity.

He knew that every sporting competition is as much a psychological battle as a physical one, a duel between characters. Each participant calls on his inmost resources to achieve that final edge. And since the nature of each opponent is the material of his victory or defeat, there comes a point at the end of the competition when the two participants look at one another from their new status as victor and loser, in the final assessment of the other.

When he shook hands with Ericson after the last race, Jim looked with this same interest into his rival's eyes. A strange, hunted expression flitted across Ericson's face. He seemed unable to return Jim's gaze, to look him in the eye. At that moment Jim understood that Ericson had thrown everything, every last psychological reserve into beating him, and his failure was unbearable. He now seemed to Jim like a man haunted by his failure.

This final meeting had a more profound effect on Jim

than any other event in the past few months, though its consequences were not immediately obvious. In the small spaces of time between his commitments and allotted duties, he tried to focus on the problem, but it continued to elude him. He suspected that it lay in the wholly different attitudes of Ericson and himself towards each other. In the course of the competition, he had come to develop a genuine respect for Ericson's ability and the almost matchless performance of the *Shadow* crew in close-quarter combat. It had been a pleasure to go out and meet them and do battle – more than a pleasure – an honour. But Ericson had no such respect for him. It was as if he despised Jim, and to be beaten left no final barrier against anguish.

Ericson could have left honourably, but chose to leave the very next day without warning. The Lagonda was gone. His crew were not due to depart for another several days, and Jim took this opportunity to strike one final blow against Ericson.

In the next two days he persuaded two of *Shadow*'s crew, Mat Polaski, the greatest of the winch-grinders, and Franky Haldane, mainsheet trimmer, handshaker and grinder of metacarpals, to change sides. In a meeting with Jim and Jack the night before the remainder of *Shadow*'s crew were due to leave, Coach Johnson approved these recommendations. The new crew members were duly signed on.

On the twentieth of June the *Ghost Train 5* circus moved out. The crew of *New World* tied a large, inflated balloon in the shape of a banana to the bumper of the English bus which had come to carry them away. Only fourteen of the sixteen Ivy League thugs left on the double decker bus. The gates were swung closed and almost immediately they were poised to move into the final stage of their preparations. Before they did so, the exhausted crew and back-up teams were given a week of leave.

Some of the crew stayed in the camp, protected now by the military security against the outside world. They slept in deckchairs, played backgammon and table tennis, read books or magazines. Jim, part of him still high on elation, and another part still recoiling from the nature of Ericson's defeat, decided to return to Weepeq.

But before he left, Coach Johnson delivered a letter addressed to him in a flowing, confident hand. It was from Tom Stuttaford, congratulating him on his sailing performance and inviting him to a meeting on his yacht at ten-thirty the following day.

Thirty-seven

Tom Stuttaford's big yawl, *La Reine*, lay against the wall, flying its Stars and Stripes. A small, irregular swell from the harbour mouth caused it to rise and fall majestically against its fenders. Its traditional lines, with a magnificent counter stern, seemed to suspend it in time; a sleek, rich object invested with an ancient pedigree.

When one drew closer, studied the immaculate bright-work, the scrubbed teak decks, the rich gleam of the copper binnacle, the ropes laid out in perfect coils, it carried the unmistakeable aura of permanent crew, of deck hands and loving attention; the aroma, intoxicating to the senses, of a combination of good taste supported by limitless expense.

Tom Stuttaford was on board, dressed in blue blazer and white trousers, welcoming his guests down to the saloon. Several large cars were parked nearby, their sleek bonnets protruding from behind a low, brick wall. Inside, behind the discreetly dark glass, their chauffeurs waited. Jim arrived on foot.

'Come right on down,' said Stuttaford. 'Let me take your raincoat.' He looked up at the unsettled sky. A large bank of cloud was scudding across, carrying the threat of thunder in its grey folds. Tom Stuttaford said: 'Goddamn weather.' And Jim understood from this that he was uneasy.

In the saloon, in the eerie light before a thunderstorm, the polished wood exuded a rich, honeyed glow. Three men were seated around the hardwood saloon table. He recognised General Walters, Colonel O'Reilly, and Senator Sam Hickstead.

Jim had a curious premonition, the sense of some illicit meeting, of card-playing or a gambling den. He had seen a film once in which certain Mafia hierarchs had met in a country retreat to negotiate the apportioning between them of some territory of mutual interest.

For a brief moment no one appeared to take any notice of Jim. Then Tom Stuttaford descended the wooden gangway ladder behind him, and called out. 'We're all here.'

The eyes of the seated men rose. Senator Sam Hickstead stood up and shook Jim's hand. General Walters and Colonel O'Reilly remained seated but nodded perfunctorily to Jim. Tom Stuttaford said cheerfully, 'Make way round the table, you guys, for two more.'

When they were seated, Senator Hickstead, who seemed to be their spokesman, said: 'Congratulations on your selection, Jim. You certainly showed you're a fighter.'

Jim glanced at General Walters, who remained impassive, then returned his attention to Sam Hickstead.

The Senator put his hands together on the table. He looked around at the others, as if to gather support. Then he addressed Jim directly.

'Tom has kindly lent us the use of his yacht today so that we can maybe put across a couple of thoughts to you, following your fine victory in the selection trials. Perhaps you'd bear with me.'

This time, Jim thought, there's no pun on the word 'bear'. It was getting darker outside; no one had seen fit to put on the yacht's accommodation lights.

The saloon seemed suddenly silent. All he could hear was the occasional slap of wavelets on the hull, the creak-

221

ing of the fenders against the sea-wall as the yacht rose and fell gently.

'I'm not breaking any state secrets,' Senator Hickstead continued, 'when I tell you that we're in an important and interesting negotiating stage with the Russians. We're coming up to our next round of arms limitation talks. Both parties are looking for big reductions in current weapons stockpiles. We're hoping for concessions right across the board, nuclear and conventional. There's a good chance the Russians will concede something major regarding their continuing preponderance of conventional forces. I'm not telling you anything that hasn't been aired, at one time or another, in the newspapers. Naturally, it's very important that the Russians come to the table in the right frame of mind.'

The senator paused, considering a delicate matter of nuance.

'Now, how exactly does this affect you? Well, maybe it does and maybe it doesn't. But consider this, young feller, if you will. It's clear to everyone, including, I have to say, the Russians, that in the last decade their industrial restructuring has not worked out quite as they hoped. I don't have to quote the latest figures on the output of leather shoes in Siberia to tell you that. Sure, there have been successes, but the Russians are very status-conscious people, and if you consider the respective economic positions of our two countries, not a great deal has happened in the last decade to change the fact that they're still well behind, and not making much headway. Frankly, that puts them in a defensive state of mind. They're looking for something, anything, that will bolster them, that will give them a little added status.'

The Senator studied him carefully.

'Now that's where this current America's Cup thing is kind of interesting. Maybe there's something here we can, uh, look at. It's quite clear that the Russians are treating this with a great deal of attention. They made the challenge and it's obviously an important event to them, an expression of their national identity. They're treating it like a ritual trial of strength.

'That's fine by us. We're not averse to that. All I'm saying to you is this, young man. We all want our side to win, and we're doing everything we can to help you, but in the wider, strategic sphere, it would clearly help if the Russians didn't lose too badly, if I make myself clear.'

He looked at Jim directly, studying his face for an answer.

At first Jim could not quite believe what he had just heard. He looked around the table, at the firm, expressionless eyes of General Walters, the diffident expression of Colonel O'Reilly. Finally he glanced at Tom Stuttaford, who smiled at Jim his usual, good-natured smile, though Jim thought he detected an edge in it.

'Frankly,' continued the Senator, making the best of Jim's silence, 'we don't expect you to make any reply. We'd just like you to consider what we said. We felt there'd be no harm in talking to you and making sure you are aware of the higher priorities.'

For several seconds, it seemed as if even the waves had become still.

Sam Hickstead turned to General Walters.

'Want to add anything, General?'

General Walters did not move in his chair. Keeping his eyes directly on Jim, he said: 'Just to back you up in what you said, Sam. These concessions from the Russians are of vital importance. Anything, anything which can be done to bring them to the negotiating table in the right frame of mind, so as to commit themselves to significant arms reductions, is a help to us.'

Sam Hickstead nodded.

'Tom,' said Sam Hickstead. 'You got anything you want to add?'

'I don't think so, Sam,' Stuttaford replied.

'Right,' Hickstead said. 'So there you have our collective view.'

The storm moved slowly past them to the south. Jim could hear the occasional rumble of thunder.

Senator Hickstead said, deliberately lightening the conversation, 'What the hell are we all doing talking seriously about politics on a magnificent craft like this? Tom, may we avail ourselves of some of that fine bourbon you promised us?'

'Sure can,' said Stuttaford. 'I know that underneath all this foreign policy stuff, that's your only reason for coming here.'

'He knows me too well,' said Sam Hickstead to the company in general.

But their humour was uneasy. They drank a glass of bourbon each, and then, after perfunctory small talk, the company split up. The General and the Senator walked away side by side, the General talking, the Senator listening, and this struck Jim as an odd reversal of roles. The two men reached their chauffeur-driven limousines. The General's drew away first down the cobbles to the muted screech of rubber tyres.

'Surprised?' asked Tom Stuttaford, from the companionway. Jim still didn't know where Stuttaford's own view lay. As if by way of explanation, Stuttaford said, 'Those people are my closest acquaintances. My head tells me they're right in what they're saying.'

He looked at Jim and smiled.

'But all we old buffers can do is talk, put across our views. In the end it's up to you.'

Remembering the Senator and General walking away, Jim wondered whether this was true. He said: 'It doesn't need me to make Ivan Illich look good.'

Then he shook hands with Tom Stuttaford, thanked him for his hospitality, retrieved his raincoat from the wet locker beside the companionway stairs, and stepped out onto the cobbled quay.

Until then, it was as if the import of the conversation had numbed him. Only as he walked away from the yacht did his mind begin to work through its sudden, inexpressible load of turmoil and anger.

Thirty-eight

What had been said, apparently so casually, struck at the heart of Jim's assumptions. It had never occurred to him, not once, that if he and his crew came through the elimination trials with Ericson, the competition would be anything other than a straight battle between Illich and himself.

As he walked along the cobblestones his anger began to build. He went over Hickstead's little speech as carefully as he could, searching each word, each nuance, for hidden meaning. At the centre of the speech was a veiled suggestion, one which was hinted at but never fully articulated. And yet the more he considered what had been said, the more this hidden aspect began to grow, to take on form and weight. A question of a truly terrible nature now began to haunt him. When they asked him to 'make the Russians look good', were they actually asking him to lose?

The thought was so astonishing that he was forced to pause some several hundred yards along in his walk and stand still, taking deep breaths.

A few seconds later he started to walk again, but almost immediately, the notion that he was being asked to lose produced a fresh cycle of question and counter-question. At one stage, he almost walked into the water, pausing just in time as a sudden change in the direction of the harbour wall brought him face to face with a twenty-foot drop.

He grew furious with himself for remaining silent, for not asking them to clarify their request. In retrospect, he wanted to shout at them that if they wanted someone to 'take a dive', they should find someone else. But he had a sudden, sobering thought. Maybe that was exactly what they had tried to do. Perhaps they had tried to replace him with John Ericson. And as he walked around the outer perimeter of the harbour, a fresh cycle of thoughts assailed him. Was that what they intended for Ericson? Was he their man because they would expect this kind of sacrifice from him?

An unexpected wave of sympathy for Ericson struck him. Perhaps it was more than parental ambition and Ericson's own, unachievable goals which had caused him to break down. Perhaps the thought of deliberately losing to Illich, if he won through the selections, had preyed upon him.

He pulled in at a small café, one of those places in which he felt at ease, amongst working people. The coffee was strong. He drank several cups. He would have eaten something but he had no appetite.

The café had a phone booth in the corner, an enclosed booth that was private. Glancing at the amiable graffiti, he guessed it was mainly used by the clientele to put bets on the horses. He had waited an hour to give Stuttaford time to get home. He dialled Stuttaford's number and waited for the phone to be picked up.

The maid answered. Jim gave his name and asked to speak to Mr Stuttaford. Several seconds passed, then he heard footsteps approach the telephone.

Tom Stuttaford's voice said: 'Hi, Jim, did you forget something?'

'Not that I know of, sir.'

'How can I help you?'

'I'd appreciate it if I could check with you about the meeting that we had this afternoon.'

There was a moment's silence. Jim decided, for no good reason, to press ahead.

'I don't understand why it was called, or what I'm supposed to do exactly as a consequence.'

It is remarkable how intently one can listen.

'I appreciate your sentiments, Jim. I'm not sure I'm the right person to add my interpretation of the meeting.'

'Maybe it wasn't quite clear to you, either?'

'I have to say that the import of it was clear to me, but I'd hesitate to say directly what I thought about it.'

Jim allowed several seconds to pass. He felt fear slide into his heart. He decided it was now or never.

'My own impression was that they want me to lose to Ivan Illich.'

There are silences and silences. What the pause which followed lacked in longevity, it made up for in depth. At length Tom Stuttaford said: 'That has to be your interpretation.'

'It's not yours, sir?'

'That I can't say.'

Another long silence followed, and Jim felt his fear filling out, becoming large. But then Stuttaford unexpectedly asked: 'May I ask you a question, Jim?'

'Sir.'

'If your interpretation is correct, what do you intend to do about it?'

Jim said: 'I can answer that one directly.'

Tom Stuttaford paused. Afterwards, when Jim tried to remember this part of their conversation exactly, it seemed to him that he recalled a click, as if a switch had been pressed, or a recording machine turned on.

'Go ahead.'

Jim said:

'If my interpretation is right, and I am being asked to lose, I intend to ignore the advice, sir.'

Tom Stuttaford said evenly:

'I thought maybe you might.'

Jim waited, hoping for some clarification of Tom Stuttaford's view. At length he said:

'Goodbye, sir.'

'Goodbye, Jim.'

It was shortly afterwards that Jim began to experience the curious sensation of being followed. He knew the notion was absurd, and he could find no physical evidence, but the impression persisted. When he crossed streets he glanced up behind him, looking for some sign of a shape which was familiar, a figure following in his tracks. But he could find none. There was no single common denominator amongst the figures walking behind him. It was like being haunted by a ghost.

Thirty-nine

Back at the base the following day, as he was about to leave on his week of holiday, Jack asked: 'What exactly are you suspicious about?'

'It's difficult to express.'

'Try me.'

Conflicting emotions assailed Jim. He considered that he owed it to Jack to say what he felt, that he at least should clear the air.

'Yesterday I was called to a meeting on Tom Stuttaford's yacht. Senator Hickstead, and General Walters were on board. O'Reilly was also there, but he didn't say much.'

'Go on.'

'The Senator said we're coming up to the next round of negotiations with Russia, and the Russians are feeling paranoid because their economy is failing. They need bolstering if they're going to negotiate in the right frame of mind. That was more important than any other goal.'

'So?'

Jim paused. Even now it seemed absurd. 'They near as damn asked me to lose.'

'They asked you directly?'

'They asked me to make the Russians look good.'

Jack's face did not register either confusion or alarm. His slightly pale eyes did not move. Jack's security, the great, unflappable nature which made him a tactician of genius, this confidence was an object of considerable admiration to Jim. But now, Jim felt, it was close to blindness.

'You must have misunderstood them.'

Jim turned away, suddenly angry, not wanting Jack to see what was inside him.

Jack insisted: 'That's really absurd. You must be mistaken. They couldn't have meant that.'

Jim felt the spasm of rage leave him. It lasted only seconds. Then he was back in control of his feelings; as much, at least, as he ever was.

'I telephoned Tom Stuttaford afterwards to ask whether my impression of the meeting was right.'

'What'd he say?'

'He said he couldn't comment. I asked him to tell me that my impression wasn't the right one, but he wouldn't. Instead, he asked me whether, if my impression was right, I intended to take the advice.'

'Hold it a moment,' said Jack. 'You asked him to deny something that had never been said. And he refused to deny it. Jim, for Chrissakes, this is bizarre. If no one asked you to lose directly, how can you be expected to act on it?'

Jim replied with a trace of sarcasm he later regretted (because irony had no effect on Jack), 'Sure, Jack. It seems unlikely, therefore it couldn't have happened.'

One further event occurred before he left.

Jim was packed and ready to go back to Weepeq. He was about to lift his suitcase and carrier bags out to his old car, when the telephone at the end of the dormitory rang. He was half expecting a call from Coach Johnson and for a moment was unsettled by a woman's voice.

'Jim?'

'Yes?'

'Angela Stuttaford here.'

Jim tried not to allow his consternation to show.

'Good afternoon, Mrs Stuttaford.'

There was a brief pause at the other end of the line.

'I don't quite know how to say this, but I feel I may be able to help you clarify something.'

It was Jim's turn to pause, to feel his way carefully.

'Could you be a little more specific?'

'This isn't the time.' Her tone in this matter at least was decisive, confident. 'It would be best if we met. Could I suggest the White Hill Hotel, Fifth Street? Six this evening?'

Jim looked at his watch. It was four-thirty. There were so many unanswered questions, his mind began to race. He said: 'I'll be there.'

The line went dead.

He killed time for half an hour by drafting a report on training progress that week. Coach Johnson insisted on a weekly summary, not least because it helped to clarify matters in the mind of the writer. The subheadings were 'problems', 'proposed solutions', and 'future goals'. Coach Johnson placed emphasis on conciseness of exposition, applying military training, and Jim had begun to enjoy the discipline of these reports. This time he found the concentration especially welcome.

At twenty-five minutes past five he left the base, checked through security, and walked the two miles to the White Hill Hotel at a brisk pace. The weather was warm, the pavements more crowded as he moved in toward the centre of town.

The White Hill was one of those small, plush private hotels which had survived on its highly personal, somewhat idiosyncratic atmosphere. Though its exterior was bland concrete and tinted glass, inside it was a mass of greenery and fountains, a place of almost tropical profusion.

He was several minutes early. Glancing into the foyer, he could see no sign of her. He left the foyer, returned to the street, and windowshopped idly outside.

At two minutes past six, with a small rush of anticipation, he saw Angela Stuttaford, in dark glasses and an expensive sable fur, climb the stairs and enter the foyer. He waited a minute and climbed the stairs after her.

She was sitting in a small room off the foyer, reading a magazine. When she saw him she rose to greet him and said: 'Let's go somewhere quiet.' She turned and walked past the lobby. He followed her through a second set of revolving doors and out into a small side street. She hailed a cab. They got in.

She made small talk while they drove through the city. The cab travelled northwards, bearing right off the motorway, along a detour, across a traffic light and into a secluded residential street. She got out and paid the driver. Jim followed her to the door of a house. He noted the number. Eighty-seven. A cardkey opened the door. Inside the magnolia-painted hallway was a large cork board, on which messages had been placed apparently at random. He caught sight of one. 'Hi. I'll collect you at eight this evening. Brad.'

She removed her glasses. He was aware of her remarkable eyes.

'This place is used by our two youngest daughters when they're back from college. They're at an age where they like a bit of independence, and here Tom can't cross-question them about the intentions of their boyfriends.' She smiled, leading the way to the sitting room, with its low furniture and glass table.

Jim recalled something Stuttaford had said about living among a female tribe. Angela Stuttaford was saying: 'Sit down. Would you like a drink? Coffee?'

'No thanks.'

She removed her coat, threw it over a chair, and sat down opposite him. He had the impression that she felt at ease in the house, that she was familiar with it.

'I apologise for the cloak-and-dagger. It's just a precaution.'

'Against being followed?'

She shrugged and lit a cigarette. He remembered Tom Stuttaford saying she forbade smoking in their own house. He wondered if different rules applied here.

'I'm sorry I was so abrupt on the phone,' she added, and exhaled. Then she said, almost brutally: 'The reason

I asked you to meet me was this. I happen to know people in my husband's world. Maybe I mentioned to you, his world is my world too. I'm quite active in that world, on the social side mostly, but I know its main figures well. As I think I told you, I come from an old political family.'

He waited for her to speak her mind, but in the safety of the house she seemed in no great hurry. She drew in on her cigarette.

'I understand you recently attended a meeting on my husband's yacht. Some advice was given to you.'

Jim's mind froze.

He was aware of her eyes surveying him, fathomless. He nodded. She said: 'That advice might seem a little difficult to swallow.'

He would not help her. His anger extended to her, he could not help himself. So he continued to wait. Outside, a car started and drew away down the street with a low growl. Opposite him was a large casement window. He could see occasional pedestrians pass, mostly young people, young professionals, returning home. The windows of the buildings opposite were hidden by plane trees.

'I would like to reassure you that I'm not here on behalf of those who gave the advice. I wanted to meet you so that I could offer some advice of my own.'

She exhaled carefully. 'It's more in the nature of a friendly warning. The people who gave you that advice are very powerful. They have powerful connections. In my world, you get to know that immediately. You could say it's automatic.

'They can help or hinder you. If you accept their advice, they can help you, make connections for you, assist in your career. If you don't, they can make things difficult.'

She drew in on her cigarette and leaned back in her chair. He was aware of something else, sitting opposite her. The neatness of her ankles, the shapely fullness of her calf. She was sitting cross-legged, and her right foot was moving slowly up and down, as if she was tapping to the rhythm of some internal music. He was aware too, that on some level she was aware of his thoughts.

232

Jim said: 'I appreciate your taking the trouble to tell me this.' He knew that, in the formality of his answer, he might appear to be offering her a rebuff.

She studied him.

'I wonder if you do.'

And he understood then the bargain that she was offering him, the unspoken question that lay between them, as sinuous as the curve of cigarette smoke she blew so fearlessly, so freely, into the air between them.

He felt the anger inside him sharpen. He could have accepted her invitation, but he was suddenly tired of games, suggestions, insinuations. Instead he said: 'You're a beautiful woman. I'd like nothing better than to go to bed with you. But I go to bed because I want to, not as part of some bargain.'

He saw her eyes narrow briefly. And in that curious moment, he knew he had severed all relations with Tom Stuttaford's clan. But what he did next was worse, was full of childish stupidity and bravado.

'That meeting we had yesterday. I thought about it all last night. The more I thought about it, the more disgusted I became. I'm not interested in becoming involved in someone else's power games. As far as I'm concerned, playing with other people's lives isn't my idea of how to live.'

Mrs Stuttaford smiled. He felt he saw a great deal in that smile.

'The young can be so pompous.'

She opened her handbag and powdered her face. After a few moments, she said: 'And when you try to beat your opponent on the water, what else are you doing but gaining power over him?' She pressed her compact shut. 'I heard you almost destroyed John Ericson's son.'

'I really don't know what I'm doing, to tell you the truth. Maybe one day I'll work it out.'

Angela Stuttaford stood up. She closed her handbag with a small snap and said: 'I'm glad you find me beautiful. Would you like me to call a taxi?'

'No thanks,' he replied. 'I can find my own way.'

She let him out. It was starting to get darker. He felt her amused, patronising eyes on him as he walked away down the street.

Forty

It was freak weather for early summer.

Large, solemn snowflakes fell slowly. The light had an almost violet tinge, turning the ground dark, except where the snow had begun to gather. Outside the harbour mouth the sea was grey, the colour of chased mirror.

Jim ascended the path up the hill from the shoreline, between the old factory buildings, the disused warehouse cranes with their rusting pulleys, the piles of decrepit machinery in the long, empty yards.

As he climbed, the terraced houses of the working men gave way to larger houses, houses with a certain amount of room about them, where the factory owners and their managers had once lived. The snow was thicker now, falling softly but determinedly, beginning to shape itself on the pavements and the streetlamps. It grew thick enough on the ground for him to feel it underfoot; a soft, almost animate presence.

It was midday, and the sky was nearly dark. Lights had appeared in some of the windows, though most of the windows seemed empty. A number of the houses had windows which were opaque, suggesting newspaper or boards had been placed behind them. Little had changed since his last visit, except that the district had become, in its quiet manner, even seedier than Jim remembered.

Grandfather's house was, like its owner, an oddity, a small house amongst these larger mansions, hidden away from the sight of the road. Jim walked up the series of gravel runways that formed the path, up the familiar flight of stone steps, and across the spread of old lawn. The grass was not trimmed, but cut with a scythe in order to prevent overgrowing. He noticed that some of the slates had fallen: several, merely chipped, had been laid in a small, neat pile for future use.

Jim let the big dolphin knocker drop and heard the sound of Sam Shaw's footsteps in the hallway.

Sam Shaw stood looking at him, with that incomprehension which is almost blindness. 'Goddamn,' he said. Sam Shaw appeared to have aged. His bones seemed finer to Jim as he hugged the old man.

'Mind if I stay for a few days?' asked Jim.

'Son, you stay as long as you like. Hell, this is your home.'

Inside were the familiar smells of paraffin and naptha, the fishing nets spread over the chair, the other constituents of a spartan order.

'What are you doing in these parts?'

'We've got a week's leave before the final part of the training.'

Sam Shaw looked more closely at Jim. He could see the strain in Jim's face, the signs that were deeper than the welts and bruises from training or the big livid burn scar that ran across his right hand.

As the evening progressed, Sam Shaw gained the impression of someone angry and cold, someone who is wound like a spring. He wondered if this was the being that Coach Johnson had talked about, the man in whom the devil is present but not yet entirely in control.

Sam Shaw found his grandson frighteningly detached. He did his best to put him at his ease, but it was no more than a helpless gesture.

Jim slept in his old bed that night, listening to the familiar siren calls of the steamers moving down the river and out into the bay. They had opened up a new docks upriver for container ships, and the river traffic was becoming heavier. There was some congestion in the fog. The foghorns were almost continuous. But Weepeq Bay had been bypassed. The foghorns were from further away, from the curve of the bay near Highton. He went to sleep to the lowing calls of the steamers.

In the morning Jim woke early, listening to the chorus of birds through the grey square of open window. After the freak snowfall yesterday, it was warmer now. He could hear Sam Shaw bustling about below, tidying the house for his guest. He washed, dressed, and went downstairs.

Sam Shaw was kneeling at the stove, feeding pieces of pinewood into the red heart of the woodburner from an old wicker basket at his side. He was sufficiently engrossed not to notice Jim standing in the doorway.

Jim laid the table and Sam Shaw made toast, eggs and coffee. Jim realised he must have gone down early to the store. Sam Shaw had brought back a newspaper which lay on the table, and which he knew was meant for his guest. But Jim had had too much of the news to want to read it. It was left unopened while they ate their breakfast in silence.

Jim went fishing with Sam Shaw that day, helping him load up the dory with lobster pots and nets. The weather had changed to low fog, but it was milder. The snow of the previous day had melted. He let Sam Shaw row him out to the area where, nearly ten years before, he had helped his grandfather lay his nets and lobster pots.

Neither said much. That afternoon, when they had returned and had delivered the catch to the local offices of Sprawl and Sons, Fish Merchants, Jim went down the hill to Mrs Chednik's store with a list of groceries drawn up by Sam.

The store had not changed much, except that a show-case window had been installed and painted with light blue paint, and the name was up in small lights above the door. Inside there was the familiar fug of warmth.

He rang the bell at the counter.

Mrs Chednik was larger than he had remembered, with lines of veins beneath her eyes which make-up did not entirely hide, and some streaks of grey had appeared in her hair. But apart from that she was the same woman that he remembered. She came to the counter, looked up at him, and remained staring at him for several seconds until he felt uncomfortable. It was as though she were making out his outline first and then moving towards his centre. 'Well, well, well,' she said at last.

She turned away and went into the interior. He heard her nose being blown and realised, with astonishment, that she must be crying. He was at a loss as to what to do. It would have been right for him to go and comfort her, but it was as alien to his character as that of a wolf. He waited until she had recovered, and could return to the counter, asking him what he wanted to buy.

He gave her the little list drawn up by Sam Shaw. As she bustled about the store the initial embarrassment of their meeting wore off, and she started to show some of the liveliness he remembered. After a few minutes of stocking food and other items in the cardboard box which she had placed on the counter for the purpose, she started to become cheerful.

He asked her, casually, the question that he had been wanting to ask ever since he had arrived yesterday.

'Maria?' replied Mrs Chednik. 'She's fine. Living in Tucane. Seems pretty happy with life.'

For the second time he was at a loss as to how to continue. Mrs Chednik continued to pull items down from the shelves.

He said: 'Does she come down here occasionally?'

'Sure,' said Mrs Chednik. 'They were down here a month ago.'

'They?'

'You didn't know?' He sensed again that she was searching his outline, trying to understand him. 'She's engaged. A nice guy called Jock Henshaw. An attorney.'

He was glad to get out into the already falling dusk with the box of groceries, angry and ashamed at the depth of his reaction. She had a perfect right to get engaged, to make her own life.

Back at Sam Shaw's house he unpacked the groceries, helped his grandfather fix back some skirting boards that had come away from a wall. 'You'll be lonely down here,' said Sam Shaw after supper, adding 'away from the action'.

'Maybe,' said Jim.

Sam Shaw said nothing.

In the mornings Jim kept up his exercises, working out on the small lawn in the morning, taking a run in his tracksuit along the empty foreshore. During the day he helped Sam Shaw with his fishing and the repair of the house. The wooden fence at the back of the house had fallen down in one of the winter storms, and Jim made it his task to fit up a new one. He went down to Sam McLuskey to buy some wood.

McLuskey's shed door was locked. Jim went round to the sidedoor and knocked at it. He thought he heard some movement inside. He knocked again. A bolt was slid back. A young man in dungarees and a wool hat appeared, staring at him without answering. 'McLuskey here?' asked Jim. He did not reply, but called out something into the interior of the building.

McLuskey came to the door. 'Shit, the goddamn conquering hero.' McLuskey's fat, powerful hand grasped Jim's.

'Hey,' he called into the interior. 'Frankie, this guy's the one that's gonna tear apart the Russians. Come and shake hands with the guy.' There was no answer from the taciturn young man.

Jim was hauled in, given a cup of coffee, interrogated about the merits of John Ericson. 'All the papers were predicting he was going to be the helmsman. That's right, is it?' asked McLuskey.

'I don't think so,' said Jim.

'His father gave an interview saying that they were on the point of knocking you guys right out,' McLuskey continued. 'Said you guys were dinghy racers and predicted you couldn't take the punishment of the big boats, particularly on the start line.'

Jim was glad he hadn't read those papers. Clearly,

238

Ericson was not only weighted with his own ambitions, but those of his father.

He bought from McLuskey ten four-inch by four-inch spruce poles, a can of wood preservative, two pounds of three-inch nails. He carried them up the hill to the house, and began to use the claw hammer to rip the planks from the poles that had fallen.

He needed cement and couldn't find any close by in the little maze of old shops on the seaward side of the town. He had to travel several miles along the foreshore, out towards Highton, to a new gardening centre. Highton had changed considerably. The old cottages and out-houses had been replaced by smart new estates. Areas of land had been set aside for parks. New lines of trees had been planted on the wide streets. Executives from the new electronic industries on the other side of town had chosen to live there. Now their attorneys, accountants, realtors had set up new offices there.

Back home he used a gardening spade to dig five holes, about two feet deep, in which he could pour the cement. There was a pile of sand behind the shed he could use to mix. He borrowed an old, almost rotten sheet of ply on which to mix the cement, and went to work to fill up the holes with the grey slurry. He had to cross-brace the poles while the cement dried around them. Dusk was falling when the cross-braces had been installed and the final slurry poured. He left his work for the day and went inside.

On the second day there was fine weather. The sky was a little hazy, but the air was dry and warm. Since the old weatherboarding for the fence was rotting in areas, Jim took advantage of the dry days to buy some new timber palings, and to protect it with copper-based protective which he bought from Chednik's store. By the time he had finished, the fence was almost completely renewed.

When the fence was finished, he spent the next two days out fishing with Sam Shaw. It was good to be out on the water. Except for the following day, when the fog descended once again for a few hours, and the bay was

239

full of congested traffic upriver and the sounds of lowing steamers, the fine weather continued.

On Friday afternoon, a fleet of Optimist dinghies set out from the area of the bay close to the Weepeq Bay Sailing Club, and raced around a course which took them quite close to where they were collecting pots. Sam Shaw noticed how Jim kept his eye on their progress, watched certain of the small craft take advantage of windshifts.

'A couple of those guys are pretty good,' Sam Shaw said. 'Good enough to be asked to attend summer sailing school.'

'That so?'

'Your example, you see. They all want to be like you. Famous old boy of the club.'

Jim returned his attention to the fishing.

The haze had cleared. The pale sun had grown hotter through the day. A long slow swell came in from seaward, rocking the boat gently as they worked, their sleeves rolled up, to bring in the pots with their rustling, iron-blue captives.

Forty-one

Jim painted the rebuilt fence with a final coat of protective. It was already dusk by the time he had finished. He picked up the can of protective and carried it to the old lean-to woodshed where Sam Shaw stored his garden equipment.

It was dark in there, and he had to wait for his eyes to adjust. He put the can and brushes on the shelves. Returning to the house, he paused outside the back door to kick his boots against the wall and remove the mud. As he crossed the threshold he thought he detected an unfamiliar smell, a trace of musk. Inside, Sam Shaw moved about in the kitchen. Jim removed his boots in the outside hall and walked inside in his socks. He walked into the kitchen and saw, in a chair facing away from him, the dark glossy back of a woman's head.

'Look who's here,' said Sam Shaw.

Maria said, 'Hi, Jim.'

The house was unheated. She had kept on her black overcoat. She stood up and hugged him like a sister. He felt oddly embarrassed in front of Sam Shaw, determined at least not to let his feelings show. Only afterwards he realised this was why she had come straight to Sam Shaw's house, knowing perhaps that she was safe.

He did not remember what they talked about, except that in the course of the conversation he tried to pick up, like a dog a scent, the construction of her present life. She was animated. He noticed that she often said 'we'. 'We' went shopping last Sunday.

He assumed that the other part of this 'we' was back at her mother's house. From her conversation, he had already assembled in his own mind a vision of a fresh-faced young lawyer, a city man, already becoming slightly plump.

He let Maria talk. She was animated and happy. He himself said very little. He had hardly any small-talk, and the artificiality of their situation inhibited him. Sam Shaw poured them each a drink, asked her about her work in an attorney's office.

She said finally, 'I really came over to sympathise with you about what's happened.'

He returned her look, nonplussed. There was something he did not understand.

She tried again. 'It must have been terrible for you to get so close to being selected.'

He was no wiser.

She put her hand to her mouth and said, 'Oh God, don't you know?'

He looked at her.

'John Ericson's been selected as helmsman for the defence. It's all over the papers this morning.'

Always, in moments of crisis, something prevented Jim from reacting immediately. He watched her, and it occurred to him, quite slowly, that what she had said conceivably might be so. He felt his stomach knot tight. Maria said, 'I didn't know. Are you all right?'

'Do you still have the newspaper?' he asked.

'No, not here.' She added, 'Back at my mother's house.'

'Could I see it?'

She nodded, frightened at what she had done.

He walked with her to the door. Sam Shaw said nothing. She hugged and kissed Sam Shaw goodbye. Jim put on his shoes and walked out into the cold with her. They went down the path together, saying nothing, and then the several hundred yards along the sea road to Mrs Chednik's store. A 'closed' sign had been placed across the door, but the lights had not yet been turned out.

Maria pressed on the doorbell.

A tall figure came to open the door, a young man in a pullover, with glasses and a small beard and with his necktie loose. Jim was aware of the blue eyes, slightly quizzical, and small moustache. He reminded Jim of a young academic. They studied each other briefly. 'Jock,' said Maria, 'this is Jim Shaw.' Jock's face showed no sign of hostility. A pleasant, confident smile spread across his face. He leaned forward and shook Jim's hand.

Jock stood aside to let them in, and closed the door behind them.

'Something really awful has happened,' said Maria. 'Jim didn't see the papers this morning. Do we still have that copy of the *Washington Post*?'

'Sure.'

Jock, who had stood back a moment, without taking his eyes off Jim, said 'Yeah, upstairs, I'll go and get it.' He turned around and ran up the circular, wooden staircase.

Too many impressions were occurring too quickly. Maria said, 'Do you want to stay a while? Would you like a drink? Mother's upstairs cooking a meal. You're really welcome to eat with us.'

'I'm fine, thanks,' Jim replied.

Jock came down the stairs again in long strides, holding a paper. 'It's right here.'

Jim looked at the headline. It said '*Ericson selected for Cup Defence.*' He read the opening paragraph.

In a surprise announcement today, the defence syndicate for the Americas's Cup defence against the Russian challenge broke the news that they had decided to select John Ericson, the helmsman of the trial horse, Shadow, *as the helmsman and skipper of the America's Cup defender* New World. *Although internal sources say that Jim Shaw on* New World *won a number of races, John Ericson's superiority early on in the races, particularly in the crucial pre-race manoeuvres, led to a careful re-evaluation of the contending helmsmen after the selection trials had ended.*

The announcement that Ericson had been chosen was made by General Marcus Walters, who has acted as the driving force in the syndicate. Tom Stuttaford, the syndicate Chairman, later confirmed that decision.

Jim glanced up. He felt nothing. Maria and Jock looked at him.

Jim heard himself say, absurdly, 'Thanks.'

Maria put a hand on his arm. 'You'll stay for supper, Jim?'

But Jim was already opening the door. Maria released her grip of his arm. Jim closed the door quietly behind him. He started to walk steadily along the coast road towards Sam Shaw's house.

A door hesitantly opened and then closed behind him. He started to walk up the hill. Out there in the dusk, with the lights of the bay starting to shimmer and wink, it suddenly seemed absurd to him. He knew his anger would take several hours to build. In the meantime he was aware of a kind of rapid hysteria, almost of relief, mounting inside him. He felt like laughing uproariously.

The unreality of the situation flooded him. Other explanations of what had happened assailed him. He wondered if the announcement had been misreported. He turned the corner of the hill before the final ascent towards Sam Shaw's house. The lights of the bay seemed closer from up here, brighter, reflected in the water.

Maria's footsteps caught up with him. He felt curiously calm. He turned round to face her as she came up to him.

Her face was in shadow. He tried to peer into this shadow to see her, to find further explanation in her expression. In this unfamiliar territory, he took a step towards her and found she had flung herself into his arms. Her mouth was dry on his, the wet brush of her tears on his cheek.

Her sentimentality evoked the cruelty of his passion. He half lifted her towards the wall, placed her against it, and drove against her strongly with his pelvis, felt her gasp at the blow. Then, suddenly ashamed, he released her. She put her hands over her face.

He left her standing there and walked up to Sam Shaw's house, too ashamed even to apologise.

Forty-two

That evening he piled his things in his old car, said goodbye to Sam Shaw, and drove through the night.

Throughout the journey he tried to work out what might have happened, but every line of thought became more absurd and the events which followed inexplicable. His early numbness gave way to rage. As the dawn started to come up, a pale glow in the rear view mirror of the old Studebaker, his rage finally caught up with him and he could have leapt out and howled his anguish.

The road came up in front of him; its pale coil unwove behind him. The lights of towns moved past on one side or the other. He remembered what Sam Shaw had said to him about lights long ago.

About five o'clock in the morning he stopped and emerged from the car to urinate by the side of the road. The big headlamps of occasional night trucks cut swathes behind him. Otherwise traffic was light. He got back into the car and took to the road again. The car radio burbled, and he thought he might perhaps catch some news of his own demise, but there was no reference to it on the early morning news.

He hadn't eaten since breakfast the previous day, but his stomach was knotted so tight he didn't feel hungry. To try to calm himself down, he pulled up outside a roadside café and went inside. A middle-aged, buxom woman in a blonde wig served him a plate of eggs, sausages, rashers of bacon. He forced himself to eat. He washed it down with a cup of coffee, paid at the till, picked up some things from the car and went round the back to the washrooms. He spread lather on his face and began to shave. Above the lather his eyes were bloodshot from the night's driving. Out of pride he was determined not to look too ragged when he approached the training camp. The routine of shaving cooled him down. He threw cold water over his face, combed his hair, pulled the creaking door closed behind him, and hit the road again.

It was eight-thirty, and the traffic had become heavier. He followed the freeway to the outside of the harbour. The car was running out of gas and he filled it up at a small station.

There was the usual security at the camp when he drew up outside the checking office, but the individual guards had changed. He did not recognise any of the three figures he could discern through the darkened glass. He pressed his horn. A few seconds later the door opened and one of them came over to him. The man who approached him had the familiar walk of guards and policemen, letting his weight pull him forward, his feet splayed. Jim rolled down his window and held up his identity card. The guard glanced at it, then more closely at him, and walked over

245

to his office to consult. Jim looked through the window. One of the three lifted a radio-telephone and began to talk rapidly.

The first guard returned and put his big paws on the window, leaning down. 'Centre says you aren't supposed to be back here for another three days.'

Jim said: 'I've got an urgent meeting.'

'Who with?'

Jim said quietly. 'That's my business.'

The guard stood up and walked over to the office. There was a rapid exchange between the three guards inside which he could not hear. One of the guards, the senior one, a tall, thin, angry man with sergeant's stripes on his sleeve, picked up the radio-telephone. The other two seemed locked in some kind of discussion.

Jim thought, 'It's true. The whole thing is true.' Up to now a part of him had not believed it, a part was still agnostic.

He got out of the car and walked over to the guard hut. He pushed open the door. The two guards stopped talking and turned to look at him. The sergeant ignored him and continued to talk into the telephone.

Jim said: 'Get me a line to Colonel O'Reilly.' Neither of the two guards moved. The third, on the radio-telephone, turned round to give him a brief, angry stare.

The sergeant put down the radio-telephone.

'Colonel O'Reilly was just speaking to me. He says you aren't scheduled to return until Friday. He looks forward to seeing you on Friday. Now I'm asking you to get the hell out of my office.'

'Let me speak to him.'

'Sorry, he's not available.'

'But you've just been speaking to him.'

'That's right. That was a few moments ago. As of now he's not available.'

'Then let me speak to Coach Johnson.'

'Sorry, sir, Coach Johnson is not in charge here. I take my orders from Colonel O'Reilly.'

'Coach Johnson runs the sailing programme.'

'Sir, I don't know anything about the sailing programme. This is a military base and right now you're causing a disturbance of the peace.'

Something inside Jim snapped. He felt himself go cold. The scene in front of him seemed to waver. In part of his mind he realised that he was a little faint from having driven through the night. A headache was spreading over his left temple. He wanted to sleep. The guards watched him with that mixture of cheerful, detached hostility which is the hallmark of a certain type of the military policeman.

'Sergeant,' Jim said evenly, 'Until I'm told otherwise, I'm running the defending yacht, which happens to be on the base. As far as I'm concerned, you're preventing my access. I'm reporting this to the authorities, and then I'm reporting it to the press. Maybe you'd just like to telephone Colonel O'Reilly because I feel it's your duty to let him know the consequences of these actions.'

The sergeant was a tough man, a man not unfamiliar with obstreperous behaviour. But Jim felt, rather than saw, him hesitate.

'Sergeant,' repeated Jim, 'you've got just ten seconds to pick up that radio, and report this. After that I can't answer for the consequences. Those will be Colonel O'Reilly's responsibility. I think you owe it to him to tell him that.'

The sergeant swallowed carefully. His mouth hardened. He didn't like to back down in front of the others. But something about the attitude of this young man worried him.

'Now I'm going to step out of here,' Jim continued amiably enough, 'because what you say exactly is not my business. Perhaps you'd be kind enough to report Colonel O'Reilly's answer to me when you receive it.'

Jim walked out of the hut.

It was already starting to get hot even though it was hardly more than half past nine. He opened his car door, got in, started the car up, and pulled over to the side of the road, so that he was no longer blocking the entrance.

Several other vehicles drove up, were checked by the guardhouse, and were ushered through. Through the window he could make out the shape of the sergeant leaning forward, speaking on the radio-telephone, his back turned away.

It seemed to him that a full five minutes elapsed before the sergeant put down the telephone, and another minute passed before he emerged again from the office.

The sergeant leaned down towards the window. He seemed angry in that white-faced way of those who feel the rules are being flouted.

'Colonel O'Reilly will see you at two-thirty.' He repeated, 'Two three oh.'

'Thank you, sergeant.' Jim put the car into reverse, a little faster than the sergeant expected, and backed away, turned, and drove off. In his mirror he saw the sergeant standing, his hands on his hips.

He had five hours to kill.

Guessing he would not be able to spend the night at the base, he went looking for some hotel accommodation. He found a place down a sidestreet which was cheap and simple, dumped his luggage there, and used the hotel room telephone to try to contact some of the other crew. Eventually he got through to Jack's parents' house, but Jack was out for the day. He tried to obtain Coach Johnson through the switchboard at the base, but the base telephone operator consulted someone else. A man's voice asked, 'Who is it speaking?' 'Jim Shaw,' he replied. There was another silence. 'I'm sorry, Coach Johnson is not available.'

Jim put down the phone. He closed his eyes and his exhaustion overcame him. He slept for several hours, a fitful, uneasy sleep. He woke up with a headache, walked over to the handbasin, threw water over his face to clear his mind a little. To keep alert, he went through the small foyer into the harsh light of the street, walked through the streets of the town for an hour, and killed another half hour in a coffee bar. Then he went back to get his car.

At half past two he was at the gates. The sergeant was off duty. Another guard came to his window, looked at his identity card, and opened the gates.

Inside, a corporal was waiting to take him to see Colonel O'Reilly. Jim noticed that a series of futher security measures were being put into effect around the base. An extra three feet of barbed wire had been added to the high security perimeter fence. Two more watchtowers were being installed inside the base. The telephone connections were being changed. A further group of prefabricated offices had been added. The base seemed alive with the military.

The corporal, a thin man in his early thirties, with glasses and standard army crew cut, led the way to O'Reilly's offices. Several rooms adjacent to O'Reilly's offices, previously empty, had been taken over. The rapid drill of typing came from one. In another a machine, perhaps a photocopier, was being run. The corporal said 'Wait here.' He knocked on Colonel O'Reilly's door, and went in. Jim waited outside. A few minutes later the corporal emerged with a sheaf of papers under his arm and beckoned him in.

O'Reilly was seated behind his desk, working on some papers. Jim stared for what seemed a long time at the smoothly parted hair, at the square hand holding the paper steady while the other wrote a report. Jim waited while O'Reilly continued to write. At last O'Reilly put down his pen and looked towards Jim. He did not stand up.

'Sit down.'

Jim did not take the offered chair. Instead he put the copy of the newspaper in front of O'Reilly, and asked: 'Is this true?'

O'Reilly did not look at the newspaper. He said instead: 'You're causing us a lot of unnecessary trouble.'

Jim indicated the newspaper lying on the desk between them.

'You know about this?'

O'Reilly still did not look at it. He sat back in his chair, bringing his hands together so that his fingertips joined. There must have been ten people working in the offices around him. Jim could hear voices, somewhere a telephone. He wondered what would require this amount of people to administrate.

'Maybe I can explain something to you,' O'Reilly said, 'something that clearly isn't obvious to you.' He paused. Jim heard someone come into the outer office, then leave, closing the door quietly behind him. O'Reilly was studying him without expression. 'This is a military base, and I am its commander. Now, my brief is what happens here, not what I may read in the newspapers. What you tried to do this morning is my immediate concern.'

'What was that?'

'You used threats to gain unauthorised entry,' said Colonel O'Reilly evenly. 'You intimidated one of my soldiers.'

'O'Reilly,' Jim said, 'I am not military personnel, I am not under your command. These little security games are starting to annoy me. As far as I understand it, they're meant to protect us from outsiders. Now they're being used against me. I just happen to have read that I'm no longer the helmsman for the defence. No one has ever said that before. Maybe I could ask you again. What's going on?'

'I repeat to you, that's not my business. As far as I'm concerned, who helms the boat is not my decision. You'll have to take that up with someone else. I'm in charge of base security, and I'm warning you, you're causing considerable trouble. I have nothing more to say.'

'Is Coach Johnson here?'

'I can't answer for him.'

'You have no objection to my looking around?'

'I certainly do. This base is off bounds for the next three days.'

Jim wondered, if he hit O'Reilly, how soon O'Reilly's minions would be at hand to arrest him. Instead he said: 'You're offering no explanation for this newspaper article.'

'I'm not responsible.'

'But your superior, General Walters, made the announcement.'

'I don't question my superiors.'

'You confirm he made the announcement.'

'I'm not in a position to deny it.'

Jim was suddenly tired of fencing with O'Reilly. He had seen enough to gain a clear impression that his fears were justified. He couldn't see any further benefit in trying to get O'Reilly to say something he didn't want to say. Instead he said: 'Thanks, O'Reilly, that's about the best I can get out of you, I guess.'

O'Reilly remained seated. He pulled a paper towards him on which he had been writing, and began once again to fill in columns in his precise hand.

Jim walked towards the door. He closed it behind him. The corporal, who had been sitting at a desk in a nearby annexe, sprang forward. Jim ignored him and walked out of the offices into the quadrangle outside. He heard agitated footsteps behind him. The corporal plucked his elbow. 'I'm under instructions to take you to the gates, sir. I hope you aren't thinking to cause any problems. Sir.'

There were a number of possible inflections on the word 'sir' that made it feel like a loose knife in the corporal's hands. When he added 'sir' to the end of a sentence you felt the knife being passed into your ribs.

Jim let the corporal guide him to the gates. He looked down the quay at the two yachts, hidden, except for their decks, behind their security covers.

'Please,' said the corporal. 'Just move in a straight line with me. That's real good. Just keep moving, sir.'

Back at the hotel, Jim phoned Jack's parents' house. Jack's mother, Mrs Peabody answered in her sure, musical voice. 'I'm so sorry to hear the news, Jim. Jack's back. He's in his room.' Jim heard Mrs Peabody call upstairs. A few moments later, Jack came on the line.

'Did you read the paper?'

'Yes,' Jack said. 'And I heard on the TV news.'

'You any idea what's going on?'

'None,' replied Jack. 'I guess I'm as surprised as you.'

'Why would they do it? I mean, in that way?'

'I just don't know. Look. Do you need any help? Anything I can do? Want me to come up and show some solidarity?'

'I'm OK,' Jim said, and felt, as he did so, an unassailable rush of gratitude. 'Don't worry about me. For the time being I'm trying to find out what's going on.'

'Call me if you need me. Promise me you'll do that.'

Jim went out, walked around the town, stared down at the base from one of the vantage points in the low, surrounding hills. He returned to his hotel and lay down on the cover of the bed.

The phone rang. He assumed it must be Jack ringing back. But it was Coach Johnson, sounding brisk and matter-of-fact.

'I got your number from Jack. I heard from the base that you were causing some real trouble there today.'

'I was looking for an explanation.'

'About the announcement?'

'That's right, about the announcement.'

There was a silence on the end of the line.

'What do you want to know?'

'Just about everything.'

There was another pause.

'OK,' Coach Johnson said. 'I'll square with you. Ever since John Ericson came to sail *Shadow*, there has been a pressure group above me who has favoured him as the helmsman. You're familiar with the arguments. He's perhaps the most successful big-boat sailor in the world. He comes with a complete team. He's got a long track record. The only way I could stop his automatic selection was to ask him to come and trial-sail *Shadow*. It was a gamble. I gambled you'd beat him. I guess you proved I was right.'

Jim's mind started to race. He would take a long time

to come to terms with what Coach Johnson had just said. Instead he replied 'So what happened?'

'What happened is that this lobby wasn't persuaded by the result. They thought it best if Ericson sailed for us.'

'Why?'

Coach Johnson sighed almost audibly.

'Jim, do you realise what a goddamn trouble-maker you are, how much you put people's backs up? You're not part of the establishment. They don't mind that. It's just that you act as if that's a hell of a good thing.' Coach Johnson had said more than he wanted to. He added: 'Just take that as read, will you?'

Jim said nothing.

'They look after their own. John Ericson is one of them. His father's one of the biggest defence contractors in the country. He's on first-name terms with the highest military, with the political establishment. I shouldn't be telling you all this.'

'I'm glad you are.'

There was a pause. At length Coach Johnson said: 'OK, just let me add one other thing. I also have more information than you do in other areas. I'm talking about John Ericson. About his medical condition, that is. Let me put it like this. It's pretty damn obvious to those involved, those who've seen him recently, that he's not in a position to run a defence. I don't know whether it's psychological or physical, or maybe a combination of those things, but what he needs is a long rest. You understand what I'm saying?'

'I think so,' said Jim.

'Do me a favour and just lie low. Let things work out on their own. John Ericson's undergoing extensive medical tests. When that's over my guess is they'll have no choice but to reinstate you.'

Jim felt his tiredness close in on him again. The pain above his eyes increased. For several seconds he considered Coach Johnson's words. He knew he had more information than he had hoped for. But a devil inside him wanted something more. Jim said: 'I think I see the picture. But there's one thing that puzzles me.'

'Shoot.'

Jim chose his words carefully.

'Whose side are you on?'

There was a pause on the other end of the line. Then, with a hardly audible click, the line went dead.

Forty-three

In the booking lobby of the small hotel the surprised clerk was told Jim Shaw would no longer be needing the room. His business in the town had finished, and he had to be off. He wished to pay his one night's overstay for the use of the hotel room and the telephone.

He still had nearly three days of holiday, and he wanted to get back as soon as possible.

Because of the extra traffic on the road during daylight hours, the journey took him an hour longer. He called his grandfather from a callbox, told him he would be arriving late, not to wait up for him. The rest of the journey was without mishap. He arrived back at 11:40 in the evening, saw that Sam Shaw was still working in the kitchen, and rapped several times on the knocker.

Sam Shaw peered out through the window, pulled the lock on the door. 'You must be tired as hell. I'm just about to brew up a cup of coffee. You look awful.'

Sam Shaw pushed aside the nets, put the kettle on the stove.

When he was seated in the kitchen Jim tried to explain to Sam Shaw what was happening, that Ericson had a powerful lobby behind him, and this lobby seemed to have won in the selection of the helmsman. He also recounted what Coach Johnson had said. With a pang of shame he refrained from telling Sam Shaw what his final question to Coach Johnson had been.

The old man did not say much. He listened while he worked on some lobster pots that a strong riptide had dislodged and which had been damaged by being dragged a long way across the bottom.

Finally Sam Shaw asked: 'What do you think of Ericson as a helmsman?'

'Best I've ever seen,' replied Jim, and then added, 'except for Illich.'

'You really think he's good?'

'He's not just good, he's great. He's considered to be the best big-boat helmsman in the world. He really deserves that reputation.'

'You wouldn't mind being beaten by him?'

'It's an honour to be matched against him.'

'You really mean that?'

'Why would I lie about it?'

Sam Shaw paused to consider his grandson for a while. He'd wondered what lay underneath that exterior, what drove him. Sam Shaw did not delude himself that his grandson was a likeable man – he was too concentrated, too deadly for that. But somehow Jim had attained a psychological attitude of detachment. Sam Shaw asked himself, was this something Coach Johnson had implanted in him, or something which was there already?

Once, a long time before, Sam Shaw had read about a mystic who had advocated that one should be, at the same time, both wholly involved and wholly detached. He didn't know whether this applied to his grandson's attitude. Instead he repeated 'You look tired. You should get some sleep.'

The morning was bright. A few small specks of cloud, as insubstantial as lace, hung in the sky. The air was so still you could hear every small wavelet on the beach.

Jim, waking late for the first time for almost a year, could hear the rowlocks on Sam Shaw's skiff creaking as he rowed the boat down the coast to the fishing grounds.

Jim dressed, made himself a cup of coffee and some toast, and went on a run along the sea shore.

He needed it to clear his head. He took the route along the beach. The tide was out and the sand was hard where it was still moist at the water's edge. He turned inland and followed a route through the small park at the water's edge. The route took him through Highton, and then past his old school. A new wing had been added, a science block with large wooden window frames and a dedication copper plaque which was too far away for him to read.

He followed the route inland, aiming to do a full circle and emerge on a hillside at the back of Sam Shaw's house. As he came down the hill he was able to see both the foreshore and, in staccato glimpses, the few straggling buildings that lay along the seafront there. Occasionally he caught sight of the grey-tiled roof and blue window frames of Sam Shaw's house. He turned and ran inland. The morning, though sunny, was nevertheless cold. He felt its chill in his lungs. Between individual elm trees he could see the sea, far below, hardly a ripple on its surface.

He could just discern a solitary figure walking along the foreshore, a figure almost wholly indistinguishable. He detoured out into the road so that he did not lose sight of it. A green pick-up van, emerging from a sidestreet, accelerated out and almost knocked him over. He sprang back onto the pavement and began to increase his pace downhill, running fast, up and over the sidewalks, cutting corners. A small wiry dog, excited by the drubbing of his feet, darted out of a back alley and chased him for fifty yards, snapping at his heels. He turned another street corner and began to sprint downhill towards the shore.

The streets here were short and confusing. The area had been built up in the last few years, and there were extra roads. He swung round a corner and realised he was in a cul-de-sac. Two more streets ran parallel to the hillside. Finally he found a downhill track which led past the backs of several rows of delapidated houses. Back on more familiar territory, he could find his way. Now he was approaching the foreshore fast. He used a short cut down the hill along the pedestrian path, descended a flight of stone steps. He came out at about three hundred yards along the foreshore, panting hard, and looked right and left.

There was no sign of her. He started to run along the foreshore in the direction he guessed she would have taken, looking up the streets as he passed. It was hopeless. Only an irrational expectation kept him moving. All the streets he looked up were empty. He felt the breath racketing in his lungs. The rapid sprint down the hill had exhausted him. He was forced to slow down.

He was about to give up when he saw that she was walking parallel to him, a little higher up the hill. There was no obvious way he could reach her on this stretch. He kept moving along the foreshore parallel to her. She seemed to have stopped, changed direction. He lost sight of her and was struck by the thought that now she must have seen him and, in order to avoid him, had turned inland.

At last he found a small street that connected the two levels. He ran up it and reached the upper level. Turning around, he saw that she was hardly more than twenty feet away. Maria had stopped and was watching him with an odd look, without surprise or consternation.

Finally she said, 'You really are pretty good at this, aren't you?' And he realised, as she said it, that there was no forgiveness here, and that was hardly surprising. He stopped in front of her, waiting for several moments to catch his breath. He said: 'Can I offer you a cup of coffee?'

He watched her try to harden her expression against a grimace or a smile. He said, 'I know a little place just up the hill here. One cup of coffee isn't going to hurt anyone.'

Maria said: 'The last one hurt quite a lot.'

She walked up the hill with him, but he could find no way of making polite conversation. They found the coffee shop, Fabrizi's, and went inside.

There were a couple of old men in the corner, sitting opposite each other. The milk-shake machine was as he had remembered it, except that a notice on brown paper, with 'out of use' scrawled across it in blue ink, had been taped to the pull.

It was self-service. Jim ordered and collected two coffees. He sat down at the table with them.

'What's happening with the sailing?' Maria asked.

'I don't know exactly. I managed to get confirmation that Ericson has been announced as the helmsman.'

Maria studied him for a while. Jim felt, remembered, that he sometimes resented this intensity of interest.

'Then it's true.'

Jim said nothing, stirring his coffee. Maria watched him. In another part of the building music was playing, but the melody had been abstracted by the walls, and all one could hear was the beat, like an animal stirring.

'Why aren't you up there fighting?' Maria asked.

Jim shrugged. 'Not much I can do.'

'But you beat him, didn't you?'

He could see doubt in her eyes, real consternation now, even a flash of anger.

'In the final races, by nine to three.'

'But that's disgusting. How come you look so . . . relaxed about it.'

'There's nothing I can do. I told you. It's out of my hands.'

'But then why did you go up yesterday? Weren't you going to confront them?'

'I went up to find out what was going on. They confirmed that Ericson has been selected.'

Maria was angry. 'Am I missing something here?'

'No,' said Jim, 'I don't think so.'

Maria took a deep breath. 'You're going to let them walk all over you? Just like that? Without doing anything? Without raising so much as your little finger?'

'Now wait a minute, Maria. Let's be mature about this.' Jim was starting to enjoy himself. 'Sailing's just a sport, you know.'

For a moment he thought she was going to hit him. She controlled herself.

'From what I can see, John Ericson's just a spoiled brat. He's had it all his own way. Now he's using his contacts to get himself the place that rightfully belongs to you.'

'There is something I didn't tell you. Ericson over-played his hand in the trial races. He pushed himself beyond his limits. He's getting treatment, but it's likely that he won't be sailing anything for the next few months.'

Maria considered this for several moments. 'It still stinks.' She looked at him. 'Doesn't it?'

'Yes,' he said.

'Are you sure you're not too complacent?'

'Maria,' said Jim quietly, 'if you think I'm complacent, that's fine by me. I've worked pretty hard to get this far. But I really don't get agitated about things I can't help.'

Maria watched him for a while. 'I guess that's true. Maybe that's what keeps you sane. On the other hand,' she added, 'maybe you just couldn't give a damn about anything very much.'

'Look,' said Jim. 'You've asked me quite a lot of questions, and you've offered me a certain amount of advice on how to run my life. Can I ask you a couple of things?'

She looked at him blankly. Jim pressed on. He said: 'You're definitely marrying this guy?'

Her eyes gave nothing away.

'Tell me it's none of my business,' he suggested.

She didn't answer for a moment. He could see she was considering whether to leave, so he continued neverthe-less. 'You thinking of running away again, Maria? All you have to do is just back smartly out of that door and you'll leave me behind for good.'

He thought, this must be it. There was no way Maria was going to sit here and take this.

But Maria was still sitting there, as if nothing had happened. After a while she said: 'What's the alternative?'

Forty-four

'The alternative,' Jim suggested, 'is that you marry me.'

'Why would I want to do that?'

'Because you take sailing so seriously.'

'You think that kind of flippancy is going to do your case any good?'

'It couldn't do it any worse.'

A group came into the shop, noisily, a husband, wife and three children. They sat next to the counter. The children scampered between the chairs.

He saw that she was serious, and felt for the first time a lightening of tension.

'Why don't you come back with me?' he asked.

'Where would I stay. In the camp?'

'I'd find you a place in the town.'

'And you'd sneak up occasionally and see me. When no one was looking.'

'I'd live with you.'

'But don't you have to stay in the camp?'

'They didn't allow me back in the camp this week. I figure I have a legitimate reason for sleeping out if I want to, on the grounds that I can't rely on being let back in.'

'That'd be telling them.'

'It'd only be for two months.'

'If it was only two months, maybe I could manage it. But it won't be. You'll never leave the water. It's the one thing in your life. I don't deny you that. It's your own choice. I just don't want to be part of it.'

Maria stood up. Fabrizi, the old gentleman, came to the door to escort Maria, asking her to give his compliments to her mother. Jim walked out into the street with her.

'I don't understand you,' he said. 'One moment you're telling me not to let Ericson walk all over me, then you're saying I'm too close to the water.'

They turned a corner. Maria turned to face him. She

pulled his face down to hers. Her lips parted on his. He felt himself drawn down into their softness.

They walked down to the foreshore, his arm round her waist, past the rows of old houses, the deserted factories, towards an area of sand dunes. The air was warm. There were few people about. They lay down on a patch of rough couch grass. He kissed her. She responded. But there was something nervous, perhaps even cold, in her response to his further efforts. He fumbled with her dress but somehow she became heavy, she resisted him.

He grew increasingly angry, but he could not break down her resistance. He said 'What's wrong?'

'Nothing,' Maria replied. Her eyes narrowed, and he steadied himself for a display of temper.

Finally she said, 'You're an American, of course.'

He stared at her. 'So are you.'

She shook her head.

'You think when I say I'm from a Russian family it's just a joke. It's just something I'm supposed to shrug off.'

Jim remembered what Sam Shaw had told him about Agnes Chednik and her background. A Russian trading family who came from Estonia, their home for generations.

'I don't get it.'

'You will,' said Maria. She stood up. She brushed the grass and sand off her dress.

For a few moments he lay there, staring up at her, while she looked down at him.

He stood up. He said: 'I'm sorry if I've offended you.'

'You haven't offended me. I have to tell Jock. I don't know what he'll do.'

For the first time he felt a trace of sympathy for Jock Henshaw.

He was at a loss. She slipped her hand around his arm and they walked back. It was early afternoon. Maria said, 'I only went out to post a letter for Ma. I've got to go back and tell her about my change of plans, too.'

They parted at the bottom of the hill. Jim walked up to his grandfather's house, hardly daring to think.

When he heard Jim and Maria were intending to marry, Sam Shaw let out an uncharacteristic whoop. He danced a hornpipe around the kitchen. It seemed to Jim that marriage, a sober and solemn ceremony of great portent between two people, was also a cause of temporary madness in all those closely connected, not only in Russians.

Sam Shaw insisted that Jim should do no more work that holiday, that he and Maria should take the car and go away for a few days.

'You won't have another opportunity.' It was an order. 'It'll do you both a lot of good. I'm insisting.'

Sam Shaw went upstairs. Jim heard him dragging something across the bare floorboards. He came back with a brown parcel in his hands. He put eight hundred dollars, packed tightly into an old brown envelope, on the table in front of Jim.

'Just take it and go. You're only young once.'

'Maria's got to break the news to Jock Henshaw. And her mother doesn't take too kindly to breaking off engagements either. I think it's best if I give her a bit of time to sort things out before we take off anywhere.'

'Keep it anyway,' Sam Shaw insisted, 'for when you do.'

Jim knew how hard he'd had to slave to save that sum. He couldn't accept it. But he couldn't refuse it either, for Sam Shaw's sake.

He said 'thanks' and hugged the old man, aware again of his frail bones, and at the same time of the force of Sam Shaw's will.

Two days later, the newspaper headline was brief:
AMERICA'S CUP HELMSMAN RESIGNS.
Jim studied the text carefully over his cup of coffee.

The America's Cup helmsman John Ericson, who was set to replace Jim Shaw in the defence against Russia in two months' time, announced that he is retiring from the America's Cup due to health problems.

The announcement was made through Ericson Traction

Corporation, at the company headquarters yesterday. A spokesman for Mr Ericson said that he was honoured to be chosen for the task, and that he had not sought the job, but that he had overstressed himself during the past five years' hard campaigning on his successful Maxi-yacht Ghost Train 5. *The spokesman continued that although the selectors had decided John Ericson was the better helmsman, he wished Jim Shaw, the other helmsman, every possible success.*

Syndicate spokesmen confirmed that they had reluctantly accepted John Ericson's resignation, but they felt that Jim Shaw, the runner-up in the competition, was nevertheless a helmsman of great promise. Other sources, of a more informal kind, revealed today that the syndicate's main worry concerning Jim Shaw was that he is a very individualistic, even temperamental young man. He does not take kindly to the military discipline which the syndicate feel is necessary to prosecute a successful defence against the forthcoming Russian challenge. The Russian challenge, these sources say, has the full backing and technical support of the Russian military, and a matching effort is required by the American side. They say Shaw has already been in direct conflict with the authorities who are running the technical back-up, and that he objects to the security procedures which are now being enforced in the final run-up to the defence.

Jim Shaw put down his coffee and walked out into the small garden. The sunny weather was continuing. The bay was blue and serenely quiet. Sam Shaw's skiff was a small dot to the north.

He opened the gate and walked down the stone steps to Mrs Chednik's store. The small bell rang as he pressed open the door. He had hardly time to adjust himself to the darkness of the shop's interior before Maria was in his arms, her mouth was on his and his head was pleasantly swimming.

A moment later Agnes Chednik was holding both of them, spattering them with her tears, and Jim realised what was meant by the warmth of a Russian family.

Maria was saying 'Congratulations, Jim,' he guessed about being back as helmsman, and Agnes Chednik was congratulating them both about their marriage. At least that was what he assumed. There was such a great deal of crying and commiseration, tears and laugher, that it was difficult to know precisely what was being said or meant. To Jim, raised in a lonely, masculine household, this was something new, not unpleasant, but something he would take a little time to get used to.

Book Three

Forty-five

While Agnes Chednik spattered Jim Shaw and her daughter with her tears, a small task force was approaching the United States coast.

The group consisted of three main ships and several smaller ones. At its centre steamed the *Moscow*, a converted landing ship, carrying no weapons now except for two helicopter pads, but with a quarter deck bursting with sensors and sophisticated telemetry. She was driven by her two Vorok turbines, her diesel held in reserve. These two power-plants, discharging through her propellers, threw out a powerful wake above which the seagulls turned.

Accompanying her, at port and starboard stations, but a little aft as if out of deference to her important cargo, were two Udaloy destroyers, more overtly offensive, with their missile batteries hidden by thick covers. Further back were three supply ships; two tankers, and a second ship carrying spares appropriate for the small task force.

Visibility was good, but a south-westerly force six wind had been blowing on the beam all day and had brought in an uncomfortable, quartering swell. The two Udaloy destroyers, almost beam on to the sea, rolled slightly, but the advanced stabilisers on the *Moscow* minimised roll. Beside her stately solidity, the motion on the smaller support vessels was sufficiently pronounced to be uncomfortable.

The force moved in towards the sunset, towards a horizon which, in the final hour of daylight, was turning a deep shade of purple.

For all its great size, the *Moscow* had almost a skeleton crew, no more than were strictly necessary to take the ship to America and back. Her usual component of marines and their equipment had been cleared to make way for her current mission and personnel. The weapons store rooms had been emptied and, in some cases, reformed entirely to suit its new task. Within the hull of the *Moscow*, there lived another community of approximately two hundred and fifty persons, mostly engineers, technicians, highly skilled workers, with machine rooms, independent generators, and a set of workshop and storage rooms which contained complex engineering equipment.

As at the centre of a termite mound, living under the permanent disclosure of racks of artificial light, this community worked in shifts at the complex tasks of placing its systems in readiness. Apart from the rumble of the ship's turbines, the main background noise was the whine of the ventilation system designed to carry away the heat produced by the racks of lighting, and to regulate the temperature and humidity exactly to the task of the work undertaken there.

A key to this frenetic activity lay in the largest cabin of all, in the aft sections of the ship, above the engines. Here, attended by a dozen artisans each, like queen ants, two large yachts were stored. Entering the central cabin from the technical director's office complex, an arresting sight met the eye. Raised several feet from the ground so that their keels could be worked on, positioned alongside one another, bow to bow and stern to stern, were two sculptures of shining symmetry, highly tuned from several years of exhaustive trialling and racing. Several groups of men burnished the hulls using sanders with soft heads. Beside the yachts lay some eight masts each, several of which were formed of titanium, and several (hidden under security covers) of a new alloy which had only recently found use in the most modern tactical bombers of the Russian air force. Alongside these stood a series of spare sections for repair. A rigging bay was situated nearby, and adjacent to that a machinery room which contained the lathes and cutting machines used for the sophisticated materials deployed on the structures and working mechanisms of the yachts.

The second largest bay, aside from that which contained the two sailing vessels, was the cutting loft for the

268

sails. Like a star with its satellites, this large bay also had its ancillary rooms, where machines were used for cutting and repairing. A specialised computer etched out the precise geometrical shape of panels of cloth for the sails. In a store room close by, kept dark in order to minimise damage from ultra-violet light, were racks of sail-cloth, enough for fully thirty new suits of sails for each yacht. Each bale was stored in its own sealed pack, and the entire room was kept at a precise temperature of 12 degrees Centigrade and at constant humidity.

Every four hours a shift was changed, each shift working eight hours. This was maintained throughout the twenty four hour day, relentlessly, so that the community – aside from senior personnel – lived almost entirely independently of the daylight hours, like the crew of a space capsule or a nuclear submarine.

The *Moscow* was unusual in its accommodation. The members of its community lived in their own small rooms, with as little as two or three to a room, and sometimes – for the senior scientists or technicians – the luxury of a single room. For this purpose a great deal of the crew accommodation had to be changed, new partitions created, new offices and even leisure facilities installed. A number of the technicians and scientists on board had been seconded from the space programme or military research, and were used to a level of luxury not found elsewhere.

'Breathe in,' said Natalia Lishkaya.

Ivan Illich breathed in through his flared nostrils. Dr Liskaya placed the instrument on the right of his chest and admonished him again. 'Breathe.'

Illich's chest rose and fell.

Dr Lishkaya was often troubled in her examinations of the helmsman. She tried to dismiss her own nervousness as a residue of the adolescent cult of hero-worship. A grown woman, showing nervousness in front of a mere child – it was absurd.

She let the stethoscope fall back to rest across her ample

bosom. As if in compensation for her nervousness, her instructions were sharp and clear.

'Turn round.'

She tapped his shoulders, directed her hand to the area of his left kidney. 'Still painful?' He had strained a muscle here in the recent training programme. Illich merely drew down the corners of his mouth. 'Here?' She tapped and saw him flinch.

'It hurts still,' she said matter-of-factly. Her hands mapped out the area of strain.

'Your exercises?'

He nodded. He was conscientious, she knew, in the matter of maintaining fitness. His body, nevertheless, bore the traces of numerous scars, rope burns. Sailing at this level punished the body remorselessly. She noticed his hands, the thumbs pronounced, the fingers strong. For some reason they perturbed her. She turned her attention away.

She was in front of him now. She glanced at his eyes, finding them distant, without obvious response.

'You must continue with the special exercises until further notice.' The eyes also troubled her. Dr Lishkaya folded her stethoscope and placed it in its hand-made wooden box.

To do so, she bent forward slightly and noticed, as if from far away, that Illich's slender hands adorned her breasts. For a curious moment she felt that, just as she had physically examined him, so now she herself was being physically examined, and a part of her sensed that this was appropriate.

There are certain times in a person's life when a moment's hesitation can dictate the course of events. Dr Natalia Lishkaya did, at that moment, reach towards his hands in order firmly to remove them, but by the time her own hands had travelled that unbridgeable gulf, they had lost their direction. Instead of removing his hands, her own hands merely settled on his, reinforcing their presence. Her mind swam.

If she had been a reflective woman, Natalia Lishkaya

would perhaps have noted the perfect timing of Illich's response, his intuitive understanding of the moment at which to assert himself. She might have reflected on the subtleness and casual authority with which he had chosen to strike back, to reverse the roles. Instead she watched his hand gently disengage and begin to undo her apron. He turned her so that he could undo the buttons at the back of her dress. Like a good patient, her own hands assisted him.

Forty-six

Maria turned over and faced Jim in bed.

Jim lay with his eyes open, staring at the ceiling. Outside he could hear the faint slap of the waves on the wooden piles of the jetty.

Maria propped herself up on her elbow. Her face was indistinguishable against the bright light of the window behind her. She said: 'Do you really know what you want in life?'

Jim didn't like the way this conversation was going. His life had a direction, a goal. For the first time in his career, he felt his existence had meaning. He didn't want to even discuss it.

'To beat Ivan Illich,' he replied warily.

Maria paused, pursed her lips, considered.

'And what do you want in the long term?'

'To marry you.'

'In that order?'

Jim detected an edge in that last question, enough of an edge to roll over onto his side and face her.

'You'd prefer a different order?'

'Yes, I'd prefer a different order.'

'Can I marry you now, and then beat Ivan Illich?'

With a sudden movement Maria swung her legs away and with her back to him, threw on a dressing gown. She went to the window. She looked out.

'Don't make a joke of this, Jim.'

'I'm not.'

'I'm not prepared to marry you until you're finished with sailing.'

Jim paused. Her statement took the breath out of his body.

'But sailing is my life.'

'No it isn't, Jim. Competition is your life. Beating the other guy is your life.'

'I'm starting to lose you. Of course beating the other guy is part of winning.'

But Maria was relentless. 'It isn't part of it, Jim. It's the whole thing. That's what drives you.'

'It's what drives a lot of people. I just happen to be . . . quite good at it.'

People were starting to move about in the street below. Far away a motor car started. The sun streamed through the window, turning the edges of Maria's dressing gown a glowing red.

'Ever since you came back from that summer sailing school with Jack Peabody, ever since Coach Johnson took control of your life, you changed.'

'Yeah, I started to build up confidence. I started to grow up.'

'Grow up?' Maria stared out of the window. The words seemed to hang there, turning like dust in the morning sunlight. 'You think winning is growing up?'

Jim bit his lip, perplexed and angry. 'So what do you think I should do? Give it all up?'

She was silent. Her quietness unnerved him. She said slowly: 'I want you to grow up.'

'OK, OK. Can I just try to win one cup first, just one tiny little cup?'

'You're trying to make a joke out of this again, Jim.'

Maria left the room. When angry, she could move as

quietly as a cat. He stared at the ceiling again, bit his lip, shook his head from side to side in perplexity.

The Russian fleet had arrived.

The three main ships, *Moscow*, *Zamyatin*, *Mikhail Gorbachev*, anchored off the main roads, in the arm of the bay. *Zamyatin* and *Mikhail Gorbachev* had taken a different route to the main convoy. The two missile destroyers *Uzbekan* and *Salud*, like waiting watchdogs, anchored half a mile away to the east, closer to the protective sweep of the shoreline. Half a mile to the west, the tankers and support ships swung at anchor.

Within two days of anchoring, the *Moscow* had opened her doors. Engineers swarmed on the surface, locking and welding the parts together, laying down an even non-slip surface. The flame of welders' torches could be seen at night as two large derricks were fixed in place. Two further pontoon arms, each ninety feet, were positioned to provide a breakwater against the swells that traversed the bay in the fresh westerlies. Fast patrol boats, launched from the deck of the *Zamyatin*, moved between the three ships, transferring stores and personnel. The Helix helicopters of the *Mikhail Gorbachev* hovered over the bay, collecting local information on water temperature, salinity, the precise shape of the sea-bed, the tidal shifts about the bay, and the predominant wave-patterns. Weather balloons were released each day.

It was reliably reported that a surveillance satellite had been rerouted over the bay, and that there was an intensive burst of signal traffic between the *Zamyatin* and the satellite at each orbit.

On the fourth day two yachts were brought out on motorised cradles, as helpless and beautiful as flying ants, and lowered into the protected water of the little artificial harbour at the stern of the huge amphibious ship. Several fast patrol boats kept at bay the spectator craft and television launches which tried to record the event.

Forty-seven

The arrival of the Russian ships seemed to unsettle Ernie. One evening, returning to Maria's flat, Jim saw his tall figure facing out to the distant shapes of the grey warships anchored in the bay.

'So what's your angle on the Russians, Ernie?'

Ernie turned round, surprised. He smiled: 'They're our opponents.'

'Come on, it's more than that.'

They started travelling in the same direction. Ernie was silent as they walked along the street.

'We're in this together. Unload.'

'Fuck you, whitey,' Ernie said quietly, without apparent malice.

They turned a corner. A strong shaft of sunlight between the buildings hit them, so that they had to shield their eyes. They crossed the street and walked in the shade on the other side. There were few people about. Ernie started to talk.

'My father was a union official. He struggled to put me through college. He was an idealist, I guess. I was brought up to believe in the natural rights of man. I joined an organisation called the League of Concern. I believed all that stuff about the brotherhood of man. I wore out my shoes going from door to door, raising funds.'

Ernie lapsed into reflective silence again as they walked.

'Look,' Ernie said eventually. 'I may as well give you some background. Let's hook over to my place. Got a few things you might be interested to hear.'

'OK.'

They turned away from the beach front and started to walk inland. Jim asked: 'Do you know of a guy called Sam Hickstead? He's an expert on the Russians.'

Ernie turned his face, and Jim noticed the curious blankness of intense thought, as if a nerve had been touched.

'Senator Sam Hickstead?'

'Yeah.'

'Sure, I've heard of him. He a friend of yours?'

'No, he's not a friend.'

The flat was reached through a side alley in the older part of town. The common entrance hall was a clutter of mail and bills for the four units.

'Typical students,' Ernie said.

The door was unlocked by a plastic cardkey. A small green light glowed.

'I installed this myself,' Ernie said. 'Simple paranoia. Better security than a key. If someone does get through, it registers on a little memory disk. Every time I come in I wipe the memory disk.'

He closed the door behind them.

The flat was small, neatly kept. On one wall was a group of textbooks on computer software. Two computer screens, one above the other, stood on a table. Against the wall, stored like books, was a library of computer disks.

'Why are you so nervous about security, Ernie?'

Ernie smiled raffishly. 'My father told me there's only one thing people hate more than a dumb nigger. That's an intelligent nigger.'

'Boy, you got it bad.'

Ernie was already through in the adjoining room, searching for something.

'Look,' he called from the other room, 'let's leave my psychological state out of it, OK? That wasn't why I asked you to my humble pad. Just tell me why you asked me about Senator Hickstead.'

A car started outside, revving up down the street. Sunlight poured through a small skylight above Jim, placing a gold oblong on the nearest wall.

'He makes me nervous,' Jim said.

Ernie was suddenly in the doorway, all attention. 'He makes *you* nervous?'

'Sure.'

275

'You know him personally?' Ernie asked.

'We met a couple of times.'

'So why does he make you nervous?'

'Look who's asking all the questions now.'

'Come on, whitey. Unload. We're all in this together.'

'I think maybe he wants us to lose.'

'Why?'

'To make the Russians look good.'

Ernie's face went blank for a moment. Then he said: 'Why don't you just sit down. I got some things to look up.'

He went back into the small adjoining room. Jim could hear him shifting cases.

'You asked me about the Russians,' Ernie called through, a few minutes later. 'I'm interested in their attitude to other groups, other races.' He was searching methodically, moving about the room from one place to another. Through the partly opened doorway Jim could see him kneeling beside a storage trunk, lifting small boxes of computer storage disks. Ernie continued to discourse amiably while he worked.

'There are huge racial tensions inside the Russian empire. Estonia is a European country on the Baltic Sea. Uzbechistan is purely Asian. There are, if anything, greater cultural differences between the groups which make up the country than between, say, black and white Americans. You better believe it. At least we talk the same language. The Russians are trying to hold a huge tract spanning parts of western Europe and the most eastern outposts of Asia.'

Ernie came back into the room carrying a small recorder and several storage disks. He put the recorder down on the table and clicked in a disk. Quickly he punched several buttons.

The voices were indistinct at first. He turned up the volume.

'We missed a couple of sentences,' Ernie commented. 'But it doesn't matter, you can pick up the thread.'

It was an interview. The interviewee's voice was familiar.

'Senator,' the interviewer was saying, 'as this current administration nears its end, you are considered to be perhaps the dominant figure outside the government. You have more experience of political life than virtually anyone in Washington. I'm going to put to you a potentially loaded question.'

'Fire away.'

'You talk as if helping the Russians is the most important thing we can do, that if we look after them we look after ourselves. Is that a fair summary?'

'Yes, I think it is. We live in a frightening world, a world which could quite easily descend towards chaos. In the twentieth century, we have depended upon a confrontation between the superpowers. Frankly, as we move into the twenty-first century we are groping for a new world order. I for one think this should be built on collaboration rather than confrontation.'

'But, Senator, what exactly does that mean?'

'We're starting to explore that now.'

'Do these initiatives have the support of the government?'

'Governments are transitory. We're talking about broader, deeper movements in geopolitics.'

'You don't have the support of the government?'

For the first time Jim heard a sharper, colder side to Hickstead's voice.

'I don't know whether those of us who are engaged in this dialogue have the support of this current government or not. As I say, this is far longer term than any span of government.'

'Senator, your critics say that you are conducting foreign policy independent of any presidential election mandate. They say you have taken advantage of a fluid stage in world politics to step into the vacuum of foreign policy.'

'Is that what they say?' Senator Hickstead asked, and he sounded amused.

'Do you agree with them?'

'This is a free country. I can talk with whoever I like.'

'Including the Russians?'

'Including the Russians.'

'Senator Hickstead, thank you for your time once again.'

'You're welcome.'

Ernie switched off the machine. 'That was all I recorded on that one. I got other disks. In fact I got a whole box full of them. I'll just look a couple of them up.' He disappeared into another room. Jim heard the sound of furniture being moved, a heavy box being lifted onto the floor.

'Put on some coffee,' Ernie called through the open doorway.

Jim went to the kitchen. It was neatly laid out, precise. He filled a kettle with water and put it on the gas cooker.

Ernie came through with more disks. He placed several of them in small piles beside the player. 'Russia is my obsession. I just try to find out as much as I can, whenever I get the chance. Anything I can get on foreign policy relations.' A voice coughed out of the machine. Ernie turned the knobs and, while the fastback made a sound like an angry squirrel, doubled back on an interview.

'Here, listen to this.'

The machine seemed to give a short, metallic rasp. The voice of an interviewer said: 'Senator, what is it about foreign relations that interests you?'

'The slow march of history.' Hickstead's tone was familiar. 'The apparently inexorable nature of developments.'

'You're a distinguished observer of the relations between America and Russia. In a sense, you're this country's most experienced and consistent expert in the foreign policy field.'

'You're very kind. Consistency is a word I take very seriously. As do the Russians.'

'Some people would credit you with most of the behind-the-scenes diplomatic activity between ourselves and the Russian political community.'

'They're entitled to their view.'

'In dealings with Russia, how do you regard your

opposite numbers?'

'I have the greatest of respect for them.'

'Why in particular?'

They don't live from moment to moment, like politicians in the US. That means their foreign policy is longer-sighted than ours. That's a huge advantage. Long-sightedness in foreign policy is everything.'

'Could you say that's what you've been trying to do in American politics, introduce this element of long sight?'

'That's a pretty good summary of my position.'

'That's on the wider level. What do you feel about your opposite numbers as people?'

'Again, deep respect. They know where they're going.'

'That respect seems to be mutual, doesn't it? It seems to most commentators that you are the person the Russians most like to speak to.'

'I'm sometimes criticised for participating in foreign policy without a direct electoral mandate. What you have to remember is that, to a Russian politician, the term of an American Presidency is relatively short. Four years, even a two-term eight years, is short. No sooner have they got to know an administration, worked out a relationship with it, than it is replaced by another. They're constantly looking towards us for consistency, and the American political process does not provide it for them. That's why there's some kind of role for someone like me.'

'But the Russians have elections, too.'

'Their elections don't much affect their élite.'

Ernie moved towards the machine and switched it off.

'The rest of that interview is just platitudes.' He put in another disk, pressed a switch. The machine gave a high-pitched whine as it rewound a tape. Ernie was moving fast, Jim noted, with that calm swiftness of a man in the grip of an obsession. He noticed that Ernie's coffee remained untouched beside his chair.

The high-pitched whine came to a halt. Two clicks of the switch, another cough.

'Listen to this,' Ernie admonished him.

The sound on this tape was blurred. It was not a formal

interview. Instead there was a great deal of noise, as if someone were blowing across the top of a microphone. It sounded like a lot of people in a hall.

'I recorded this myself,' Ernie said, 'at a foreign policy group discussion at Princeton University when I was doing my Master's. Senator Hickstead was the main guest speaker. I was in the audience. It's a lousy recording.'

Someone was talking in the background, almost indistinguishable above the squeaks, trills and clicks of the machine. It could have been the underwater song of a whale as much as any human meeting. Suddenly, a clear voice said from nearby: 'Senator Hickstead, may I ask a question from this part of the floor? From what you've been saying, how important would you say our relations with Russia are in terms of our own national destiny?'

Someone groaned in the audience. It seemed like one of those portentous questions that mean nothing.

'Listen to this,' whispered Ernie, and Jim saw that his face was rapt, that his whole concentration was on the little machine in front of them.

There were more crackles and squeaks, like an entire school of porpoises, then Hickstead's voice could be distinguished above them.

'No, that's a good question. I would say that the relationship between our two countries is more important than our individual destinies. In fact, I would say that I look forward to the day when the importance of that relationship takes precedence over our individual national rights.'

There was a buzzing on the tape. Another question was asked from somewhere else, but it was indistinguishable against the returning background noise.

Ernie switched off the tape and took hold of his coffee cup.

'That's what haunts me,' he said. 'Just that one sentence. That was one hell of a statement.'

But Ernie didn't look haunted now. He was like a man released. He had communicated something that had been on his mind. He said: 'This is cold. I'll make another cup. You want a refill?'

While Ernie set another cup of coffee, Jim had time to look around the room. The decorations were mainly posters, an old one of Aretha Franklin, a blown-up photograph of the great 50-foot racer, *White Cloud*, thundering out of the roads off Cowes, Britain, into a big green sea. A huge black train, bedecked with red flags bearing the hammer and sickle, moving across a brown-and-white desert.

Ernie saw Jim staring at this last poster: 'Trotsky's propaganda train crossing the Gobi desert,' he explained, then nodded cheerfully at the picture of the yacht *White Cloud*. 'Great name for a boat with a black navigator, huh?'

'How do you think the campaign is going?' Jim asked.

'Real good. Boat feels fine to me, teamwork's good. Now we got us a grade one mainsheet trimmer, we're going to come out well.'

But Jim felt there was something Ernie was holding back. 'So what's bugging you?'

Ernie took a gulp of his coffee. He took his time answering.

'The atmosphere in that camp,' he said at last. 'It keeps reminding me of something. Been working so hard I didn't fully realise what it was. Only came to me the other day exactly what I felt.'

Jim waited.

'My father was arrested once for his union activities. I went to visit him.' He paused. 'That security system,' Ernie said slowly, 'the feel of the place. Reminds me of the way I felt in my father's prison.'

Jim did not answer. He was too surprised to comment.

'I expect that sounds real strange.'

Jim didn't have the heart to reply. He drank his coffee and then, a few minutes later, left for the street and Maria's flat, assailed again by his doubts.

Forty-eight

Maria was Jim's safety valve, his excuse for being outside the enclosure. He wanted nothing so much as to get to the flat, where he knew she would be waiting for him.

In the days which followed, he did his best to concentrate on other things. He flung himself even more determinedly into the daily routine of gymnastics, training, sailing, debriefing, into the cycle of comforting exhaustion.

He applied Coach Johnson's advice and concentrated his thoughts on beating the ultimate opponents. But he could not help becoming a little obsessive about the nature of his Russian challengers. One day, in the flat after a long day's sailing, he asked: 'What are the Russians actually like?'

Maria turned from the ironing board. 'Much like everyone else, I guess.'

'You really mean that?'

Maria continued to iron, turning over one of Jim's pairs of grey trousers. She paused long enough to consider: 'Emotional, volatile, friendly, generous,' Maria said. 'How's that?'

'Like you, then.'

She stopped ironing to snort with laughter.

'Why do you want to know?' Maria asked.

'Ambassador Brent told me their society is based on violence. Ernie Stead, our navigator, says they make the Ku Klux Klan look like liberals. You say they're friendly and generous.'

'They come from a big country. They have big emotions. They're extremists.'

'They sound like Americans.'

'Maybe.'

'So when I think of the Russian crew, if I carry in my mind this image of a bunch of big, generous, violent, warm-hearted racists, I won't be far wrong.'

'Maybe not.'

She put down the iron on the board, and turned her head to look at him. They burst into laughter.

Forty-nine

It was quarter to six in the morning.

Jim and Maria were lying in bed; the radio had been switched on by the automatic alarm and was humming gently in the background. It would be ten minutes before the local weather forecast. The announcer said:

'Before we go any further, I'd like to introduce you to Senator Sam Hickstead, Chairman of the Foreign Relations Committee, Chairman of the Presidential Commission of Enquiry on Weapons Proliferation, and a prominent member of the Senate.'

'Shall I turn it off?' murmured Maria. A sweep of hair fell across her face, blurring her mouth.

'No,' Jim said. He reached across her to find the tuning knob. The voices were indistinct. He moved the cursor until he could hear Hickstead's answering drawl more clearly. Maria made a small sound, half way between a moan and snuffle. He noticed that her eyelids fluttered.

'What are your own views on the current state of play of US–Russian relations, Senator?'

Jim turned up the volume slightly. Maria opened her eyes and looked at Jim. He was staring at the radio, transfixed, his hand still on the volume control.

'Something wrong?' Maria asked.

Hickstead's voice was carefully practised, familiar and authoritative.

'We're approaching a time of great historical significance for all of us. The next round of bilateral arms negotiations between America and Russia is due to start in six months' time.'

'Why is this historic, Senator?'

'We are at a point where our two great countries are not only facing each other across the negotiating table, together we're facing a world in which the most pervasive threat to the well-being of humanity is the proliferation of nuclear and other arms in the hands of other, smaller countries.'

'Why is this dangerous?'

'We and the Russians have lived with our own frightening nuclear potential for a long time now, for nearly sixty years on our own part and almost that time on theirs, so that we've become reasonably used to its management and containment. Other countries, newer to these weapons, have not developed our methods of control.'

'You see ourselves and the Russians on the same side with regard to the potential threat posed by these other countries?'

'What's the matter?' Maria persisted, but Jim put his finger to his lips, shushing her.

'That is correct. Above all,' the Senator was saying, 'what we have to do is get together, establish a non-aggression treaty with verifiability securely built in. Then, with our own relations made more secure, we can turn our joint attention to these other problems.'

'The proliferation of weapons?' asked the interviewer.

'That's right. We have to make a major success of our own mutual defence pacts before we can seriously tackle these other problems.'

'Senator, how do you react to the suggestion, made in some quarters, that what you have been advocating is a kind of US/Russia hegemony over the world?'

'My answer to that is that America and Russia already exercise a hegemony over the world, except that this hegemony is based on mutual distrust. I think we can do a great deal better for humanity if we get together, if we spend less time acting to prevent one another's influence in the world, and concentrate on what we can do jointly.'

'What's preventing us from reaching such an agreement?'

'Frankly, it's the Russians' own current domestic economy. At the end of the last decade they made a decision that they would bring their economy into line with other developed nations. They wished to do so within the formal structure of socialism. Unfortunately, that hasn't worked. They've been falling behind relative to the other economies, particularly in relation to ourselves and some Far Eastern economies like Japan.'

'How does this affect the forthcoming arms control negotiations?'

'The Russians are in a defensive frame of mind. They're starting to feel as if they're losing badly against the other major economies of the world. The latest statistics on Russian production per capita of population simply confirm this. The Russians have a very powerful sense of national destiny, one which is as great as our own. But the lamentable condition of their own internal economy, increasingly cruelly exposed, is making them paranoid. That means we are going to be looking across the table at negotiators who are ill-at-ease, who are not in a position to negotiate with any fullness of heart, who are not capable of thinking of the greater issues at stake but are looking simply to save face.'

'You're saying it would be better if they could come to the negotiating table with some sort of feeling of achievement, maybe some kind of international triumph?'

'Yes, I am. Any ideas?'

'Thank you, Senator, for your analysis.'

The weather forecast came on; a bright day, with local showers, winds northerly, breezes ten to thirteen knots. Jim rolled back onto the bed. Maria, still watching him, said: 'You look as if you've just seen a ghost.'

'Maybe.'

'Do you know Sam Hickstead?'

'We've met.'

'What does he have to do with sailing?' asked Maria.

'He's like you, Maria. He doesn't think winning yacht races is very important.'

Jim pushed aside the bedclothes, stood up and started to get dressed.

Maria rolled over to watch him.

He hesitated, and Maria said, 'Do I embarrass you, watching you?'

'No.'

'You sure?'

'Yes.'

'You look embarrassed to me.'

'You trying to wind me up?'

She turned away again, smiling.

He went through to the bathroom and washed, shaved, brushed his teeth.

On his way out he kissed her goodbye. Her mouth was warm under her hair.

Outside it was chilly. He had glanced at the clock face as he left. Six-fifteen. He pushed his jacket up around his ears and set off through the misty darkness, walking fast, keeping to the lighter side of the street. Lights had come on in the flats above the shops. Their muted radiance made luminous squares and lozenges of the mist. He crossed a corner of Harbinger Street and went into John's Row. There was a café called Harry's in Heidel Street, an early morning café where he liked to catch an early breakfast. It was a place frequented by working men, early morning shift-workers, night janitors. It was good and cheap and the coffee woke him up.

In Beech Street he knew someone was following him. He knew it for certain.

Whoever was there was expert. Not a sign of footsteps, no visible presence. It was a curious thing, but he could feel someone watching him, someone behind him. Not wishing to look nervous, to give his pursuer the satisfaction of knowing he was afraid, he did not turn round.

In Harry's he sat in a window seat and there, just out

of the aura of lights, he felt but did not see a shadow go by on the other side of the street.

'What'll it be?' asked the waitress.

'Coffee, bacon, two eggs, sausage, liver, tomato, two toast.'

'What an appetite.'

It was true. Fear hadn't allayed his hunger.

Through the window he could see a sliver of dawn above the sloping roofs of the street opposite. When he had eaten and paid and left, the sliver had grown deeper, had widened into an arrowhead. He still could not see into the deepest shadows. He kept on the lighter side of the road, taking a different route down to the shore.

The guard at the training camp gates was slow to come out and let him in. When he did finally arrive, he unbolted the door loudly, standing aside slowly, breathing heavily with disapproval as if he had been running. Jim went to the changing room and emerged several minutes later in his exercising shorts and tracksuit.

They were assembled on the concrete, all twenty-six of them, the two crews and the four reserve winchgrinders. Jack was loosening up. From their mouths came plumes of breath like the speaking captions of cartoons.

Benny Haldeman said: 'Haven't you had enough exercise for today, Shaw?'

The rest of the team laughed.

Jim started to work in with them.

Marty Green, one of the army instructors, put them through their morning exercises. Afterwards they showered. Jim avoided the communal breakfast. He made his way to his tiny office, picked up a torch which he kept in a drawer, and walked down the quay to *New World*.

The confidence of the military in the security screen around the camp was such that they did not believe in the necessity of guarding the yachts themselves. Each day after racing the crane lifted the yachts, draped in their security skirts, from the water and over the high security fence that separated the compound from the water.

He climbed the ladder up the topsides, flipped over the

top onto the decks, sprang down softly into the cockpit. The hatches were drawn closed but not bolted. It was light enough to see inside now. For the deepest recesses he used the torch, drawing its milky beam slowly back and forth across the internal bracing structures.

The boat's wooden interior was covered with a sealant coat of epoxy which acted like varnish, bringing out the glow of the structural wood with its sallow, golden fires. He looked with particular care at the laminated ring frames.

One day, he thought, he would build a boat like this, out of laminated veneers, with hardly any interior furniture, just a few seats bonded into the rich, living walls of wood.

For half an hour he checked the internal structure, feeling his way with his hands where he could not check with his eyes or the torch. He could find nothing.

He went up into the bright sunlight, made a cursory search of the cockpit. But he felt exposed to prying eyes up there, and after a few minutes he descended the long ladder again.

As his foot touched the ground he realised O'Reilly was standing there, about five feet away from the base of the ladder. O'Reilly's feet were placed slightly apart, in the position of a man standing at ease on the parade ground, except that he was slowly rocking backwards and forwards on the soles of his shoes like someone in deep thought.

'Boat all right?' O'Reilly asked.

'Seems to be.'

O'Reilly gave him a wry smile. 'Glad to see you so conscientious.'

Jim watched him walk away, his footsteps slightly splayed, his back straight, his hands swinging easily. Not for the first time, he found himself admiring O'Reilly's easy self-confidence.

Fifty

No sky could be clearer, no breeze more refreshing.

A lay-day had been called while the boats were thoroughly checked and overhauled, prior to final measurement the following day. After the morning's work on checking the yacht, he and the crew had been given the afternoon off.

For the first time for several months, as he walked along the shore, Jim felt a sense of freedom. It was good to know they were so thoroughly prepared. No campaign is perfect, but he felt sure that he and the crew had taken themselves to the limit of their capability. The cares of the compound temporarily left his shoulders. He walked fast for two hours, simply for the sake of movement. It is said that the brain has a structure, the cerebellum, which is responsible for simple repetitive motor activity. Those who pace up and down rooms are exercising this cerebellum, freeing the more conceptual part of their minds for some work of a more demanding nature, perhaps simply for contemplation.

So Jim walked as the evening drew down. He crossed the park on his way back to the foreshore, cut in through the shopping centre. While his legs moved him across town, he considered the final stages of the training programme.

The training was shaping up well. Perhaps it was their vanquishing of Ericson's group that had given them that final cohesion which characterises the best of teams. Their co-ordination began to seem so spontaneous, so flawless, it was almost easy to take it for granted.

Unthinkingly, his legs carried him in the direction of the compound. Rounding a corner, the familiar shape of the protected area loomed before him in the half-light. In the centre of the compound, the shapes of the two yachts, their underbodies protected by security screens, burgeoned out from the two supporting derricks.

It was growing darker as he walked along the shoreline just inland of the compound. A group of buildings temporarily blocked his view. When he emerged from behind them a brief feeling of suspicion caused him to look more closely at the shapes of the yachts. He felt sure he had seen a light flash on the closest, which he knew to be *New World*. He paused. The light had disappeared, and he was no longer sure he had seen it. He was about to walk on again, kicking himself for imagining things, when it appeared again, a small but clear firefly glimmer; it flickered again, disappeared. There was someone on the deck of *New World*.

A stream of four or five cars moving along the road caused him to run parallel until they had passed and he could sprint across the road towards the entrance gate. As he approached, he could make out the silhouette of the guards in the partly lighted temporary offices adjoining the entrance road. The entrance gate, as was normal at this time, was closed.

He rapped on the gate. One of the two guards peered out of the window, stood up, and came outside.

The guard recognised him. 'Good evening, Mr Shaw.'

'Open up, please. I want to get in.'

'You going someplace, Mr Shaw?'

'What do you mean? I'm cleared to enter the compound.'

'Sorry, there's a special security check in progress.'

'Security check?'

'Yes, sir.'

Jim looked at the guard's face, trying to make out his expression in the uncertain light.

'What the hell does that mean?'

'Just what I said, sir,' the guard answered. 'I got orders to challenge any person, inform them of the situation, and if they try to pass after my warning, shoot on sight. Sir,' the guard added, 'that is a serious order.'

'How long's it going to last?'

'Just as long as I'm ordered, Mr Shaw.'

Jim felt his anger harden.

'OK, I understand.' He willed himself to relax. Something caught his attention. He looked over the guard's shoulder. 'But then why's he allowed in?'

It was the oldest trick in the world, but the old ones are sometimes the best. Caught unawares for a half second, the security guard turned away. Jim reached through the mesh, snapped the bolt back on the gate, thrust into it with his shoulder and broke through. He ran hard for the nearest building. The guard unclipped his pistol, but the sights of his gun traversed deep shadows. The perpetrator had rounded a corner and was out of sight.

The guard, a heavy man, gauged from the speed of his assailant that he would not be able to catch him on foot. He drew out a whistle and blew it piercingly three times, at two-second intervals. Then, the alarm raised, he ran in pursuit.

Jim moved along the side of a building, keeping to the shadows, praying that he would not strike some hidden object and fall headlong. He paused, gathered himself and sprinted past the entrance to the biggest shed. Detouring to his right, he followed a gangway down to the dock and maintenance areas.

Behind him he could hear footsteps. A dog had been let loose and was yelping as it tried to pick up his scent. Perhaps it had already.

As he reached the dock, weaving between the bollards, something struck him hard on the shoulder and he cursed under his breath as he went down, sliding forward along the rough surface of the dock. He rolled onto his side. A stab of pain struck his shoulder as he raised himself to his feet. He was bruised, but that seemed all. Partly winded, he continued his crablike run down the dockside area. The outlines of the two yachts were suddenly almost directly above him. The dim shape of *New World*, suspended above a flat working area, rose up above him, covered in its security skirt.

He could hear the search spreading behind him above his own hoarse breathing, the whistles and shouts.

Arclights of searchlamps cut the sky and then beamed down, illuminating the area of the docks. In the main buildings, someone had punched the floodlight switch. An area of bleached light opened behind him.

A ladder had been laid up against *New World*'s side. Two men were standing at the foot of the ladder. They were both quite still, listening to the commotion on the other side of the compound as the search spread out. The noise of the chase covered the noise of Jim's own movements. He moved closer, using the shadows. A third figure was descending. A patch of shadow hid the faces of the figures, so he could not recognise them.

He made a final dash towards them, running fast. Aware of him now, they bunched themselves to take on their unexpected attacker. A few feet away the descending figure put a foot on the ground and turned into the light. Jim saw his face clearly, and felt his mind spinning.

'O'Reilly!'

He tried to check himself, but his feet were already sliding. He hit the ladder with his bruised shoulder. The two henchmen were reaching forward towards him when O'Reilly snapped: 'Wait.'

He had to give O'Reilly credit. He was cool.

O'Reilly pulled off a pair of gloves, speaking slowly, almost pleasantly.

'Why, Jim.'

The other two stepped up behind O'Reilly. They were faces he didn't immediately recognise. One of them carried a small object under his arm, a box.

Jim said: 'What the hell is going on?'

'Perhaps you can tell me,' O'Reilly said evenly. 'I thought there was full security cover.'

Jim could hear the footsteps of the approaching guards. O'Reilly and his two men stood motionless.

'What's he got there?' Jim asked, pointing to the box.

'Nothing to worry about,' O'Reilly commented, as if he were talking to a child. 'Say, you're mighty concerned.'

Jim lunged towards the man with the box. As he did

so he was seized expertly by the other man, who was exceptionally powerful.

After a few seconds O'Reilly said calmly: 'OK. Let him go.'

The grip was loosened. Jim punched aside the remaining arm and the man started towards him, but O'Reilly said, more sharply: 'Leave him.'

O'Reilly turned towards Jim again.

'You shouldn't have bust through security like that, Jim. You could have been hurt.'

'What were you doing on the boat?'

'Checking. We can't be too careful.'

'Checking what?'

'Checking our Russian friends haven't got up to any tricks.'

'So why didn't you inform me? Why did your guards keep me out?'

'They aren't *my* guards, Jim. They're our guards. I don't understand your attitude.'

'They were ordered to shoot if I passed.'

'We wanted full security so that we could undertake a thorough check. Jim, I don't like your attitude. I have to warn you that I'm going to have to report this incident to the authorities.'

'Who are these authorities, O'Reilly? Who are these goddamn authorities and what do they think they're doing?'

'You're starting to sound downright unpatriotic. Now listen, Jim. You break any more security orders and I have to warn you, there will be serious consequences. I hope you heard what I said.'

The flatfooted guard whom Jim had outmanoeuvred appeared out of the shadows at a run.

'At ease,' snapped O'Reilly. 'The situation's under control.'

O'Reilly and his two heavyweights pushed their way past Jim. Jim watched them walk up the gangplank towards the main offices. O'Reilly issued a brief command to the guard, and several others who had now collected at the top of the gangplank dispersed. The guard came towards him.

'Sir,' said the guard. 'I'm going to ask you, just once, to remove yourself from these premises, or I have the authority to arrest you and detain you in the guardhouse.'

'Fuck you,' Jim said.

'Sir,' said the guard with admirable restraint. 'I have a gun and you do not. Experience tells me I'm in a position to fuck you.'

'OK, I'm going.'

'I will walk right behind you to the gate, sir, with this thing pointing at your back.'

Jim started to walk up the gangway with the guard following.

In front of him, O'Reilly and his two companions disappeared through the office door, carrying their box with them.

Fifty-one

Jim waited half an hour at the coffee shop before Coach Johnson arrived.

Coach Johnson looked angry at being invited to this absurd assignation. He nodded cursorily and sat down opposite Jim.

'OK, what's the problem?'

Jim ordered him a cup of coffee. It took some time before it came, brought by a harrassed young woman with light streaks in her dark hair. Coach Johnson did not speak immediately. He was breathing slowly and deeply, as if restraining his anger.

'So why did you ask me here, Jim?' Coach Johnson asked again. 'Don't tell me. Let me guess. You wanted to apologise for that stupid incident last night.'

Jim stirred milk into his coffee.

'Do you know what trouble you cause me?' asked Coach Johnson.

Pedestrians were passing outside the window, throwing moving shadows across the table. A small boy put his face to the window and made faces at them. Jim said evenly:

'Maybe you can tell me what's going on.'

'Perhaps you better tell me.'

Jim paused. He wasn't going to be hurried by Coach Johnson. Not now. He said: 'Those guys seem to be taking over.'

'What guys?' Coach Johnson asked.

'You know who I mean.'

He looked at Coach Johnson and saw the anger in his eyes, a few flecks of red as if he hadn't slept too well. Maybe, Jim thought, O'Reilly had called Coach Johnson to a post-mortem on last night's incident.

'OK,' Coach Johnson said resignedly. 'I know who you mean.'

Jim paused again. Finally he said: 'Who is this guy O'Reilly? I mean, what's his game in all this?'

Coach leaned forward, and for the first time that meeting he spoke, not with exasperation, but with his customary directness and force. 'Jim, do you know who Colonel O'Reilly is married to? Tom Stuttaford's sister. Our syndicate head is his brother-in-law. Jim,' said Coach Johnson, and Jim saw that he spoke with the cold passion of someone who knows he is dealing with a profound truth, 'it's not a question of these guys wanting to take over. They have taken over. They took over before this even started. These are the guys that are always there.'

'Christ.'

'Yeah, that's right. Now what am I supposed to do, mount some kind of moral crusade? Against what? Against the natural order? What good would that do? Give me a break, will you?'

'OK, they run the operation, they play their games. But we run the sailing side, don't we?' Jim could hear the

295

edge of rancour, of desperation, in his voice, but he could not prevent it. 'We run the boat. Don't we?'

'That's a stupid question.'

'Is it?'

'It isn't our business to worry about things like that.'

'Isn't it?'

'You're working real hard, Jim. Working without a break. You need a holiday. Maybe we all do.'

Coach stood up. He was about to go. Jim put a restraining hand on his arm. Coach stiffened.

'A holiday's not what I need,' Jim said.

Coach Johnson looked down at the restraining hand pointedly, but Jim didn't remove it.

'That guy Walters rolled in first. Said it's a security operation. Ever since then, security's been running us.'

Coach Johnson continued to look down at Jim's hand. It seemed like a stalemate. Having made his point, Jim removed his hand.

Coach Johnson said, with unexpected mildness, 'What exactly are you suggesting?'

'I don't know what I'm suggesting. That's what I'm asking you.'

'Look,' said Coach Johnson, and Jim could see that he was, despite everything, still angry. 'You let them play their games. They're nothing to do with us.' He paused. 'It's for our own good.'

'Their good or our good?'

Coach Johnson sat down in his seat again and tried to compose his anger. He seemed resigned. 'What's the difference?'

'I don't know. Maybe there is a difference.'

'Listen, Jim, you're a great guy. I'm one of your fans. But this isn't helping either of us. Somewhere out there is Ivan Illich. He's the one you have to beat. Do you think he asks himself a lot of damnfool questions about the motives of his own side? I don't think so. I think he just gets down to the job.'

'Is that what you want me to do, Coach?'

'Yeah, that's what I want you to do.' Coach Johnson

paused. 'Listen, Jim, do you have any idea what those guys can do, if they put their minds to it? They can bug your every movement. They can listen so close to you that they can hear what you're thinking before you even thought it. You need friends who can help you.'

'Friends?'

'Yeah, friends.'

'You call O'Reilly a friend?'

Coach did not answer. He drank his coffee. Jim leaned forward.

'Coach, when I find O'Reilly or one of his guys has been going over the joint in the middle of the night, I don't feel I'm with friends. I feel I'm dealing with woodlice.'

'You're getting paranoid.' Coach waved a hand to ameliorate Jim's response. 'OK, OK, maybe I wouldn't choose some of these guys as my buddies. But they've got a job to do, like us. It just seems to me that you are being . . . mighty intolerant of them.'

'You're prepared to put your hand on your heart and tell me, for certain, that these guys are our friends?'

Coach stood up again, and Jim knew this time he could not restrain him.

'Listen, son,' Coach Johnson said, 'if you can't take the pace, if you find the pressure is getting to you, just tell me and I'll do something about it. I mean that. Otherwise, I don't want my best helmsman to be wasting his time complaining about his own side. That's just stupid. So help me, my job is to help you win this thing.'

Coach Johnson nodded and left. Jim watched him depart and pushed his coffee away.

The café was starting to fill up. Two elderly women approached the table.

'May we sit here?'

'Sure, I'm going anyway.'

They smiled and simpered. He got up and put on his jacket. As he was waiting to pay at the till, he heard one say to the other: 'Isn't he on television?'

'I think I recognise the face,' the other replied. 'It's one of those police movies, isn't it?'

'Is he the cop or the bad guy?' asked one old lady.

'I don't know, Martha,' responded the other. 'You never can tell, these days.'

It was the only cheerful thing he heard that morning.

Outside the weather was still edgy. Small rain clouds were scudding across the sky. Behind them a thunderhead was building. Against the greyness, lights were starting to come on in the buildings overlooking the street. There was nothing he could do about O'Reilly. The reality of his position set in as he made his way back to the compound.

He did his best to put last night's incident from his mind. That day he worked exhaustively over the sail programme with Tom East, checked over the list of spares that would be needed for the races with Eddie Cantor, then went into the shed where *New World*, stripped of her mast and rigging, was due to be thoroughly checked by the measurement officials before the races began in five days' time.

Fifty-two

A wave exploded against *New World*'s hull; a geyser of spray lifted from the impact, reaching up towards the light like a hand.

The boat was taut as a bow string. He felt the familiar surge of adrenalin as he aimed *New World*'s bow towards *Shadow*'s midships. *Shadow* passed in front of him like a sleek animal. *New World*'s bow missed their stern by several feet, but he felt the surge and lift of his heart as, with a sound like a tearing cloth, they hit *Shadow*'s wind train;

he lifted the bow upwind a few feet to take advantage of the curve *Shadow*'s sails made in the wind.

Sunray Jones, returned to take the helm of *Shadow* after Ericson had left, tacked on top of them. Jim felt the whole yacht's nerve tighten as he eased *New World* downwind a few degrees now, trying to pull out maximum speed.

With the honed instincts of a predator, he watched a flutter in *Shadow*'s genoa as she came through the wind, a flutter that was a little too long. *Shadow*'s winchgrinders were getting tired. Her tack was a fraction slow, and that was all the latitude he needed to strike back at her.

He watched Moose's face, saw him spit on his hands, saw him punch the air several times to loosen a muscle, take hold of the coffeegrinder handles, nod, ready to tack when needed.

But the flurry of nine rapid tacks they had forced on *Shadow* had already done its work. They had broken through *Shadow*'s wind, and were neck and neck. Now it was a matter of looking for those tiny fractions of a knot of extra speed which would lift their bow clear.

Jack in these close quarter fights changed from tactician to tuner. He was already moving forward beside the genoa, tightening the leach line half an inch to remove a tiny flutter in the upper portion of the sail, signalling to the genoa trimmer with his hand to ease the sheet a fraction, gesturing to the mainsheet trimmer to ease his sail a fraction too. Moving along the deck he dropped cat-like down the hatch to transmit an instruction to the sewerman about the next sail-change. In his traverse he had instructed two Olympic Gold medallists and a legendary crew-boss. It was a tribute to his hold over the crew that his advice was accepted and implemented with such speed.

New World was starting to work at its peak. As helmsman, Jim felt like a pilot of a fighter aircraft with superior performance in every field. He could burn out *Shadow*'s mid-deck crew with his big-hearted winchmen, his trimmers could tune the sails and pull out those fractions of knots of speed which were decisive in racing. He could engage in close quarter manoeuvre and know that their own sailhandling was faster, crisper, subject to less error. And he felt that when he had the opportunity to turn this full armament on Ivan Illich, the world's greatest helmsman would need all his talent to survive the onslaught.

But it was one thing to beat a good second crew, another to face an individual helmsman at the peak of his powers who had never lost an international regatta. There was always the factor of the unknown in the other boat and its crew. And the time was drawing rapidly closer.

Fifty-three

In the final stages of the build-up to the big races, Ernie's obsession with the speeches of Senator Sam Hickstead was a small and welcome diversion from the worries of organising the defence.

On his occasional visits to Ernie's flat, he would use the time to work out navigational strategy. Then they would work over the tactics of the following day. Afterwards, if there was time, Ernie would bring forth more material from his archives on the collected sayings of Senator Hickstead. It was like tracking an extraordinary and fabulous animal.

'Listen to this one,' Ernie said. He turned the switches again. The machine whined. Numbers flew past on a liquid crystal indicator.

The machine came to a halt. Click. The end of a sentence, then the by now familiar, confident voice of Senator Sam Hickstead. He had been answering questions about Russian defence policy. Now he unexpectedly turned the tables.

'You've asked me quite a few questions. Maybe I can

ask you one. Have you ever thought about what the Russians think of us?'

The interviewer was startled for a moment.

'Can't say I have. What do they think of us?'

'Then consider this. To the Russians, we're a nation of refugees, who revolted against Europe, threw off colonial status, and then proceeded to become the most powerful nation on earth.'

'What are you saying, Senator?'

'What I'm getting at is this. To them, America is a revolutionary state. Actually, it's *the* great revolutionary state, red in tooth and claw, exporting its revolutionary culture aggressively worldwide. Our own intellectuals may laugh at the Coca-Cola culture, the culture of materialism, but it has the popular vote of every third world country in the world. Allowed free rein, no other culture would stand a chance.

'Against our own truly revolutionary culture, the Russian use of revolutionary rhetoric is hollow. Despite phases of *glasnost*, some attempts at *perestroika*, despite tinkerings with the election process and the limited independence of industry, Russia remains a highly élitist, centralised state. They look across at us, and what do they see? More real revolutions, in society, in morals, in commercial practice, in computers, in the way we organise our local communities, more real revolutions per decade than in their entire history.

'This poses a very real threat to them. Our revolutionary energy extends, for example, into armaments. We invented the atomic bomb, the hydrogen bomb, the intercontinental missile, the multiple re-entry warhead, the nuclear submarine. They've done their best to keep up with us, but we're always pressing ahead with new and more terrifying weapons systems, with Stealth, for instance, or with the Star Wars programme. When we try to look at the US from the other side of the fence, it's easy to see that we could easily represent, to an essentially conservative Russian administration, a truly frightening and demonic aspect.

'We should understand that to the Russians, we're considered to be the source of revolutionary energy in the world, and this makes them justifiably nervous of us. Even countries like Japan or West Germany or South Korea are economic clones of the United States. In our diplomacy, we need to be considerate of Russian fears. We have to realise that there is a real basis for their terror of us.'

Ernie turned off the machine.

There was a moment's silence while Ernie rewound the tape, clicked off the machine, sat back in his chair.

'You see why I'm so interested in this guy? I don't necessarily agree with the conclusions he draws. But I have to admit, there's a current of logic in what he talks about. He's dedicated himself to these problems over a long period. He's trying to find solutions.'

Jim moved in his chair. Senator Hickstead had a way of transfixing his attention. He said: 'Let's come back to our own role in this. What if part of his solution is to make us lose?'

Ernie turned away.

'That's where I think he has to be stopped.'

'But you just said, he's so logical.'

'A lot of people have been logical,' Ernie replied. 'Like Hitler, like Stalin. It depends on your assumptions.'

'You don't mind him being logical, as long as it doesn't affect us.'

Ernie, who was studying the label of another disk, looked up suddenly.

'I'll tell you what I think. I think looking into the future is fine. Putting yourself in the other guy's position is fine. But trying to manipulate the outcome of sport to suit political ends is exactly what people like Hitler and Stalin used to do. You can always find good reasons for that, but the principle stinks!'

'So,' Jim said wonderingly, 'I gather you don't think we should take a dive.'

He believed, in that instant, that he actually saw Ernie go white with rage.

'You want to take a dive, maybe you just better tell me right now. Because if you do, I'm going to get my black ass out of here so godamn quick you won't even believe you ever saw me.'

Ernie was touchy about the Russians. Jim could see the tension was getting to him, too.

Fifty-four

Sam Shaw broke his previous rules to see the America's Cup. He hired a television. Mavis Blatsky allowed him to lead a cable from her house to his house so that it could be connected up. She owed him, she said, for mending the fence between them. So it turned out that Sam Shaw could watch television without being reconnected with the municipal electricity supply. That saved his face and his principles.

On the day of the first race he switched on the set. He studied the screen as it turned from dark to light. The announcer said:

The thirtieth challenge for the America's Cup is starting today. Over to our mobile studios at the scene of the racing and to our two commentators, John House and Larry Peters.

JOHN HOUSE
Hello everybody. Today is an historic occasion. The thirtieth America's Cup defence will start in forty minutes' time in what appears to be magnificent weather. It's a bright, clear day with fifteen knots of wind.

Helping me in my commentary on the series will be our technical expert, Larry Peters, a former member of the American Olympic team and a highly successful competitor in offshore racing. He is a recognised authority on the deadly sport of match-racing, as epitomised by the America's Cup. Larry, can you say a few words?

LARRY PETERS
Thank you kindly, John. America's Cup competition is more like boxing than racing. There are only two competitors. The competition actually starts ten minutes before the starting gun goes.

The ten-minute gun is the signal for the two competitors to enter the ring and start to manoeuvre against one another. These pre-start manoeuvres can be very interesting to watch. One boat will try to get behind another. In this position it can, according to the rules, drive its rival away from the starting line. The boat that is driving the other way is therefore closest to the starting line, and can break back at will towards the starting line with a lead over the other yacht.

JOHN HOUSE
That's before the race even starts?

One more thing, Larry. Sometimes the boats are pretty level with one another, and they'll be sailing towards one another. Then one boat will turn away. What's happening there?

LARRY PETERS
In sailing, the boat with the wind on its right-hand side, its starboard side, has right of way. That's the main rule in understanding who has racing right of way, John. Once you understand that rule, a lot of the manoeuvring starts to make sense.

JOHN HOUSE
Just one last question, Larry. It's not a sailing question, exactly, but maybe you can help with the answer. Just why are the Russians putting so much effort into this challenge?

LARRY PETERS
I've been asking myself that question quite a lot over the last few months.

JOHN HOUSE
OK, that's the disclaimer. Now what's the answer?

Well, I guess if I was in their position, with an economy that's been falling behind, and with pretty much an international military stalemate, I guess I'd be looking for other ways to demonstrate national prestige. If that's the case this is an opportunity to show how good they are.

JOHN HOUSE
Thank you, Larry, I don't know whether everyone out there will agree with you, but it's an interesting point of view.

Fifty-five

They had never seen so many vessels.

From horizon to horizon the sea was filled with yachts, motor-boats, spectator craft. The surface of the water was churned with a thousand wakes. Behind the lines of smaller craft, tall ships were anchored, pleasure steamers and cruise liners. Beyond those, more sombrely grey, a smattering of military vessels stood like sentinels. In the foreground the milling smaller boats crossed and recrossed. Amongst them moved the Coastguard cutters, already beginning to remove yachts from the area of the course, a large square of open sea.

Above them, gathered like the birds of the air, were the aircraft. At the lowest level helicopters swooped and whirled. Above them, fixed wing aircraft turned and banked slowly, while at a higher altitude still the airships hovered, hardly moving, bedecked with sponsors' names. Airships had undergone a resurrection in the last decade. Helium was incomparably safer than the volatile hydrogen of the old airships. For the first time the sky was filled with their quiet, hovering shapes; at a lower level the smaller, more nimble ones, and above them the great transoceanic airliners, larger than the largest Zeppelins, some containing as many as several hundred people.

As the crew prepared the boat, Jim had looked out beyond the harbour mouth to this vast concourse of human vehicles.

The day had begun without wind. In the compound Jim had stared out at the greenish dawn beyond Cauldron Bay, and searched the sky for the predicted eighteen knots of breeze. Cloud cover was sparse. It was eerie, before a soul was about, and the trafficless city was quiet. He gazed out across the imperturbable waters of the empty bay in the knowledge that a few hours later the sea would fill with a huge armada of vessels, the sky would darken with aircraft.

A military band was playing as they loaded sails on board, and made their last minute check-ups of equipment. The tow boat cast them a line. They threw off the mooring ropes and followed obediently, like a great seabird with its wings folded. The squat shape of the towing launch drew them out towards the battleground.

Their fast support launch, capable of sixty knots at full gallop, closed in behind them. It carried the spares, the extra sails, the spare winch hydraulics, rigging and ropes, the great wire cutters that could be used to clear rigging in an emergency.

On either side a Coastguard cutter closed in and escorted them, in close formation, pushing back the small group of press boats and television launches which snapped at their heels. The roar of the crowd became louder as they reached the packed harbour mouth. On board *New World*, the crew waved enthusiastically.

Outside the harbour mouth Jim could see more wind. A few white sea-horses dotted the areas of sea not occupied by the milling swarm of spectator craft. Groups of Coastguard cutters were acting in concert to herd the fleet into its appropriate spectator areas.

He could feel small gusts on his face as the yacht turned through the harbour entrance and the crowd's roar reached a crescendo. He felt the wind in the tall mast, the soft singing of the metal rigging. His nerves became keyed to the quick shifts and swirls which occurred just beyond the harbour mouth.

And here the sheer size of the spectator fleet astonished him. Seeing the little squadron emerge from the harbour mouth the sirens began, at first the higher pitched yelps and wails of the smaller yachts and motorboats, spreading through the fleet, through the ranks until the liners themselves joined in a hoarse, raucous welcome.

'We'll be exhausted by the time we get there,' said Jack above the din. They proceeded forward through the fleet, the Coastguard cutters carving a furrow through the milling, turning, reversing yachts. Diesel and petrol fumes filled the charged air.

Wavelets from the ruffled waters punched against their bows. They rolled in the swell caused by a large passing spectator craft. The tow-rope went slack and suddenly taut, hauling *New World* alarmingly forward.

'Keep off the fore-deck,' shouted Jack. He had once seen, on a tug manoeuvring a liner, a hawser break under strain and convert the man standing behind it into raw flesh against the tug's dark wheelhouse. He did not want a subdivided Virus, or Jingle to lose his bells. Not before the race, at any rate.

The accompanying flotilla now formed a phalanx, a convoy of small hooting yachts crowded in on them, kept at bay by the thin line of the Coastguard cutters. The convoy proceeded out to the course.

Approaching them from the warship *Moscow*, another convoy was set on a converging course. At first it was only identifiable by the single tall mast in its midst. Afterwards, he would remember the scene clearly. The intervening craft seemed to clear away, like milling sheep before the quick, attacking dashes of the Coastguard cutters. Almost without warning there was clear water between them.

The approaching convoy, now more discernible, drew forwards. In station above it two Hind D military assault helicopters thundered. On either side were two fast motor

torpedo boats, like greyhounds. Several grey support launches brought up the stern.

The two convoys slowed to drift speed. The Russian
challenger was towed forward, and for the first time they
could see its red hull clearly, and appreciate its sleek lines.
The tow launch turned into wind, so that the two yachts
were parallel, and they could see *Leningrad* broadside on.
A huge red battleflag with hammer and sickle floated
from its forestay. It was a moment of tension and interest.
They could see the blond head of Ivan Illich in the stern,
as he discussed a point with his tactician. Above them
the red battleflag waved slowly in the wind.

JOHN HOUSE
It's clear and bright out there today, in this historic race between
Russia and America. This isn't the first time the Russians have
competed in the America's Cup, but it is widely believed that they
have been training for this particular confrontation with
determination over the last decade.

Each of these magnificent yachts is like a warship in action.
Everyone must perform their function flawlessly, as part of a
single, cohesive unit. Each crewman on each yacht is the best in
his field. Of the Russian winchgrinders, two are Olympic
weightlifters. The reserve is a champion of heavyweight wrestling.
Getting in those huge sails as fast as possible is critical. Here
too the Russian team have truly awesome power.

Despite our experience of America's Cup sailing, we're
considered to be the underdogs in this event. I hope our boys are
going to turn the tables and prove me wrong.

So here we are, lined up and ready to go, with the day bright
and the wind at twenty-two knots according to our weatherman.

On the deck of the tender to *New World*, Coach Johnson
called out 'Good luck.'

Jim said quietly to Jack, 'No more excuses, we're on
our own.'

An eerie silence pervaded the yacht. Gino Compostella,
the winchgrinder, 'Mace' to the crew, worked his hands
carefully into his gloves. Georgie Riga, starboard genoa
trimmer, turned his winch slowly. The staccato clicking

of the perfectly engineered mechanism was the only sound on the yacht. Inside, everyone was preparing himself for the fray.

Beneath decks Marvin Toller, the sewerman, tied a series of sailcovers on the sails. Around him the sails were stacked up as neatly as sheaves of wheat. While he was tying he heard a slight thump against the hull, hardly distinguishable from the patting of wavelets. He stopped stacking sails and stood up, listening. The sound, so faint he could only just separate it from the background noise, occurred again. After that he heard nothing, aside from the slow, even threshing of the tow-boat's propellers as, with hardly two knots of forward speed, it held them facing into wind. He shrugged, and returned to the task of preparing the sails.

Fifty-six

No one in *New World*'s cockpit spoke for several minutes. It was Jack who broke the silence, instituting a final gear-check before the race. Ernie was crouched over the radio, earphones on, listening for the race instructions as the incoming wind swirled and settled.

The first leg of the race was always upwind. The race officers were obliged to wait until the wind had established a clear direction before setting the course buoys. This was the time of tension, before the action began, a time when all jokes seemed uneasy, when action seemed futile, a time of waiting.

Greenback patted his gloved hands together rhythmically. The only other sound, above the race officer's reportage through the radio, was the slap of the wavelets on the hull.

By now the Coastguard cutters had cleared the area of

the course. Helicopters dipped down low above them to photograph the decks of the two yachts and their waiting crews. A television launch bristling with cameras and microphones had broken through the cordon and was firmly escorted away by two cutters.

The wind was settling in. At twenty minutes before the ten-minute gun, Ernie switched to a pre-set waveband to receive the most recent weather report. The wind strengths were consistent with the sails they had on board.

On deck Jim said: 'OK, let's get the sails up. Twelve minutes to the ten-minute gun.'

They emerged from their trance.

'Fast,' Jack roared.

Hand over hand, swinging their full respective weights, Jingle and Big Ape hauled the mainsail up the mast. At its full height the halyard was tensioned precisely on its winch. On all the ropes small markings were set out to reproduce the precise tensions required for different wind strengths and different wave conditions.

The tow rope was cast off.

'Code fourteen genoa.'

The big foresail was attached to its sheets and hauled up.

'Tension her to load three,' shouted Jack.

'Course to upwind buoy zero one eight degrees,' Ernie sang out.

'Turning to port,' Jim shouted.

The thundering sails quietened, filled. The coffeegrinders pulled the genoa in the last few inches. *New World* heeled and began to pick up speed.

The small support fleet was moving away, backing nervously from her as she slowly came to life.

'Settle down,' Jim said. 'Let's get the numbers up.'

Jack turned to study the Russian yacht. The battleflag had been lowered, furled, and was handed over the side to the support vessel. The mainsail was already rising, the genoa following a few seconds later.

'Jeez, look at that,' Jack said.

Jim watched the spectral sails fill. Then *Leningrad* began to surge, punched forward into a swell, bore away to pick up further speed. Now the entire crew on *New World* swung to watch her slicing the waves, bearing away on a reach, running at speed, gybing through the wind with the controlled crash of boom, swinging upwind, settling down close hauled on the other tack.

It was perfection. From the rake of the mast, to the cut of the sails, from the powerful quarter wave which started to sing out white as she picked up high speed, they were mesmerised by the Russian machine.

'Settle down,' Jim urged. He and Jack began to bring the crew down to earth.

'Tack.'

They tacked onto port, and set up the yacht on the other side.

'Tension main halyard up to load four,' roared Jack.

'Numbers, Ernie.'

'Better on load four,' Ernie answered after a short interlude studying the instruments. 'Yeah, definitely better.'

They turned and went back to the starting box.

'Two minutes to ten-minute gun,' Jack warned.

Three hundred yards away the *Leningrad* was wheeling, tacking. Like two knights at the starting lists, they waited for the seconds to count down.

JOHN HOUSE
On the Russian boat, with its gleaming hardware, the crewmen are making a final check on the instruments as they turn and tack.

The sails of both boats are setting well, and they're both moving back and forth smartly, as the seconds slide away. We're counting down to the ten-minute gun. Ten, nine, eight, seven, six . . . Both boats are hauling in sails and picking up speed as they head towards the perimeter of the starting box. There goes the gun. And here they go. They're closing fast, slicing in towards one another, the winchgrinders working furiously, the sails being tuned and retuned for maximum speed. And as they move in towards the close manoeuvre, it's over to our match-racing expert, Larry Peters.

The cordite had hardly cleared from the ten-minute gun

before both yachts had entered the starting area. Taking advantage of beam winds, they swung in towards each other fast.

Before they started Jim had said to himself, 'I cannot help but be frightened by a yacht driven by one of the greatest sailors of all time. Remember that we are also an unknown quantity to them.'

Reason, however, had no effect on his feelings. As they closed he could feel his own terror mounting. Ernie sang out the speed numbers, but he could feel the nervousness of his crew rising as *Leningrad* swung towards them. To break this tension he would move in closer to confront them directly, to blood his crew.

LARRY PETERS
In each of these manoeuvres, John, there is frantic activity on both boats as they start to swing, and the sails are powered in and out by the winchgrinders. The trimmers are having to control the set of the sails every second while the boats turn.

Every time a grinder hauls in a big genoa, he's generating enough power to pull a small car up the mast. In this type of manoeuvre, the grinders are working virtually continuously.

'Boarding party.' Jim gave the signal for a close grappling duel.

Leningrad was swinging low now, adopting his own preferred tactic, picking up speed for the duel. To avoid collision, Jim was forced to sail *New World* high.

Leningrad turned savagely, swooping up towards them, and they were engaged. Jim used this fleeting opportunity to spring downwind towards them, turning fast above them so that he could punch the wind out of their sails, slow them down to his own speed. In a close turning battle events occur so fast they are a matter of reflex. Pandemonium breaks out, the sails thunder and slam as they cross the decks. Like two warhorses, they spun around each other angrily, each boat engulfed in the action of the other. They could hardly hear their own voices for the roars of the Russian commands.

Then they were out on the other side, in clear air, neither yacht with any advantage. Both yachts broke away to pick up speed, to regroup. A cheer went up briefly from the crew, a cheer of astonishment and pleasure that at least in the close engagement, they had not been bested.

LARRY PETERS
There appears to be nothing in it during the turns, but then this isn't the strength of the Russian yacht. Illich is a master of sheer speed. They've broken off from this preliminary skirmish, and as the seconds tick down towards the start, each of the two competitors is driving towards the start line, picking up speed as they go.

Twenty seconds of turning had seemed like several lifetimes. Jim let them cheer for a few seconds. It released tension. The sudden explosive engagement had cleared the air. But now it was Jack's turn to close in, remorseless, to harangue and encourage them back to absolute concentration.

They were engaged now in a bitter battle to build up speed. It seemed to Jim, probing for advantage, that they accelerated more easily than the other boat, a small but not insignificant detail that he would build into his future tactics.

'Ernie, where are you?' Jim shouted.

But Ernie was perched over the flickering screen of the computer, cool as a cucumber, detached from the heat of the battle, studying the flowlines on its white surface. 'Eight-four,' Ernie said, 'Speed rising, eight-six, and six, eight-seven. Wind is backing. Bias on port end of line now. Stay on this side.'

'They're going down to the other end of the line,' Jack said.

'Timed run,' Jim called.

A 'timed run' was an individual approach by each yacht to the start line, with enough distance between them not to require immediate counteractions. The two yachts were well separated now, turning in their own halves,

313

tuning their sails for the burst to the line. In ten-second intervals Ernie called out the time, until the final thirty seconds, when each second was counted off.

'Harden up. Sheet in. We're going for speed.'

'Nine, eight, seven, six, five, four, three . . .'

Fifty-seven

JOHN HOUSE

Down come the seconds. Five, four, three, two, one. There's the puff of smoke and the report from the starting gun. They cross the line, about a hundred yards apart, both on starboard tack. And now Leningrad *is tacking onto port tack. Looks to me like a flawless manoeuvre. How do things seem to you, Larry?*

LARRY PETERS

We won't be able to say for sure until these yachts come together again. At the moment they're both driving hard up the windward leg of this course.

They were two seconds behind the start line when the gun went, a fine start on starboard tack, heading parallel with *Leningrad* while they built up speed.

Leningrad tacked away from them.

They continued on the same course, building up speed slowly, moving well, easing the sheets in and out as the small gusts struck them. They heeled and feathered. The numbers were climbing steadily. The boat felt good. When the crew was concentrating the boat became silent. Jim watched the display units with their rows of moving numbers, feathering the boat up slightly into wind as each gust touched them.

'Tack now,' Jack said. It was a fluent, quick tack. They were going well.

'How are we looking, Jack?' asked Jim.

314

He would remember that moment for a long time afterwards. Jack was silent while he considered the position, making his mental calculations.

Jim glanced towards *Leningrad* and saw why. It had already climbed on them.

'Did they get a lift?'

But Jack answered this time, and Jim felt a hollow in his stomach.

'No, I don't think so.'

Jim felt the wind crushed out of his lungs. That could mean only one thing. *Leningrad* was faster. Much faster.

JOHN HOUSE
Both boats have tacked and are heading in towards each other, on a converging course. From this distance, it looks as though Leningrad *is ahead. As they get closer the impression is building that the Russians are gaining ground. The two boats are closing fast.*

LARRY PETERS
New World *is at least four boat lengths behind after this part of the course. At least four, maybe five. This doesn't look good for our chances. The Russian challenger would appear to have a speed edge, maybe a substantial speed edge.*

JOHN HOUSE
They've crossed tacks again, and New World *is a significant distance behind, even at this early stage in the proceedings. How does it look to you, Larry?*

LARRY PETERS
They're crossing tacks again now, and if anything New World *looks to have dropped a further two lengths behind.* Leningrad *is powering towards the first weather buoy, having already established a strong lead. I have to admit, reluctantly, that* Leningrad *appears at this early stage to be a gear faster than* New World. *This is already starting to look ominous as* Leningrad *rounds the weather buoy at least ten lengths ahead of* New World. *The Russian challenger does a perfect spinnaker set and steams off on the downwind leg.*

'Let's see how much we can catch up downwind,' Jim said. It was weak, but it was essential to keep up morale.

Leningrad turned the upwind buoy a full fifty seconds ahead. Morale might have taken a hammering, but the boat was still being sailed well, and any action committed with competence helps to raise spirits.

'Where's the best wind?' Jim shouted out to Virus on the foredeck, as he scanned the water ahead.

'Port, twenty degrees.'

'Check,' Ernie said, watching the flowlines on the display screen. 'More turbulent, but faster.'

'Fifteen degrees to port.' It was a good tactic for another reason. The extra windspeed generated by sailing closer to the wind caused them to surf down the faces of the small waves. They concentrated their efforts on driving hard down these wave fronts, taking advantage of each surf, trying to claw back distance.

Extra wind came in from port. The wind strength increased by an extra two knots. They had to concentrate on filling the spinnaker, as the wind direction swirled and changed. It demanded a level of concentration which kept their minds off their own difficult position.

After several minutes Jim shouted, 'Gybe!' The bowman released and reset the spinnaker pole. They swung through the wind quickly and came out well on the other tack. So far they had made no significant mistakes. On the other tack Jim asked:

'Distance between us?'

Jack was cautious:

'They've pulled out another thirty-five seconds, I think.'

'Check,' said Ernie, reading out *Leningrad*'s position on the flow-screen.

It was then, Jim realised, that only a miracle would provide a single race win, let alone the series.

Ernie, cool Ernie, spoke for all of them, repeating 'Fuck, fuck, fuck,' to the screen, as if gently mocking its recalcitrance.

To trail lamentably in a race, without even a chance

of challenging, has all the pain and none of the excitement of beating a slow bruise. They concentrated on the mechanics of sailing.

As they closed with the downwind buoy now, they could begin to gauge the damage. In the course of the downwind run, the great red yacht had pulled out a further twenty-second lead. To the trailing boat in a race, the leader carries with it an air of invincibility. When the trailing crew looks at the leader, it seeks reasons for its success, and inevitably it finds them. *Leningrad* looked magnificent as it crossed broadside, its sails in perfect aerodynamic curves, its motion through the small chop powerful, settled and assured. It began to tack up the final leg.

It is normal for a match-racing yacht which has gained an advantage early in a race to place a cover on its opponent, to position itself between the source of the wind and its opponent's sails. But *Leningrad* did not do so. It simply crossed and proceeded on its path as if they weren't there, and that struck home even more forcibly than their rival's superior speed.

Jim tacked – for psychological reasons more than anything else. He could feel the intimation of hopelessness over their position closing over the crew. He wanted above all to shake them out of their shock. *New World* thundered through the wind, the winchgrinders valiantly flung themselves into hauling in the genoa. It was a good crew, another flawless tack.

Now they were on the same tack as *Leningrad*, running parallel, sufficiently well placed to be clear of *Leningrad*'s bad air.

Jack's eyes were glued to the other boat's stern, studying her progress.

'OK, Ernie, sing to me,' Jim said.

'Eight-four, eight-four, eight-five, eight-five.'

He concentrated on their own speed. The crew was silent and the numbers were coming up nicely. After several minutes, Jim said:

'Jack, how're they doing?'

'They just pulled out another estimated twenty seconds of lead.'

'We got any excuse?'

'No, I don't think so,' Jack said quietly. 'They're just faster.'

JOHN HOUSE

The Russian boat is driving now towards the finish line. On each of the legs of the course, it has pulled out a further lead. The distance between the boats is now a full three minutes.

LARRY PETERS

We're starting to see a rout here. At no time has the American defender even looked as if it was in the match. On no leg has New World been able to reduce the distance between them. Ivan Illich and his crew have sailed their formidable yacht to a three minute and ten second lead. This looks to be an ominous first race.

JOHN HOUSE

Here she comes now, the great red-hulled yacht, not even bothering to turn into wind as she crosses the line. There goes the finish gun.

Leningrad has won this race by what looks to be at least three minutes. Here comes her tender moving in towards her as two fast patrol boats of the Russian Navy take up position to escort her back towards the warship Moscow.

LARRY PETERS

Leningrad's crew are jubilant as she sails towards base. The siren in the background is the warship Moscow, a call of triumph on this day of victory.

JOHN HOUSE

And only now, New World crosses the line, three minutes fifteen seconds behind.

LARRY PETERS

It's amazing what an effect defeat, particularly a defeat as decisive as this, can have on crew morale. The American crew looks shell-shocked. Like rowers who have lost a race, they're doing the equivalent of leaning on their oars, drained by defeat. The headsail has been dropped, and Jim Shaw sails tight-lipped under mainsail while a tow rope is placed on New World's bow.

318

There are going to be some tough post-mortems in the American camp, John.

JOHN HOUSE
That's the end of the first race of the America's Cup defence. The Russians, who have been developing their campaign over the last decade, powered impressively into the lead in this race. After that decisive win, American hopes are looking bleak.

New World glided in to a silent quay.

Coach Johnson stood tight-lipped on the quay, ready to debrief them. But today Jim would not acknowledge his presence. Although it was the helmsman's privilege to walk ashore directly, today he would help the others lift the sails off, check through the gear. Jack and Ernie, following his example, helped them too. Then they helped to check the boat's gear before the lifts were put on. Her security skirt was put in place. They remained on board while the yacht was lifted by the crane over the perimeter fence, and placed on its cradle in its pallisaded enclosure on the other side.

Beneath them, Coach Johnson walked back up the quay.

With his experience of racing, Jim knew that the real damage to the crew's morale had not yet been done. That was yet to come. They were still in shock. Only afterwards, in the privacy of their own thoughts, the experience would eat into them like acid.

And he knew, above all, that with the terrible *gestalt* of the loser, they would seek and find reasons for *Leningrad*'s success, and having found them, believe them. Believing them, they would enter a cycle of further demoralisation. He was aware too that if they were to achieve their best professional efforts at holding back *Leningrad*'s speed superiority, he must break this dangerous cycle, and that to do so he must initiate some drastic action which would restore morale.

Fifty-eight

Maria flung her arms around him as soon as he opened the door. He could smell the perfume of her scalp, the shining roots of her hair.

'You all right?'

'I'm a little shocked, that's all. The amount they beat us by was rather large.'

She smiled. 'Good old Jim.'

He sat down. It was the first time he'd been able to relax for what seemed like a century. The compression of time on such a day made it seem absurd that only eight hours had passed since he left the flat. His tiredness overcame him.

Maria bustled around him, brought him coffee, put a plate of his favourite cookies in front of him, as if he were a small child.

In bed that night, he said:

'Talk to me about the Russians.' So she did; not about Russia, but about Estonia, where her family had lived for four generations. She told him stories her grandmother had passed on to her mother and her mother had transmitted to her about Tallinn; of her grandmother's life as the daughter of a minor merchant, the narrow, winding streets, the many languages of the sailors and seafarers, the factories that belched smoke across the bay, the markets and constant influx of steamers and merchant ships, the trade with the other Baltic states. And Grandma's house. It was astonishing how much detail had been passed on about the house, the layout of the kitchen, the big entrance hall, the carpets that were hung on the wall, Eastern-fashion, the upstairs landing with its five small rooms (in two of which were lodgers, an old Karelian landowner in one, in another a retired pilot and his tiny wife), in winter the porch full of discarded furs and boots, the smell of the *shchi* cabbage soup, the bubbling samovar in a corner, the old servant Anya whose whispered '*prosti-tye*' and soft curses filled the house as she worked.

And then there were the myriad recipes of food. Frozen sides and legs of meat which were hung from the upper windows to preserve in the cold of the freezing winter. Her grandmother was half Hungarian, and she brought with her a nostalgic yearning for Hungarian dishes, for Tojasos Borju Velo, the thick layers of breadcrumbs, sour cream, paprika, and the full use of the animal in its entirety – recipes for heart, sweetbreads, kidneys, liver and brain; for foot, knuckle, jowl, ear, and even the tail; and when meat was scarce, main courses of cabbage or brussel sprouts with a handful of smoked bacon.

Sometimes Jim would prompt her, ask a question, but mostly he lay quietly listening to her.

The medieval city of Tallinn, with its narrow, cobbled streets, perched on a hill, with its saint, *Starie Tom*, and its weathervane overlooking the square was, by a curious coincidence, the centre of the Russian sailing effort. Coach Johnson had told him so once or twice, but it had generated no living image, nothing for his mind to grasp except, perhaps, a picture of a soulless modern Russian seaport. Maria had put flesh on those bare bones. Beneath the hill with its fortified walls and towers, Ivan Illich had drilled his crew over several seasons to their current peak of efficiency. He passed into sleep with the two images, the warmth of the old city, and another, as his fears showed themselves, of the menacing, implacable opponent who rode out like a medieval knight from its gates and whom, whether he wished to or not, he would face again tomorrow.

Fifty-nine

The following day brought perfect weather. The sky was almost purple. Dotted here and there were small patches of cloud, as delicate as blossom. Jim made his way on foot through the back streets towards the compound.

It is sometimes said that on a yacht which is fast the tactician can do nothing wrong, on a yacht which is slow he can do nothing right.

That morning Jim was prepared to start the difficult work of rebuilding the morale of their crew, beginning with his tactician. But when, having cleared the security screen, he approached *New World*, he found Jack organising the transfer of the sails on to the craft, his quiet, unflappable self, and he thanked God silently for his great ally. Ernie was beside Jack, helping with sails. He too seemed, on the face of it, in reasonable condition. But it was the internal damage, the damage which one could not see, that he must deal with.

They heard him coming and both turned towards him. He looked at their faces for signs of that wasting of morale, that ennui of spirit which eats away at those who believe they are likely to lose.

'He looks all right to me,' said Ernie.

'We were worried about you,' Jack explained.

'All that responsibility,' Ernie said.

They studied him with concern and sympathy.

'Look, I was worried about you,' Jim protested.

'That as well,' said Jack.

'Yeah, on top of everything else,' Ernie said. 'He was worried about us.'

They were studying him with real concern now, watching his face for any sign of adverse reaction.

'Are you sure you're feeling all right?' Jack asked him.

Ernie turned sideways as if he were about to sneeze. But he was trying too hard to stifle his laughter. It came out in short hiccups and gulps. The disease was spreading fast. Jack too was now doubled up, wheezing and gasping for breath.

'Look at his face,' Jack said.

'Yeah, look at that schmoz.'

They hobbled around, weak at the knees.

'How can you joke at a time like this?' Jim asked. 'Think of all the people watching you.'

They pulled themselves together, but only with difficulty.

At least he didn't need to work on the morale of his afterguard. A clear case of clinical hysteria, yes: low morale, no. A huge sense of relief overcame him. He looked at the rest of the crew. There had been no signs of special stress the day before. But he knew people took things in different ways. That each of his men would put on a brave face for the sake of their fellow crewmen.

On the way out to the course, in the mêlée of the spectator fleet, as *New World* bucked and kicked behind the towboat through the disturbed water of a thousand wakes, he called the crew around him.

Raising his voice over the sound of the nearby engines, he said: 'I don't know what each of you does to keep up his morale in difficult situations. I only know what I can do – that's to try to be brutally honest about the position, take it on the chin if I can, and then see what can be done. That's what works for me, so here goes.

'As things stand that boat is faster than us. Let's not even try to deceive ourselves. The strong likelihood is that it's too fast for us to catch on boatspeed alone.'

He looked at their faces. For the time being they were undecided as to where he was leading them. They seemed to be giving him the benefit of the doubt.

'Those are just the facts, and like I say, I prefer to deal with the facts. I want you to take those facts on board if you haven't already. Throw your arms in the air, tear your hair out. All those facts mean to me are that if we're going to win this series, we have to achieve it by superiority in things other than boatspeed – in better

323

crew-work, superior tactics, in just outthinking and out-working our opponents.

'In an average crew, the kind of defeat that was handed out to us yesterday would demoralise them. They'd make mistakes, they wouldn't be able to help it, and they'd lose by an even bigger margin today than yesterday.

'Our task today is to sail the best race we can, and pull back on some of that loss. Even if we can pull down the margin between us, that'll be a victory, a step on our road to recovery.'

Big Ape was rubbing his chin thoughtfully. Jim looked from face to face: Virus, Jingle, Greenback, Moose, Mace, Georgie. It was a gamble, but he'd judged each in his way as a sophisticated man, mature enough to come to terms with the problems and work on the situation without delusions. At this stage they must be given something they know in their hearts is achievable, however small. To hold out the prospect of victory in this race, immediately after the catastrophic and comprehensive defeat of yesterday, was unrealistic. He could lose them that way.

He saw one or two smiles.

Big Ape said: 'We'll do that.'

There was a small chorus of assent. They went back to their places.

JOHN HOUSE

This is the second race of the thirtieth America's Cup defence. The two competitors wait, sails up, for the ten-minute gun to go. They're both hardening in sheets for this second contest.

There goes the ten-minute gun. They move into the starting box, picking up speed. Both boats appear to be waiting, like wrestlers circling. Now, as if by common consent, they move in towards the centre. Here they go, driving hard towards one another. They're closing now. New World *bears away, pointing down to leeward, and rounds up.*

LARRY PETERS

New World *is in a fierce turn.* Leningrad *responds, but* New World *seems to have sprung into that one so swiftly that she's out-turned* Leningrad, *is positioned on* Leningrad's *stern, and*

is driving the Russians away from the starting line. Jim Shaw
is forcing the Russian challenger further and further away from
the starting line. Fifty seconds to go, and Shaw has manoeuvred
into the superior position at the start. Now he's turning away for
the line.

JOHN HOUSE
As New World *turns back towards the line, Ivan Illich is*
swinging Leningrad *to follow back to the start line. Twenty-*
five seconds to go. New World *is two boat lengths ahead of*
Leningrad.

LARRY PETERS
Ten, nine, eight, seven, six, five, four, three . . . Here goes New
World, *crossing the line fast on starboard tack, having won the*
start against Leningrad. Leningrad *follows some two boat*
lengths behind. This is a good beginning for New World,
John.

JOHN HOUSE
It certainly is, Larry. Jim Shaw has hit back smartly after the
defeat of the last race. Leningrad *tacks to port now and* New
World *tacks to cover. Here they go, both picking up speed.*

LARRY PETERS
Leningrad *tacks again to try to clear her air and* New World
responds immediately by tacking again. This is classic match
race play. Jim Shaw on New World *is determined not to let*
Leningrad, *potentially the faster boat, pass her.*

JOHN HOUSE
Now Leningrad *is driving forward fast, keeping on starboard*
tack. What's going on here, Larry?

LARRY PETERS
Leningrad *is persevering on this tack, hoping that* New World
will tack away. But already something interesting is occurring,
right under our noses. Leningrad *is starting to bear off to*
leeward of New World. *This really is a terrifying display of*
Ivan Illich's greater confidence. Leningrad *is bearing off,*
accelerating, and starting to drive through New World's
windshadow.

Jim felt it like an icy cold.

To leeward *Leningrad*, which should have been gripped by *New World*'s windshadow, had merely born off slightly and was slowly and inexorably powering through.

The shock moved through the *New World*'s crew. After their superior start, they had started to pull back on some of their lost morale. They had established a classically advantageous position. It was as if a wrestler, having pinned his opponent, feels himself being bodily lifted as his opponent rises to his feet.

To leeward of them, *Leningrad* continued to gain. He could see from the fluttering of the telltales on her sails that she was in disturbed air, that she was not operating at peak efficiency. What was truly shocking was that it seemed to have virtually no effect on her performance.

Jack breathed out behind him a sigh of angry astonishment.

JOHN HOUSE
New World *achieved a brilliant start, outmanoeuvred* Leningrad, *placed a close cover on the Russian challenger, which would have held any other match-race yacht we know of, yet somehow* Leningrad *has simply used her greater performance to break* New World*'s cover and move into lead position.*

LARRY PETERS
Ivan Illich has opened up a three length lead here as both boats tack towards the windward mark. Leningrad *tacks across the bow of* New World. *John, this is heartbreaking. There's just no way one can counter this type of boat superiority.*

Beneath the brutal demonstration of *Leningrad*'s speed, something else became apparent to Jim. His crew fought back without complaint. They rounded the top mark some twenty seconds behind *Leningrad* and produced the fastest and crispest spinnaker set he had yet seen.

They hunted the windshifts in the downwind leg. Although they lost another fifteen seconds in the downwind leg, another brilliant tack call in the second upwind leg put them into a shift and they held the increase in

Leningrad's lead. But it was a hard and bitter fight. Jim was reminded again of the sensation, whenever he sailed against Illich, of being on an escalator taking you in the wrong direction. If you fought with every fibre, you stayed in the same place, but if you even paused, you slipped backwards.

The result, once again, seemed inevitable.

Sixty

Maria had been shopping. There was a smell of good things cooking in the flat. Jim followed her into the kitchen.

'You angry?' she asked.

'Sure.'

In fact, he wasn't so much angry as exhausted. In defeat he felt as if someone had punched him; defeat didn't only happen once; it wasn't one dimensional, it came in all shapes and sizes. Every second on the course, falling behind *Leningrad*, seemed to him like a body blow of a new and different kind.

Afterwards, to see whether they could repair the damage, they had a brainstorming session with Tom East about the sails. But they could think of nothing radical that would not itself entail a risk of falling back further. In the history of America's Cup racing, the losing yacht would often gamble on some radical revision of sailing or tactics. Almost without exception, it generated a greater disaster than before. It was necessary to hold one's nerve. They went through every aspect of their performance, and though there is always room for improvement, nowhere did it seem to them was there any hope of achieving the gain in speed to equal *Leningrad*.

In the kitchen Maria cut up carrots and parsley, strips of fresh cabbage into a soup dish.

The television was on in the sitting room. He listened with half an ear to the news summary, and barely reacted to the announcer's initial statement. It was the next news item that caught his attention:

'The peace conference between America and Russia has been brought forward by several months, to a date six weeks from now. The new move is understood to have the support of an influential group of senators and congressmen, led by Senator Sam Hickstead. Critics of the peace negotiations say that it has been brought forward as a means of gaining credibility for the final stages in the current presidential term.'

'You all right?' asked Maria.

He pulled back to concentrate on her. 'Yeah.'

'Sure?'

The voice of the television announcer continued. 'Senator Hickstead denied that the move to bring forward the peace talks was motivated by any desire to add a feather to the cap of the current presidential administration. He said that the signs were now looking good for agreeing a wide range of new arms limitation and verifiability pacts with Russia. Our correspondent asked him why the signs were good. Senator Hickstead said that he detected in the last few days a new mood of confidence in the Russians.'

'Jim,' Maria was saying. 'Jim.'

'Yeah?'

Maria was studying him carefully. 'Why don't you tell me what's worrying you?'

'I'm just tired.'

He sat down on one of the breakfast chairs.

Maria poured chopped liver into the soup. It smelt good. He knew he was lucky.

'What was your day like?' he asked.

Listening to her talk was like therapy to him. It was the very ordinary details. They took his mind off his own problems. He watched her cooking, moving plates about the stove.

Sixty-one

JOHN HOUSE
This is the third race of the thirtieth defence of the America's Cup. The score stands at two nil to the challengers. The Russians need only two more races to win this best of seven series. It looks as though the US is already in a difficult position. Over to you, Larry.

LARRY PETERS
The margins of win for the previous races were in the area of three minutes in the first race, two minutes in the second – a very big lead. These figures hide the fact that the American team counter-attacked in a very determined way and won the start yesterday. But the almost unbelievable speed superiority of the Russian yacht Leningrad *allowed her skipper, Ivan Illich, to break cover up the first windward leg. After that, no matter how hard* New World *fought back, the race became something of a procession.*

JOHN HOUSE
Thanks, Larry. Back to the course. There goes the ten-minute gun, and the two boats are moving in to the starting box. Neither appears intent on closing the distance between them. In fact, they're both of them keeping to their own side of the box. What's this, Larry?

LARRY PETERS
Match-racing is very much a psychological battle, John, so one side is never sure when the other side is bluffing. But right now it looks as though neither boat wishes to engage directly. They're both loitering in their own corners as the seconds are counted down.

Fifty seconds to go, and Leningrad *is picking up speed and heading for the far end of the line. They're sailing straight past each other. Obviously Ivan Illich believes there is more wind on the starboard side of the course, while* New World *believes the port-hand side is favoured.*

JOHN HOUSE
They can't both be right, Larry.

LARRY PETERS
That's right, John, only time will tell. Ten seconds to the starting gun. . . . Five, four, three, two, one . . . They're crossing the start line at opposite ends, and each driving away from one another.

JOHN HOUSE
It's as if they're in different races. Each boat is beginning a series of tacks up towards the windward mark on courses which will eventually converge. Are these the right tactics for New World?

LARRY PETERS
Jim Shaw has to accept right now that the other yacht has a major speed advantage. So he's got to find a way of beating the other boat which doesn't rely on speed.

One way to do this is to look for windshifts which will help him and not the other boat. The risk is that the opponent, on another part of the course, may find better conditions.

JOHN HOUSE
Back to the race course. It doesn't look as though Jim Shaw is losing any ground here, Larry.

LARRY PETERS
No, it doesn't. In fact, it looks as though his bold guess may even be working. They're converging now. This is starting to be exciting. Jim Shaw is tacking in towards that upper mark. He looks to me to be ahead, but we can't say by how much.

JOHN HOUSE
Here they come now. New World *is turning round the mark some five boatlengths ahead of* Leningrad! *This has been a superb counter-attack by Jim Shaw. He obviously chose the right side of the course.* New World's *spinnaker sets perfectly as she drives off on the downwind leg.*

LARRY PETERS
And here comes Leningrad. *Even when behind in the race, she*

looks threatening. A faultless spinnaker set, and she's powering away down the course in hot pursuit.

'How much time between us?' Jim asked.

'Twenty-three seconds.'

'More wind out to port,' Virus sang out.

'It checks on the flowscreen,' Ernie confirmed.

Jim knew he would be forced to keep taking risks. His first move had paid off, but like money in a current account, the lead gained would soon be spent. He glanced round at *Leningrad* hauling them down.

'They catching us?' he asked Jack, knowing the answer in advance.

'Fast.'

'Turning to starboard fifteen degrees.'

The winchgrinders began to haul in the spinnaker. He swung the wheel and as they came up he could feel, without looking at the instruments, that they were starting to drive faster. The move would also help to prevent *Leningrad* powering up to weather and stealing their wind.

This was the essence of tactics, trying to do several things at once, to preserve your own advantage while making things more difficult for your rival.

'They've changed direction to follow us,' Jack informed him.

'Where's this extra wind, Ernie?'

'About two hundred yards ahead.'

Jim looked back. The bow of the Russian yacht was looking closer as it steamrollered down towards them.

But the wind was playing them tricks, acting skittish. Like a mirage the dark patch on the water moved constantly ahead, always receding.

'Here it comes,' shouted Virus.

Jim could feel it in the sails, the way the boat seemed to pause and then drive forward. The bow lifted out two long flutes of water and they started to surf down the forward face of a wave.

He looked behind again. *Leningrad* too had now caught the gust, and was closing remorselessly.

JOHN HOUSE
Jim Shaw has just managed to hold off Leningrad*'s counter-attack on the downwind leg. As these boats round the leeward mark,* Leningrad *is only a boatlength behind.*

LARRY PETERS
Leningrad *tacks, and Jim Shaw tacks immediately to keep close cover. For a moment or two the boats seem to be holding their respective positions. Ominously,* Leningrad *is continuing on this tack. This was what Illich did yesterday. And as he does so, it is becoming increasingly obvious now that the same terrible thing is happening.* Leningrad *is driving out from under* New World*'s lee, using her superior speed to bear off and break through* New World*'s windshadow. This looks like a tragic repeat of yesterday's race.* Leningrad *is on the point of breaking through the lee of* New World *and is starting to overtake the American boat. This is absolutely tragic. What can Jim Shaw do now?*

Leningrad was neck and neck with them, about fifty yards to leeward, and once again Jim had to strain to compose his mind against the subconscious assumption of Illich's absolute superiority.

'Ease sheets slightly,' said Jim. 'Let's drop down on them.'

'You hear him, guys,' Jack shouted. 'Ease a fraction. We're going for speed.'

JOHN HOUSE
New World *has changed her course heading a few degrees, Larry. What's Shaw up to?*

LARRY PETERS
My guess is he has decided he just can't sit idly by and let Leningrad *power through his lee. He's decided to ease sheets, sacrifice his temporary position, and get in closer to* Leningrad. *The closer he gets, the more damaging his windshadow on* Leningrad.

JOHN HOUSE
Seems like a desperate move.

LARRY PETERS
It's the cold and brutal move of a trained match-racer, who seems to have judged the odds correctly. If he does nothing, Leningrad *in a few minutes will have powered through his lee. He's certain to lose if he does nothing. This way maybe he can hold back the inevitable.*

Ernie sang out:
   'Speed rising. Eight-four becomes eight-five, Eight-five. Eight-six.
   It was nerve-wracking, watching the boats come together, praying that *Leningrad* was not already too far ahead.

LARRY PETERS
I have to say, Jim Shaw timed that bold and aggressive move to perfection. New World *swooped down on* Leningrad, *and punched the wind out of her sails.*
   Every ounce of experience tells me that Leningrad *must accept it has been thwarted, and tack away.*

JOHN HOUSE
But she isn't. She's holding course.

LARRY PETERS
Leningrad, *her mainsail buffeted by the turbulence of* New World*'s wind, is bearing off a few degrees. And she's brazening it out. This is arrogance or confidence on a monumental scale. They're neck and neck. This is absolutely terrifying.* Leningrad *has recovered from Shaw's deadly blow, and is simply moving ahead, inch by inch, foot by foot. Now she's forward of* New World*'s windshadow. And now* Leningrad *is counter-attacking. She's using clean air to squeeze up to* New World. *In this leeward position, she has the right of way. And she's squeezing up, forcing Shaw to tack.*
   There goes New World, *tacking now, forced to tack away by* Leningrad.

Losing this time was more difficult than last. It felt to Jim as if he had been beaten to the ground, as if all the sap had been drawn from him.

On their way back to the dock, Ernie said: 'The speed instruments are reading high.'

'What do you mean?' Jim asked.

'I tried to check using an alternative means of calculation. Using the laser rangefinder, I can get an exact distance reading on where we're going, take the time to get there, and get the speed.'

'So?'

'Measured against that calculation, the speed instruments are always high.'

'How much?'

'About one tenth of a knot. Of that order. Not much, I admit, but it's consistent.'

'You sure it's not just an instrumentation error?'

'I couldn't be absolutely sure. Look, I'm just passing on an opinion.'

Jack said: 'It doesn't mean anything unless we know what the cause is.'

'I'm not causing trouble, you guys. I'm the navigator. I'm in charge of the instruments, and in my view they're reading artificially high relative to our actual speed. Enough said.'

'Thanks, Ernie.' Jim said. They were all edgy and their nerves were strained. He would think about what Ernie said later.

First they would hold a detailed post-mortem on the day's performance, and prepare for what seemed, even to him, to be inevitable defeat the following day.

Sixty-two

Jim sat in the semi-darkness, leaning forward, his elbows on his knees, his face in his hands.

The footsteps down the corridor clearly belonged to

Coach Johnson. He could hear the slight drag of Coach Johnson's bad leg.

The door was opened and the light was switched on. 'Hi, Jim. Thought maybe I'd find you here.'

Jim raised his head from his hands and nodded, without turning round.

Coach Johnson paused, then walked past him to the table at the head of the room. Jim noted that he wore a suit, as if he'd just met someone important. He sat down and indicated with the open palm of his hand that Jim should sit opposite.

Slowly, Jim stood up. It was difficult to shake off his depression. There seemed to be no power in his limbs. He walked slowly to the table, pulled out a chair, and sat down opposite Coach Johnson.

'I got word from on high.' Coach Johnson paused, considering his words carefully. Jim was staring at the opposite wall, as if only part of him was listening. Coach Johnson studied him for a moment.

'They wanted me to pass a message on to you.' He continued to study Jim's face, as if assessing his response. 'Frankly, they wanted me to tell you they're grateful for what you're doing.'

Jim considered the incongruity of this statement.

'Grateful? But we're losing.'

Coach Johnson shrugged. 'OK, we're losing now, but other places . . . things are going OK.'

'I don't understand. What are you saying, exactly?'

Coach seemed both expansive and evasive. 'I'm saying things are fine.'

Jim was more alert now. 'You're saying they're pleased we're losing?'

However much he and Ernie might react against a hint or suggestion that they should 'make the Russians look good', Jim realised that he never fully believed that this could be the case. But here was Coach Johnson apparently offering final confirmation.

Coach Johnson was patient. He could see he was getting

into troubled waters. His helmsman had just had the stuffing kicked out of him. He wasn't feeling too happy.

'Look, Jim, you and me, we don't know what's going on. Could be something to do with the summit meeting that is coming up. The Russians have had a bad time economically. Maybe this'll put them in a good frame of mind.'

Jim thought he recognised Hickstead's phrases. He said instead, to give himself time: 'Summit?'

'Yeah, something like that.'

In the pause that followed the air itself seemed to grow still.

'You're saying our guys are pleased that we're losing?'

Coach Johnson sighed. 'Jim, to us this is a big thing, the biggest thing in the world. That's our view, OK?'

'They really want us to lose . . . '

'We all got different priorities.'

'You're agreeing with them?'

'Now look, Jim.' Coach Johnson waved a hand through the air, as if warding something off. 'That's putting me in a difficult position.'

But Jim was already rising to his feet. 'You goddamn taught me,' he yelled. 'You taught me when I was a child. Never give up. Never give up!'

Coach reached forward, attempting a conciliatory gesture. But Jim threw off his hand.

'Jim!' Coach Johnson lunged to his feet. But Jim had moved away and was already at the door, throwing it open.

Pushing the table aside, Coach Johnson lumbered to the now empty doorway, shouting at the security guard at the other end of the corridor. 'Stop him!'

Jim tried to break past, but the big security guard was surprisingly nimble. He hit Jim from the side in a sprawling tackle, slammed him against the wall and pinned him there.

'Hold him!' shouted Coach Johnson.

He closed in on the struggling guard.

Jim could smell the sweat of the big man's body. Every

336

movement he made seemed to deflect off the bulk of his assailant. The guard applied a ruthless procedure; each movement Jim made, he was slammed hard against the wall. He managed to work an arm free briefly. He swung as fast as he could, throwing his weight into his free elbow, feeling his elbow strike into the solar plexus of the guard. The guard doubled up in agony. The grip on Jim slackened. He broke free, sprinting down the corridor.

Coach Johnson shouted 'Dumb bastard,' and ran after him. Emerging from the corridor into the open, Jim sensed that, for the time being at least, he was safe. Coach Johnson could have shouted to the guard to press the alarm system, but a crowd was standing at the iron grille. To arrest his helmsman publicly would have caused a scandal. He watched Jim show his security card to the guard at the perimeter gate, saw the gate opened. Then Jim had disappeared into the crowd.

Coach Johnson turned to look at the guard, still doubled up. 'You did your best,' he said.

'That little bastard was like an eel.'

The guard rose slowly, a big man with a reddish face, taking deep breaths.

'You all right now?'

'It's the indignity,' the guard said, 'more than the pain.'

Absurdly, Jim remembered a stray phrase of Mao Tse Tung's: 'A guerrilla hides amongst the people like a fish in the sea.'

For a while he kept to the crowds that had packed the town. He traversed two blocks and then, moving apart, sprang over a fence. He landed five feet down the other side of the beach, dusted the sand off his clothes and started to walk, his hands in his pockets.

A woman looked up to watch him passing. Perhaps she half recognised him, for she turned to the small chihuahua at her side and said 'nice man, Elmer'.

Three children beside a sandcastle stopped playing as he walked past.

The attention made him nervous. He turned towards

337

the old disused amusement arcade. A barrier with a notice sprawled across said 'Do not cross. Dangerous.' Jim vaulted the barrier and began to walk along the echoing planks.

Beneath him the sea lapped against the piles. Seagulls called close by. He was passing through a tunnel, and he could see the shadows of gulls in the open end. On the decaying footwalk his footsteps made an odd, hollow sound. He stepped round old piles of rusting plant and machinery, several old deckchairs with the canvas long since rotted, discarded cartons.

An old man, dressed in a ragged overcoat, was lying beside some newspapers. He looked up at Jim's footsteps, eyes sightless with drink.

Jim stood on the end of the short pier. Some distance away crowds milled, children shouted. He tried to gather his thoughts, to quieten his outrage. But instead he felt rage building inside him.

Fifty yards further on there was an old, rusted bench. He pushed some newspapers aside and sat down. He must have waited several hours. It was already early evening when he started to walk back. The crowds for the most part had deserted the shore. Only the occasional, lonely figure could be seen on the beach in the gathering dusk.

Early streetlamps were starting to shine.

Keeping to the backstreets, he walked downtown, towards the area of bars, seedy cinemas, the other face of the big seaside port. To avoid a main thoroughfare, it was necessary to make a detour towards the beach again. Part of the beach was hidden from the landward side by a short sea wall. It was now dark and the beach was deserted. Only his shadow, thrown by the lights of the *Moscow* out in the bay, kept him company.

He had heard on *New World*'s radio, as they were towed back to port after their third successive defeat, that the Russian president had flown in that afternoon, and was intent on viewing what would almost certainly be the final race tomorrow. Ivan Illich, the announcement said, would be dining with him, reporting on the races so far. In official circles on both sides, the outcome was widely regarded as a foregone conclusion.

He didn't begrudge Illich his victories. It was the hopelessness of his own situation, the final realisation, at a visceral level, that the matter had been decided beforehand, that began to eat like acid. Senator Hickstead, General Walters and Tom Stuttaford would have their way.

His anger started to burn inside him. He wanted a drink.

Drinking didn't loosen it. It just kept coming back more strongly, like waves.

The interior of the bar was bottle green from the lights on the ceiling. It was underground, with walls in rough colourwash.

He drank steadily. The barman approached him at first, trying to open up a conversation, but when he saw his customer was morose he moved back to the other end of the bar. Occasionally he came forward to refill a drink. Two tall girls and a short man in a loud shirt appeared and settled down at the other end. The barman seemed to know them. He raised a telephone to speak to someone and for some reason Jim grew nervous. He guessed, from the look of the girls, that they were hustlers. One of them glanced in his direction, and when he did not return her look, turned away.

The bar started to fill suddenly, and drink did not blunt his dislike of being with too many people in a room. He put down his glass and made his way out.

Outside it was dark. The night-lifers were beginning to come out onto the streets. A taxi's wheels squealed a block away. Several girls walked by in twos or threes. The loneliness of the town at this hour descended on him. He found another bar in a quieter, older part of the town, the haunt of elderly men and their women. After a few more drinks he felt uneasy again and moved out.

He bought a bottle of whisky at an all-night store. The middle-aged man serving there would not look him in the eyes, and Jim supposed, aware suddenly of his external condition, that at this stage he must appear dangerous. Rows of bright green dolls stared at him from the shelves. Outside it was starting to get chilly. The clear night sky let out the heat. He made his way down the less populated streets. He turned down an alleyway and thought he caught sight, at the other end, of a movement in the shadow. He made a detour back towards the beach.

The wall was difficult to scale in his condition. He landed badly on the other side, and sprained his hand lifting himself up. Switching the half empty bottle to the other hand, he weaved his way back to the amusement arcade.

It was starting to drizzle. He made his way under the piers of the amusement arcade. He sat down on the sand and finished the bottle. Then he smashed the empty bottle against a pier.

Across the water the floodlights of the *Moscow* spread tiny points of light across the waves. Its helicopter launch pad was lit. Occasionally launches moved towards it and away, carrying guests. Sweeping aside the broken glass with his fingers, he rolled over and slept.

Sixty-three

Grandpa Shaw rowed out his lobsterpots. Jack flicked his dinghy onto its side, driving past with the wave hitting the pier under Jim like a drum roll. Coach Johnson shouted from the stern of the cutter as the dinghies milled. Charlie Grist's shadow puffed small black clouds. Maria walked away from the window.

Something was nudging him, pushing insistently at his shoulder. With the return of consciousness, he felt suddenly cold. The shove against his shoulder became more insistent. He tried to open his eyes, but the sun was beating down fiercely, and he could only see, as if out of the bottom of a well, the outline of figures above him.

A voice said: 'Well, just blow me through a hoop.'

Another said: 'Goddamn.'

Sun and shadows moved across Jim's face. He held up a hand against the light, but his eyes were so sore he had to screw them up. His whole body ached.

There were two of them standing against the sun. He caught a glimpse of a leather jacket.

'Remember him?'

'Jee-sus. Hell, it's coming back to me.'

'Do you see what I see?'

'It's coming, it's coming.'

'This is one of those guys who stole our chicks in José's.'

'Hell, damn. You mean about a year ago?'

'I do surely.'

'Ooh-wee. That's just awful.'

'Fact. Kiss my doodle if this isn't the guy who started it.'

'Hell, damn, that's just terrible.'

He could see them now a little better, their faces indistinct, but their figures had a distant, unpleasant familiarity.

'Doris Swarze.'

'Sam.'

'Remember them?'

'Remember them, asshole?'

A pain began to thunder in Jim's head. He felt his mouth go dry.

He heard one of them say, almost lazily, 'I think we should beat the shit out of him.'

'Sounds right to me.'

He tried not to brace himself for the first blow, knowing that to do so would bring about what he feared. He could hardly think, his brain was clattering so.

The first kick struck him in the rib cage, just a friendly starter, perhaps too high to do any immediate damage but it crushed the wind out of him, sending a pain through

341

his lung so violent that he rolled on his side in agony. He doubled up and put his hand over his face, and knew that he had done something which had almost certainly sealed his fate.

Another kick sent a stab of agony into his kidneys, and they were just warming up. The pain helped to clarify his mind. Now kicks began to rain in on him.

'Hold it.'

A kick from a boot glanced off his elbow.

'What?'

'Wait a bit. Wait a bit.'

'What's going on?'

'This guy's something special.'

'He's what?'

Another blow struck him, a really painful one, just below his ribcage. He could hear the squeal of his own breathing. He waited for the blows which would follow, but there seemed to be a temporary respite.

A hand grabbed him by the ear and roughly pulled his face towards the light. 'He's that goddamn guy who's . . . ' Fingers were clicked.

'He's what?'

'That motherfucker.'

The fingers went click, click.

The snapping stopped.

'That guy who's sailing against the Russkies.'

A second face drew close.

'You got to be kidding.'

'I am not. This is the little pig-squealing sucker that's taking a hammering from the Russkies.'

A hand shook his face, 'Ain'tcha?'

'Look at the sucker.'

'He's got it bad.'

'He looks in bad shape.'

'It's shocking to see.'

'What we gonna do about that?'

'Put him out of his misery, maybe.'

'Yeah.'

'Best we can do.'

'Looks like it.'

Jim quailed again, waiting for the next blow.

'No. wait.'

One of the figures straightened up.

'You on the level about this guy?'

'Sure.'

'Hell, I have one juicy idea.'

'You have?'

'Hell, damn.'

'Lemme have it.'

'Damn, damn, hell.'

'Come on.'

'We pick up this little pigshit asshole, we put him on a machine, and we deliver him just like he is to the public, man.'

There was a pause.

'To the public at large, man.'

'Hell, damn.'

'Yeah, man.'

'Hell, damn. That is plain evil.'

'To public scrutinee.'

'Shit.'

'We didn't touch him.'

'Us?'

'We found him.'

'We sure did.'

'Lying in his own goddamn vomit under a bench. Chickenshit little creep.'

'That's how it was.'

'We did our best.'

'We got to help him to get transport.'

'Come on, brother.'

Hands lifted Jim. He couldn't stand. He was being raised by one on either side, pushed, shoved, dragged towards the beach. The pain in his chest and kidneys almost made him pass out.

One of the voices said:

'I could do with a drink.'

'Big, big.'

'Buckets of ice.'

'Cool, cool.'

'Pig-sniffing cunt-sucking fist-fucking Pepsi.'

Jim fainted.

He didn't remember much of the ride through the streets on pillion, the whooping and yelling, the swerving from side to side through the traffic as his head rolled like an empty melon. His arms were locked under the rider's arms to prevent him falling off. The motorbikes halted along the sea-wall. A sudden stench of seaweed rose up towards him. He was being part pushed, part helped down stone steps. He tried to open his eyes, and the world came towards him on a vertical spine of pain.

They were in the stern of one of the powerboats tied up against the wharf.

One of the bikers was grunting, pulling hard on the throttle of the outboard. A voice was raised in consternation. 'Hey, that's not your boat.'

'It is now.'

The motors started to roar.

'This is important luggage.'

'National business.'

'Hey, you can't do that.'

'You better believe it.'

'Take this rope, old man,' he heard one of the bikers say, followed by the thud of a coil hitting a body.

The throttle was opened and they swung away in such a steep curve they almost turned over.

They had allowed Jim to collapse in the well of the boat. Behind the pain of his head, the first beginnings of coherent thoughts were beginning to form. He eased himself back against the aft thwart of the powerboat, then slowly upwards into a sitting position.

Every time they hit the swell of another boat, the impact went through Jim like a red-hot lance.

Spray doused him once or twice. The salt stung his eyes, but in spite of it, his vision was clearing slightly.

The motorboat was jinking right and left avoiding other boats. There were shouts. Someone called out: 'Slow down, you moron.'

One of the bikers said: 'I could get to like this.'

They went through a small gap between two boats so close that the stern wave exploded against the two topsides and doused them.

'Damn, hell, damn, this is good.'

'Ride her, cowboy.'

The throttle was gunned into full. They jinked and swerved, sprang over a wave in a full turn, approached a wall of spectator yachts at full power. By rights they should have spread themselves on it like marmalade. But a gap showed and they thundered through.

They were in the space cleared for racing. Ahead, half a mile distant, were the tall masts of *New World* and *Leningrad*. Sail was being hoisted on *Leningrad*. *New World* stood idle.

A Coastguard vessel picked up speed, swung towards them, and accelerated like a greyhound.

'The posse's picked up our trail.'

'Shi-it, this is good.'

The Coastguard boat was coming in from the side at an interception angle.

A megaphone was sounding. 'This is forbidden water. Halt immediately. Halt immediately.'

'Damn, hell, damn.'

'Too fucking cool.'

One of the bikers went below and emerged from the small cabin holding a megaphone.

He put it to his mouth.

'Out of my way, you motherfucker, or I'm going to blow your ass off.' He turned sideways. 'How's that?'

'Real good, we're communicating.'

The megaphone on the cutter said laconically. 'Message understood.'

The Coastguard boat was a magnificent sight. Two perfect peeled flutes of waves, each forty feet, swept back from its bow, a bow of unimpeachable aggression, knifing towards them.

'Halt immediately, halt immediately for your own safety.'

The biker put down the megaphone, turned round, and dropped his pants.

'I read you loud and clear,' said the cutter megaphone.

'Hell damn, hell damn, this is good.'

'Hold on, brothers,' the biker at the wheel said.

They began to jink and swerve. The Coastguard cutter held back, like a greyhound studying a fleeing hare, waiting to pounce.

They were closing with *New World* fast; three hundred yards of wavering, fuzzy distance.

The Coastguard cutter swung across their bows. They dethrottled to avoid full collision, turned, and struck a glancing blow against the cutter's topsides. Two guns were aimed at them from the deck of the Coastguard boat.

'You're under arrest.'

The sun beat down fiercely. Jim stood up shakily, looked into the small hole of a level barrel, swayed several times, steadied himself against the spray awning and said. 'I request safe passage. I am the helmsman of *New World*.'

There was a silence behind the levelled gun-barrels.

The sun beat down on Jim. He felt faint again, swayed, and held himself upright by holding onto the side. Another figure joined the two on the rail.

Wavelets tapped against the hull.

A voice, the laconic voice of the skipper, said clearly, 'And I am the Queen of Sheba.'

Sixty-four

JOHN HOUSE
The two yachts have been towed out to their preliminary positions. There they sit, on either side of the starting box, sails not yet up. The crew on both yachts are checking instruments, leading ropes through fairleads, preparing themselves for the contest. But there seems to be something a little out of place on the American yacht.

Over now to Larry Peters, who's monitoring the latest information as it comes in.

LARRY PETERS
Thank you, John. Unfortunately, there does seem to be an unforeseen development on the American defender. The skipper and helmsman, Jim Shaw, does not appear to be on board.

The American camp is keeping a tight lid on these developments. As you viewers out there may know, this has been one of the highest security operations, with the two camps maintaining absolute secrecy.

However, a well-informed source appears to confirm that there had been friction between Jim Shaw and the security authorities on how the campaign should be conducted. Shaw has been dissatisfied with the interference imposed on the American defence by security.

My informed source says that this may be the root of the problem. If so, it's a terrible end to this defence. We stand at the point of no return, before an ignominious defeat. The Russians need only one more race to take the Cup. That's hardly the time to let a rift like this appear. That's about as much as I can say right now. Back to you, John.

JOHN HOUSE
Thank you, Larry. Maybe I can speak for most of the viewers out there when I say we're really sorry to hear that.

We go back to the competitors now. This is straight from the helicopter. There are signs of activity on the Russian challenger. They're putting on their mainsail, getting ready for action. The

347

Russian support boat is drawing away. There are only twelve minutes to go before the ten-minute gun.

Now let's look at the American boat. Sails aren't yet being hauled up. Will you look at that? There's some kind of conference going on in the back of the boat. The tactician Jack Peabody, Jim Shaw's right hand man, appears to be in discussion with Hal Johnson, the coach of the American team. The support launch is still tied up alongside.

Well, what could one possibly make of this? I really don't know. For those viewers who have just joined us, we are at the start of the fourth race of the thirtieth America's Cup.

Jack's eyes hunted anxiously through the spectator craft.

Coach Johnson said: 'You're going to have to steer the boat.'

'There must be something wrong.' Jack looked out across the slowly heaving sea to the solid grey of the spectator fleets beyond the course. 'He'd be here if he could. Something is wrong.'

'He flipped, Jack. Pressure gets to some people that way.'

'No! He'd be here.'

'You steer the boat. That's an order.'

Jack turned. His face was white. 'You got one minute to get off the boat before I throw you off. You overstay your time, we get disqualified, then I'm going to blame you personally for losing the Cup.'

Coach Johnson, his jaw hard with anger, removed himself to the launch tied up astern. On board he reversed the engine, swung in a half circle, then punched the gear into full forward throttle, moving away towards the spectator positions without looking back.

Jack watched him go. He steeled himself to tell the crew the series was over. His watch indicated forty-five seconds to go. Soon the navigational clock would start to trill out the last thirty seconds of countdown.

Ernie, standing beside him, pointed to another area of the course, and asked: 'What's happening over there?'

LARRY PETERS

There's some commotion in the screen of Coastguards and Naval boats around the starting area. A small speedboat has broken through the screen and is being pursued by a fast coastguard boat. The speedboat is zigzagging about, dodging the efforts of the fast patrol boat which is trying to intercept it.

Maybe it's carrying some message for New World. *But time is running out, time is down to forty seconds before the ten-minute gun, after which Jim Shaw is going to miss this America's Cup race. What a tragic end to this series.*

The speedboat has been intercepted by a Coastguard cutter and has been placed under arrest. There are signs of a discussion there. We aren't in a position to say what's going on. And now the Coastguard cutter seems to be pulling back, it's pulling back and allowing the speedboat to pass.

Ten, nine, eight . . . The speedboat has reached New World, *and someone has been pulled aboard. There goes the ten-minute gun . . .*

A cheer has gone up on the New World. *It looks as though, yes, it looks as though Jim Shaw is aboard.*

Jack said, 'Jesus.'

He could have wept. Instead, he hauled Jim aboard.

'Goodbye, motherfucker,' the biker on the wheel of the speedboat said. The speedboat revved and turned away. The Coastguard cutter was hovering now, ready to escort it away from the racing area.

Jack shouted, 'Up sail.' And to Ernie: 'I'll attend to this.'

Turning towards Jim, he said: 'Am I glad to see you, you drunken bastard.'

Jim swayed on the sidedecks. His head felt as if it was in two halves, and they would never join. He wondered whether he had sustained a broken rib from the bikers.

Of the less than half dozen items they kept on board not related to racing, a light, plastic bucket with a lanyard was one. Jacked fetched this up, held on to the lanyard, threw the bucket overboard, and scooped it up full of water. Standing in front of the swaying helmsman of *New*

349

World, Jack said laconically: 'Hold still. This is going to be great television.'

Then he emptied the contents of the bucket over Jim.

JOHN HOUSE
Did you see that, Larry?

LARRY PETERS
I sure did, John.

JOHN HOUSE
Must've overslept.

LARRY PETERS
Looks to me like a humdinger of a hangover. At least, though, with Jim Shaw finally on board the crew have sprung into action. They're pulling up sail now.

Sixty-five

JOHN HOUSE
Jim Shaw is steering New World *as it closes with* Leningrad. *In the stern of* Leningrad, *spoiling for a fight, is the great Russian sailing champion Ivan Illich.*

LARRY PETERS
And it looks as though even now the Russians have the advantage. Each sail is perfectly set as they power reach down the line towards their rival. The two yachts start to close in on one another from opposite sides of the box.

JOHN HOUSE
They're hauling in their sails. Like old battleships, they're manoeuvering to board. They're closing with one another.

LARRY PETERS
From here you can see the winchgrinders putting their power into

the sheets, the trimmers easing the sails in and out with each small
change of boat heading or wind.

JOHN HOUSE
And here comes the red hull of the Russian challenger, with the
hammer and sickle etched against its topsides, already taking a
fast turn towards the American boat. In the stern Ivan Illich
aims that sleek bow straight towards the Americans.

LARRY PETERS
Now they're closing, they're almost broadside. Already both yachts
are turning around each other, each struggling to turn
faster . . . The yacht which manages to get behind its rival is
likely to hold the advantage and drive its rival away from the
starting line.

JOHN HOUSE
The audience is quiet as we watch this deadly game unfold. Looks
to me as though the Russian boat has gained an advantage.

LARRY PETERS
The American boat is forced to bear away, with the challenger
in close pursuit.

JOHN HOUSE
Now what's happening here? New World *is heading towards*
the spectator fleet, with Leningrad *hot on its tracks. The US*
boat is going to try to lose its pursuer by weaving and ducking
through the spectator fleet. You can hear the Coastguard
loudspeakers warning the spectator fleet not to move, to stay in
position.

LARRY PETERS
The sirens have become silent now. The loudspeakers have stopped.

JOHN HOUSE
New World *is continuing to drive into the spectator fleet, drawing*
the pursuing Leningrad *after her.* New World *is making a*
detour around a motor yacht, gybing. It's so quiet now, you can
hear the swish of their bow waves and the crash of the boom as
New World *gybes.* Leningrad *swings in behind them,*
relentless. The Russian yacht gybes too. They're a long way
from the start line. How are we for time, Larry?

351

LARRY PETERS
We're starting to run out of time before the start now, John. Two minutes ten seconds to go before the starting gun, about one minute forty seconds to get back to the line.

JOHN HOUSE
New World *is now close to the stern of the Soviet warship* Moscow. New World *is turning around the warship, with* Leningrad *still in close pursuit. How do you see the situation developing now, Larry?*

LARRY PETERS
Well now, look at this, both yachts are in the lee of this big ship, starved of wind, slowing down. It's turning into a drifting match here in the lee of the Moscow, *as both boats ease their way forward on every tiny little breeze. The first one to reach the clear air on the other side of the* Moscow *is going to be able to break first towards the line.*

'Ease it,' Jack hissed.

They were only able to catch the faintest zephyrs, and every tiny breath of wind had to be grasped by the sails, shaped and deflected. In the light conditions in the lee of the *Moscow*, both sails required adjustment from second to second.

'Keep the mainsail fuller. That's too flat,' Jim said.

Jack had sprung forward and was helping Georgie, the starboard genoa trimmer, to ease and tighten in during the zephyrs, hauling in the sail directly by its sheet, easing where necessary. The concentration of the crew was intense. The boat still had way, though it was only gliding now. You couldn't even hear the rustle of the bow wave.

'Two knots,' Ernie sang. 'Two dead, one-nine, one-nine, one-eight.'

The metal sides of the warship towered above them. Grey covers hid sensitive instrumentation and radars. The rail was lined with Soviet sailors and technicians off duty. The red flag with hammer and sickle floated from its stern.

But they had no time to study the details of the *Moscow*.

Each tiny vortex of wind cast from its giant bulk was a small source of power, a tiny battery in the mirror calm, a matter of a few inches of distance.

JOHN HOUSE
New World *is still ahead.*

LARRY PETERS
That's right, John. And maybe the tactics of the American yacht are becoming clearer now. It is starting to look as if Jim Shaw may be in the process of turning his difficult position into a clear lead. It looks almost as if the Russian yacht may have been drawn into a trap.

How ironic it would be, in this battle of wits, if the US boat has used the windshadow from the Russian warship to turn a helpless position to its own advantage.

JOHN HOUSE
Will you take a look at this! The first boat to emerge from the Moscow's *windshadow is* New World. *Look at her sails catch the wind. She heels now and accelerates, swinging in a huge loop towards the starting line.*

LARRY PETERS
And Leningrad *has not yet emerged from the windshadow of the Soviet warship. The seconds are ticking away as the American boat powers towards the start line. There is now something like a full minute between these boats.*

JOHN HOUSE
This is incredible! I cannot believe . . .

LARRY PETERS
There goes the starting gun! Thirty seconds later, the American boat sweeps across the start line, and begins to tack up the first leg of the course, putting a full two minutes of time between them. What an unbelievable reverse for the Leningrad. *With cool audacity, Jim Shaw has turned this race into a potential disaster for the Russians.*

Now here at last Leningrad *is emerging from the windshadow of this enormous Soviet warship. The wind is catching her perfect sails. She is heeling and accelerating fast, swinging in a wide*

loop to avoid any further windshadow, and now Leningrad *is
streaming towards the start line in hot pursuit.* Leningrad *crosses
the line and tacks. Look at this astonishing yacht change course
and accelerate out of the tack.*

On *New World* they were wound up tightly.

Jack was coaching the crew. 'We have a chance here,
a slim chance. Concentrate every second on what you
have to do.'

'Tack,' Jim shouted.

They came through the wind fast, slicing out on the
other side strongly and well, the winchgrinders winding
in the last few inches slowly as they gained speed again
and could flatten the sails for the close haul.

Jack saw a couple of the crew glancing nervously back.

JOHN HOUSE

*They're now on the second to last leg of the course. And the
American boat is still leading by one minute,* New World*'s lead
is being whittled away on every leg by the ferocious counterattack
of* Leningrad. *Every tack it hauls in an extra couple of seconds,
every time it sets one of its flawless spinnakers, it pulls back more
valuable seconds.*

*Slowly the distance between these boats is closing. Now here
we are at the final mark.*

'Jesus.'

Jack said it involuntarily as he glanced back and
watched the Soviet boat round the last buoy, twenty-eight
seconds behind them. Being remorselessly overhauled like
this was almost more unnerving than being beaten fair
and square on the course.

'Bring in that mainsail one inch,' Jim said. 'That's it.
Feels a little better. How's it on the clock, Ernie?'

'Solid on eight-two. Eight-two. Eight-two. Eight-three.'

'What'd I tell you?' said Jim. He was determined to
keep their morale up. It was also necessary to counteract
the splitting headache against which he struggled.

'Next person who turns round to look at *Leningrad* I'm
gonna drop my pants and moon him,' said Jack.

Jim had a nasty recurrence of memory.

'That's some bad magic,' said Big Ape.

But they didn't need to look back. They could hear, in the silence of their concentration, the sliding rush of *Leningrad*'s bow wave, and the almost musical whine of her winches as her trimmers eased and hardened sails with the gusts.

JOHN HOUSE

As they come towards the finish line, it's the American boat, New World, *now some twelve seconds ahead, which is going to cross the line first, which is now slicing strongly towards the finish line. The gun goes in this fourth race. An American victory, yes, an historic American victory in the face of defeat.*

Jim swung *New World* into the wind to shoot the finish line. For a few seconds she hung there, the shadows shaking out of the sails, while the smoke from the finish gun drifted past.

The crew turned round. Jim remembered that moment. Their victory had not yet fully dawned. Slowly they turned. He saw, in slow motion, their faces lighten. They began, almost imperceptibly, to smile. They turned towards him like flowers towards sunlight. The silence filled slowly with their cheering, growing until it became a confused roar.

The crew sprang towards Jim, whooping and shouting and thumping him and Jack and Ernie on the back. Behind them the sirens were wailing. A fire-ship shot a jet of water into the air.

'Excuse me,' Jim said. Turning aside, he vomited copiously into the sea.

Sixty-six

In front of the cheering crowds on adjacent jetties, *New World* tied up at the dock. The crew stepped on shore.

The sails were piled up on the quay, ready to be taken away for the nightly check and recut at the sail loft.

A screen of security guards held back the crowds while the lifting strops were placed on the yacht and the secrecy skirt was manoeuvred into place. The yacht was lifted over the high security fence into the compound.

Jim and the crew made their way through the cheering crowds. Holding his carrier bag on his shoulder, Jim found himself blocked by cheering, swarming, backslapping people, harried by small boys with autograph books. His aching, bruised ribs made him wince every time someone jubilantly hammered him. He did his best to sign his name as he walked.

The crowd closed and expanded in front of him. He glanced sideways up one of the alleys that led down to the waterfront, considering how best he could make his dignified escape. The crowd seemed to part for an instant and drew back, then swirled forward again. In the instant of its parting, he saw a familiar figure standing beyond the crowds, in the alcove of a shop front, talking to another man. Jim recognised the neck and back of O'Reilly. The man to whom he was talking was hidden, except for his soft hat.

Jim turned and started to push his way through the crowds towards O'Reilly. It was difficult to make progress without actually forcing people aside. The crowds opened and closed again. Tantalisingly, he only caught occasional glimpses of his objective. He saw O'Reilly glance back once, perhaps distracted by the hubbub of the crowd. Then O'Reilly was shaking hands and was starting to walk away from the man in the soft felt hat who, Jim saw now, also wore a grey raincoat.

Jim shouted: 'O'Reilly!'

He was forcing his way through now, ignoring the angry comments of the people he thrust aside, towards the entrance to the alleyway. O'Reilly had disappeared. A few yards on there was a cross-roads of narrow walkways. Two other narrow pedestrian streets snaked away on either side, both empty except for some windowshoppers. A figure in a grey coat, with a felt hat, moved away from a window and walked at a brisk pace away from him.

Jim set out in pursuit. Moving as quickly as he was able along the wharf, it seemed an interminable time before, weaving amongst and through the passers-by, he was able to catch up with the walking man.

Out of breath after his short burst, Jim drew level.

'Excuse me. Hey, excuse me, sir.'

The man turned round. He had an impressive face, broad, with short, iron-grey hair. He was well-dressed. His overcoat looked expensive. A banker, Jim thought, or perhaps a politician? He had the assurance of privilege. Now he was regarding Jim with the impassive, frankly calculating eye of one who is not used to being stopped on the street without good reason.

'That man you were talking to back there. I wonder if you could tell me where he went. I'd really like to speak to him.'

'Which man would that be?'

His accent was Eastern seaboard, New York, maybe. Jim drew in his breath.

'Colonel O'Reilly.'

'I don't know anyone of that name.' The man was courteous, but firm. 'If you'll forgive me.'

He turned and walked on, but Jim ran after him.

'You were speaking to him. Right back there.'

'You are mistaken. I do not know anyone of that name,' the man repeated.

Jim held up his palms in a gesture of peace. 'OK, you don't know him. I'm sorry I troubled you.'

The man glanced at him for a moment, then continued his even, precise walk.

Jim watched him go. Something about the man jogged

his memory. He was certain he had seen him somewhere before. The image of his face teased and frustrated him. The man disappeared around a corner. Jim could have howled with fury at the ineffectual churning of his memory.

'Hey, Jim.'

Jack was walking towards him. 'Why'd you head off like that? I thought maybe you needed some help.'

'I thought I saw O'Reilly talking to someone.'

'So?'

Jack's face was open. A half smile played on his face. Jim hesitated.

'Nothing, Jack. Just my paranoia.'

'What's troubling you, buddy?'

'Generally or right now?'

'Try generally.'

'We're slow. I can feel it. Our speed is down.'

'I don't get it.'

'Our speed is down. You're not on the wheel. I can feel it.'

'How much by?'

'Not a lot. I don't know exactly, but maybe enough so that if we got it back, we'd be in contention.'

Jack pursed his lips.

'Something's slowing us,' Jim repeated. 'I can feel it, goddamnit.'

'The readings say different. They don't show up any difference to speak of.'

'We aren't as fast as we were,' Jim said slowly.

'Now hold it a minute ... We're busting a gut, Jim, and if you ... Just suppose I agreed with you that we're going a little slower than in practice. What are you trying to say? The Russkies are sabotaging us?'

'Not exactly.'

'Look, Jim, I believe anything you say. You're the skipper, but ... '

'Ernie pointed it out first,' Jim said.

Jack halted.

'Ernie?'

358

'Yeah. He thinks there's something odd going on with the instruments.'

For the first time in a little while Jim felt amusement steal over him; not much, just a little.

'Looks like I'm dealing with two paranoiacs here,' Jack said with resignation. 'Maybe we better talk to Ernie.'

'Can we get hold of him quickly?'

'I sure can try. Where should we meet? At the base camp?'

'No. Let's go downtown somewhere. Let's meet at Ernie's flat.'

Jack paused.

'Paranoia,' Jim said. 'Just put it down to that.'

Jack shrugged: 'OK. See you later.'

Jim watched Jack walk away, with his slightly ambling, tall man's gait, and he felt, as he often did, a mixture of affectionate envy and frustration at Jack's trusting nature, his assumption of the best.

His own mind, on the other hand, despite his headache and the pain in his ribs, was starting to work like a squirrel in a cage. He began to walk back to the flat so that he could change clothes. He kept to the quiet alleys and narrow streets to avoid the crowds.

Down Brewster Avenue it was quiet. He walked fast.

It was only when he was passing Wheeler Street that he gave an involuntary exclamation as a thought struck him. Like a computer which searches its memory banks, his mind had lifted up out of its deeper recesses the image of the man whom he had seen talking to O'Reilly. He remembered him at Tom Stuttaford's party, standing in a little group talking to a group of politicians and diplomats. General Walters had walked over to him, and engaged him in conversation. They seemed like old buddies.

He had found the connection he had suspected, a small connection, but enough. And if it did not explain much, it made him all the more anxious to see Ernie.

Jim rang the door of his flat. As Maria opened the door, he rose slightly on his toes to give himself sufficient spring

359

to take avoiding action. The door was opened fully and he ducked. Maria looked down at him.

'What are you doing down there?' she asked.

Jim straightened up carefully. 'You're not mad?'

Maria made no comment. She stood back so that he could come in. Warily, he edged past her. She closed and bolted the door behind him.

She was cold but she was clearly in control. He was glad at least that she wasn't going to make a scene. This was a sensible girl. He knew she wouldn't take his absence last night too badly.

He followed her through into the tiny living room. 'Maria, look . . .'

She struck him with such force on the face that, apart from the shock, the weight and ferocity of her forehand was enough to send him staggering limp-kneed back against the wall. For a brief moment he thought she was coming after him to finish him off. But she had turned smartly on her heel and walked through into the tiny kitchen.

'Coffee?' she called, a few seconds later. He couldn't speak. She took his silence for assent and started to fill the kettle.

With one hand on his burning, throbbing face, he managed to lever himself to his feet, and made his way gingerly into the kitchen.

'Look, Maria, I just went out and got drunk.'

'I don't want to hear anything about that,' Maria said calmly. 'Ever again.'

'You don't?'

The pain had moved inwards. His whole jaw felt as if it had been re-arranged. The sensation on one side of his face was altering and changing, giving it a subjective impression of a pounding, balloon-like enormity. He leaned against a kitchen cupboard while the kettle boiled and watched her calmly fill two cups.

'Look, can I just make one wholly objective statement?'

'Concerning what?'

'Concerning the physical effects of assault.'

'If you have to.'

'It's true about seeing stars. You don't mind my telling you this? There are yellow and blue ones, but the prettiest are the red ones.'

'Is that so?'

She handed him his coffee. The coffee was hot but the hand that held it out to him was ice-cool.

Sixty-seven

Ernie opened the door.

'Wow,' he said. He drew his breath sympathetically through his teeth. 'That is an absolute Lulu.' He called back into the apartment, 'Hey, Jack, come and look at this, will you?'

Jack came to the door, and looked round carefully. 'Well, I'll be. Just look at that.'

'Cut the crap and let me in, will you?'

They stood aside to let him pass.

Inside, he found them peering like a couple of school-kids at his black eye. There was real reverence there.

'That's some woman.'

'Full on.'

'Hey, take a seat. You must feel awful.'

Ernie said: 'There's something I forgot to tell you about the Russians, Jim. Those Russian women. Don't ever get on the wrong side of them.'

'Amen,' Jack said.

Jim tried to freeze them out, but it was difficult trying to look forbidding with a black eye as big as a tennis ball.

'Look,' Ernie said. 'Let's talk about something else.'

'Yeah.'

'He's embarrassed.'

'He sure is.'

361

'Would you like an ice-pack?'

'A raw steak maybe?'

'A soft cushion?'

They sat down round Ernie's small working table. It was covered with manuals and disks. It seemed from the spreadsheets and tabulations as if Ernie had been working all night. Ernie cleared a space, then went to make some Bolivian coffee.

With the coffee-maker hissing and hiccupping cheerfully in the background, they started to look at some of the data that Ernie put in front of him. Tapes, graphs, print-outs, spreadsheets.

By the time Ernie finished, Jim, for his part, was feeling low on humanity and high on aggression.

The three of them – he, Jack and Ernie – had been through their performance averages several times. They could find no significant reason for the major speed difference between *New World* and *Leningrad*.

The set of figures that Ernie had derived after spending much of the previous evening punching the data into his own portable computer were, Ernie felt, conclusive. The results of his calculations had emerged as a graph, the graph of real performance against the erroneous speed performance on their instruments.

Ernie explained: 'The direct boatspeed readings I'm obtaining on the instruments correlate with the performance we were getting in the practices. That's why I haven't really pressed this until I checked my facts.'

'But there are cross-checks that I made as well. For example, the laser rangefinder provides accurate ranging of the buoys on the course. I also know the time accurately that it takes us to reach those buoys. I've programmed the boat computer to use the laser measurements to provide an alternative means to check speed. Checking our speed using these other means, we're definitely not going as fast as we were in practices.'

Ernie had drawn out a graph with three lines. He pointed to the first line: 'This line is today's recorded speeds. It matches up with this second line, which is our predicted speed. But the line just below them is the actual speed obtained on the laser rangefinder.'

'So what's going on?'

'Let's deal with the facts alone. The first fact is, we are definitely going slower than we were in the practices.'

'You're absolutely certain?'

'I'd stake my life on it. Consistently slower. An average of about a tenth of a knot. That means something like an average of just under three minutes around the course.'

'So why do the direct readings tell you that we're going the same speed as before?'

'I've lain awake thinking about that. It's a difficult one.' Ernie paused. 'It's almost impossible to explain by accident.'

They watched his face while they digested this statement. Ernie continued: 'Just let's consider one alternative. Suppose that someone had some means of making us go slow. And – just for the sake of argument, you understand – suppose this person didn't want us to get suspicious. He'd adjust the direct speed instruments to make sure that although we were going slow, the instruments were reading a little higher – giving us the same apparent speed as before.'

'Isn't that a little absurd?' Jack asked. 'I mean, it assumes someone who has access to our boat wants us to lose.'

Jack looked from Ernie's face to Jim's.

'You really believe this?' asked Jack. But he didn't need to ask to know that he was in a minority of one.

Jim said, 'Ernie, just tell me again. Our actual speed is lower than in the practices, but the direct speed log is reading artificially high by just the right amount to make us think we aren't losing any speed.'

'You got it.'

'You sure that the instruments haven't been reading high all the time, including the practices?'

'I checked our readings on the instruments against the

363

information on the laser rangefinder during the practices as well. I had to work back through a lot of data.'

'And?'

'They correlated perfectly.'

Jim breathed in deeply. 'And now they don't?'

'That's right. Since then our actual speed has gone down, and somehow our instruments have been adjusted in such a way that it looks as though we haven't lost any speed.'

Jack said: 'You sure there's no other explanation?'

Ernie looked at Jack directly now, then nodded once, hardly more than a single inclination of the head.

Jack breathed out audibly. He said: 'So what do we do now?'

'We try to live to fight another day,' replied Jim.

In the silence that followed, Jim felt the hopelessness of their position closing in. He said: 'On that subject, I've been thinking about something Ernie told me about how the Russian system works. It might just help us tomorrow.'

'What's that?' asked Ernie.

'You told me that the Russian system of command is a little inflexible. There's a standard, textbook method for doing everything.'

'Sure, I said that.'

'Well, maybe we can test that one out tomorrow.'

'We're all ears,' Ernie said.

As if in sympathy with the painful beating in his head, Jim's paranoia was moving into higher gear. Before he explained his proposal, he insisted they turn on the radio. There was a soap opera on, two people arguing. To someone entering the advanced stages of a persecution complex, it was just the right background to confuse the ears of any listening device.

Sixty-eight

JOHN HOUSE
This is the fifth race of the America's Cup defence starting now.
There goes the ten-minute gun as the yachts move into the starting
box.

The score stands at three to one in favour of the Russian
challenger in this best of seven races. The Russians need only
one more race to win, whereas the defence needs to win three in
order to win. These look to be pretty slim chances for the defence.
Over to you, Larry.

LARRY PETERS
Jim Shaw pulled back a remarkable win yesterday by
outmanoeuvring the Russians in the pre-start skirmishes,
establishing a lead of three minutes over the start line which
Leningrad was unable to pull back.

JOHN HOUSE
Is he going to be able to do something like that today, Larry?

LARRY PETERS
The starting manoeuvres seem relatively conservative today.
Neither boat seems to be gaining. Leningrad appears to be
playing it safe. She hasn't managed to get on the stern of New
World, but neither has the American defender managed to come
out on top.

JOHN HOUSE
It's getting down to forty seconds before the start gun, and both
yachts have broken away to sail in parallel towards the line.

LARRY PETERS
As the start gun goes, Leningrad tacks away to port. And off
she goes. She seems to be taking advantage of a slight change
in the wind which is providing lift. She tacks now and so does
New World. They're converging, with Leningrad on
starboard tack, holding right of way. As they close, Leningrad
is a length ahead. They're crossing now. And Leningrad tacks

on top of New World, *placing a close cover on the American defender.*

JOHN HOUSE

New World *tacks in order to break away from this cover, but* Leningrad *tacks with her.* Leningrad *continues to place a close cover on* New World, *tack for tack, so that she can dump her bad wind on the American boat. Over to you, Larry, for a technical appreciation.*

LARRY PETERS

These are classic match-racing tactics. The Russian skipper may be a little hurt by yesterday's race, in which he was outwitted. Ivan Illich is not used to losing. Maybe that's why he's placing an aggressive close cover on the American boat. In all the other races up to now, he's used the greater speed of Leningrad *to go ahead. But now he seems to be saying 'OK, buddy, get out of this one.'*

What's interesting now is the rate at which Jim Shaw is tacking. Every time a yacht tacks, it loses speed, and these big yachts need about forty seconds to regain full speed. But Shaw is tacking at a ferocious rate, once every twenty seconds, as if he's daring the Russian yacht to follow him.

JOHN HOUSE

And follow him they do. Every move New World *makes,* Leningrad *follows. This is an absorbing duel. These are two tough, determined players out there. What's going on now, Larry?*

LARRY PETERS

It's difficult to know exactly, John. The earlier indications are that the American keel may have a slight edge in tacking. Maybe Shaw's relying on that to help. But let's look more closely at what's going on here.

JOHN HOUSE

My count says this is the twenty-third tack by both boats on this leg. The pace is unrelenting, the pressure on the winchgrinders is merciless.

'Now!' roared Jack.

New World shuddered as the sails swept her decks and

were hauled in by the winchgrinders, until they became taut with wind on the new tack.

After each tack the winchgrinders hung heavy over the winches, fighting for breath. Mace would throw himself back, hauling big draughts of air into his lungs.

Jim said: 'Ready again, you guys.'

'Ready,' roared Moose.

'Tack!' Jim shouted.

Immediately afterwards they could hear the answering calls on *Leningrad* as she followed each tack with one of her own.

It was starting to be a straight fight between the American and Russian winchgrinders.

They had worked out these tactics the previous evening, in the seclusion of Ernie's flat. Their assumptions had been that the navigator and tactician on the Russian boat would not play any part in the winchgrinding. So when their winchgrinders were feeling the strain, they would throw in Jack and Ernie for a few tacks, giving their men time to recover. Then they would see if they could burn out the Russians.

'Rescue Party,' Jim said.

Jack and Ernie moved forward. Moose and Mace moved back from the big coffeegrinders.

'Ready,' shouted Jim.

'Ready!' they assented.

'Tack!'

One southern dude and one black navigator wound their little hearts out to get in the big genoa. Moose and Mace were collapsed against the cockpit sole, breathing with heavy, reeling sighs.

'Ready?'

Jack couldn't speak for breathing, for the heavy gasps of air that were filling his lungs against the vast effort of grinding. He held up his thumb.

'Tack!'

The same furious, gruelling process was repeated.

Leningrad followed. Their speed was still about even with the Russian boat.

'Can you take another one?' shouted Jim.

Jack's thumb came up. A little hesitantly perhaps, but it came up. Maybe it was the thought that Moose and Mace had already used up twenty-six consecutive tacks that pushed them towards their third successive tack.

'Ready,' roared Jim. 'Tack!'

Ernie and Jack put in their final spurt of power. Then they fell back. Jack said afterwards at that moment you could have hung them over a washing line.

'OK, Moose and Mace,' shouted Jim.

By contrast, Moose and Mace looked almost fresh now. They pushed the other two aside. Jack and Ernie slumped against the cockpit.

'Ready!'

This time Mace and Moose hit the pedals like two boxers putting a flurry of punches into an opponent, as if they would turn the coffeegrinder into smoke.

They were through the tack and on the other side, picking up speed fast.

'Ready?' shouted Jim.

Up came Moose's gigantic thumb again.

'Tack!'

To a matchracer, all movement is relative. They were slowing down with each tack. But *Leningrad* was starting to slow further. It was hardly evident at first, but each time they tacked now, each time Mace and Moose hit the pedals with redoubled force, punching into them with the balls of their hands, they were starting to come up on *Leningrad*.

Leningrad was still above them, move for move. A feeling of excitement, as sharp and intense as fear, began to fill Jim's stomach. For the first time in the series, *Leningrad* was starting to look vulnerable.

JOHN HOUSE

Manoeuvre and counter-manoeuvre, both boats are slowing down dangerously. The Russian boat is almost dead in the water, without steerage way, and is drifting down. The American yacht is closing! New World *is closing at about two knots, perhaps two and a half knots more speed. There's going to be a collision!*

New World *is going to ram* Leningrad*! The American boat is refusing to change course and is about to ram the Russians! No! No! No! There it goes. Crunch! A major collision. This is just incredible. What's happening here, Larry?*

LARRY PETERS
What's happened, John, is that almost certainly the American boat has rammed the Russian boat right out of the race.

JOHN HOUSE
Is that in the rules?

LARRY PETERS
Yes. The boat to windward is obliged to keep out of the way of the boat to leeward. Leningrad *lost its speed in the tacking duel and drifted down to leeward out of control, across the path of* New World. New World, *with almost two knots more speed, pursued its legitimate course, and was within its rights to make contact with the opponent.*

JOHN HOUSE
So what's it mean?

LARRY PETERS
It means that almost certainly, subject to verification, Jim Shaw has won another race. He's outwitted his Russian opponent, lured him into a trap, notched up another win.

JOHN HOUSE
Let's get back to the action. What's happening out there on the course right now?

LARRY PETERS
New World *has unfurled its red protest flag. Both boats are picking up speed.*

JOHN HOUSE
Thank you, Larry. For those viewers who have just joined us, Larry Peters is explaining an incident that has just occurred in this fifth race of the America's Cup. After a fierce tacking duel, the Russian yacht slowed down to the point where it drifted

down on the American yacht, which appears to have been within its rights in maintaining a course leading to a collision. Almost certainly *Leningrad* will lose this race as a result. Now, Larry, how do you see the series going? Can Jim Shaw pull something out of the bag again?

LARRY PETERS

I don't know, John. If I were those Russians, though, I'd keep well clear of this guy in future. He's cunning, he's determined, he's resourceful, and if you get in too close, toe-to-toe, he's gonna bloody your nose.

JOHN HOUSE

So what happens right now? The two boats are continuing to race, and it looks as though *Leningrad* is ahead again.

LARRY PETERS

Frankly, John, it doesn't matter who gets ahead now. Jim Shaw's going to complete the course, as he's obliged to do, and as long as he does so, to all intents and purposes the race is over.

JOHN HOUSE

You sure that protest is going to stand up?

LARRY PETERS

I've spent more time sitting on sailing protest committees than I care to remember. Without meaning to sound arrogant about my judgment, I'd say that if that protest isn't upheld, it'll be the biggest scandal in sailing history.

JOHN HOUSE

Thanks Larry, that's pretty emphatic. If that is indeed the case, the score of races will stand at 3–2 to the Russians. It looks as though the Americans may live to fight another day. Just one thing, Larry. That was a pretty hard knock Jim Shaw gave the Russians out there. I accept that he was within his rights, but did he really need to hit them quite that hard?

LARRY PETERS

It wasn't friendly, John, but then I guess Jim Shaw isn't in a friendly mood.

370

JOHN HOUSE
Larry, something odd is happening out there. The Russian boat does not appear to be sailing to the course. In fact, she seems to be heading back towards her floating mother ship, the warship Moscow. *What's going on? Is she damaged?*

LARRY PETERS
No, John, she isn't damaged. That collision sounded fairly dramatic, but neither boat appears to be holed or unseaworthy in any way. I think what's happening out there is much more interesting than that.

You have to understand that Ivan Illich is quite possibly the greatest helmsman in the world. What he seems to be saying is 'You won that one fair and square. I'm not going to resort to the protest room to fight you. We'll meet again tomorrow.'

JOHN HOUSE
If that's the case, Larry, it's truly awesome confidence.

LARRY PETERS
He has every right to feel confident, John. He's got the faster boat, he's in a 3–2 lead right now, and he needs just one more race to clinch the Cup.

JOHN HOUSE
I hope I don't sound critical of our Russian friends, but isn't giving up on a race like that going to lead to some harsh words back at headquarters? I mean, I know we're in an era of increasing Russian liberalism, but a few years back the guy would have ended up cutting salt in Siberia?

LARRY PETERS
Like I say, he's the most highly decorated Russian sportsman. He's a celebrity in his own country. He can probably get away with it.

On starboard tack, they held their breath and watched *Leningrad*'s tall sails grow smaller as she made her way towards the *Moscow*. It was a strange sensation.

For the next two hours they sailed the course, tacking up the beats, launching spinnakers, in an eerie race of

371

one, while their great rival was being hauled out and examined for damage.

Their own damage seemed to be limited to an area on the bow of about one foot square, where the topside had curved in at the point of impact with the other boat. Eddie Cantor would be able to set it right that evening, epoxying in a replacement panel that would be dry enough to be coated with quick drying paint early the following morning. There had been some moments of fear that during the glancing collision the rigging might become entangled, and the masts torn down, but the boats had drifted apart without further incident.

Rain was falling as they approached the finish line. A dense line of cloud had approached from the east. The sudden white hissing on the surface obscured the salute of the spectator fleet as the finish gun boomed. With rain pouring down their necks they lowered sails and stowed them to be dried later.

The rain continued clean and cool as they were towed back to the base camp in a hooting convoy of spectator yachts. If anything the rain had increased when they stepped ashore, dispersing all but the most intrepid spectators to the shelter of overhanging balconies and doorways. It was still hissing and frothing on the tarmac and pavements as Jim made his way through the backstreets to the flat.

Maria helped him take off his soaked clothes, set them out to dry by the radiator. Perhaps she felt guilty about the black eye she had given him the day before. Perhaps his look of a damaged raccoon appealed to her maternal instincts. While Jim's clothes dried on the radiator, and gusts of rain applauded on the panes, with an airy deliberation that always excited him, she carefully removed her own.

Sixty-nine

JOHN HOUSE
And here we are some two minutes before the start of the sixth America's Cup race in this, the thirtieth defence of the Cup.

It is turning into an extraordinary series. The Russian team began with a series of three decisive victories, requiring only one more win to take the series and the Cup. But in the last two races the American yacht New World *has struck back with two astonishing wins. Both of these two victories were made possible only by outmanoeuvring the Russian boat. There is still a major speed difference in favour of the Russians.*

Despite this plucky comeback, the situation looks almost hopeless for the American yacht, unless Jim Shaw and Jack Peabody can pull out of the bag another one of their remarkable wins. Over to you, Larry, for some technical comment.

LARRY PETERS
If I were Ivan Illich, I wouldn't mix it with these guys at all. I'd go for the other end of the start line. Jim Shaw and Jack Peabody are about as clever as a barrel load of monkeys in tactical exploitation. I would keep clear of any tacking duels, and just let my superior speed blow the other guys out of the water.

JOHN HOUSE
If the Russians do that, do you think the chances look pretty hopeless for the American boat?

LARRY PETERS
Much against my own wishes and hopes, John, that's what I have to say if I'm honest.

JOHN HOUSE
One thing is certain. With the score standing at three two in favour of the Russians, and because there's a chance of a fight here, the spectator fleets have almost doubled in size. Have you ever seen so many boats together in one location, Larry?

373

I have to say I haven't, John. They seem to be pressed tight to the horizon, almost certainly the biggest spectator fleet of all time.

The tow-boat turned up into wind and *New World* began to haul up her mainsail.

Ernie was busy with the instrument console and the information panel in the aft cockpit. He sang out:

'Compass heading for first mark, zero two three. Wind velocity 22 knots, fluctuating between 19 and 24. Seems to be set constant upwind. No big shifts, maybe a slight veer five degrees in ten minutes time.'

Jack's console included the stress readings on the rigging. He wanted more forestay tension. Virus went below to crank up the hydraulics on the forestay. Jim said to Ernie:

'Pin end of the line slightly favoured, right?'

'Check. Nothing in it, though.'

While they were talking, Jim glanced at the massive spectator fleet being forced slowly back off the course by the coastguard boats, sheepdogs driving sheep.

Punching the course data into the computer, he thought he saw, about sixty feet away, a bubble break the surface.

He fed in the last of the data and turned to look more closely. There was no sign of further bubbles.

Jim said 'I'll be back,' and went below.

The inside of the boat was dark after the sun. As his sight cleared, the laminated frames stretching away forward reminded him, as they always did, of the ribcage of a huge animal.

Marvin Toller, the sewerman, was packing sails forward, stowing them in neat lines in likely order of use.

'Hi, Jim.'

'Marvin, this is important. Do you ever hear any odd bumps or thuds against the hull? I mean, apart from the waves.'

'When?'

'Like now, for instance, before the race starts.'

Marvin Toller considered matters.

'No.'

'You sure?'

'I'm not sure. I just can't recall anything like that. I haven't been listening, though.'

'OK. Thanks.'

Jim felt relief mixed with irritation. He moved back out to the cockpit.

JOHN HOUSE
OK, now we've got a shot from the airship above New World. It's two minutes to the ten-minute gun. There she is. It looks as though the skipper, Jim Shaw, has moved from the cockpit and has gone forward and down the hatch, maybe to check on something, maybe to issue last-minute instructions to Marvin Toller, the sewerman, who's responsible for packing and repacking all the sails below decks. Anything unusual in this, Larry?

LARRY PETERS
Not necessarily, John. Looks like a plain case of passing on some instructions, possibly regarding sail choice. It's getting close to the ten-minute gun.

'Everything OK?' Jack asked.

'I think so.'

'We're getting close to casting off from the tow-boat,' Jack warned.

Ernie tapped Jim on the shoulder.

Jim turned round. Ernie was pointing to the hatch. Marvin Toller was signalling, beckoning Jim forward.

'Excuse me again,' Jim said.

He went down the hatch, waiting for his eyes once again to become accustomed to the interior darkness. Marvin Toller's figure emerged from the gloom. He had his finger to his lips, signalling quiet.

Jim listened. He applied all his concentration to the sound of wavelets slapping the hull, to the sigh of the rising breeze in the rigging above, to the light drubbing of a halyard internal to the metal sides of the mast.

But Marvin Toller was still signalling quiet, pointing with his finger to the hull.

He heard nothing, and glancing towards Marvin again, he was about to make his exit, when Marvin pointed and nodded.

Only then did he hear it, hidden in the background slapping of the waves, the slight touch of a solid object against the hull, no more than the faintest contact. It seemed everything in the boat, the whole dark ribcage, started to turn slowly around this tiny sound.

JOHN HOUSE
Here comes Shaw now. Looks like he's moving pretty fast to the stern. He seems to be taking off his shirt. Is he too hot, or what?

Jim's heart was beating fast.

Jack said: 'For Chrissakes, Jim, what's bugging you?'

But Jim was lifting the coil of rope from one of the running backstay winches, was looping the end around his torso, and tying a bowline. He pulled the completed loop up under his arms.

He put the coil of rope in Jack's perplexed hands.

'Hold on to that. Just keep paying it out until I tug on it. I'm going over the side.'

JOHN HOUSE
Well I'll be! The skipper, Jim Shaw, has just dived over the side. What's he up to now? Is he going to check on something down there? What's going on, Larry?

LARRY PETERS
John, this is getting too much for me. I just don't know. Jim Shaw arrived late for the fourth race, and his tactician threw a bucket of water over him. Maybe the guy just likes water! I really don't know. Right now my mind is just boggling quietly.

The water was colder than Jim expected. Visibility was less than six feet. He could just make out the vague outline of *New World*'s midsections. He swam forward until he made contact with the hull, feeling his way down to the

376

keel. The two curving scimitars of the vertical keel foils came into view. He checked one side, then the top of the endplate. His lungs were starting to burst. He kicked out from the keel and swam to the surface.

They were all peering over the side. He saw Jack gesture frantically at the watch on his wrist.

The yacht was drifting at about a quarter of a knot through the water and he had to swim hard to reach the keel again. He began to swim under the hull, aft of the keel, feeling his way along the perfectly smooth surface.

JOHN HOUSE
Larry, are you still boggling quietly, or can you talk?

LARRY PETERS
I can talk, John.

JOHN HOUSE
Do you think this type of behaviour, just seconds from the ten-minute gun, is a trifle odd?

LARRY PETERS
Frankly, I'd forgive Jim Shaw anything after those last two races. I just have no idea what is going on.

JOHN HOUSE
OK, this is a shot from the airship. It's fifty seconds to the ten-minute gun. Leningrad, *maybe the greatest match-racing yacht in history, has its sails set and is picking up speed, impatient, waiting for the gun to enter the box.*

On the American boat, on the other hand, the crew have not yet hauled up sails because their skipper is over the side fishing on the end of a rope for something underneath the boat. If you viewers out there are confused, I have only this to say. So are we.

Jim's lungs were starting to burst again. He was moving slowly towards the rudder, sweeping his fingers across the polished surface of the hull. His progress was painfully slow. He was on the point of leaving, his mind hovering uncertainly between fear and regret, when he located it.

It was like an animal, an organic parasite, and his fingers, once they touched it, pulled back with an almost instinctive loathing. He brought his face close to it and saw clearly, at one foot's distance, a drogue, attached with a suction disk to the hull.

His lungs were full of fire.

He gripped the drogue, placed his legs against the hull, and hauled against it with the full strength of his legs. It seemed to hold, and he was in danger of passing out. He tensed himself and hauled once more. On the point of blacking out, with a curiously obscene sound it came away from the hull. He jerked on the rope and at the same time kicked out towards the surface.

Breaking the surface, he sucked lungfuls of clean air. Jack and Ernie, working hand over hand against the clock, pulled him in to the side of *New World* on the rope. Anxious hands hauled him on board. He was too weak to stand, and lay crouched on the deck for a few seconds coughing and wheezing.

JOHN HOUSE
Five, four, three, two. . . . The skipper's aboard. There goes the ten-minute gun. Leningrad is under full sail and is swinging in towards them, and our guys haven't even got sail up. What do you call this, Larry?

LARRY PETERS
Showmanship, I guess.

'Sails up!' shouted Jack. 'You OK?' he asked Jim.

Jim nodded.

Ernie was kneeling down, studying the strange object Jim had brought up: 'What the fuck is this thing?'

In the background, Jack was organising the setting of the sails, barking out orders. Jim said, between heaves of air: 'About a tenth of a knot, is my guess.'

Eddie studied the drogue briefly with a mixture of fascination and revulsion. Lying on the deck, with its black suction pad and the strange fan of its tail, it looked like

378

some primitive animal, something you'd expect out of the Eocene.

'Take it below, Ernie.' Jim could sit up now. 'Let's see what effect this has on our speed.'

Jim stood up. A little while later he had recovered enough to take over the wheel from Jack.

He bore off and picked up speed towards *Leningrad*. But as he suspected, Illich was intent on different tactics this race. As the two boats closed with one another to lock antlers, Illich changed course elegantly to avoid them.

Seventy

JOHN HOUSE
Leningrad *seems to be sailing relatively wide of* New World. *Larry, I expected that, given the unprepared position of* New World, Leningrad *would swoop on her like a hawk.*

LARRY PETERS
We're seeing Leningrad *pass some fifty yards wide of* New World, *driving past at great speed, not bothering to turn and manoeuvre. This is very much as Ivan Illich should play it. He's going to keep out of trouble if he can help it, and use his yacht's overpowering speed to drive into a lead position.*

JOHN HOUSE
By the same token, Larry, if New World *is good at close quarters fighting, we should expect her to go looking for trouble, should we not?*

LARRY PETERS
I'd agree with that, John. That's what is starting to be perplexing about these pre-start manoeuvres. New World *is not giving chase to* Leningrad. *On the contrary, she appears to be moving towards the other end of the box.*

JOHN HOUSE
It's as if neither boat is acting concerned about the other. The seconds are ticking away now. Thirty seconds to go to the starting gun, and Leningrad *is starting a run towards the line. At the other end,* New World *is beginning to move in towards the line. Both boats are powering up, accelerating to full speed.* Leningrad *has reached the line, some fifteen seconds early, and is turning to drive at speed along the line so that when the gun goes she can cross in full flight. And here comes* New World. *Five, four, three, two, one . . . There goes the starting gun.* Leningrad *is across three seconds after the gun,* New World *about five seconds down.* Leningrad *had a slight edge. Over to you, Larry.*

LARRY PETERS
Leningrad *is driving away on port tack.* New World *is on starboard. On all previous occasions, when these boats raced upwind,* Leningrad's *greater speed enabled her to cross in front of* New World. *We are likely to see the same thing happen again.*

'Eight-two, eight-two, eight-three, steady eight-three, steady eight-three,' Ernie called out in his crooner's imitation.

'Ease mainsail slightly,' Jim said. 'Half an inch. That's it.'

'Eight-three, steady, eight-four.'

'Keep mainsail right there,' said Jim. 'How's the other boat, Jack?'

'Can't say yet,' Jack said.

New World was cutting nicely through the short swells, sending out small blasts of rainbow spray from her bows. Jim cast a quick glance at *Leningrad.* It was difficult to tell anything at this stage.

'Jack, shall we go?'

'Yeah, let's go.'

'Ready!' Jim shouted. Then: 'Tack!'

JOHN HOUSE
*Both boats have gone about. They're on a converging course.
They're closing in fast.*

LARRY PETERS
Now in the previous races at this point Leningrad *was already
several boat lengths ahead. But this time there doesn't seem to
be much in it. There's nothing in it!* Leningrad *is now on starboard tack, so* New World *will have to give way. They're neck
and neck! Either* New World *picked up an extra gear in speed
somewhere, or else she had a favourable windshift out there.*

JOHN HOUSE
New World *is opting to tack under the lee of* Leningrad, *right
under her lee. Look at the confidence of this boat as she goes
about! A flawless tack.*

'Ready to hoist spinnaker.'

New World closed in on the top mark. *Leningrad* spun
smoothly around the top mark a length ahead. Nose to
stern they followed her around. The spinnaker was
hoisted, and began to fill, opening the rubber bands that
held it in position like a zip fastener, until five thousand
square feet of perfectly cut sail burst into shape with a
surge of power.

They were in a position to counter-attack, to hunt *Leningrad's* wind. More than any increase in speed, it was this
almost physical contact with the other boat, the punch
and counterpunch delivered by grinders, sailhandlers,
helmsmen, the cut and thrust of the tacticians, whose
every move must be perceived and reacted against instantaneously, which up to now had been missing. Two match-
racers, separated by a distance no more than the length
of a single boat, seem as close as two lovers in a bed.

Rounding the leeward mark, they were still close to
Leningrad's stern. With the spinnaker still being hauled
into the sewerman's pit, Jim shouted: 'Tack!'

New World spun through onto starboard.

'What are they doing, Jack?'

'Nothing.'

'Now?'

On separate tacks, the distance between them was opening rapidly.

'Now?'

'Nothing.'

'Settle down, you guys, let's start cranking up the speed.'

Out of the corner of his eye Jim could see *Leningrad* continuing on port tack. The gamble had worked. Despite the fact that they were on divergent courses, Illich was still so confident of *Leningrad*'s superior speed that they were not applying a cover. The two boats continued to diverge, opening up a large sea area between them.

Jack moved up and down the boat, exhorting, questioning, helping to trim. The crew were settling into that trance of concentration when nothing else matters.

'Eight-five, eight-five, eight-six, steady eight-six, eight-six,' Ernie crooned.

'Wind's shifting,' said Jack. 'We're being knocked two degrees down. Want to tack?'

Jim felt his adrenalin surge. By rights he should tack now, keep in contact with the other boat. But there looked to be more wind a little ahead.

'Ernie?'

'Wind shifting around quite a lot ahead. Six of one, half a dozen of the other.'

'We'll keep going.'

'VMG?' Jim asked.

VMG was speed made good to windward. 'Good.' replied Ernie.

'OK,' Jim called. 'Let's keep going.'

JOHN HOUSE
These two skippers, each with monstrous confidence, have decided to go their own ways, to risk everything on a single great gamble. Something like half a mile separates the two yachts now. They might be on different planets. How do you read this, Larry?

LARRY PETERS
It's just like you say, John. Half a mile of distance between them is the measure of the confidence of each skipper that he has taken the right decision. You have to understand, however, that this is not an equal gamble. If Illich loses, he returns to fight again. If Shaw loses, he loses everything. So it's a small gamble for Illich, a big gamble for Shaw.

JOHN HOUSE
Why didn't Illich cover the other boat?

LARRY PETERS
He could have placed a loose cover on Shaw. But remember that Illich is a chess champion. Maybe he's encouraging Shaw to go out into clean wind, daring him to take the gamble.

JOHN HOUSE
And Shaw's bitten the bullet?

LARRY PETERS
I'd say he's chewed off the whole barrel of the gun.

JOHN HOUSE
What do you think the crews are feeling out there?

LARRY PETERS
My guess is the tacticians will be going quietly mad on each boat. A tactician's whole focus of attention is the other boat, and how to deal with it. He hates to be out of contact.

'Tack!' Jim shouted.

Jack heaved an almost audible sigh of relief. Like a planet which has been flung by its orbit into dark, cold space, they had reached the outermost limit of their trajectory, and were now starting on the long return swing.

Over the water, on another part of the ocean, a universe away, *Leningrad* tacked.

This was a nervous time. As the yachts converged, it would only gradually become clearer which was ahead. Now it was Jack's turn to play the icy game of nerves, to hold out on information until Jim was stretched to breaking point. And it was Jim's role not to ask, to affect nonchalance while every fibre in his being wanted to scream out 'Who's ahead?'

But there were other clues. Ernie was watching the position of the two yachts on the radar screen. Between bursts of calling out speed, he was beginning to whistle. From this Jim began to suspect that his instincts were correct, that his long strike out into empty space had been worthwhile. They were ahead.

JOHN HOUSE
Ladies and gentlemen, you cannot see my colleague Larry Peters at the moment. He is so nervous of the outcome of this terrifying tactical battle that he has put his hands over his eyes and is quietly boggling here. Larry, can you speak?

LARRY PETERS
Only just, John. We have a monitor here from an airship above the race, and it looks as though the incoming boats are close, but if anything Jim Shaw is slightly ahead.

They are starting to close fast now, and the distance between them is becoming more apparent.

More than any violent encounter, Jim would remember the moment of sliding round the buoy, some six lengths up on *Leningrad*. No one said a thing. Maybe eleven silent prayers of relief went up into the thin, sunfilled air, but he didn't hear them. The spinnaker filled, and in eerie silence they struck down toward the leeward bouy. On the misted horizon, a strange noise began to make itself apparent, as thousands of horns, trumpets raised their raucous salute.

JOHN HOUSE
And as these two yachts approach the finishing line in this sixth race of the thirtieth America's Cup defence, it's New World *which is ahead by a short distance,* New World *which has found that tiny fraction of a knot of extra pace in a race where both yachts have stood off and tried to blast each other with their speed. It's Jim Shaw now who is on the brink of pulling back three races in succession, as* New World *comes head to wind to slip over the finish line. Only eleven seconds, but it's enough.*

Jim Shaw pulled the biggest surprise yet out of the bag. He's shown that in speed New World *is now the equal of the magnificent Russian challenger.*

Seventy-one

It wasn't the sail back to the harbour, with the biggest fleet of cheering spectator boats pressing thick-walled against them, hooting and shouting and screaming, or the revelry and laughter, that was occupying Jim's mind.

When they reached their own pontoon, the fenders on *New World* had hardly kissed the sides before he stepped ashore, carrying under his arm a most unusual object. He patiently waited until the crowds had parted sufficiently for him to enter the high security gate. Then he walked fast up the pontoon, up a gangplank, followed the path alongside the main repair buildings, struck right into the main office buildings, pushed past a corporal in the outer office, and burst his way through into the inner office of the camp commandant.

O'Reilly was at his desk, dictating into a microphone. He clicked the switch off and looked up.

Jim raised the drogue and brought it down hard on O'Reilly's desk. The impact must have triggered some internal mechanism. With a little squeal of motors, the drogue spread its tail like some small sea-peacock.

'We won't be needing this any more,' Jim said.

O'Reilly looked at him, expressionless.

Jim turned round and walked out, pushing past the orderly who stared past him at the object on the table.

Only when Jim had gone did O'Reilly permit his eyes to travel from the closed door of the outer office to the object on his desk.

During their return from the course, Jim had gone below with Jack and Ernie to examine the strange object that had been placed on their hull. Jack, ever practical, had a Swiss Army penknife with a small screwdriver. He unscrewed the outer case and removed a waterproof, rubber lined gasket. The internal parts could be drawn out from the case. Inside was a battery, a servo-mechanism for activating the tail. By pulling one of the gleaming rods, the tail expanded causing a hollow like a small umbrella, creating more drag. By pulling another rod, the tail contracted, reducing drag. It was a fine piece of engineering, simple and effective.

Ernie, their electronics expert, indicated a small object the size of a plum, connected by wires to the other parts of the mechanism. 'It's a receiver of some kind,' Ernie said. 'A sonic receiver, is my guess, responsive to underwater sonic impulses. Sonic impulses beamed to it through the water could be converted into commands to the tail to open or close.' Ernie smiled up at them. 'It's real pretty.'

'Commands from where?' Jim asked.

'Could be from any one of the spectator boats.'

'So some guy sitting in a spectator boat could increase or decrease the amount of drag on *New World*.'

'That's about it.'

An expletive came to Jim's mind. The outrage was so great that it beggared the imagination. They had spent their lives learning how to sail, how to squeeze that final fraction of a knot, and someone was sitting in a boat with a lever, controlling their speed. It didn't bear thinking about. Ernie was turning the mechanism over in his hand. 'Hey, look, there's more.'

There was another little motor connected to the suction disc. 'Look at this,' Ernie said. 'This valve on the suction disc is operated by this little motor here. It's also connected to the receiver. My guess is that if it receives a pre-arranged signal, it pulls the valve on the suction disc, and the thing detaches itself from the hull and sinks to the bottom. No need to recover it. Easy to make, if you've got the facilities. They've probably got a box full of these things.'

'Who's they?' Jim asked.

Ernie said: 'Now that's what I call a question.'

In Ernie's flat that evening, with the radio turned up as background noise, Ernie asked Jim: 'What did O'Reilly say?'

'Nothing,' replied Jim. 'Nothing at all.'

'You think it's him, not the Russians?'

'I couldn't be sure. O'Reilly didn't give anything away when I dumped it on his desk. My guess is yes.'

'Whoever it is,' Jack said, 'how do you think they attached that thing to our hull?'

It was something that Jim had wrestled with since coming ashore.

'We'd have spotted it straight away if it had been on when we launched the boat. It must be put on when we're out on the water.'

'How?' Jack asked. 'A frogman?'

The notion was bizarre.

'In the compound, after launching?'

But underwater gates were drawn across the entrance to the compound, and how could a frogman get into that small area of water unobserved?

'In transit to the course?' Jack asked.

But they were towed at eight knots, and no frogman could swim that fast. And even if, for the sake of argument, there were some means of underwater propulsion which enabled him to do so, he'd have to dodge the propellers of hundreds of milling spectator boats, quite apart from identifying *New World*'s hull amongst all those decoys.

They tried to work through their suspicions logically.

'The only time we're stationary,' Jim said, 'is when we're waiting close by the start line prior to the ten-minute gun.'

'Go on.'

'Say the frogman loitered in the area of the start line,

387

keeping at sufficient depth to avoid the spectator craft, until the area was cleared. Then he'd have a better target. No spectator boats, and two boats waiting, almost stationary, for about twenty minutes behind the towing launches, pointing into wind. Not even a knot of speed. That's when it might be done.'

Jim recalled the slight knocks against the hull that had deepened his suspicion when he and Marvin Toller had waited, listening, in the deck below *New World*. That also had occurred when the two yachts were stationary prior to the start.

'Think they might do it again?'

The prospect was appalling. But he didn't want to take any chances.

'How do we stop it happening?' Ernie asked.

'If the frogman waits until we're stationary, let's use a different procedure this time. Let's cast off from the towing launch before we get there, hoist sail, and keep moving. If we keep up speed to over five knots continuous, he shouldn't be able to keep up with us.'

They talked about other means of prevention, but that seemed the most sensible.

Jack was looking pensive.

'What are you thinking about, Jack?'

Jack shook his head. 'I thought this was a goddamn yacht race.'

Good old innocent Jack, Jim thought. When they left Ernie's flat, he and Jack walked through the streets in silence for a while before Jim had to turn off to his flat.

'Don't worry about things you can't help,' Jim said when they parted, quoting something Jack had said to him not so long ago.

He felt differently. Uncertainty had been the greatest torture. Now that he was sure in his own mind of the threat, he could face up to it more easily.

Seventy-two

JOHN HOUSE
This is the final race of the America's Cup coming up. The weather is slightly overcast, wind speed predicted to come up to about twenty-five knots, rising thirty. A blustery day. Over to you, Larry. What's your prediction on the racing today?

LARRY PETERS
The betting still has to be on the Russian challenger, John. Illich is going to lick his wounds and come out fighting. Remember, he's never been beaten in an international series, and he isn't likely to allow this to be his first. That being said, I think that the metal of the American team has been tested under adverse circumstances, and these guys are real fighters. I think it should be a great match.

JOHN HOUSE
Thanks, Larry. Out on the course the two boats are being towed out from their respective camps . . .

'About forty minutes to ten-minute gun,' Ernie commented.

'Prepare to hoist sail,' shouted Jack. Approaching the area from downwind, they were facing sufficiently close upwind to haul up the main with reasonable ease.

Although the Coastguard cutters were driving back the spectator fleets, as *New World* approached the start line, the area was still heavily clogged with milling craft.

'Up mainsail!' Jack shouted.

Virus and Big Ape hauled it up in long swigs, until it was tight at the mast, the leach thundering in the rising wind.

They had been towed at their normal eight knots to the course, but approaching the starting area the launch was starting to slow.

'Six knots,' Ernie called.

'Prepare to cast off,' Jim ordered.

Jack moved forward to explain to the towing launch operator they wanted some sail practice.

He unfastened the tow rope and cast off. Jim spun the wheel to bear away and pick up speed under mainsail.

'Genoa up!' shouted Jack.

There was plenty of breeze, and the forecast was for more. Under full sail Jim bore away for an opening space in the spectator fleet.

'Nine-two,' Ernie called.

They were close reaching, a fast point of sailing.

'Nine-six.'

Virus stood on the foredeck, at the foot of the forestay, to warn Jim of any craft approaching under the blind side of the genoa.

JOHN HOUSE
Larry, looks like New World's *getting in some early practice here. As we're growing accustomed to some unusual antics from* New World, *what's going on?*

LARRY PETERS
Looks innocent enough to me, John. They may wish to have a look at a new sail. It's slightly unusual. The modern computer cutting techniques are so precise even a new sail comes up with exactly the calculated shape. But practice hurts nobody.

JOHN HOUSE
You were saying earlier that New World's *comeback has gained the sympathy of the crowd.*

LARRY PETERS
That's right. I think just about everyone out there recognises we owe New World's *last three victories to the pluck of Jim Shaw and his crew. I think they'd forgive him anything now.*

JOHN HOUSE
What about his conflict with the authorities?

LARRY PETERS
He's probably got a lot of sympathy there, too. I guess at some level most of us support the individual against the big corporation.

Twice, at Virus's signal, they had to swing sharply into wind to avoid spectator boats approaching on the blind side beneath the genoa, and were forced to wait, sails flapping, until the boat in question had changed direction. But now the course was clearing, and they had an open path.

'Nineteen minutes to the ten-minute gun,' Ernie called.

Several hundred yards away, *Leningrad* lay head to wind behind her towboat, her huge red battleflag whipping in the strong wind. Above her a Russian military helicopter hovered. *Leningrad*'s tender, after loading fresh sails on her deck, was drawing away.

There was enough sea-room now to turn upwind and tune *New World*.

'Let's set her up on port first,' Jim said.

The crew settled down. Several minutes later they tacked onto starboard. The waves were short and quite steep today. Occasionally *New World* would plunge her bow, and water would run over the decks.

'Twelve minutes,' Ernie called. '*Leningrad*'s hoisting sail.'

Their upwind practice had taken them nearly half a mile upwind of the starting area, and they bore away to return to the line.

Closing with the line, Jim saw a slight disturbance in the water about fifty yards ahead, slightly to port of their course. It might have been a fish breaking the surface.

Thirty yards away he saw it again, and it occurred to him, with a curious tightening of his stomach, that it was the breaking of bubbles. His mouth went dry and a cold rage gripped him. A whitecap had broken and there was no more trace of bubbles on the surface of the water. He made a decision. Swinging the wheel, he changed direction fifteen degrees upwind and aimed the bow directly at the place . . .

Did he imagine he heard a bump as the keel struck

391

something? They were over and past the area, and were preparing to change genoa to a heavier sail as the wind increased.

JOHN HOUSE
One minute before the ten-minute gun, and something odd has happened. New World, *which put up its sails remarkably early this morning, and cast off from its tow-boat, was sailing along when a frogman broke the surface some sixty yards astern. Larry, have you anything to add?*

LARRY PETERS
I guess it's possible, John, just possible, that New World *might have accidentally rammed a frogman below the surface of the water. I guess this could have damaged the frogman's breathing equipment and forced him to the surface.*

JOHN HOUSE
If so, Larry, what do you think the frogman was doing down there?

LARRY PETERS
Put it like this. I think he's got some explaining to do. Maybe he's clearing some underwater obstruction on the course.

As I speak, a helicopter has spotted the frogman and is moving in to assist. It's hovering above the frogman, who's waving an arm at it. From its insignia, it looks like a US military helicopter.

Jim was only aware of the commotion when the US Army Black Hawk helicopter moved in behind them. He saw the black arm of the frogman reach up for the sling and then, a few seconds later, begin to be raised upwards.

Ernie said quietly, 'Jee-sus.'

Jack, watching from the stern, also had seen it. He bit his lip and turned away. Jim looked at his face and saw an expression close to recognition.

JOHN HOUSE
OK, Larry. We'll be reporting back on that later. Now it's thirty seconds to go before the ten-minute gun.

The two yachts are already up to full speed as the gun goes,

392

and both sweep in towards the centre. They're on a collision course with one another. Oh, my, these guys look determined.

LARRY PETERS

They're converging fast, both on a close reach. Now they're starting to wheel. And as they turn against each other the winchgrinders are pouring power into their machinery, the trimmers are letting the heated ropes through their gloved hands. They're wheeling rapidly and powerfully, each boat trying to gain the mastery over the other, neither boat appearing to gain.

JOHN HOUSE

New World *is the first to break away. She's picking up speed rapidly and driving off. This manoeuvre appears to have caught* Leningrad *off guard. She's completing another half wheel and is now driving off after* New World, *which has accelerated towards the spectator fleet, and is aiming towards a group of anchored yachts. It's as if* New World *is saying 'Come and get me.' And it's getting down now to two minutes before the starting gun.*

LARRY PETERS

Leningrad *is following. She's going to keep driving* New World *into the spectator fleet. And* New World *is now passing through the first boats. It's a minute and ten seconds to the start.* Leningrad *is breaking off! She's turning now and she's going to power back to the start line.* New World *continues on course. Can she get to the start line in time?*

JOHN HOUSE

Leningrad *has hit the start line some twenty seconds early, and is driving off down it, building up speed before she crosses. And in comes* New World. *Ten, nine, eight, seven . . .* Leningrad *hardens up and drives towards the line. There goes the starting gun.*

LARRY PETERS

Both boats are exactly two seconds after the gun at the start. What incredible timing, as both boats drive away on the same tack.

JOHN HOUSE
What was happening there, Larry?

LARRY PETERS
Another psychological display of confidence on the part of Jim Shaw. He dared Leningrad to follow him into the hurly burly of the spectator fleet. Leningrad wisely declined after the terrible trap it fell into in the fourth race. Leningrad broke for the line early, Jim Shaw, on the other hand, managed a perfectly timed run at the line. It looked casual but it requires colossal nerves. It is a curious thing, but psychology plays a great part in match-racing, and New World is starting to display that combination of nerve and arrogance which signals confidence.

JOHN HOUSE
Leningrad is tacking away to port, looking for windshifts on the port side of the course. Will New World follow? No, it doesn't look like it. She's continuing on port tack, looking for wind on the starboard side of the course.

LARRY PETERS
Each of these skippers believes he'll find more wind on his side of the course. The two boats are confidently driving away from one another.

JOHN HOUSE
Each is starting to tack up his side of the course. They're converging now on the buoy. And still there's nothing in it.

LARRY PETERS
Nothing in it, perhaps, but New World is coming in on starboard tack. New World has right of way, and is going to exercise this ruthlessly to drive Leningrad outside of her. Ivan Illich is going to have to tack, and he's leaving it late. Is he going to collide? His yacht is swinging through the wind, turning fast, and now it's not going to touch. This is split second timing. Illich has thrown Leningrad onto a close parallel course. To turn that close requires nerves of steel.

JOHN HOUSE
Now Shaw is being forced wide of the mark by Illich. Illich has the inner position, turns around the buoy and in so doing

394

establishes a clear lead of about one and a half boatlengths as the two boats raise spinnakers and pour down towards the lower mark.

LARRY PETERS
The wind is rising thirty knots, with a sharp sea, and occasionally each of these boats starts to surf. You can see on the decks that every time either boat begins to accelerate down a wave, the winchmen grind in the spinnaker to prolong the surf.

There's also a strong luffing match going on there. Each time New World *tries to climb to windward in order to steal* Leningrad's *wind, Illich responds by driving upwind to clear his air. This luffing match is taking the yachts in a huge loop above the course.*

JOHN HOUSE
They're starting to close in on the leeward mark.

'Look behind you,' said Jack.

Jim turned. Two waves back was a shape of water which, although not much larger than the others, had an almost vertical face.

'Think they've seen it?'

Jack said, 'Maybe not.'

'Can we distract them?'

'Shall we gybe?'

Jim glanced back at the wave. He felt his stomach knot with excitement. He nodded.

Jack shouted: 'Gybe!'

Virus swung out along the spinnaker pole, hand over hand over the white sea. With a savage jerk of his right arm, he punched out the shackle pin with a sound like a rifle shot. The huge sail floated free. He moved quickly back along the pole, and landed on the deck as lightly as a cat. He and Jingle swung the pole, clipped the spinnaker on the other side, and reset the pole.

Leningrad's tactician watched their manoeuvre closely. He debated rapidly with Illich whether they should gybe in response.

On *New World* the square wave hit their transom hardly

more than five seconds after their completed gybe. They felt the boat lift and surge.

'Grind,' roared Jack.

Moose and Mace hit the pedals in a furious co-ordinated burst.

'Grind, grind, grind,' screamed Jack.

Hemdale Sondheim, 'Moose' to his frinds, gold medallist decathlon, and Gino Compostella, US champion weightlifter, 'Mace', burned out their shoulders, arms, and then found something extra, some fine drug which raised them above agony, made their muscles seem frictionless, and drove harder still.

With the extra power introduced into the spinnaker by grinding it in, the big boat surged on the wave face. The speed numbers rose from fourteen knots rapidly to eighteen, twenty, and with a sudden, blasting rush, twenty tons of *New World* emerged from the water like a dinghy as the numbers flickered and levelled out at twenty-one knots on a full plane.

LARRY PETERS

New World *is starting to surf! They are surfing down on the inside of* Leningrad. Leningrad *is responding ferociously by luffing up. There could be a collision! And still they're surfing on, parallel,* New World *has established an inside overlap.*

In finding an inside overlap, they've taken the wind from Leningrad, *whose spinnaker has collapsed.* New World *has struck back. She used a big wave to surf into an inside position, punching the wind from* Leningrad's *sails, and she's driven right over the top of* Leningrad. *She's turning at the mark, dropping spinnaker fluently, climbing upwind under main and genoa. What a piece of opportunism! In the course of a few seconds, Jim Shaw overtook* Leningrad *in an explosive burst of speed down the forward surface of a wave. He now emerges with nearly one and a half boat lengths ahead as they start the second windward leg.*

JOHN HOUSE

Here they are, tacking up the final leg now. What do you think of that, Larry?

I'm just getting my breath back, John. That must have been a demoralising experience for Ivan Illich who is now in the second position, trying to clear his air from Jim Shaw. I'd say we're right back in the race.

Behind them, with a clatter of winches, *Leningrad* tacked away.

'Do we cover?' asked Jack.

'No,' Jim replied.

Jack glanced at him, detecting something in his voice, then turned back to keep an eye on *Leningrad*. The crew settled down, entering that eerie trance of concentration in which all thought is subsumed into a tiny fraction of a knot of extra speed.

Three minutes later, they tacked back. As they converged, Jack said: 'We've increased our lead by two more boatlengths.'

They tacked again ahead of *Leningrad*, keeping a loose cover.

Seventy-three

Jim said: 'OK, trust me. We're not going over the finish line. We're going to bear away.'

Several seconds passed.

Then Jack said: 'Sweet Jesus.' He turned to face Jim: 'Don't do this to us. We're one minute away from winning the America's Cup.'

'Prepare to bear away.'

'Tell me you're joking, Jim. Don't do this to me!'

'Bearing away!' Jim shouted.

But Jack was beyond further objection. Whatever other thoughts went through his mind, he thought simply: What God giveth, He also taketh away.

Jim was already spinning the wheel.

By reflexes alone the genoa trimmer eased the big, blind foresail. *New World* bore away and swung downwind.

'Gybe!' shouted Jim.

The boom crashed over. The genoa was hauled across. *New World*, having turned a hundred and eighty degrees, was now closing rapidly on *Leningrad*.

JOHN HOUSE

I do not believe what I'm seeing here! This is astonishing. Just short of the finish line, assured of certain victory, New World, the US defender, has turned around, seconds from the finish line and is now sailing downwind towards Leningrad. What in God's name is going on? The two yachts are closing rapidly.

On board *Leningrad*, Ivan Illich exclaimed aloud, and then was silent. His tactician turned around in consternation and saw that Illich too was at a loss, his face white, his jaw clenched.

At such moments, time becomes frozen. It seemed to them that *New World* turned in slow motion; a single crest exploded against her bow, the plume climbed like a geyser. Then, like a sudden fast forward, *New World* was almost on them. Illich felt, for perhaps the first time in his life, a brief surge of hysteria. His sight clouded and then returned. He left the wheel for a few seconds to stand up on the sidedecks. Holding the leeward wheel for support he raised his fist and roared out, 'Amerika!'

New World swept by him.

Illich returned to the wheel, aligned *Leningrad* once again on the wind, and drove her towards the finish line.

JOHN HOUSE

I do not believe what we're seeing here today. On the point of winning the America's Cup, Jim Shaw has turned away from the finish line, spurning victory and honour. His yacht New World is even now sweeping past the Russian challenger, which he was on the point of defeating in the final race of one of the greatest series ever, and is now swinging back towards the shore. I am lost for words.

The television screen clouded and became wavy in front of Maria's eyes. She whispered through her tears 'Jim.'

The crew of the *New World* were only now beginning to realise what had happened. Their faces were still uncomprehending. Big Ape shook his hand, expressionless. Virus, on the foredeck, scratched his head. Ernie raised his eyes to the sky in a gesture of helpless appeal.

Jack started to shake, a little at first, then almost as if with a fit. The laughter silently filled his body, taking control. He started to laugh out loud. The crew listened to him as if to a madman. One by one their faces began to unfreeze. First one and then another began to laugh with Jack, seized by the absurdity of their position.

The laughter dissipated itself. They looked back at Jim, driving the boat on towards the promontory of the harbour.

'Spinnaker!'

The spinnaker was launched and filled. *New World* accelerated, driving along the shore, past the uncomprehending crowds who silently watched her pass. She was moving fast now, picking up speed with each wave.

Mace pointed to the silent crowds and called back: 'You got some explaining to do, Jim.'

And it was true, The silence of the crowds was like the peace at a funeral.

After a while Jack said: 'Listen, you guys. Listen.'

A whisper seemed to be running through the silent crowds, like the first sign of a breeze.

Jack said, with more confidence: 'Listen to that.'

The crowd seemed to be regaining its voice. At first it was like a hum, then a cheer. As they wheeled towards the harbour entrance the sound grew until, when they had drawn abreast of the harbour entrance, it was a roar that filled their ears.

They sailed in with dazed faces, staring about them.

A launch came out to meet them. Coach Johnson stood in the prow. He was ready with a tow-line, standing with his feet braced apart. He prepared to throw it towards them. The long rope came out like a snake towards them. No one touched it. The rope slithered off the foredeck.

They drove past him, still travelling fast. The launch bounced once or twice against the topsides, and then was past them.

Close to the harbour wall they handed the spinnaker. Under mainsail alone they glided in towards their berth.

The crowds had been cleared from the mooring area. The high security wharf was silent. They tied up and stepped ashore.

A single figure stood facing them. Jim stopped, face to face with O'Reilly. O'Reilly's features showed nothing. He returned Jim's stare. Jim pushed past him and walked up the quay.

The crowds that had gathered at the base were held back from the compound by the high security fences. In the forecourt a cavalcade of three large, black limousines waited. Occasionally one would gun its engines. In the middle car, just discernable behind the grey glass, was the profile of General Walters. Jim walked past them towards the entrance.

At the gate the security guards made a perfunctory effort to stop him, but he forced his way determinedly past. The other security guards, disoriented without instructions, watched with an almost childish helplessness as Jim raised the huge cross-bar on the main gates. The crowds streamed in like water. He stood by to let them pass.

While the security guards tried ineffectually to hold back the crowds, Jim began opening the subsidary gates, drawing in a fresh flood with each gate.

In his car, General Walters leaned forward to say something to his driver. The driver spoke on his radio telephone to the forward car. The cavalcade moved forward towards one of the open gates, pressing its way through the incoming crowds. Revving its engine, the first car moved onto the main thoroughfare.

The second and third cars followed. Jim watched their tailgates swing and accelerate out onto the open road.

He turned and walked down a footpath along the side of the buildings. He opened a door and stepped into the bare hall, like a schoolroom, where he and the crew had gathered and been briefed on so many mornings.

A beam of sunlight fell through the silent air. Dust swirled there, a vortex of shining tiny sparks. He sat down in one of the chairs and, leaning forward, took his head in his hands.

Bob Judd
Formula One £3.99

'It's bloody good! Bob Judd has a deep knowledge and understanding of the sport. And he has used it to tell the story of the excitement and the politics of motor racing at the highest level. I couldn't put it down'
MURRAY WALKER

'I thoroughly enjoyed it(s) mixing fact and fiction and drama with reality. Formula One is a Dick Francis on wheels'
JACKIE STEWART, three times World Champion

'What a good novel. Judd's car-racing knowledge is superbly integrated onto this passionately told story . . . a perfect read'
TOM KENEALLY, Booker Prize winning author of *Schindler's Ark*

'Racing cars . . . sex . . . lovely turns of phrase, and a feel, a gloss, a surface tension that, at its best, captures what Grand Prix Racing is really about'
CAR MAGAZINE